New York Blues

Book Two in the Virex Trilogy

To Keith and Alison Brooke
(thanks for all the hard work, Keith)
and to George, Molly, Daisy and Edward

Prologue

Sergio Mantoni's ambition was to travel back in time.

He stood and gazed through the window as his technicians gathered themselves around the long table. They showed as reflections in the tinted glass, nervous ghosts aware that he would be dissatisfied with whatever they had to tell him. He always was. As the head of Mantoni Entertainments, it was part of his job never to be satisfied with the work of those in his employ. They might call him a bastard behind his back – they certainly wouldn't have the balls to call him that to his face – but he had long since ceased to care about the opinions of others.

The greensward sloped away from the villa towards the cliff-face; beyond was the grey, choppy sea, and on the horizon the smudged, snow-bound coastline of New York. It looked cold out there. He would remain on the island until spring came round again.

On Laputa it was forever summer, and the sun shone down for twenty-four hours a day. The island was his retreat. He'd had it built in order to escape from the past, from the streets of New York which were a constant reminder. He lived alone on Laputa and tried to forget, which of course was impossible.

And yet here he was, with his assembled technical team, attempting to revisit the past – a past altered radically from that which had so hurt him, a past edited of pain and rearranged to resemble paradise.

But he knew they were going to tell him that the past was unattainable.

He turned and took his seat at the head of the table, clearing his throat to commence the proceedings.

He looked around at the dozen faces. They were among the top hundred VR technicians in the world, a bizarre assortment of creeds and colours, ages and, goddamit, sexes – if what they said about Tannahill was true.

He had assembled them at great expense and effort over the course of the past five years. Thanks to these people, Mantoni Entertainments was leading the field in the advancement of virtual reality. Thanks to these people, Sergio Mantoni was one of the richest men in the United States of America.

But what good were riches when he was denied his dream?

'Lew,' he said, 'I think you'd better get it over with.'

Beside him Stephanie, his PA, fingered the touchpad of her soft-screen and began recording the meeting.

Lew Kramer nodded. He was the head of the R&D team, a petrified yes-man but brilliant in his field.

Kramer glanced at the soft-screen on the desk before him. 'As you know, we've been working for the past three months on the cortical-interface parameters. Shelly has come up with some interesting findings in this area. Shelly . . .'

A blonde woman in her early twenties, looking more like a VR starlet than a scientist, began reading off specifications from her soft-screen.

Mantoni tuned out. He watched the woman, noticing the shape of her upper body beneath her white blouse. A year or two ago, when he had still indulged in the pleasure of real-world flesh, he would have made it obvious to Shelly whatever-her-name that he found her attractive, and he would have embarked on a short and ill-fated affair. Life was much simpler, now that he could lose himself in the impersonal, no-consequence sexual hedonism of VR.

'We're looking at an exponential increase in the absorption of axon receptors, resulting in a reduced failure rate—'

'Lew,' Mantoni said, silencing the woman, 'give it me in language I can understand, okay?'

Kramer cleared his throat, nervous. 'Sure, ah . . . What we've found is that, although we've developed the tech-nology, the software, to substantially increase the success of

2

immersion times in volunteer subjects, we still can't forecast with any degree of confidence a time when we'd be happy to go ahead with across-the-board immersions of any more than forty-eight hours.'

He stared at Kramer. 'Forty-eight?'

'The situation is that we've managed to increase the neuro-tolerance in test subjects from the current upper safe limit of twelve hours to forty-eight. However, after being immersed for so long, subjects suffer certain anomalies and irregularities in the functioning of their motor neurone systems.'

Mantoni raised a hand. 'Forty-eight hours? You told me, last meeting we had – you said yourself, Lew, that you'd get it up to a week inside three months.'

Kramer nodded, his eyes avoiding Mantoni's level gaze. 'I was being . . . ah, somewhat optimistic, sir. My team forecast certain breakthroughs that never occurred.'

'You're telling me!'

'However, we are working on software that actually cuts in and simulates the function of the motor neurone system, thereby gaining longer periods of immersion. Once we have certain glitches in the matrix straightened out, I see no reason why we can't achieve, say, a hundred hours by the end of the year.'

Mantoni nodded, considering what the tech was telling him. A hundred hours. He looked around the table.

'Word is,' he said slowly, 'that the bastards over at Cyber-Tech have already conducted successful immersions lasting in the region of ten days.'

A young black man in a kaftan raised his stylus. 'Imposs-ible, sir. They're feeding you false data – it sounds like scare tactics.'

'I have it on good authority. Ten days. Where are we going wrong?'

As his gaze swept around the table, he saw glances fall one after another. No one offered a reply.

'Very well, if you can't satisfy me with immersion limits, how about the time-extended zones, Lew?'

3

This time Shelly spoke up. 'This is proving an even harder nut to crack, Mr Mantoni. I have a team of a dozen scientists working on the various problems.'

'And?'

'So far we've succeeded in accomplishing something in the region of a four to three ratio. For every four subjective minutes the volunteer spends in the tank, three minutes elapse in the real world.'

'That's not good enough.'

'It's what our present understanding of the problems dictates.'

He looked at Lew. 'I told you I wanted an equal time ratio.'

'And we're doing everything within our powers to achieve that, sir.'

'How long before you come up with any real progress?'

Kramer consulted his soft-screen, pursing his lips. 'That's hard to say. We're dealing with concepts and paradigms we hardly understand—'

'Okay, okay.' He looked around the table. 'I want you to go back to the labs and keep at it. You've done well. But "well" isn't good enough. You've got everything, money, the latest software, the very best hardware we can design – you're the finest brains in the business. So maybe I'm pushing you harder than it's fair to push, but you don't get results if there's no one behind you, pushing.' He stopped. Even to himself, he sounded like a tired baseball coach.

'Okay, enough. Get out of here and back to work.' He looked along the length of the table. 'There's just one thing, before you go. Who's heading pharmaceuticals?'

A middle-aged woman raised a hand. 'That's me, sir. Frazier.'

'What's the latest on the memory-suppressants, Frazier?'

'We're still conducting tests, sir. But the results so far are disappointing.'

'Why am I not surprised?'

At least, she had the guts to smile. 'We can't target specific memories and effectively block them,' she said. 'When we

4

attempt to localise and aim at certain memories, we find that other areas are affected, too. The procedure just isn't safe enough to even think about beginning selective trials.'

Mantoni nodded. 'I've heard enough. I want you all back here in three months. And I hope a few positive results will be forthcoming.'

As the techs stood and moved to the door, Mantoni turned to his PA. 'Download that to my files and take the boat with the rest of them. I won't need you until the weekend.'

She nodded, never allowing her stern expression to slip, folded her soft-screen and followed the techs from the room. As she went, he watched the way the tight material of her skirt hugged the contours of her voluptuous bottom. The sight brought back a sudden, intense memory he would rather have kept buried.

He stood quickly and moved from the room. He left the villa and caught up with Lew Kramer as the head of R&D was halfway across the greensward. The others had reached the cliff-top and were queuing to negotiate the precipitous steps which led down to the jetty and the waiting launch.

'Lew, before you go . . .'

Kramer stopped. Mantoni took the man's elbow and steered him across the gravel path which circumnavigated the island.

They walked until they were directly above the jetty, then stopped and stared down. The launch rose and fell on the heavy swell.

Across the water, North America shivered under the usual winter onslaught. Here, on Laputa, artificial sunlight gave the illusion of a perpetual summer.

'Okay, Lew, let's cut the bull and talk straight. Everything you gave me back there was all very well. Safe limits. Strictly monitored volunteers . . .'

He looked into the eyes of the tech; he saw fear in there, and at the same time the desire to please.

Not for the first time, Mantoni wished that he could elicit an honest personal response from the people he met. He had

5

long ago given up trying to learn the truth from acquaintances in the real world. In VR, where he could surf anonymously, at least contacts treated him without the bias of prior knowledge, without the fear and respect that his wealth and power elicited in the real world.

'Between you and me, Lew, I want to know the upper limits of immersion, no matter what the physiological and psychological consequences. And the memory suppressants – I want to know exactly the extent of the resultant amnesia.'

'Ah . . .' Kramer glanced down at the launch beside the jetty. He looked at Mantoni. 'We might have trouble recruiting volunteer test subjects.'

Mantoni nodded. 'Fine. Then I'll volunteer myself, okay?'

'I'll discuss it with the team,' Kramer said, 'see what they suggest.'

'Do that. Then contact me as soon as you've come up with something.'

Kramer, his gaze unreadable, nodded and made his way along the gravel path towards the steps.

Mantoni moved to the edge of the cliff and watched the tech join the others on the jetty. One by one they boarded the bucking launch, all of them quickly pulling on winter coats as they left the ersatz summer of Laputa Island.

He watched the launch chug from the jetty and head towards the city. He stared down at the concrete jetty thirty metres below. It would be so easy to step forward, close his eyes and fall. The news media would be full of his tragic accidental death, while his business rivals would gloat at his passing.

No one, he thought, would mourn his demise.

He wanted so much to escape into the past, a past when he had been happy and in love for the only time in his life.

He had to admit that the chances of achieving his dream were becoming rapidly more unlikely.

He turned and made his way to the villa and the mindless diversions of VR nirvana.

New York City
Summer 2040

One

Halliday lodged his feet on the desk and listened to the night rain. He'd dimmed the lights of his office and the only illumination came from the glowing screen of the desk-com as the file downloaded. The ceiling fan clanked monotonously overhead, doing little to cool the room but folding the humidity to the consistency of uncooked omelette.

He pulled at his collar, sweat trickling down over his chest. The file was taking an age to come through.

He smiled to himself. Casey would never understand. She'd be quick with one of her barbed teenage put-downs, and he'd just laugh and take it. She was too young to appreciate the value of something she had never experienced.

He stood and opened the window, hoping to admit a little breeze. The monsoon rain pounded against the fire escape, and the wind that blew into the office was suffocatingly warm. He heard running footsteps on the stairs, and seconds later Casey burst into the office, barefoot and soaked to the skin.

She passed Halliday a tub of chicken noodles and crouched on the chesterfield, toes scrunching into the threadbare cushion. She ripped open her take-out and speed-forked food into her mouth. So much of her behaviour, he decided, was the result of being the youngest of eight siblings.

He put his own take-out on the desk and moved to the adjacent bedroom. He came back with a towel and threw it at her. She draped it around her head like a boxer, or a novice nun.

He opened the chicken and began eating. 'Busy day?'

'Citizens always want food,' she said. 'One after the other. So many faces, Hal. Where do they all come from?'

He wanted to say that they came from the same place that she did, but he'd promised himself never to remind her of that.

'Hey,' she said, pulling at the front of her T-shirt to bite at a stray noodle, 'why so dark in here?'

He smiled. 'Why'd you think?'

She pointed at him with her fork. 'You got the file, right? You finally decided to buy the file?'

'It's downloading. Taking its time, though.'

She couldn't help grinning. 'They probably saw you coming, Hal. Sold you some corrupted old Mexican shit.'

'Like to bet?'

'Yeah, why not? The file's corrupted, even the teeniest glitch, and you take me to Silvio's, okay?'

'Deal. And if it works like a dream you bring me beef instead of chicken. Deal?'

He knew he was onto a winner. He'd ordered the file from a reputable dealer over in Newark, with a year's guarantee or his money back.

Casey finished her noodles, crushed the tub, and rim-shot it into the trash can. 'How 'bout you? Busy?' she asked in her pronounced Southern drawl.

She always asked that. He wondered if she was really so unobservant that she didn't notice how the question rankled him. He told himself that she was only sixteen, and uneducated in the niceties of social interaction.

Business was bad, and here he was buying files to while away the hours when he should be out hustling for commissions.

She stretched her arms and yawned with all the gauche immodesty of a simple kid raised in a big family of Georgian white trash. 'I'm beat, Hal.'

It was eight o'clock on another steaming June evening in El Barrio, and Casey's working day was ending just as Halliday's was beginning. He was glad she wouldn't be around

10

while he watched the file: it had been bad enough trying to explain why he'd ordered the thing in the first place. To talk her through what the images meant to him would be just impossible. Some experiences were too personal to explain.

'Hey,' Casey said now, sitting up. 'You got a customer.'

The dollar icon at the top right of the desk-com was flashing on and off. Someone had passed the Chinese laundry on the first floor and was heading this way.

Halliday upped the lighting, revealing a long room barely wider than his desk, wallpaper the colour of yesterday's noodles and a green threadbare carpet that actually looked better with its topcoat of mould.

He switched on the wallscreen and watched the shadowy figure of the potential customer climb the steps. He wondered what would deter this one from hiring his services – the state of his humble office or his own dog-tired appearance.

He glanced at Casey. 'Hey, get yourself outta here!' In the cruel glare of the fluorescents, the frail elfin beauty she possessed in shadow was revealed as the honed-down, ano- rexic consequence of a malnourished childhood.

But she was staring, oblivious and big-eyed, at the figure on the wallscreen. ''Christ-o . . .' she whistled. 'Look who it is!'

The woman had stepped into the light outside the door. She was a tall laser-sculpted beauty with a fall of hair like midnight made liquid and a silver-scaled Gucci overcoat. She would have looked fabulous on a Milan catwalk, but in the mildewed confines of the low-watt landing she looked like an angel in Alcatraz.

Halliday peered at Casey. 'Who is she?'

Casey stared at him pityingly. 'Just Vanessa Artois, is who. Wise up, Hal. You know – she was a big holo-screen star, five years ago? She's a VR queen now.' She shook her head. 'Where you been, Hal? Don't you know nothing?'

He looked back at the screen and the staggeringly beautiful woman outside the door of his office. 'A VR queen? What the hell does she want here?'

11

Casey gave a pantomime shrug. 'Beats me, Hal. Maybe she's lost?'

'Talking about lost, Casey. Get.' He pointed to the door of the adjacent bedroom. 'Go on.'

'Hey, too late.'

She jumped up, pulled the chesterfield away from the window and ducked down behind it.

Halliday had no time to argue. He pushed his half-eaten tub of noodles into a drawer and wished he could do something about the lingering odour. He managed to turn off the wallscreen, button up his shirt and smooth down his hair before the door opened.

Vanessa Artois strode into the office with all the predatory languor of a jaguar on the prowl. Halliday sat back and tried not to look impressed.

But she was impressive, and she knew it. She sat down on the chair opposite Halliday and crossed her legs, her coat splitting to reveal a startling length of thigh tanned to perfection. In the flesh, she was even more striking than the wallscreen had suggested. She had a long face, cheekbones like the chevron of an arrowhead and a wide, mobile mouth, which she employed now. The quick twist of vermilion lips adequately indicated that she would rather have been elsewhere.

Halliday was not to be outdone. 'If you want the All Star Casting Agency, you've come to the wrong place.'

And why not? Like Casey had said, Artois was probably lost.

From behind the chesterfield, Halliday heard a barely suppressed snicker.

Artois ignored his witticism. She lit a long cigarillo and exhaled twin jets of cannabis smoke through perfect nostrils.

He noticed, as she removed the cigarillo from between her lips, that her hand was shaking.

She looked at him, her blue eyes intense.

She said, 'I need your help, Halliday,' and for all her beauty

12

and confidence, her poise and hauteur, those five tremulous words spoke of someone in distress.

They also had the effect of making her suddenly human.

He leaned forward. 'That's why I'm here.'

She took another shaky draw on her cigarillo. 'I knew Barney what, six, seven years ago.'

Halliday tried not to let his surprise show. 'You did?'

'In the early days of the agency, after he quit the police. He was hired by the studio to act as my bodyguard. He was with me for more than a year. You get to know a person in a year.' She shrugged, her eyes distant. 'He was a good guy, Barney.'

'The best.'

'I was shocked when I heard about . . .'

'It was a terrible thing,' he said. He kept his tone neutral. Even now, he didn't like to dwell on what had happened.

'I met him not long before he died,' Artois went on. 'I came out of the Mantoni building, and there he was.' She smiled. 'I wish we could have chatted longer, talked about old times. Barney . . . I don't know. Maybe Barney was the father I wished I had.' She paused there and considered the glowing tip of her cigarillo.

'He talked about you,' she went on. 'I asked how the agency was doing, and he told me he'd expanded, taken on a partner. He said you were good, a hard worker.'

He smiled to himself. In the early days he supposed he had worked hard. Then, last winter, Barney died and left him the agency and a bit of money, and with that and what he'd made from the Wellman case, he'd slackened off, become lazy.

'Barney said you specialised in missing people. He said you were the best.'

Halliday grunted. Years ago, perhaps, before the reality of the city had taken away the shine of his optimism.

'How can I help you?'

'I want you to find someone, Mr Halliday. I want you to

13

drop whatever you're doing now and work exclusively on this case.'

'That'll rack up quite a bill. I'm a busy man, you understand? I have dozens of cases ongoing.' He stared straight at the VR star. The fact was, he was working on nothing at the moment.

Artois nodded. 'I understand that. What's your hourly rate?'

Halliday took in her Gucci overcoat, the tooled leather shoulder bag beside her chair. He considered what journeyman actors were raking in for dumbshit VR dramas these days, according to media reports – and he doubled his usual rate.

'A thousand dollars per,' he said. 'Plus expenses. And a bonus of five grand if I come up with the missing citizen.'

Artois didn't even flinch. She tapped the ash from her cigarillo into the tray on the desk, regarding him all the while. 'I'll go even better than that, Mr Halliday. How about fifteen hundred dollars per hour and a bonus of ten thousand if you do the business? How does that sound?'

She was effectively buying him for what to her was no more than small change, and all he could do was nod his head and say, 'That sounds perfectly acceptable, Ms Artois.'

She buckled her cigarillo in the ashtray. From her shoulder bag she produced a silver envelope and passed it across the desk.

He glanced at her and opened the envelope. There was a pix inside. He slipped it out and looked at the glossy image of a young girl. The kid had a round, pretty face. Her only resemblance to Artois was her jet-black hair, cropped short, though. He guessed she was about eighteen.

'Family?' he asked.

Artois nodded. 'Kid sister, Canada. She's fifteen.'

Fifteen? He found it hard to believe that she was a year younger than Casey. He supposed that one of the privileges of wealth had always been the ability to deny one's true age, whether young or old.

'I want details. How long's she been gone? Where she was last seen, and who by. I want a rundown of her daily habits and a list of all her friends and acquaintances. Let's start with where and when, okay?'

Artois nodded, lighting another joint. She looked at him over the flame, fanned away the resulting smoke and said, 'She's been missing two days now. She lives with me at my apartment on Madison. She often stays with friends for the odd night without telling me, so I wasn't too worried at first. Then yesterday, when she didn't show . . .'

'Do you two get on? No jealousy? You haven't rowed lately?'

Artois shook her head. 'We're close, have been ever since our parents died five years ago. I don't try to be her replacement mother, tell her what to do. She's a sensible kid.'

'School?'

'Turner's Drama College.'

'Wants to follow in the footsteps of her big sister?'

'And why not?'

'She's not resentful of your success?'

'Absolutely not. I share my good fortune, Mr Halliday.'

'And you're sure there's no ill-feeling on her part? I mean, she's still a kid, a teenager. They go through stages, irrational moods. You're everything she wants to be. Have you noticed any changes in her behaviour lately?'

'What are you trying to suggest?'

'Just that ninety per cent of all the cases I deal with are the result of domestic . . . dissatisfaction, let's say. There's resentment from one party that the other sometimes never even suspects.'

'I assure you there's nothing like that. We're close. Canada would never dream of running away to spite me.'

'When did you last see her?'

15

'Monday morning. We left the apartment around the same time. I was picked up by a studio chauffeur and taken to a publicity event. Canada took a taxi to college.'

'What were her plans for the next day or two? Did she tell you what she was doing?'

'I was meeting her Tuesday evening for a meal at the Ritz. Monday I got back late, midnight. She wasn't home, but as I said, that's not unusual. Then yesterday she didn't show at the restaurant.'

'Wednesday dawns, and no sign of Canada, and the alarm bells start ringing.'

'You could put it like that. I've never known her to stay away for that long without contacting me.'

'So you get in touch with the police and they tell you to go home and not to worry and she'll turn up in a day or two, right?'

For the first time since he'd started firing questions at Artois, her level gaze faltered. She lowered her eyes, regarded the fragrantly smouldering length of her cigarillo. 'Actually, Mr Halliday, I haven't contacted the police.'

Halliday sat back, considering. 'Why not?'

'You must understand my position, Mr Halliday. It isn't as if I'm an anonymous citizen. The media make my business their business. Canada is fifteen, I'm her legal guardian, and if the news media got hold of the fact that she was missing . . .' She smiled at him. 'Need I go on?'

'You think the police would leak the fact that your kid sister's missing?'

Artois pulled a formula sneer from the Thespian's Manual of Method Acting. 'What do you think, Halliday? The studio is constantly warning us to steer clear of the city police.'

'Wise. So . . . you contacted me instead?'

'I made enquiries. I spoke to her friends and teachers at college. I got nowhere, and then I remembered what Barney said about you.'

'I'm honoured. I thought you might have tried one of the more reputable Manhattan agencies.'

16

Artois glared at him. 'Why so cynical, Halliday? I told you, I was close to Barney. I'd like to think he'd be pleased I was putting work your way.'

'So you're doing this for the memory of Barney?'

'I'm doing this,' she said, controlling her anger, 'in an attempt to find my sister. Barney said you were good. I trust what Barney said. Therefore, here I am. Satisfied?'

Halliday held up a hand. 'Okay. I'm sorry . . . It isn't every day I get hired by a VR star. The idea takes some getting used to. But give me time.'

'You think you can find Canada, Mr Halliday?'

Raking in an hourly fee of fifteen hundred dollars, he was damned sure he'd find her . . . though it might take him a week or two to do so.

If, that was, Canada Artois was still alive.

'I'll do my best, Ms Artois. Can you tell me if Canada used VR?'

'Of course. Doesn't every kid?'

'Does she have her own jellytank?' he asked. Not many people did, but he'd heard the super-rich were buying their own these days.

'No way. I said I'd get her one when she's completed her studies. I bought her a card for one of the uptown VR Bars. Ten hours a week.'

'How has she been healthwise lately? You haven't noticed any lethargy, jaundice?'

'What are you trying to suggest?'

'You know that some places turn a blind eye to the maximum four-hour stipulation.'

'I bought her a card to a *reputable* Bar, Mr Halliday. They allow minors only ten hours in the tank per week, and no longer than four hours per immersion.'

'I know that, you know that – but try telling that to some of the more shady jellytank operatives. I know you gave her a card, but what if she wanted more, and paid for it herself?'

'She wouldn't do that. Okay, she liked VR, but it didn't

17

rule her life. To answer your question, she was perfectly healthy. No tiredness, jaundice. I would have noticed.'

Halliday nodded. 'You'd be surprised at how many missing kids turn up three, four days later, blasted and strung out from too long in the jelly.'

'I don't doubt your word, Mr Halliday. But I know Canada wouldn't be so stupid.'

Halliday let it drop. Over the years he'd come to realise how little supposedly close family members really knew about each other.

'I'll need more pix of your sister,' he said. 'Also her address book. It'd help if I could visit your apartment, take a look at her room. Whenever's convenient.'

Artois nodded. 'Of course. I have engagements in the morning, but I'm free in the afternoon.'

'I work nights, Ms Artois. The earliest I can make it is eight.'

'Very well. I'll see you at eight.' She bent over to open her shoulder bag on the floor and fished around for her card, an expensive silver foil affair engraved with her name and address.

'One more thing,' Halliday said. 'You said you didn't want the police on the case because they might tip off the media.' He waited. 'But what makes you think that I wouldn't do just that?'

She smiled at him. She leaned over again to open her bag, and lifted out a black container about the size of a shoe box. She left her chair to place it on the desk before Halliday, and that simple action saved her life.

The laser fire lanced through the open window, passed over Halliday's head, and hit the back of the chair where three seconds earlier Vanessa Artois had sat.

Casey danced out from behind the chesterfield, yelping. Artois was kneeling on the floor, peering over the desk. 'What the hell?'

Halliday leapt to his feet. 'Casey, take Vanessa into the bedroom! Move it!'

Artois stared at Casey in her cut-down shorts and ripped T-shirt . 'Who is this?'

'A friend. Look, just get into the next room, lock the door and turn the lights out. And don't move from there, okay?'

Casey ran to the bedroom door and yanked it open, gesturing Vanessa Artois to follow her.

Two

Halliday took his automatic from the top drawer and slipped it into his body-holster. He jumped through the open window and took the steps of the fire escape three at a time.

The downpour had stopped, and the hot night enveloped him in its overbearing and possessive humidity. Each drawn breath was more like a draught of fluid as he struggled to fill his lungs. He jumped the last six steps, landed in the narrow, darkened alley and began running. From the angle of the laser's entry into his office, he knew exactly where the sniper had fired from. The derelict warehouse opposite was being renovated, its floors removed to provide space for a proposed skyball court. The sniper must have been on the roof of the building, and the only way he could have climbed up to the roof was via the fire escape on the far side of the warehouse.

He ran along the alley and turned left, down a delivery lane. He came to another, wider alley and turned left again. Two hundred metres ahead was the rusted skeleton of the fire escape. He kept to the shadow of the building and ran as quietly as possible towards the escape. He would climb up to the roof on the off-chance that the assassin had remained in situ in order to get a second shot at the VR star. He came to the extremity of the fire escape and was about to jump for the lowest rung when he heard a sound from along the alley.

He peered into the darkness. A hundred metres ahead he saw a fleeting shadow drop ten metres down the side of the warehouse and land in a heap in the alley. He drew his automatic and set off, sure that whoever it was must have injured themselves in the fall. A second later he was startled to see the figure pick itself up and sprint off. He gave chase.

The figure vanished into the shadows. Halliday came to the section of façade which the sniper had scaled, but could see no sign of any physical aid, ladder, rope or fire escape. As he ran he experienced a surge of dread: what was he chasing that could drop ten metres with no apparent injury, sprint off at speed, and scale a sheer red-brick façade without resistance?

The alley continued for a couple of hundred metres before the first turning, but there were dozens of broken windows the sniper might have escaped through on the way. Halliday ran, pausing from time to time before the gaping, empty window frames to listen for any sound from within. He imagined the sniper long gone, by now merging with the crowds on the busy thoroughfare to the south.

The laser fire caught him by surprise. It speared through the jagged fangs of a broken window – an instant lapis lazuli flash – coming so close to frying his skull that his forehead was flash-burned and his heart almost stopped with fright. He dropped to his knees, cursing his complacency, and scuttled towards the next window. He peered into a vast chamber of darkness and made out a series of concrete columns, the occasional bulky shape of a packing crate, but no sniper.

Then he heard footsteps crunching over broken glass, coming from the far side of the room. The timbre of the footfalls changed, and he tried to make out why – then he had it. They were moving away, and up, accompanied by the infrequent creak of old timber: the sniper was climbing a flight of stairs.

He climbed through the window and moved across the chamber, stopping from time to time to judge the progress of his quarry. The footsteps continued. In the dimness he made out a flight of enclosed steps. He came to the rectangular entrance and paused, listening. The sniper's footsteps had ceased. Halliday imagined the guy lying in wait on the floor above. He crouched and took a deep breath, considering his next move.

Then the footsteps began again, tracking across the floor above his head. They were moving towards him, and he guessed what the assassin was doing: heading for the next flight of steps that gave access to the roof.

He sprinted back across the chamber towards the grey rectangle of the window. He climbed out and ran along the alley. Ten metres away was a fire escape zigzagging up the side of the warehouse. If he moved quickly, and luck was on his side, he'd surprise the sniper as he emerged on the rooftop.

He had to climb onto a window sill and leap for the bottom rung of the truncated escape. He hung, his legs paddling air, then hauled himself onto the metal steps. He regained his breath and then climbed, trying to combine speed with silence.

He came to the edge of the rooftop and slowed. Cautiously he raised himself and peered over. After the twilight of the chamber, the open air was illuminated by the neon lights from the main drag three hundred metres away.

The assassin was crouching beside the exit of the stairs, laser rifle aimed and ready. At least, Halliday assumed he was crouching.

As he peered, at first disbelieving, he realised how the sniper had dropped ten metres down the side of the warehouse without benefit of rope or ladder.

The sniper was not human.

It was not crouching but standing upright, a small hunched figure with long arms and bandy legs like grammatical brackets.

The sniper was a chimpanzee, one of the boosted-primates Halliday had heard were being used by companies as little more than slave labour. This was the first boosted animal he'd seen in the flesh.

He experienced a surge of fear. With humans, with most humans, he had some hope of judging their strengths and weaknesses, both physical and psychological: he could second-guess their motivations. With a boosted-chimp, an

animal not even in control of its own actions, but programmed to commit acts of savagery without conscience or a
second thought as to the consequences, he had no rational
way of understanding the enemy.

Then he came to apprehend the larger picture, beyond the
fact of his personal safety or lack thereof: someone, somewhere, wanted Vanessa Artois dead, and was prepared to go
to the extreme of programming a primate assassin to do the
job. Could this have anything to do with the disappearance
of Artois' sister, Canada?

A small voice deep inside his head whispered that he
should turn back now, escort Artois into the safe custody of
police protection, and wash his hands of the case.

Then he thought of Barney, and what his boss would have
thought of that line of defeatist reasoning.

He gripped his automatic, sweat making its butt slick in his
palm. He ducked beneath the edge of the building, considering. From time to time he cautiously lifted his head to peer
over and watch the chimp as it waited.

Five minutes passed, and then ten, and he wondered if the
animal would ever give up its vigil. For all he knew, the
chimp might have been programmed to wait indefinitely,
cover every eventuality and risk nothing.

Halliday took another look. Something in the chimp's
augmented sensorium counselled that the danger was over.
It moved away from the stair exit, towards the centre of the
rooftop, in a swift knuckling lope, and then dropped into a
sitting position. As he watched, the chimp quickly and
efficiently folded away its laser rifle and slipped it into a small
pack on its back. It adjusted the backpack and scratched its
groin, the casually obscene gesture at odds with its role as a
programmed killer. Then it stood and loped away along the
rooftop, fisting the ground with every other step to stabilise
its progress.

Halliday considered disabling the chimp with a well-aimed
shot. He would follow it, get within range, and then fire.
He had contacts who could access the assassin's software,

perhaps supply him with vital information, like who programmed the chimp, and why.

The alternative, to follow it back to wherever it made its home, was fraught with problems, not least of which was that it might lose him in the busier streets of the city.

When the chimp was twenty metres away, Halliday hauled himself onto the rooftop and gave chase. He wondered whether he should warn the chimp that he intended to shoot if it didn't surrender or go ahead and wing it without warning. He was still debating when the chimp turned and saw him.

Instead of running away, the primate sprinted towards Halliday with an enraged screech that sent a frisson of fear over his scalp. He raised his automatic and fired as the animal leapt, teeth bared. The shot missed. The chimp hit him and knocked him to the ground. He was aware only of the pain as his head smacked against the stone, the rank stench of the animal, and the sight of its discoloured, improbably large teeth going for his throat.

He lashed out, hitting the animal in the jaw. It yelped and spun away, righted itself with a deft balletic pirouette and dived at him again. This time Halliday hit out with his automatic, striking the chimp across the face. He gained sufficient time to take aim and fire. The shot hit the chimp's upper arm, taking out a gout of blood and fur. The animal scrambled away at speed, squealing. Halliday gave chase, trying to sight its legs.

The chimp seemed to know where it was going. It veered left towards a catwalk connecting this building with another. It bounded across the 'walk, leaving a trail of dark blood in its wake. Halliday came to the catwalk and slowed, holding the rails to steady his crossing. The chimp was gibbering to itself, clamping a hand to its wounded bicep.

They were heading towards the neon-lighted main drag. The buildings here, century-old tenements and offices, had been adorned with the latest in cosmetic hologram façades.

24

The block ahead glowed with an unnatural halogen glare, lighting the night like an oversized Christmas bauble.

The chimp bounded from the catwalk and scampered across the rooftop. It turned once, then headed towards the edge of the building, and with a sick, sinking feeling Halliday knew exactly what it was planning.

Across the canyon of the thoroughfare was the carved overhang of an old tenement block. The chimp braced itself to jump, and Halliday realised that the chase was about to end in failure. He raised his automatic, but at that second the chimp leapt and sailed through the air, heading towards a hoarding that bore the legend: F.P. Wilson, Holo-Façades.

Halliday watched it, knowing that the leap was beyond his own ability. It was perhaps five or six metres to the other building . . . and a long drop down to the empty sidestreet.

As he watched the chimp jump to freedom, something odd happened. At first he thought it was a fault of his eyes as the animal sailed towards the hoarding on the opposite tenement. Its body seemed to disappear from sight for a fraction of a second, almost as if it had merged with the very structure of the sign. Then he caught a quick glimpse of the small, furry body as it fell – and he knew what had happened. The chimp had misjudged its flight, intending to land on the deceptive solidity of the hologram façade, but passing through the mirage of light to hit the original stonework beneath. It dropped, hit a projection on the side of the building with a sickening snap, and tumbled the rest of the way like a broken marionette.

Halliday peered over the edge at the lifeless body lying in the gutter, then made his way to the nearest fire escape and climbed down.

A street kid was squatting beside the dead chimp, a barefoot refugee in a soiled smock. She looked up as Halliday approached, tears filming her big brown eyes. She reminded him of Casey, only ten years younger.

'Is . . . is it your monkey, sir?'

'It's okay. It's just sleeping.'

He gazed down at the broken-backed mess of the chimp.

'But it's all bleeding, look.' She pointed at a dark slick of viscous blood pooling beneath the animal's head. 'It isn't sleeping at all. It's dead.'

He knelt and examined the console set flush with the base of the chimp's skull. An astringent reek of burnt circuitry pinched his adenoids. When he touched the console, it was hot.

He had hoped that something of the animal's occipital unit might have survived, but when he poked about with his penknife he found that the entire unit was fused with the surrounding skull. The blade chipped away a mess of charred plastic and shattered bone and came out dripping with brain tissue. An auto-destruct program, primed to go off when the chimp died – destroying any tell-tale evidence that might lead to the animal's owners.

He looked up and down the sidestreet. There was no one about, though crowds passed by twenty metres away on the main drag. Piles of garbage, bagged and awaiting collection, lined the length of the gutter.

He unfastened a sack and emptied it onto the sidewalk, then returned to the chimp and its infant mourner. The girl looked at him. 'What you going to do with it, sir?'

'I'm taking it away.'

She blinked. 'Are you going to eat it?'

He looked at her, wondering what experience in her short life might have prompted such a question. 'No,' he said. 'I'm not going to eat it.'

He opened the plastic-weave sack and reached for the chimp. He looked at the girl. 'Why don't you go home now?'

The expression on her face suggested that the concept of home was new to her.

He reached into his pocket and gave her a ten-dollar note. 'Here, go buy yourself a burger.'

She looked at the bill. 'With ten dollars?' She sounded mystified.

It was a while since he'd bought himself any fast food.

He dug another ten dollars from his pocket and passed it to the kid. She jumped up and ran off in the direction of the nearest street-kitchen.

He turned to the dead chimp and was about to lift it into the sack when a flashing beacon flooded the street with electric blue light.

A drone, for all the world like an airborne trash can painted in the blue and white colours of the city police department, hovered above him.

Halliday stood with his hands on his hips, cursing its arrival. The drones were never around when you needed them. It lowered itself to his eye level with a laboured whine of turbos. 'Report!'

The lens of its centrally-mounted camera regarded him, analysing his retinal signature against a database containing the signature of every citizen in the country.

'Halford Halliday! Report!'

'Nothing to report. Found this a minute ago. Boosted-chimp, looks like. It's dead.'

The drone's beacon ceased flashing. It flooded the scene in a bright white light and filmed the chimp with its video camera.

'The city police department may require a more comprehensive statement, Halford Halliday.'

'You know where you can find me.'

He watched as the drone lowered itself over the body of the chimp. Something descended from the underside of the robot, a three-pronged grab. The drone picked up the body, turned on its axis, and hovered away down the sidestreet, the dangling corpse leaking a trail of blood.

Halliday watched it go, then pulled his com from the inside pocket of his jacket. He got through to the office.

Casey answered, her face pinched with concern on the tiny screen. 'Hal? That you? What's happening?'

'Don't worry. Everything's okay. How's Artois?'

'She's fine. We were worried about you—'

'I'll be back in ten, fifteen minutes. See you then.' He cut the connection and made his way from the sidestreet into the late-night bustle of the main drag. This area of El Barrio, north of where he had his office, had been taken over by the influx of refugees from the Atlanta meltdown and the radioactive contamination of much of the country south of Washington. These people were poor, but they'd done their best over the years to make the city their home. It was way past midnight now, and still the streets rang to the sound of steel bands and braying jazz trumpets. The gutters were lined with stalls selling a hundred varieties of fast food. Revellers strolled along the wide sidewalks, taking in the atmosphere. With his worn jacket and sweat-stained shirt, Halliday himself might have been one of the more recent intake of refugees fleeing the devastated no-man's-land of Georgia and South Carolina. He walked past a row of buildings resplendent with the lie of state-of-the-art hologram façades, preternaturally effulgent exteriors concealing the crumbling brickwork and broken doors and windows of municipal neglect.

He had once asked Casey what she thought about the increased use of holo-façades. She'd just shrugged and said they looked great.

'But underneath, Casey, those buildings are falling apart.'

'So what? They look good, don't they?'

He crossed the street, dodging knots of revellers and the infrequent automobile, a luxury since the recent hike in the price of oil. He made his way towards the flashing lights of Thai Joe's Twenty-Four Hour VR Bar.

Thai Joe was standing on the sidewalk in his Hawaiian shirt, voluminous shorts and flip-flops, trading quips and jokes in broken English with every passer-by. His smile was a permanent feature, less an altruistic response to the state of the world than an involuntary muscle seizure.

He saw Halliday coming and opened his arms wide. 'Been a long time, Hal. Need jellytank? Come, come . . . one waiting. Good rate for friend.'

'I'm not tanking, Joe. But maybe you can help me.'

'Sure thing, Hal. You name it.'

'You got a capillary holo unit?'

'Chu-chu!' Joe bellowed with laughter. 'Have I got a chu, he asks me! Who you think I am, Hal – some backstreet market trader? 'Course I have a chu-chu. What kind you want?' He took Halliday's arm in meaty fingers. 'You come inside, have beer, we talk. Hey,' he said, eyeing Halliday's forehead. 'What happened there, Hal?'

He followed Joe into the dazzling, fluorescent-bright VR Bar. 'A boosted-chimp tried to kill me, Joe.'

'You joke me, Hal! A boosted-chimp! What next? You tell me you doing pokey with some VR star! A boosted-chimp! Hey, Jimmy – get Hal a beer!'

Halliday hoisted himself onto a high chrome stool while a kid opened two cheap Chinese beers. Thai Joe sat on the neighbouring stool and slapped Halliday's thigh, hard. 'Now, we do business. You want chu, okay? Man or woman?'

'Woman. And a good one. No expense spared. And I want it now, Joe. This minute. Take-out.' He took a long, refreshing pull on the ice-cold beer.

Joe rapped in explosive Thai to Jimmy, who nodded and disappeared into the Bar at a run. Customers were coming and going through the swing doors, those on the way out wearing that dreamily contented look of all satisfied jellytank customers. Halliday caught the whiff of jelly on the skin of a passing woman, a chemical reek redolent of other worlds, other times. He used the jellytanks maybe once a month on business, and then only when he had to: VR had too many bad associations. At times, though, in the embrace of the jelly and experiencing a reality wholly at odds with the outside world, he knew how easy it could be to become addicted.

Jimmy returned with three shrink-wrapped capillary holo units and laid them on the bar.

'This one latest model,' Joe said. 'Mondo. Brazilian. Over fifty different personas. But expensive. Eight thousand dollars, to you.'

Halliday picked up the Mondo, turned it over. He examined the second shrink-wrapped pack. They all looked the same to him.

'This one, French,' Joe informed him. 'Only four thousand dollars. Not so good, Hal. Not so many personas. This one, third one, two thousand. Mexican. Only ten personas.'

Halliday nodded. 'I'll take the Mondo.' He passed Joe his card and the fat Thai waddled round the bar and processed the transaction. He wrapped the chu meticulously in tissue paper and Halliday slipped the package into his jacket.

'Pleasure doing business, Hal. You come for jelly session any day. I give you good discount.'

'Sure thing, Joe. I'll hold you to that.'

He swallowed the last of his beer, saluted Joe and made his way out onto the sidewalk. He headed south, towards the office.

The colourful stalls of food-vendors, their polycarbon awnings illuminated in the harsh glare of halogen lamps, filled the night with the aroma of cooking meat. Crowds poured down the street, a racial mix of blacks, Hispanics and Chinese. Halliday found himself looking out for his ex-girlfriend, knowing that the sight of her would only fill him with hurt, but wanting to see her anyway.

His mind wandered and he summoned stray images of Kim. They had been together for less than a year. In retrospect he told himself that it had been a near-perfect relationship, but he knew he was kidding himself with the selective amnesia of hindsight. He recalled only the high points, the sex and the affection, the affirmation of Kim Long's trust in him. That had been great – after so many years without a woman, he'd found Kim's love for him almost too good to be true. But he knew that in between the good times there had been moments of tension, periods when he'd failed to communicate. She'd often accused him of being a remote, emotionally reserved person. She was the opposite, someone who could do nothing but open up and spill her innermost thoughts and feelings. Perhaps the degree of honesty she required from him, or rather his failure to deliver it, had been the undoing of their relationship.

And then, six months ago, a case he and Barney had been working on went wrong. Briefly, Kim's life had been in danger, and rather than tell her the whole truth, Halliday had elected to keep her in the dark. He thought he'd been doing the right thing in the circumstances, but Kim had interpreted his evasion as a lack of trust and honesty. They'd argued tearfully, the night she returned to pack her belongings. Halliday stated his side of the story, but always came up against the brick wall of Kim's accusation that if he had truly loved her then he would not have lied. He cited all the great times they had shared over the past ten months, asked her how she could leave him merely because he'd told her a white lie. But Kim had walked out, and he had wondered, in the cold, lonely weeks that followed, if her reason for leaving had been nothing more than an excuse: she had fallen out of love with him as quickly as she had fallen in love.

He'd seen her two or three times after that, bumping into her in the streets as she made the rounds of her food-stalls, but she had always been heart-wrenchingly cool towards him, refusing to discuss the possibility that they might get back together. One month ago Halliday heard from Casey that Kim had taken up with another guy, a Chinese street-trader, and that they planned to go into partnership. He'd never thought that the taste of jealousy could be so bitter.

If Kim's leaving him had not been bad enough, it had coincided with Barney's death.

He told himself to forget about that . . . but try as he might he just couldn't erase from his mind the sight of Barney's body lying on the bed in St Vincent's hospital.

He turned onto his street and passed the noodle stall where Casey worked, waving to an ancient Chinese woman scrubbing woks and pans in the gutter.

He'd always eaten at the stall, ever since coming to work for Barney. He'd first met Casey about a year back. She'd served him a tub of beef noodles and said, 'Hal, right? You're

Kim's new guy, yeah?' He'd smiled, hardly looked at the kid, and forgotten about her within five seconds.

From then on, every time he bought a meal from the stall late at night, Casey had made a point of being friendly, sometimes loading his tub with extra portions.

Then, on the day of Barney's funeral, she'd turned up on the fire escape. It was midnight, and a cold winter rain was lashing the alley, and Halliday was as low as he'd ever been. He'd seen her wet, bedraggled figure curled up outside the window, and had let her into the office. He'd told himself that he needed human contact to get him through the next few hours.

In the morning they'd come to an arrangement. She could use the bedroom nights, rent-free, while he worked. She had looked at him with that thin-faced, edge-on glint of suspicion, sharp as a hatchet, and asked what was in it for him. He'd actually coloured up, realising what she meant, and thought fast: she could have the room if she gave him a free meal a day. She'd regarded him for a long time, and it was a measure of her desperation for a roof over her head that at last she nodded and said yeah, that sounded okay to her.

She'd been quiet at first, wary of his motives, but the months had worked to reassure her that he was genuine. Lately, Halliday had come to admit that he liked having the kid around.

He wondered if it was a measure of his immaturity that, since Kim had walked out on him, he could only sustain a relationship with someone who demanded no affection.

The agency was situated on the second floor above the Chinese laundry. During the day, the steam from the laundry increased the temperature in the office by a stifling ten degrees and filled the place with the reek of caustic soda. During the night things cooled down a little.

He turned into the entrance and took the worn steps to the second floor two at a time. He crossed the office and opened the bedroom door.

Casey and Artois were sitting on the edge of the bed, holding hands. They looked up with wide, frightened eyes when Halliday appeared.

'What happened?' Artois said.

'Don't worry.'

'Did you get—?' Casey began, then saw the laser burn on his forehead. 'What happened, Hal?'

'I said, don't worry.' He hesitated. 'The sniper's dead.'

Artois was slowly shaking her head. 'You mean ... you mean you actually *killed* someone?' She seemed to find this more shocking than the fact that someone had tried to kill her.

He ignored the VR star and ripped open the shrink-wrapped chu. 'Have you ever used one of these?'

She shook her head and Halliday smiled to himself. Why would someone as beautiful as Artois resort to something as tawdry as holo-cosmetics?

'I've seen them. Other actresses ...' She regarded him, something like shock in her expression. 'It's that bad?' she asked.

'You need to keep a low profile. Drop out. Change your appearance for a while, until I work out what's going on.'

She took the chu reluctantly, as if it were a cobra.

'Slip the capillary filaments over your head. The lead connects to the control case. Keep the case concealed beneath your clothes, in a pocket somewhere. You programme your appearance by simply altering the various slide settings, here.' He indicated the controls on the side of the case.

Casey helped Artois ease the flimsy filaments over her head like a balaclava. The fine mesh network adapted itself to the contours of her features, dividing her face into neat squares of flesh like a graph.

Halliday connected the case and activated the slide. Casey stared, big-eyed, as the VR queen's face underwent a rapid and startling transformation. No longer was she a fine-featured, raven-haired beauty. Now her hair was blonde, her face fuller. Halliday played with the slide and the faces of perhaps a dozen different women chased each other across the malleable canvas of the capillary unit.

Artois caught sight of Casey's hang-jaw expression. 'What? All I can see is a faint light . . .'

'These are pre-programmed personas,' Halliday explained. 'If you adjust the settings you can alter individual features, customise your appearance.' He passed her the control and indicated a mirror in the corner of the room.

She peered at her changing appearance.

'It can't adjust your height, so if I were you I'd get rid of those heels. Get some flats. Change your style of dress. It'd be a good idea to change your appearance on a daily basis.'

Artois turned to Halliday, wearing the face of a middle-aged brunette, her expression serious. 'Why do you think someone wants me dead, Mr Halliday?'

He shook his head. 'Impossible to say.'

'Do you think this might have anything to with Canada's disappearance?'

'Again . . .' He shrugged. 'I'll be able to tell you more in a day or two.'

She nodded, turned to the mirror and transformed herself into a mousy-haired middle-aged woman of nondescript appearance.

'You stand out a mile in that coat,' Halliday told her. 'Leave it here and take this.' He passed her a shabby raincoat he'd picked up at a Salvation Army sale last year, and the transformation from VR star to ordinary citizen was complete.

'I wouldn't go back to your apartment for a while. Buy some clothes and whatever and book yourself into a hotel.'

'What about tomorrow night? I thought I was going to show you Canada's room?'

'If you'll trust me with your keycard, I'll let myself in and take a look around.'

Artois nodded and passed him a silver card.

'You'll also need twenty-four-hour protection.'

'The studio provides security.'

'I mean real protection. Not some studio amateurs. I'll arrange it. I know a guy who runs a security firm. Expensive, but the best.'

He sent Casey out to call a taxi.

'If you need me, you have my number. I'll be in touch if I need to question you, okay?'

Artois looked at him. He had to admit, the chu was effective. He no longer found her intimidating. Now she was just another ordinary citizen. He wondered why he had a problem relating to young, attractive women.

'Barney was right,' she said now. 'You are good.'

'Tell me that in a week when all this is over, okay? It's early days yet.'

She slipped the control case of the capillary hologram unit into the inside pocket of the raincoat. 'How much was the chu, Halliday?'

'I'll put it on the bill.'

Casey leaned around the door. 'Taxi's here. I'll show you down, Vanessa.'

Artois nodded at Halliday and left with Casey.

He sat at his desk and poured himself a strong coffee, then got through to Szabo Security and arranged twenty-four-hour protection for the VR star.

When Casey came back she made straight for the bedroom. Seconds later she stepped back into the office, wearing Artois' silver Gucci coat. She grasped the lapels and swirled in the middle of the office.

'You two got pretty close,' Halliday said.

'We talked a lot, me and Vanessa,' Casey said. 'You know, she might be a star and that, but underneath she's a real person. We talked about Canada, an' I told her that I hadn't seen my sister for years. We have a lot in common. Did you know she's from Georgia, too?'

'No kidding?'

'Hey, you think I can keep this coat?' She did another twirl, burying her cheek in the soft silver lamé.

'She'll be wanting it back, Casey.'

'Aw, *please*, Hal . . . She won't miss it.' She paused, looking at him. 'Hey, who you think wants Vanessa dead?'

He lifted his shoulders in a *beats-me* shrug.

'Okay,' she said. 'Stupid question.' Then she waved. 'Hey again – guess what came through at last?'

He lodged his boots on the corner of the desk and massaged his tired face. 'Go on, surprise me.'

'The file, dummy – and you waiting for it for so long.'

The file . . . The file he'd ordered about a century ago. He tapped the keyboard of his desk-com.

'Remember, if there's a glitch, you take me to Silvio's.'

'And if it operates smooth . . .' he said, dimming the lights, 'beef noodles for Hal.'

He pressed the play command and joined Casey on the chesterfield.

Seconds later the wallscreen flared. Casey gasped in astonishment, and Halliday had to admit that he was impressed. To the swelling sound of something classical, the wall relayed a vertiginous aerial shot of a vast and brilliantly green forest, stretching as far as the eye could see. As the helicopter-borne camera swooped and veered, seemingly tipping the room, Casey yelled with delight and gripped Halliday's arm.

'Welcome,' said a sonorous voiceover, 'to the wonderful world of trees . . .'

The film settled down after that – no more diving helicopter shots. For the next twenty minutes Halliday watched a succession of images: beech trees, oaks, elders, sycamores . . . He repeated the names, finding magic in their familiar syllables, a strange and moving beauty in the sight of their towering, powerful majesty.

But most powerful of all, most painful, was the memory.

'The last American chestnut, *Castanea dentata*,' the grave voiceover informed him, 'died in the year 2025 . . . One hundred years earlier there were over eight hundred species of beech extant in North America.'

Halliday felt something swell within his chest. He said to

36

Casey, 'Twenty-five years ago, when I was a kid living with my folks over on Long Island, we had an oak tree in the back garden. Every day I could, I was out there climbing the oak.'

Casey jumped to her feet and turned up the lighting.

'Hey, what gives?' he said.

She looked at Halliday, an odd expression on her face. 'I've just remembered! The gift from Vanessa.'

'What gift? Turn the lights back down and watch the film.'

'She left you a gift in a black box, Hal. I opened it while you were away.' She pointed at the image of a swelling oak on the wall. 'Those reminded me.'

He wondered what the hell she was talking about.

She ran into the bedroom and came back seconds later, bearing the black box on flattened palms held out in front of her face. She eased the box onto the desk and knelt beside it, her nose inches away from the gift. Halliday moved to the swivel chair, his curiosity aroused, and unfolded the sides of the box.

He stared, disbelieving, at what was revealed.

Casey stared too, open-mouthed with wonder, and the look on her face was almost as amazing as the gift from Vanessa Artois.

Casey said, 'What the hell is it, Hal? I mean, I know what it is, but *how*?'

'It's a tree,' Halliday said quietly. 'An English oak by the look of it. The art of growing them this small, it's called bonsai.'

He knelt on the carpet and brought his gaze close to the tree. It rose from a small dish, in miniature and perfect mimicry of its fully-grown cousin, a microcosmic symbol of something that it pained him to acknowledge no longer grew in the wild.

Casey saw his rapt expression, and smiled. 'Isn't it *beautiful*?' she said.

37

Three

Sanchez was nervous every time he had to leave the sanctuary of his apartment and venture out into the real world.

He caught the crosstown subway from Brooklyn to Manhattan, changed lines and got off at Astor Place. He paused at the foot of the stairs, buffeted by fellow travellers, and stared up at the patch of daylight high above. He hated the vast open spaces between the buildings in the city; he hated the crowds and the noise. He tried to remain indoors as long as possible, but there were times when he had no option but to leave the apartment. He'd received the call from Heller this morning, arranging the time and place.

He climbed the steps and emerged onto the bustling sidewalk. He turned and walked towards Washington Square, keeping his head down, his shoulders hunched. He winced as the noise, the constant cacophony of music belting from the stores to his left, assaulted his personal space. At home he played Mahler, turned low. Most of the time he preferred silence.

He passed the Mantoni VR Bar on Broadway. A holo-projection scrolled out across the street. Sanchez looked up as he passed beneath it: a mirage of some tropical paradise, so real it seemed as though he could reach up and haul himself onto the sun-soaked equatorial beach. A running caption read: Relax in style! Live like a king!

Many citizens were taking up the offer. A constant stream of men and women passed through the neon-framed entrance of the Bar. They looked to Sanchez like a pretty representative cross-section of the New York public. A hundred new Bars had opened in Manhattan over the past few months, and the entry prices had plummeted. These days, everyone was hooked on VR. Like lambs to the fucking slaughter, Sanchez thought. He had the sudden urge to scream at the mad bastards that they were riding the virtual express to hell, but they wouldn't understand him. They were too far gone in the simple, hedonistic pleasure of the ersatz reality to comprehend the danger.

He crossed Broadway and hurried towards the Square. Already he was sweating in the clammy noon heat and he wanted nothing more than to be back in the familiar silence of his apartment.

Last week Heller had assigned him a new partner, a crazy bitch called Kat. She had a penchant for black clothing and an addiction to spin. Most of the time she was wired out of her head and hyperactive, but she was good at her job. A day after they'd first met, Kat had told him, 'You're one pretty sad bastard, Sanchez.' They'd been trading backgrounds, and he'd told her of his aversion to what was going on outside the walls of his apartment. 'You hate reality, man – but that's what we're fighting for!'

He'd shrugged. 'Yeah. But some realities are even worse than others.'

He found himself attracted to Kat, despite her barbed put-downs – or perhaps because of them. He was a weak character and he liked to be dominated. His last partner, Carrie, had looked after him like a mother. Then his controller told him that the cells throughout the city were being reorganised in the interests of security, and everyone was being assigned new working partners. And, again in the interests of security, they would not be allowed to contact their old partners. Sanchez had felt as though he'd suffered a bereavement.

He tried to shut out the memories.

He crossed Washington Square, heading for the chess tables at the south-west corner. Heller spent a lot of time playing tourists at ten dollars a time. He said it was good cover. He'd been playing chess here for twenty years, before he got involved with the underground. Sanchez wondered how anyone could spend so much time out in the open, meeting strangers all day . . . it'd drive him nuts. He was a loner, always had been. Even at Tidemann's, where he'd developed the prototype VR neural-leads, he'd preferred to work alone, doing his own thing. Even the minimal contact he'd had with his bosses had irritated his sociopathic desire for total isolation.

'You're one fucked-up individual, Sanchez,' Kat had told him. He grinned to himself. Yeah, he could get to like the crazy bitch. She understood him.

Heller sat hunched over the chessboard inlaid in the old concrete table. He was playing an Asian tourist. He made a quick move and slapped the timer. He was up on time and ahead by a couple of pawns. He looked up, saw Sanchez hovering, and nodded.

Heller was in his fifties, perhaps. A tall guy with a head of silver curls and a lined face that looked like it had seen a lot and not liked much of it. He looked, Sanchez had thought on first meeting the guy, like one intimidating fucker – but his manner belied his appearance. He was slow and quietly spoken, and sometimes his sad smile dispelled the cynicism in his eyes.

Sanchez rendezvoused with Heller perhaps once a month, their meetings lasting no longer than a five-minute game. Long enough for Heller to pass on instructions and Sanchez to nod that he understood. He knew nothing about Heller other than he'd played here for years, and that his real name was not Heller. And the only reason he knew that was because the tag he'd chosen for himself, Sanchez, was not his real name, either.

He assumed a lot more about the man, of course: that he was in the underground for the same reasons as himself, and that he came from a technical-computer background.

Heller checkmated the Asian and looked up at Sanchez. 'Game, buddy? Ten dollars. Try your luck?'

The Asian tourist vacated the concrete seat and Sanchez sat

down. He handed Heller the note, for the sake of verisimilitude. Heller held out his fists and Sanchez indicated the left. White pawn.

Sanchez opened. He made a mess of a standard Ruy Lopez, on purpose. A couple of tourists, watching, drifted away.

Heller hunched even further over the board.

'What's been happening?' Sanchez whispered. 'I expected a call last week.'

Heller muttered to himself and Sanchez caught, 'Problems, Sanchez.'

He felt his scalp prickle. 'What happened?'

Heller frowned down at the board. 'Rodriguez was killed last week.'

'Jesus. You think . . . I mean, was it linked?'

Heller shrugged. 'He was murdered. Shot in the back of the head. You tell me if it was linked.'

'We safe?'

Heller looked up, and his blue eyes contained an infinity of sadness. 'Christ knows, Sanchez. I hope so. But . . . a week ago, I got jumpy. Thought I was seeing this guy tailing me all over the place. Big guy, looked Mexican. Thought I'd better cool things off, lie low. That's why I didn't call.'

Sanchez nodded and made a move. His mind was everywhere but the game. 'So what gives? Did O'Donnell—?'

Heller nodded. He took a candy bar from a knapsack on the bench beside him and laid it next to the board.

'He cracked one of the new Mantoni codes. This should get you into some of his secure zones.' He nodded down at the candy bar, a brand Sanchez had never seen before. 'Take it to Kat. She'll do the rest.'

'What about the Kulchev virus?'

Heller advanced a pawn and hit the timer. 'The bastards at Cyber-Tech came up with a counter. We infiltrated their core, but they matched the virus and effectively eradicated the threat. They even passed the specs onto Mantoni, Tidemann's and the rest. Everything we come up with, they seem to be one step ahead.'

41

'We keep trying, man,' Sanchez said. He hummed a few bars of a tune popular a few months back. *We're all riding the virtual express to hell! Yeah, all aboard . . .*

'Sure, kid. We keep trying.'

Sanchez picked up the candy bar and slipped it into the pocket of his combat trousers. The gesture seemed as conspicuous as if he were trying to shop-lift a ten-thousand-dollar gold watch from Tiffany's.

Heller swooped his queen down the board. 'Checkmate.'

Sanchez shook his massive hand. 'Good game, man.'

'Yeah, see you around, buddy. Say hi to Kat.'

'Sure thing.' Sanchez nodded and moved away from the table. Someone else took his place. He was sweating, and it had nothing to do with the heat. He wanted to be away from this place. He'd take the candy bar to Kat, then get down to work.

He heard a cry from behind him. The tourist who'd sat down across the board from Heller was standing up, staring down at Heller and retching.

Sanchez stood, unable to move, hardly believing what he was seeing.

Heller had slumped forward, face-down on the table, scattering chess pieces. Even as he watched, Sanchez saw a tiny jet of blood, a bright crimson geyser, spurt from the back of his head and trickle through his oiled grey curls.

He looked up, across the street to where the shot must have originated. But the killer might have been any one of a hundred tourists and students packing the sidewalk.

A sickening sensation of grief and fear turning in his gut, Sanchez hurried from the Square and across the street, heading for the subway. He slipped his hand into his trouser pocket, as if for reassurance. The candy bar was a melted mess in its plastic wrapper.

He caught the subway at Astor Place and kept his eyes shut all the way south to Canal Street. He knew what he was getting into when he became involved, but until now the

42

deaths had happened to people he had never met, names without personalities.

He recalled the expression of sadness in Heller's wise blue eyes and felt his throat constrict with rage.

Kat lived in a cramped apartment above a Cantonese fast-food joint in Chinatown. Sanchez walked down the back alley and climbed the fire escape. He knocked, using the pre-arranged code. Kat took an age to answer – no doubt out of her head again, sleeping it off.

She pulled the door open and, unexpectedly, Sanchez found himself crying. She blinked at him, leaning against the wall and looking wrecked. Her Chinese-style page-boy cut framed a thin, pale face that might have been pretty were it not for the effects of her addiction. Her skin was ghost pale, her eyes bloodshot.

She wore a black T-shirt and the same colour leggings, both of which made her look thin and ill.

'You okay, Sanchez?' she drawled. She moved away from the door and into the room, and Sanchez followed. The blinds were shut and she switched on a light, revealing a small room crammed with terminals, banked computer systems, a mattress in one corner and a jellytank in the other. All the usual apparatus of the professional vracker.

'Heller's dead,' he found himself saying.

Kat sat on the edge of the mattress and reached for a spray can. She held it to her mouth and inhaled, taking a deep breath. Despite himself, Sanchez stared at her breasts outlined by the material of the T-shirt.

'Did you hear me? I said—'

'I heard you. Heller's dead. What do you want me to do, write an obituary? I hardly knew the guy.'

'Heller was on our side, Kat. He was one of us.'

She stared at him. 'Did you get the pin?'

He shook his head. 'Heller died today, and all you can ask about is the fucking pin? You know what your trouble is, that fucking spin's wiped your humanity.'

'When I need *you* talking to me about *my* humanity, kid, I'll tell you.'

He chose to ignore that. He moved to a swivel chair before a terminal and sat down heavily. 'We met, he gave me the pin and when I was leaving someone . . .' He shook his head. 'They shot him dead, Kat.'

He stared at her, wanting some response, if not sympathy for himself then at least some sign of sadness at the loss of a compatriot.

She matched his gaze. 'But you got the pin, yeah?'

He pulled the candy bar from his pocket and threw it at her. She caught it cleanly, mocking his attempt to hit her in the face.

'I didn't know Heller from Joe Fuck, Sanchez. He knew the score when he joined us. We all live with the risk.' She ripped the wrapper and bit into the bar, pulling the silver pin free of the goo with her teeth. She licked the pin clean, then proceeded to devour the candy bar, wiping her lips on the back of her hand. It was probably the first food she'd eaten in days.

'We're all expendable. Individually, we're all so many insignificant fucking ants. Get that into your screwed-up head. It's the game that matters, not the players.'

She pushed herself from the mattress and crossed the room towards him. 'Now get outta my chair and strip off.'

He nodded, dazed. 'Okay, okay . . .'

She held up the shining pin. 'If O'Donnell's done his job, this should get us into some of Mantoni's restricted areas. I'll follow you in there and dump the virus.'

He vacated the swivel chair and Kat sat down, slipping the pin into a port and tapping the touchpad. She slapped contacts to her temples and jacked the leads into the terminal.

Sanchez watched. There was something about her super-efficiency that always struck him as sexy. He almost told her that, in order to provoke her condemnation.

He walked over to the jellytank and undressed, turning his back on her. The first time he'd tanked in her presence, three days ago, he'd noticed her smirking at his modesty.

He piled his trousers and T-shirt on the floor, attached the leads to his limbs and pulled on the faceplate. He felt it seal around his skin with a soft, sucking sound. He stepped into the tank, enjoying the sensation of the gel as it embraced his legs. He sat down, the jelly sealing itself around him, deadening the sensation in his flesh. He looked through the visor at Kat. She was hunched over the terminal, her fingers flying over the touchpad. She paused long enough to raise a hand, signalling that she was ready.

He lay back and felt his body at first buoyed by the gel, and then taken into its cloying embrace as he sank. He stretched out, floating free, and closed his eyes.

After his first tanking session with Kat, she'd said something that made Sanchez reappraise his assessment of her. At first he thought she was like every other tech-head he'd ever met – including himself: she was good at her job but knew fuck all about people. Then, when he emerged from the tank that first time and talked for a while, she'd said something along the lines that he liked virtual reality more than he did the real world.

The words had shocked him, at first. It was something to acknowledge one's own guilty secrets, but quite another to have them understood by someone who was still a stranger.

But the fact was that she was right. He hated the real world. He had never fit in, had always considered himself an outsider. He had never managed to form meaningful, lasting relationships. People tended, he thought, to hate him, and his own self-regard was therefore pretty low.

Perhaps the reason he'd got into the research end of VR after graduating from MIT was in a bid to escape the real world. In VR he had found a nirvana, a painless wonderland where he could shed his real persona and become anyone, anything, he desired.

45

He'd spent a lot of time in this personal heaven, until coming to the realisation that it was really no more than hell in disguise.

Nevertheless, there was still something elementally thrilling about immersing oneself in a jellytank and making the transition to VR.

He opened his eyes. He seemed to be disembodied, a random viewpoint floating through a multicoloured fractal landscape. He sank into a kaleidoscope of swirling shapes, each one possessing the infinitesimal detail of an entire world. He stared in wonder.

He heard Kat's voice in his head. 'Okay, what you're seeing is a visual metaphor, Sanchez. I'm scrolling through all Mantoni's VR sub-routines. So far, there's no sign of any counter-insurgency bugs. Fingers crossed. I'll insert you into an inhabited zone when I come across one that might be interesting. As of now, they're all occupied by manufactured personas conducting the corporation's day-to-day business and such crap. I might have to shut you down for an hour or two until I strike pay-dirt, okay?'

He felt himself smiling. Her questioning him was redundant. There was no way he could respond to her.

He blacked out. He'd experienced this sensation before, when tanking with Carrie. It was as relaxing as REM sleep, but he retained awareness of his thoughts. Like this, hours might pass in VR without his being aware of elapsing time, as Kat guided him through zone after zone.

'Okay . . .' he heard. 'I think I got something.'

He had no idea exactly how long he'd been immersed, but some intuition told him that it had been a while.

His senses exploded with a sudden shattering bombardment of colour, sound, tactile awareness.

He was in an impossibly rustic setting, like something from a painting by . . . who was that 19th-century English artist? He looked out over a rolling green meadow, with a stream curving into the distance. On the bank of the stream was a stand of massive trees. He stared in surprise and delight. This

46

was the first time he'd ever seen trees this close in either VR or the real world.

Then he saw two figures reclining on the grass of the riverbank.

Kat was talking to him again. 'I'm getting positive signals from this zone, Sanchez. It's inhabited by realos. Don't know who they are. I suggest you get in close and eavesdrop, okay? I'm establishing a route through to the zone and readying the virus. I'll pull you just as soon as I've successfully completed the upload.'

Only then, when Kat suggested that he approach the realos, did Sanchez become aware of his guise. He turned his head and regarded his brown, furry body, his long tail. He looked down at his pink, clawed feet. He was a rat. He wondered why Kat had chosen this disguise, and if it was any indication of what she thought of him.

Sanchez scurried forward, relishing the sensation of his fast, lithe rat's body as it darted through the long grass. His sense of smell was extraordinary, stunning him even though it was nothing more than a computer simulation. The scent of the wild flowers was almost sensuously overpowering.

Then he heard the sound of voices, a man and a woman's.

He concealed himself behind a stand of ferns and peered out. The man was reclining on the grass, naked but for a pair of shorts. He was well-muscled and deeply tanned. He was familiar – Sanchez was sure he'd seen his likeness somewhere before.

The woman was naked, and her body was surely enhanced. She was blonde, impossibly curvaceous and as flawlessly beautiful as a VR actress. Despite himself, Sanchez felt his treacherous rat's body responding.

Sanchez listened as they talked for what might have been an hour or more. They seemed to be talking business for the most part; the guy was negotiating a price for services rendered, or services to be rendered. Sanchez tuned out, bored.

He wondered how long Kat would take to ready the virus. The longer he was inserted into this zone, the more chance

47

there was of Mantoni's insurgency bugs detecting his presence. He told himself not to worry. He had every faith in Kat's ability to get him out in time.

Sanchez pricked up his ears. The woman was speaking.

'. . . right now, in fact.'

'You're in contact with it, Pablo?' the guy asked.

Sanchez twitched his nose. The blonde was called Pablo? Well, he supposed anything was possible in VR.

The woman nodded. 'Direct link. It's tailed Vanessa Artois to some third-rate detective agency in El Barrio, going by the name of Halliday's. They specialise in missing persons.'

'You've used the assassin before?' he asked.

The woman nodded. 'Don't worry. I programmed it myself. It'll be tracking Artois right as we speak.' She smiled. 'Say, what's Artois done to earn this kind of treatment?'

The guy smiled and murmured something that Sanchez didn't catch.

He backed into the ferns. He knew that this protective measure was futile, a mere conditioned response. They wouldn't recognise him for what he was, even if they did see him.

What the hell had they been discussing?

Had the guy hired this Pablo-in-disguise to programme something . . . a drone? . . . to kill Vanessa Artois, the VR star?

That's certainly what it had sounded like.

'Hey, Sanchez!' It was Kat. She sounded panicked. 'I'm picking something up. Christ! I'm pulling you outta there!'

Sanchez felt his heart jump with fear. If Mantoni's techs had traced the link and uploaded some insurgency-specific bug, they could ream his brain-pan and leave him so cleaned out he'd be praying for death.

The vision of the rustic wonderland flashed out of existence, to be replaced by the fractal spacescape. He felt something screaming in his head, and wondered if it was Kat.

Then he realised that Kat could not scream that loud. The noise in his head was produced by his own throat, crying out in pain as he forced his way through the heavy gel in the tank. His brain seemed to explode with the agonising detonation of a hundred migraines.

He floundered from the tank, pulling off the leads. He was aware only of the pain – and of Kat, staring at him in horror from across the room.

Then, mercifully, blessed oblivion brought an end to the nightmare in his head.

Four

The rain began punctually at eight and continued without pause for the next hour, a torrential downpour that turned the streets into canals and overloaded the storm drains.

Halliday drove down Park Avenue in Barney's old blue Ford, its wipers batting ineffectually at the monsoon deluge. He thought of the file he'd downloaded last night, the magnificent sight of trees he'd taken for granted in his childhood. It had been hard to explain to Casey that not so long ago the world had been a different place. Trees had been plentiful, monsoon rains unknown in America. All the country had been habitable then, before the meltdowns and subsequent contamination. Casey had listened, but had she really understood? He had described another world to her, a world she had never experienced and therefore could not truly mourn. This was her reality now, to make of it what she could. It was the older generation, whose lives spanned the changes, who could compare what they had now with what had been, and lament the loss.

He parked outside the Plaza building on Madison Avenue. He ducked out from the car, jumped the rainwater surging along the gutter, and ran up the steps to the luxury apartment block. A liveried concierge promptly swung open the glass-panel door and saluted. It was a taste of a lifestyle he had only ever seen in holo-dramas.

He rode the elevator to the fifth floor. Even in this small box, no effort had been spared. It was fitted with polished panels, some ancient hardwood in which he could see his reflection. He touched the lustrous timber, told himself he could actually feel its warmth. While he appreciated its beauty, he could not help but feel uncomfortable with the fact that trees had been destroyed to produce it.

He walked down the corridor and found the door of the Artois' apartment, yet another slab of timber. He took the keycard from his pocket and let himself in, found the lights and stared around at the room.

Perhaps five times the size of his office, the lounge had a honey-coloured parquet floor, white walls decorated with examples of modern art – abstract computer graphics that swirled with a slow, mood-inducing tempo – scatter rugs and ridiculously oversized sofas and armchairs in suede.

Halliday moved around the room like someone in a museum.

At first he felt the same constraint, afraid to touch *objets d'art* and ornaments lest some unseen curator should appear and reprimand him. He supposed he might have been able to discern, from the possessions in the lounge, something of Vanessa Artois' character if he had known anything at all about the graphics and sculptures on display. He had lived his life without much appreciation of the arts, perhaps a little disdainful of such profligacy. He considered himself a pragmatist who prized function over form, and had little appreciation of aesthetics. Artois, it was clear, inhabited a different world, a rarefied reality that would have its correlation in a mindset he had no hope of ever understanding.

He wondered what Casey would make of this room.

He picked up a sculpture in wood, caressed its contours. He recalled collecting wood for the open fire of his parents' house. He wished he had thought to carve the wood instead of burning it, built up a collection of pieces he would have been able to appreciate throughout his life. He smiled to himself: how was he to know that he would grow up in a world where wood was a treasured commodity?

With a warm glow of gratitude he recalled the bonsai oak on the desk back at his office. He'd caught himself this morning just staring in awe at its miniaturised intricacy.

He moved around the room, examining family pictures

51

and holo-cubes. There were many images of Vanessa Artois: a young girl acting in some stage play, ten years ago; later pix showing her on the arms of actors and directors, or on the set of some high-budget holo-movie. The pix were dated and captioned, and Halliday saw that there was nothing from the past year or so, when according to Casey the actress had moved into VR.

There were other pix of the younger Artois, Canada: a strikingly pretty and vivacious teenager from a privileged background with all of life's many opportunities ahead of her.

There was only one pix of a couple Halliday assumed were Artois' parents: a silver-haired man with his arm around the shoulders of a tall, dark-haired woman perhaps in her fifties. He took three pix of Canada from their frames and slipped them into the inside pocket of his jacket.

On the mantelshelf above an open fire stood a line of sleek golden statuettes – stylised shaveskull figurines he recognised from somewhere.

He lifted one down and sat in an armchair, collapsing into its ludicrously soft padding. He turned the statue over in his hand, wondering where he had seen something like it before.

'Holo-Oscars,' a voice said. It was Vanessa Artois.

Halliday looked around. 'I thought I said it'd be safer if you—' he began.

There was no one, other than himself, in the room.

A peal of gentle laughter. 'Now, would I disobey you, Mr Halliday? Over here – the wall to your left.'

As Halliday turned, the white wall flickered and expanded into a floor-to-ceiling screen. Vanessa Artois smiled out at him. She was close to the relay camera, and her face was monstrously vast. The effect was as if she were peering into a doll's house.

She moved away from the camera and lay on her stomach on a bed. She was wearing a pink robe and a towel wrapped turban-style around her head, the fine angles of her face emphasised by the absence of hair.

'Hi, Halliday. Thought as I'm doing nothing I'd tune in and watch someone else on screen for a change.'

'Hope you appreciate my performance.'

She lodged her chin on a palm. 'A little dour, if you don't mind my saying. You don't look too happy.'

He was disconcerted by Artois' assessment of his mental state. He had been simply staring at the statuette, thinking his thoughts, neither happy nor unhappy.

'As a matter of fact I'm not – unhappy, that is. In fact, after your gift last night—'

'You liked it?'

'Liked it? I don't usually go for . . . I don't know – things that I can't use.' He smiled. 'But the tree's incredible.'

'Thought you might like it.' She pointed a long lacquered nail at him. 'Remember, I don't want the police in on this, okay?'

'Deal.' He hefted the statuette. 'A holo-Oscar?'

'Awarded for my "life-affirming role of Joan of Arc" in the '36 bio-blockbuster.'

'Well done.'

She looked at him. 'Sorry to shatter your illusions, Halliday, but they're bullshit. You don't think for one second that they're awarded for merit, do you? If you work for the right studio, and they've put a lot of cash into the project, and you don't make a mess of your role – then the Oscar's yours and you get to perform that puke-making little speech in front of all the fat-cat Academy members.'

Halliday shrugged. He pointed to all the other Oscars on the mantelshelf, ranked like a parade of toy soldiers. 'You must have been in a lot of big budget holos? Must've been popular?'

'What do holo-goers know, Halliday? They're force-fed whatever shit makes a buck. If your face fits . . . Hey, just listen to me. What have I got to complain about?'

He draped a leg over the arm of the chair and smiled at Artois. 'You okay? No more near-misses?'

'I'm fine. The chu works like a miracle. I've been spooking

53

waiters in the restaurant, ordering a meal in one guise, then changing when the meal arrives. You should see their faces!'

'Glad you're putting it to good use,' he said.

'And thanks for the security. Szabo's got three heavies looking after me. One's right outside in the hall as I speak.'

'They're the best. You can relax with Szabo's men around, Ms Artois.'

'What's with all this formality, Halliday? Call me Vanessa, okay? And do you have a name? I mean, not a surname?'

'Friends call me Hal,' he told her.

'Okay, Hal.' She sat up on the bed, pulled the towel from her head and began vigorously drying her long black hair. In the process, the front of her robe split to reveal the tanned rise of her breasts.

Halliday replaced the Oscar on the mantelshelf with its mates.

Artois stopped towelling her hair and looked at him. She tried to sound casual when she spoke, but he detected unease in her tone. 'Last night, when you went after whoever tried to shoot me.' She stopped there, biting her lip. 'When you got back, you said the hit-man was dead.' She stared at him with a look of disbelief that seemed genuine, and not an act.

He leaned against the mantelshelf and slipped his hands into his pockets. 'Does that trouble you?'

'I've never known anyone who has killed before. You seem . . . I don't know. Well, you don't seem the kind of person who would kill someone and then act as though it never happened.'

'Meaning?'

'Well, it doesn't seem to bother you.'

'Should it?'

'You killed someone. You took a life. Don't you feel *anything*?'

'What should I be feeling, exactly?'

'I don't know. Remorse, even guilt. If not, then sadness that it had to be done.'

'How do you know I'm not feeling any of those things?'

'Because, like I said, you don't look as though you are.' She paused. 'Well, are you?'

He shook his head. 'Not at all.'

She peered at him. 'Nothing? Not a thing?'

'Vanessa, last night someone tried to kill you. They fired a laser straight at your head, and only the fact that you leaned forward at that very second saved your life. It was a contract killing, or would have been if the sniper had had his way. And you want me to feel remorse for the death of the sniper?'

She shrugged. 'Perhaps I'm not asking you to feel any voluntary regret . . . but I just wondered if you felt anything instinctively. You took a life, and subconsciously, beneath any rationalisation of the fact, you must be feeling something.'

He paused, considering her words. Artois stretched out again on her belly, hands clasped beneath her chin, watching him with an expression not far removed from amusement.

He felt like telling her that she had spent too much time acting out bad scripts in the make-believe world of virtual reality.

'You know, when Barney was murdered earlier this year . . .' he began.

'You wanted to go out and nail his killer, right? Without allowing state law to do what it was set up to do.'

How could he begin to explain what had happened to Barney? It was too complex to précis, and anyway he didn't want to stir old memories.

He just shrugged. 'Something like that.'

'What about last night?'

He looked up at her, smiled. 'Last night was different, Vanessa. For a start, the sniper wasn't human.'

Her lips twisted with amused mystification. 'Wasn't human?'

'Someone, whoever wants you dead, programmed a boosted-chimp to do their dirty work.'

55

'A boosted-chimp? I didn't know . . .'

'Listen, they're programmed to build space stations and oil rigs. Firing a laser's no problem.'

'What happened?'

'I traced the animal to a rooftop. It ran and I followed. It tried to jump across a sidestreet and misjudged the distance. Now you understand why I'm not spilling real tears?'

'But if the sniper had been human?'

Halliday pursed his lips in contemplation. 'You know something, I might even have gained more satisfaction from the death of the sniper if he'd been human. I can understand people who kill in the heat of the moment. I can even condone an act of revenge. But contract killing, an assassin who goes out and kills someone they've never even met, for money?' He shook his head. 'Call me old-fashioned, but that I find hard to take.'

'I don't understand why someone would want me dead, Hal.'

'That's something I need to talk to you about. I want answers to questions about your past: acquaintances, friends, anyone who might have a grudge against you.'

'Fire away.'

'Not over the network. We need to meet somewhere private, where we can't be overheard.'

She frowned. 'I can't make it tonight. I'm contracted to make an appearance at some dinner. How about tomorrow evening?'

'Around eight. I'll be in contact to arrange the place.'

She sat up on the bed, hugging her shins. She shook out her hair and lodged her chin on her knees. 'Won't your little girlfriend be jealous, Hal?'

He stared at her. 'Casey?'

She read something in his expression. 'Aren't you two . . .?'

'We're friends, that's all. She lodges with me.'

Artois tried not to smile. 'I saw only one bedroom last night.'

'I work nights, she works days.'

'She's a nice kid. While you were out chasing chimps, we

talked. She never got round to telling me how she came to be lodging with you.'

Halliday shrugged. 'Usual story. Her family was killed in the Atlanta meltdown. She doesn't talk about it. She was ten at the time. She left Georgia with her older sister and rode the trains north, heading for New York. Somewhere along the way she lost her sister.'

'So you found her on the streets and took her in?'

'Something like that.' He saw Artois' amused expression. 'What?'

'I don't know – you're such a bunch of contradictions, Hal. Heart-of-stone tough guy who wouldn't flinch at killing someone, and yet you go adopt a waif and stray.'

'Sounds like a cliché right out of one of your holos, Vanessa.'

'It does, doesn't it?' She sighed. 'Why can't life be simple and people conform to stereotype?'

He stared at her. 'You mean, you think I had ulterior motives in taking Casey in?'

Artois gave him a look, then, that made him realise he didn't know the VR star at all.

He changed the subject. He picked up a pix of the old couple. 'Your parents?'

She nodded. 'Died five years ago. They had their own light aircraft. Crashed in the sea off Maine.'

'So Canada came to live with you?'

She nodded. 'We were always close. It was the obvious thing to do.'

He pushed himself away from the mantelshelf. 'I'd like to look at her room.'

'Sure. Through the door to the right and along the corridor. Third door on the right. I'll follow you in.' She reached for the remote as he stepped into the corridor.

'How did she react to their deaths?' he asked as he followed her directions.

Artois' magnified face appeared on the wall of the hall, smiling out. 'She seemed to adapt very quickly,' she said.

Her face sequenced along the wall, keeping pace with him. 'Of course, for the first few weeks she was inconsolable, but after that . . .' She shrugged. 'She got over it. She was always a very private and independent person.'

Halliday turned into Canada's bedroom, and Artois' head flared into being a metre to his right.

The contents of the bedroom symbolised the life of an adolescent girl in the awkward transition from childhood to troubled mid-teens. Dolls and teddy bears lined a shelf in one corner, a nostalgic reminder of the girl she had been, but not yet discarded. They had been usurped by other toys, though – an old simulated-reality visor, a powerful computer system, various electronic devices that Halliday didn't recognise.

'Private and independent?' Halliday said. 'But last night you told me you were close.'

'We are,' Artois said. 'We share a lot. Go out a lot together. But she has her private side.'

'She does?' He looked around the room, searching for something that might indicate that not all had been right in the life of Canada Artois. 'Tell me.'

'If I could give an example, then it wouldn't be private, would it?'

Halliday looked up at her.

She gestured. 'I'm sorry. I'm being flippant.' She thought. 'Her friends. She never discusses her friends with me. When I ask her, she always changes the subject.'

'Perhaps she has a boyfriend she doesn't want you to know about?'

'I don't think so. I mean, she's had boyfriends and she's always talked about them with me. But once or twice lately she told me she was going out, and when I asked who with she just shrugged or ignored me. I don't know, perhaps it's just a teenage thing.'

'You don't mind if I . . .?'' He gestured around the room.

'Be my guest.' She climbed off the bed and padded into the bathroom.

He moved around the room, opening drawers and storage units, checking shelves and small tables. He contrasted the number of possessions in the room with what Casey had brought with her from the street: the clothes she stood up in, a carrier bag containing two T-shirts, a pair of shorts and a few basic toiletries.

Canada had all the discs of her older sister's early holo-dramas stacked on a bedside table. There were a few plastic-paged books lined up on shelves. An expensive sound system was hooked up to the wallscreen. Halliday sorted through the discs piled in a rickety drift – he hadn't heard of a single vocal artist or band. He crossed the room to the walk-in wardrobe and sorted through over a hundred dresses and outfits, going though the pockets for anything that might give him a clue as to Canada's whereabouts.

Other than a few used tickets for long-gone dances and invites to uptown parties, he found nothing. He looked around the room. Where might she conceal things that she wished to keep hidden from her sister?

As a kid, he'd stashed candy bars and war novels under his mattress for night-time consumption, and his parents had never seemed any the wiser.

He pulled the pillow and the thermal blanket from the bed, then lifted the mattress. He smiled to himself. Either the youth of today were as unimaginative as he had been, or beneath the mattress was really the best place in the world to secrete juvenile contraband.

He glanced back at the wallscreen. Artois was still in the bathroom. He propped the mattress against the wall and stared down at the revealed hoard: a personal soft-screen – probably a diary – and next to it at least a dozen VR cards.

He whistled to himself and sorted through the cards. He expected to find they were months old and expired, but to his surprise he discovered that they'd all been issued within the past month and were valid for another two. Each card was for a different VR Bar in the city, at least ten in the Manhattan and uptown districts, and half a dozen others in refugee areas. Each card could be used daily for anything up to the standard four-hour immersion.

And yesterday Artois had claimed that Canada used the VR Bars for just ten hours a week. In all likelihood she was an addict, using more than one Bar a day. He wondered how Artois had failed to notice the tell-tale signs of over-use: tiredness, jaundice, a susceptibility to colds and viral infections.

Of course, there might have been a perfectly innocent explanation: she was keeping these cards for her under-age friends who weren't allowed in the Bars. That was the story she would no doubt have told her sister in the event of Vanessa discovering the hoard.

He was no closer to locating the whereabouts of Canada Artois, but he was a little nearer to understanding the type of person she was. He knew Canada's most closely guarded secret, knew where she spent a good proportion of her free time, and that was a start.

He saw a flash of movement on the edge of his vision as Vanessa returned from the bathroom and flopped onto the bed. 'What you got there, Hal?'

He slipped the cards into his jacket pocket and held up the soft-screen. 'I think this might be her diary,' he said. 'I'd like to take it with me if that's okay?'

'Sure. Anything that might help.'

He returned the mattress to the bed and rearranged the thermal blanket. He glanced around the room one last time, looking for something he might have missed.

Artois said, 'What would anyone want with my sister, Hal?'

He shook his head. There were a dozen answers to her question, depending on the nature of that *anyone*. She was a young, pretty girl, no doubt naïve and trusting – easy prey for a man experienced in the practice of picking up innocent girls. Then again, there was always the possibility that the person who wanted Artois dead had taken Canada as some kind of lure.

A more likely explanation, Halliday thought, was that she was strung out from a VR overdose and resting up at some friend's house . . . But, if that were so, why hadn't she called her sister with some excuse?

'Do you own a computer?'

'In the study, next to the lounge. Why?'

'I want to check something.' He stepped from the bedroom. Artois' giant face followed him along the hall. 'If it's powerful enough I can get into the memory of a few surveillance cameras, probably get some indication of the direction Canada went on Monday morning.'

He stepped into the study, a functional work-room equipped with a desk and storage units and a big Senko deskcom. It wasn't as powerful as the model he had back at the office, but it would do for the time being.

The VR star's face flashed onto the wall, watching him.

'You'll need the password,' she said as he sat before the desk.

'Let me guess,' he said. 'How about . . .' He tried to recall the studio she had first signed for. Casey had mentioned it last night. 'How about "Imperial"?'

She stared at him. 'Jesus, Hal. I mean, that isn't the password now, but the first computer I bought . . .' She laughed. 'Imperial was the password I used then. How'd you know?'

'I didn't. I guessed.'

'Actually the password is "Fetish". Don't read anything into it. I was starring in a VR production called *Dead Fetish* when I bought the rig.'

He entered the password and bent over the keyboard, tapping into the cityweb and entering the police network.

On the wallscreen, he was aware that Vanessa Artois had moved from the bed. She stood with her back to the screen and slipped the robe from her shoulders, and he couldn't help himself but stare at the sight of her naked figure. She knelt, sorting though a pile of clothes, and something in the calculated poise of her movements told Halliday that this

61

little act was staged for his benefit. His mouth felt suddenly dry and he knew he was colouring. He was torn between watching her and turning away before she discovered him.

She stood, slipping a black dress over raised arms, and Halliday turned to the screen and concentrated on the keyboard.

One of the benefits of having worked in the police department was that he could make free and easy use of their surveillance apparatus. What he was doing was technically illegal, but the resources of the New York police were so stretched, trying to maintain some semblance of law and order on the streets of the city, that a blind eye was turned to relatively victimless crimes like hacking.

Digitally stored images from the thousands of surveillance cameras across the city were kept on police records for a month, then wiped to make room for the next batch. Halliday attempted to access the camera outside the Plaza building on the morning of 6th June, around nine. He fast-forwarded through the rush hour, such as it was, and slowed the scene every time a flash of canary yellow showed through the smog. Ten minutes later he came up with something. A taxi pulled up outside the Plaza and a girl, answering the description of Canada Artois, ran out from beneath the striped awning and ducked into the back of the vehicle. It pulled away from the curb and merged with the sparse traffic.

Halliday accessed the next camera at roughly the same time and monitored the cab's progress as it motored up Madison Avenue. For the next few minutes he skipped from camera to camera and charted the taxi as it made its way uptown.

'Where did you say Canada attended college?' he asked. He turned to the wallscreen. Artois was making a performance of pulling on a pair of panties.

He looked away.

'Turner's, down in Greenwich.'

'In that case she didn't attend college Monday,' he told her.

She looked over her shoulder. 'You have any idea where she went?'

'She headed north, towards Harlem. The cameras start cutting out around 96th Street. Vandalism. It could take a couple of hours to locate the working cameras.'

He decided to head back to the office and complete the surveillance on his own rig.

Artois had seated herself on the edge of the bed. 'So if she skipped college, went off in the opposite direction in a taxi . . . at least that means she knew where she was heading, for whatever reasons.' Her eyes lost their focus. 'But why hasn't she contacted me, Hal? I've never known her do anything like this before.'

He hesitated. 'Are you sure she isn't deeply into VR? I mean, so many kids are these days. It can take over their lives.'

Artois bit her lip, shook her head 'I'm certain she isn't addicted, Hal. She tanks, sure. She goes with friends every week. She told me she liked the gaming zones.'

'How many times a week do you see Canada?'

'That depends on how busy I am. If I'm doing publicity work and the session over-runs, then I might not see Canada for days. But I'd say certainly once a week.'

Halliday nodded.

'What?' she asked.

'Nothing. I had the impression that you saw her more often than that.'

'I'd like to, Hal. But you must understand that pressure of work . . .' She stopped and stared at him. 'You think she might be hooked and I haven't noticed?'

He hesitated. 'Of course not. There's no evidence at all to suggest that. I've got to look at every possibility, is all.'

'I know. I appreciate that.' She glanced at the small gold watch on her tanned wrist and twisted her lips in the universal grimace of the unpunctual.

'I've got to fly, Hal. Call me about tomorrow night, okay?'

'Sure, see you then.'

She waved fingers, found the remote and zapped off the wallscreen.

Halliday turned off the desk-com and sat in the sudden silence, considering everything he'd found out about Canada Artois.

Ten minutes later he let himself out of the apartment and took the elevator to the ground floor. As he drove north through the quiet streets, his mind strayed from the case. He considered Vanessa, and the little flesh-show back there, and he found it impossible to erase the image of her nakedness from his mind.

Five

The rain had stopped, but the downpour had done little to freshen the air. Halliday turned onto his street and slowed. Two rows of food-stalls stretched away into the distance, their rain-slick awnings bright in the wash of the halogen night-lights. Families sat on the steps of the brownstones, and other groups, refugees without homes, trooped along the sidewalk, begging food from stallholders.

He parked outside the laundry, climbed the rank staircase to the office and unlocked the door. Across the room the bedroom door stood slightly ajar. Casey was asleep on the bed, fully dressed, Artois' silver Gucci coat arranged next to her like a child's comforter. He eased the door shut and switched on the fan; the humidity in the room was not so much reduced as rearranged.

Only then did he notice that the miniature oak was no longer on the desk.

He moved back to the bedroom door and opened it. The thought that the bonsai might have been stolen created a sickening sensation in the pit of his stomach.

On the table beside the bed, next to Casey's pile of crumpled five-dollar notes, was the miniature oak. He smiled to himself as he lifted the tree and carried it back into the office.

Casey had placed a mail package on the desk. He sat down and opened the silver padded envelope and pulled out a thick, impressive-looking book. *Beyond Persephone*, he read, and on the cover below the title the name of the author – Anna Ellischild, his sister.

Anna had included a brief letter. Halliday unfolded it and

read slowly. She was enjoying life in Seattle and working hard on her next book. She asked how he was, and invited him over for a holiday; she said the clean air would do him good. Halliday thought back six months to the incident in the Cyber-Tech headquarters, and how he had saved his sister's life that night. It seemed like a lifetime ago, the events already hazy in his memory.

He laid the book aside and picked up the framed picture from beside the desk-com. It showed Anna aged five, and her twin sister Eloise. As he stared at the photograph, he felt an aching grief at the death of Eloise in the fire that had destroyed their childhood home, over twenty years ago. The agony of bereavement never went away, it just changed into something a little less painful, a little more manageable. We somehow learn to live with what at the time seems like intolerable pain, he thought; which was just as well, for the alternative was madness.

He replaced the picture and regarded the miniature oak. Something about its intricately detailed and scaled-down perfection induced a feeling of calm. Staring at the tortured torque of its gnarled limbs, its panoply of tiny verdant leaves, Halliday imagined himself reduced in size and part of its perfect landscape. He thought of the many hours he'd spent among the trees bordering his parents' garden, in countryside contaminated and moribund for the past ten years.

He made a mental note to download information about the care and upkeep of bonsai, and also to find out how much they were going for on the black market. Not that he had any intention of selling it: the tree was more precious to him than cash. He was curious as to how much Vanessa Artois had been willing to pay to buy his silence.

He took Canada's soft-screen diary from his jacket pocket and connected it to the desk-com, instructing his rig to bypass the diary's password and download its contents. Seconds later the screen on the desk flickered and displayed short sections of text.

He supposed it was the typical teenager's diary: hurried reminders of dates not to be missed, interspersed with short paragraphs of inarticulate, if heartfelt, juvenile angst.

The entries began two years earlier. He scanned the early sections, every day conscientiously filled in before she became bored with the effort. She detailed what she was learning at college and gave brief descriptions of her friends, and what they did in their free time. It was an insight, he thought, into the privileged lifestyle of a spoilt little rich kid – a round of lavish parties, meals at expensive restaurants he'd never dream of using, trips to the theatre and opera.

He had to smile at some of the entries: *J's a bitch! She told D that I hated him. D believed her and now won't talk to me! That's it with J from now on – she's struck off!*

There was no mention of VR Bars until almost a year ago.

16th June: *Van bought me a VR card for my birthday! I went with J – incredible! It's so real! I mean, we were really on Mars, exploring Olympus Mons with the colonists! And the feeling when you came out, the euphoria . . . I didn't like the feeling when I submerged myself in the tank, though – icky! We're going again next week.*

Halliday skipped to a couple of months ago. He read the entry for 20th May: *Went with D and J to the new Bar on Liberty. D had been before, said it was heavy. Me and J watched – I couldn't believe some of the things. After, J said she might try it next time. I don't know. I mean, I know it's only VR, and you're not really doing it – but it feels so real. I'll see how I feel next time. Must admit though, watching it I felt really HOT!*

Halliday read the entry again, intrigued. The next entry was just two days later. 22nd May: *J and D and me went to Liberty last night and I met X again. I went with X, and then J and D joined in. After, it was strange, out in the real world with J and D . . . We're going again in two days. Trouble is, I'm under eighteen and the Liberty Bar only issues cards for two-hour sessions. (But D says that's no problem. I can get cards for other Bars if I can find the cash!) I hope Van never finds out about this. I mean, I feel guilty, but at the same time I want to go – I can't help it. Like J says, it's part of growing up. And in VR you can't catch all the diseases out there in the real world.*

For the following month, Canada tanked in various Bars every other day. Her descriptions of the visits became increasingly less detailed as the novelty wore off and she became addicted to the sessions.

During the period of the past two weeks, she had tanked every day in a variety of places across the city. She didn't bother to describe her experience, merely noted: 24th June: *The Caribbean Club – great!*

Halliday found other entries, however, describing her home life.

27th June: *Van in a mood again. At first I thought she'd found out – but she's not angry with me. Something to do with the studio. Mantoni won't extend her contract or something. I've never seen her this down about anything before.*

29th June: *Yesterday Van told me that she told Mantoni that she wanted to quit – get out of her contract. She felt she was being exploited. Her agent is working on it. Just hope she can find work. How will I pay for the sessions without my allowance?*

1st July: *Van was crying in the bathroom today. I wanted to say something to help. What could I say? She wouldn't even tell me what was going on. J called and we went to the Cherokee.*

The last entry was dated 5th July, two days before Canada Artois took the cab ride and vanished. Halliday read the entry, then read it again, and he knew he was onto something.

Arranged to meet J and D on Monday morning. I'm skipping classes and going straight to the Bar. X said he'd arrange things.

Halliday sat back and stared at the words on the screen, wondering what it was that Canada Artois was alluding to.

He thought of Vanessa, and the trouble she was facing at the studio. How could he tell her that her kid sister was involved in something that sounded less than wholesome – with people she referred to only by their initials? X indeed!

68

He remembered that he had Canada's address book in his pocket. He flipped it open to the relevant pages. There were various entries listed under both J and D, but none under X.

He cleared the diary from the screen and patched into the police network. A minute later he was following Canada's cab from outside the Plaza apartments. They motored up Madison towards Harlem, to the point where he had lost them earlier that evening. From now on, the surveillance system was erratic. For the next ten minutes he tried to follow the taxi as it made its way through the neighbourhood – a series of staccato images as he jumped from one camera to the next, often losing the cab altogether and having to backtrack to pick it up again. His luck ran out as the taxi turned onto Lexington Avenue, about half a kay west of his office – but that was probably close enough.

There were only three VR Bars in the vicinity. He pulled Canada's VR cards from his pocket and shuffled through them. He found cards for the Caribbean and Mario's, which suggested that on Monday morning she had taken the card that would allow her entry into the remaining VR Bar in the area: Thai Joe's.

Halliday tried to access the surveillance cameras on East 106th Street, but the only working camera was situated two hundred metres west of Thai Joe's. He could look along the street and make out the neon halation that marked the VR Bar in the distance, but it was hard to identify vehicles, and impossible to make out individuals.

Canada had met the mysterious X in VR, and then disappeared. He wondered how much he should tell Vanessa of what he'd found out. That really depended, he decided, on how much more he discovered between now and when he next met the VR star.

He killed the desk-com, locked the miniature oak in the bottom drawer of the desk, and left the office.

It was two in the morning and the street was still busy. He turned right and walked, wondering despite himself what

Kim might be doing right at this moment. No doubt shacked up with the bastard Chinese stallholder, screwing . . . He cut that line of thought.

He glanced up between the enclosing buildings in the hope of catching a rare glimpse of the stars. The overcast was dense, concealing constellations that past experience told him were out there somewhere. He realised that kids must have grown up in the city and never seen distant suns. He'd try to remember and ask Casey if she had ever seen the stars. He smiled to himself: she'd probably say sure, she'd seen plenty of holo-dramas.

The main drag was crowded, as ever. Even at this late hour citizens promenaded along the street, tourists from out of town enjoying the atmosphere and locals hawking everything from ethnic foods to the latest fad in legalised drugs.

Thai Joe was patrolling his patch outside the Bar, strolling up and down the sidewalk in his Hawaiian shirt and flip-flops. He bestowed his fixed-grin indiscriminately and pointed out the Bar to anyone who met his eye. 'Hey, friend, you tried Joe's VR Bar yet? Best in town! Guaranteed! You want some fun? Step inside.'

He was doing a steady trade tonight, with a constant procession of customers passing through the neon-framed portals.

He saw Halliday coming and raised a hand for a panto-mime high-five. Halliday obliged. 'Hal, my friend! Come for discount tanking? Hey, come in. You want beer?'

Halliday followed Joe into the Bar and climbed onto a stool. Joe made a point of checking him over. 'Hey, no boosted-chimp's shot you today, Hal?'

'Not today, Joe, but would you believe it – I'm seeing a VR star tomorrow night.'

Joe raised a hand high into the air and brought it down on Halliday's thigh, roaring with laughter. 'You lead great life, Hal! Chimp shoot-outs one day, VR stars the next!' He gestured to Jimmy to hurry with the beers.

'How's trade, Joe?'

'Could be better. Things are slowing down bad. See, some of the other Bars, downtown, they been bought out, taken over. Big concerns moving in. Word is Mafia behind the buyouts.'

'Sounds bad.'

Thai Joe shrugged. 'These places, they do good deals, reduce prices to bring in customers. Citizens aren't loyal, Hal. They go any place that does good deal.'

Jimmy returned with two beers and slid them across the counter. 'And you're losing out?' Halliday asked, taking a swallow.

'Feeling pinch, Hal. Don't know how much longer I go on before I bring prices down too.' He raised his beer in a gesture of resignation. 'Hey, you tanking today?'

Halliday wiped his mouth with the back of his hand. 'That depends, Joe. I'm working on a case.'

'Missing person, ha?'

He nodded. 'That's right, Joe. I think they might've showed up here Monday morning, tanked a while, moved on ... Maybe you can help me?'

Thai Joe made an expansive gesture, suggesting unbound munificence. 'Hal, Hal ... you know me. Any time.'

Halliday slipped a pix of Canada Artois from his jacket pocket and passed it across to Joe. 'I suspect she was here around nine thirty Monday morning, with a couple of friends.'

Joe squinted at the pix, his porcine eyes lost in folds of fat. He screwed up his lips with the effort of recollection. 'Pretty girl, Hal. I'd sure remember girl that pretty.' He shook his head. 'Sorry, Hal.'

Halliday took a long swallow of beer and watched Thai Joe above the bottle. 'How long have I been coming here, Joe?'

Joe smiled, uneasy. 'Why, months, Hal!'

'And I'd like to keep coming here. I don't want to see the place closed. The other day I heard about a Bar uptown, its

71

owner jailed and his joint shut down. He had a sex zone, but you see he was letting kids in – under-age kids, thirteen-, fourteen-year-olds. The cops found out and down he went.'

Thai Joe was shaking his head in a wonderful display of rueful contemplation. 'Too bad, Hal. Risky game.'

'You see,' Halliday said, 'I know the kid was here. And I know she liked the sex zones. And I also know you run sex zones. Now, I wouldn't want the cops to come investigating . . .' He took another draught of beer, longer this time, and let Thai Joe sweat.

He gestured with the bottle. 'But I think I can help you, Joe. I was a cop, once. I still have friends in the force. If I say a place is clean, they'll believe me. If I tip them a place is breaking the law . . .' He shrugged. 'That's just too bad.' He passed the pix of Canada Artois to Thai Joe. 'Take another look. Think about it. Maybe if you think hard enough, you'll remember.'

Joe peered at the picture. He glanced across the bar at Jimmy, then looked at Hal. 'Face is familiar, Hal. I've seen her before somewhere. Maybe she did come here.'

'Monday morning, with a couple of friends. Think hard, now.'

Joe fired off a round of Thai at Jimmy, as musical as a xylophone arpeggio, and passed him the pix. Jimmy looked from the pix to Halliday, then answered Joe.

Halliday said, 'What did he say?'

Joe returned the pix. 'Monday morning! I was out . . . Jimmy says, two girls and a boy, they came and tanked. One of the girls was girl in pix.'

'Where did they go, Joe?'

The smile never shifted, but his eyes took on the startlement of a frightened rabbit's.

'Where they go? In VR?' He laughed uneasily. He spoke to Jimmy, who replied quickly, darting a hostile glance at Halliday.

'Jimmy says he doesn't know. Privacy code, Hal. You know, every citizen has the right—'

72

'I know the code, Joe. I also know that you keep records.'

'Okay, okay. We go in back, control room. I look for you. Come, this way.'

Halliday passed the empty bottle to Jimmy, winked at him and slipped from his stool. He followed Joe through a pair of swing doors. The VR Bar was a long, discreetly lighted room sumptuously furnished with couches and armchairs. Waitresses in trim navy uniforms passed among the waiting customers with trays of drinks. Imitation-timber doors led to individual VR booths.

Thai Joe escorted Halliday across the thick carpet to the control centre, the fat Hawaiian-shirted businessman oddly out of place in the plush environs of his own establishment.

The control centre was a small, dark room packed with computer monitors and half a dozen sweating technicians. Thai Joe ordered one of them from her seat and slumped into it himself. He worked at the keyboard with a surprisingly deft action.

'Name of girl, Hal?'

'Artois, Canada Artois. Where did she go on Monday morning?'

In the half-light of the cramped control room Halliday was unable to make out Joe's expression, but he saw him wipe his palms down the front of his shirt.

He tapped at the keyboard. Text appeared on the screen, jargon Halliday was unable to decode. 'Well?'

Thai Joe cleared his throat. 'It say here, Aphrodesia, Hal. But I swear, this is some mistake. I don't know, maybe girl got in with adult card.'

Halliday let it ride. 'I'm not bothered how she got in, Joe,' he said. 'How long was she tanked?'

'Just . . .' He consulted the screen. 'Two and half hours, Hal. She left just after midday.'

'Okay . . . So, what we have here is an illegal operation. If this gets out . . .'

'Hal, my friend. It was mistake, genuine lapse. I assure you.'

'I don't want assurances, Joe. I just want one thing.'

A pause. When Joe spoke, it was almost a whisper, 'What you want, Hal?'

'Can't you guess, Joe? I want playback.'

Silence, then a hurried whisper: 'Playback, and you keep hush-hush, okay?'

'Deal, Joe. I get playback and I'll forget I ever heard of Aphrodesia and under-age customers, okay?'

'Okay, Hal, I'll get it set up.'

Thai Joe barked an order at the tech on the next console and led Halliday from the control room. 'You drive a hard bargain, Hal.'

'Hey, nothing personal. I just want to find this kid.'

Joe led Halliday across the waiting room to a private VR booth and unlocked the door.

He took Halliday's arm in a fierce grip. 'I know what you thinking, Hal. You thinking – Thai Joe, evil man letting kids in sex zones. But better they do it in sex zones than out there, Hal. I provide service that people want.'

He sighed. 'Sure, Joe. No sweat.'

'You go in and I'll have playback relayed to your tank, okay?'

Halliday stepped into the booth. In the middle of the small white-tiled chamber, set flush with the floor, was the crystal-line cover of the jellytank, the suspension gel a dark shade of honey. He had only ever witnessed one or two citizens in suspension, caught like flies in amber, and he had always found it difficult to equate the unnatural sight of the immersed subject with the fact of the pleasure they would be experiencing.

He programmed the press-select panel on the tiled wall. He undressed, hung his clothes on the hanger provided, then slipped the leads around his arms and legs. He placed the faceplate over his head and stared out though the green-tinted visor.

Then he raised the lid of the jellytank and stepped down, into the warm and clutching embrace of the gel. It seemed to

74

suck at him, moulding itself around his body with an invasive and intimate caress. He lay back and floated free, his limbs curiously light and devoid of feeling. He imagined that the sensation must be much like weightlessness in space. Through the faceplate he could see the gel ooze over the visor, encapsulating him. He closed his eyes.

Gradually, over a period of thirty seconds, he lost awareness of his senses. He was blind and deaf, and without tactile sensation. As he waited, he realised that he was apprehensive about what exactly he might find in Aphrodesia.

Then it was as if he had been instantly transported. He felt a quick heat pass through his head, and he was no longer lying in the jellytank. The first few seconds of transition, when his mind refused to believe that he was anywhere else other than in the tank – even though his senses relayed the extraordinary notion that he was miraculously *elsewhere* – were always the most disconcerting. He was standing upright, and he could feel the ground beneath his feet, a light breeze and sunlight on his exposed skin.

He opened his eyes. He was in a rolling green landscape of gentle vales and meadows, the undulating monotony of the rural idyll offset by the occasional stand of trees – beech in their autumn livery of blazing russet and gold. In wonder he walked towards the closest tree, his amazement at the sight of the beech suddenly switching to the fact of his presence here. He looked down the length of his body: he was garbed in the blue default gown of all VR users who had not preprogrammed specific dress. He touched his face; he could feel the skin of his cheek, even though in the real world he was wearing the faceplate.

He circled the tree, staring up in appreciation at the dizzyingly complex ramifications of its branches. He approached its solid and striated trunk, reached out and touched the crumbling bark. The feel of it beneath his fingertips brought a smile to his lips.

From a nearby hilltop he heard a peal of joyful laughter.

He turned and stared. Situated on hilltops between the trees were timber A-frames; outside the nearest, a naked couple rolled on the grass, making vigorous and abandoned love.

As Halliday stood in the shade of the tree and watched, obscurely disconcerted, the air before him shimmered. The figure of a young girl appeared, ghost-like at first. Then the image established and gradually gained solidity. He stared: it was Canada Artois, but a version of Canada transformed from the pix he had taken from her apartment. In the real world she was a slim, almost sexless fifteen, but in Aphrodesia, as he should have expected, she had elected to programme herself an altered appearance. She was still manifestly young, but her body was fuller. Her breasts pushed at the material of her gown; her legs were almost ridiculously long. She looked like an idealised version of her older sister.

Seconds later two other figures materialised beside her, a red-headed girl and a blonde boy, both dressed in blue default gowns. Halliday was sure these two kids had also chosen altered appearances – their bodies were too slim and perfect to be true.

The three laughed and embraced each other, then held hands and walked up a hillside and sat down on the summit.

Halliday followed. He climbed the gentle slope and knelt before the kids.

The one lie to the reality of this playback of Aphrodesia was that Canada and her friends could not see Halliday. What he was experiencing now was a recording of what had happened on Monday morning. The world around him was the same as ever, a virtual construct stored in the powerful memory core of the worldwide VR-net, but Canada and the others were no more than ghosts in an electronic synthesis, albeit ghosts which looked and sounded wholly authentic.

The red-headed girl sprang suddenly to her feet and ran towards him – and before he could obey his instincts and move out of her way, she had passed through him. Halliday flinched and recoiled, disconcerted at the experience of what looked like solid flesh and bone being able to run straight through him, as if *he* were the phantom haunting this pastoral wonderland.

'Jenny!' Canada called after her friend. 'Where you going?'

The red-headed girl stooped to pluck a flower from beside the beech tree – a golden daffodil. She carried it back up the hillside and presented it to the boy.

He made a grab for Jenny, who danced laughing from his advance. From her position on the grass, posed on her side with the gown falling from her thighs, Canada laughed and said: 'Can't you even wait, David? There'll be plenty of time later.'

'What's wrong with now?' he said, collapsing to the ground beside Canada.

'Why are men always so impatient?' she said to Jenny. 'They have absolutely no sense of anticipation.' She turned to David. 'Doesn't contemplation of what we're going to do make it all the more desirable?'

'Why all the analysis?' David asked, lying on his back and staring up at the clouds. 'That's the trouble with you, Canada. You've had a great education, and you're always trying to prove it.'

Jenny said, 'Canada's right. Leave her alone, Dave.'

David pulled Jenny to him. She put up a half-hearted struggle, allowing the boy to unfasten her gown.

She lay naked on the grass, legs spread. Halliday could only stare as David tore off his gown and knelt before Jenny. Smiling up at him, she took his cock in her right hand and eased him into her.

Smiling to herself, Canada watched as her friends rolled across the grass.

Then she looked up and waved at someone behind Halliday. He turned to look. Down the hill, the air shimmered. A form gained substance, a small, deeply tanned bald-headed man in his forties, a gold stud piercing his nose. His default gown concealed a well-muscled body.

X, Halliday thought.

The man waved and climbed the hill, smiling at the antics of Jenny and David.

The guy approached Canada and sat down. 'So you made it, Canada,' he whispered to her. 'Great to see you, kid. All set for this afternoon?'

'Ready and waiting,' Canada said.

So X knew Canada by her name, even though the practice was to use assumed tags in VR. Halliday wondered if she simply used her real name in VR or if X knew Canada in the real world.

Still crouching, X rubbed his hands together. 'You don't know how good this is gonna be, kitten.'

Canada smiled with an attempt at adult lasciviousness. 'I can imagine,' she said.

'We'll meet at two,' X continued. 'The usual place. Then I'll show you around.'

'You're not at Thai Joe's now?' Canada asked.

'I linked in from elsewhere,' X said. 'Why make the journey in the real world?' He reached out and stroked Canada's cheek. 'Hey we have some time to kill. Why not have some fun?'

Halliday watched as Canada sat up. She was taking rapid breaths. Her face was flushed. She reached behind her and unfastened the gown. The material whispered down the improved curves of her body.

X smiled and shrugged off his gown. He was hung like an elephant. They came together with the urgent, practiced choreography of lust, Canada taking him in her mouth while he leaned back and gasped with pleasure.

Halliday was torn between watching and running away. There was something almost shocking in the rapid transformation from what had been to what was happening now. He felt himself reacting as he stared, felt an irrational shame at his body's involuntary response.

Unable to take much more, he touched the small quit decal on the back of his hand and closed his eyes.

When he opened them again, he was in the jellytank. He sat up, the images of the tableau on the hillside diminishing like the figments of a dream. He stood and stepped from the tank, the gel slithering from his body like so many live things returning to their lair. He was aware that he had climaxed during the immersion: a swirl of semen turned in the gel like cream in coffee. As he watched, the tank emptied, the gel sluicing away to be filtered, cleaned, and replaced.

Halliday sat on the stool for long minutes, going over what he had seen in Aphrodesia.

X had arranged to take Canada somewhere. He was meeting her – or rather *had* met her – at some prearranged locale, and from there . . .?

He showered, scrubbing the remnants of the gel from his body. As he stood beneath the blower, drying himself, he wondered how he would begin to tell Vanessa Artois what he had found out today .

He dressed and left the booth. The lounge was full of people awaiting their allotted span in the paradise of their choosing. He wondered how many of them were destined for the delights of Aphrodesia.

He pushed through the outer door, into the neon glare of the lobby, and hiked himself onto a bar stool. He ordered a beer from Jimmy and signalled across the sidewalk to Thai Joe.

'Hey, you find what you wanted?' Joe beamed at him. 'Everything okay?'

'Sure, everything's fine.'

'This one on the house, Hal.'

Jimmy passed him a beer. 'One other thing, Joe. Midday, Monday – when the tall girl quit the Bar, you know where she headed?'

Joe spoke to Jimmy. Halliday chugged his beer and waited.

Thai Joe said, 'She take taxi from here.'

'What company?'

Thai Joe reached behind the bar and pulled a plasticard

from between a row of bottles. 'Green-line Taxis, Hal. Office just around corner.'

Halliday finished his beer and jabbed Joe in the bicep. 'Be seeing you around, Joe.'

Dawn was breaking over the city. Soon, what passed for sunlight during the smog-filled summer's day would reveal the streets in all their decrepit squalor, without the ersatz glitz of the neon-filled night.

Halliday hurried down the sidewalk, turned the corner and brushed past two drunks in the doorway of the Green-line Taxi office.

He flashed his old police identity card at the fat man behind the counter. 'Monday around noon you picked up a young girl from Thai Joe's. Where'd she go?'

'Hey, we make a lot of pick-ups, pal.'

'This girl was tall, brunette.' He produced a pix of Canada and showed the fat guy.

The guy squinted. 'That's Canada, a regular customer. Hang on.' He turned in his swivel chair and spoke into a microphone. 'Lou, you pick Canada up Monday? Outside Joe's? Some cop wants to know.' He waited, eyeing Halliday up and down. 'That's right. Okay.'

He returned to his seat. 'Lou picked her up around twelve thirty,' he told Halliday. 'Took her downtown to Battery Park. She boarded a ferry.'

'You know where to?'

'That's as much as I know, bud.'

Halliday nodded. He quit the office and crossed the street. He'd check the surveillance cameras around the Battery Park ferry terminal, see if they showed anything. If they were working, and if they recorded the real-life image of X – not the big-dicked, muscled persona X had assumed in Aphrodesia – then he might be onto something. He smiled to himself. He was hoping for a hell of a lot.

The aroma hit him as he turned into his street. The air was filled with the sound of sizzling meat and loud Mandarin as stallholders called back and forth. Halliday realised that he hadn't eaten since last night. The thought of beef noodles drowned in sauce appeared before him like a vision.

He found the stall where Casey worked, a rickety mock-timber structure flanked by stacks of caged chickens and rabbits. She was leaning on the counter, flicking through a plastic comic book, and looked up when Halliday approached. 'Hey, what you doing up? The sun's out.'

'Working late, Casey.'

'You hungry? Beef noodles?'

He looked at her. 'Listen to the mind-reader. How'd you know?'

She crossed her eyes. 'The other night? The tree file? Remember our bet?' She shook her head at him. 'You won. No glitches. It worked fine.'

He smiled. 'Beef noodles, then. I could eat a horse.'

'Hey, that's probably what the beef is today.'

She turned and scooped noodles into a tub, passed it over to him with a plastic fork. 'You got a minute, Hal? I need to talk.'

He hesitated. 'Sure. Why not?'

'It's quiet so I'll take a break.' She spoke to the old woman behind her in the stall, who was intent on decapitating a struggling chicken.

Casey pushed through a swing-gate at the back of the stall and pointed across the street to a flight of steps in the shade.

Halliday walked across and sat down, forking noodles.

Casey sat beside him, legs drawn up to her chest. She reached down and held her soiled toes, chin fitted in the gap between her knees.

Eating, Halliday watched her. 'So?'

She glanced at him without moving her head. 'Promise you won't laugh?'

'That depends. If you're gonna tell one of your jokes, then I promise.'

She jabbed him viciously with a pointy elbow. 'I mean, don't think I'm dumb, okay?'

81

'Hey!' He forked the spilled noodles from the front of his shirt. 'Okay, okay. I won't think you're dumb. What is it?'

She pulled at her toes, not looking at him. 'I've been saving up,' she murmured.

'That's great. How much you got?'

'About five hundred dollars.'

'On your wage? I'm impressed.'

She shrugged. 'I mean, I don't spend much. Food's free. I don't pay you cash for the room.'

'What you saving up for, Casey?' He tried to imagine what she might want to buy. She was a kid of few possessions. Halliday had only ever seen her spend money on second-hand comic books from the stall down the street. 'Don't tell me. New clothes? A dress, right?'

She scowled at him. 'Yeah, sure. A dress with pink ribbons and lace.' She shut up, staring down at her feet.

'Well?' Halliday tipped up the carton and drank down the last of the beef sauce.

'The other night, you brought back that thing for Vanessa? What you call it? A chu, right?'

He tried not to make disappointment evident in his reply. 'Yeah, a chu. Capillary holo unit.'

'How much was it?' She was whispering, as if in fear of his reaction.

'Eight thousand,' Halliday said. 'I bought her the best. There were others for much less than that. You could pick up a second-hand unit for around eight hundred, a thousand. They wouldn't have the range of personas . . .' He shrugged.

Casey sighed. 'The other night, in the bedroom. It was like a magic trick, wasn't it, Hal? All those faces. I mean, she was beautiful to begin with, but she put the chu on and adjusted the slide and she was just another plain Jane. But it'll work the other way around. A unit can make you beautiful, right?'

'That why you want one, to make you look like some VR star?'

Casey bridled. 'No.' She flashed him a look. 'Not a VR star. I just want to look . . . different, that's all.'

82

He let the silence stretch, wondering what to say. At last he said, 'Would you say I'm handsome, Casey?'

She graced him with a sidelong look of exaggerated dubiety. 'You?'

'I know I'm no leading man.' He laughed 'Look at this nose, all leaned over to one side. Chin the other way. Hair hasn't seen a comb for ten years.'

She smiled.

'Why try to be something you're not, Casey? Accept who you are.'

'That's easy for you to say. You're a guy. It's different for guys.'

He shrugged. 'Maybe.'

'You see, boys expect girls to look good. If you don't . . .'

'Casey, listen to me. You look fine. You're a nice kid.'

'Yeah, sure. Look at me – face like a chicken. Ears that stick out.'

'Hey, chickens don't have ears.'

She laughed, despite herself. 'I want to look good, Hal. I just want to look different.'

He nodded. 'So, okay. What's brought all this about?'

She shrugged, not looking at him. At last she said, 'See that boy over there, at the tea stall? Chinese kid.'

Halliday looked across the street at a thin, short-haired boy around fifteen. 'You like him?'

She nodded. 'Sure. Just look at him. He's great. But would he take a second look at me?'

'You talked to him?'

'As if he'd talk to me!'

'You don't know that. If he's a nice guy, he'll talk. Show interest in him and he'll respond. Trust me, I know about these things. Hell, if I were younger I'd be flattered if you came on to me.'

Casey blushed. 'Just saying that,' she murmured.

'What I'm saying is, before you go spending a lot of money on something you don't need, go talk to him. Suggest you go see a holo-drama.'

She shrugged with marked reluctance and said nothing, but now and again shot glances across the street at the Chinese kid.

Halliday considered the contrast between the confidence of the kids he'd watched in Aphrodesia and Casey's timidity. They were like different species.

He took the back of Casey's neck and squeezed. 'It's time I wasn't here. Catch you later, okay?'

'Yeah, later.'

He crossed the street and climbed the stairs to his office. The Chinese laundry was doing its best to make the place uninhabitable. The old mercury thermometer read in the high nineties. He turned on the fan and sat behind his desk, then pulled the tiny oak from behind the computer and stared at it. The sight of its self-contained, couldn't-give-a-shit perfection was therapy in itself.

Ten minutes later he switched on the desk-com and patched into the police surveillance cameras. He accessed the Monday early afternoon files and watched a green cab motoring away from Thai Joe's Bar. He never got a good close-up, but he thought he could see Canada's bobbed cut through the grime-smeared windows. He followed the cab all the way downtown to Battery Park.

He patched into cameras around the ferry terminal about the time the cab should have showed. Three cameras relayed good close-ups of the terminal entrance, a couple of others longer-range shots.

Halliday leaned forward when the Green-line cab pulled into sight outside the terminal. He saw a girl jump out and sprint for the departing ferry. The digital timer in the corner of the screen read 13.15. So she was catching the boat to Liberty Island.

He patched into the surveillance camera on Liberty Island and fast-forwarded until the 13.15 ferry docked. Perhaps a hundred passengers alighted. Among them he made out the tall dark-haired figure of Canada Artois.

She passed out of frame, and Halliday patched into a camera overlooking the path that led to the Statue of Liberty.

The silver dome of the Liberty arboretum scintillated in the distance like a dew drop. Canada walked up the path towards the dome, then stopped. She stood outside for a while, watching street magicians perform their tricks.

He waited, tense, for X to show himself. If he came down the path where the camera was situated, then Halliday's luck was in. He'd be able to patch together some identifiable pix to show around the area in case locals should recognise the guy.

Someone emerged from the Arboretum, briefly. He gestured and called something, and Canada waved and joined him. They disappeared into the dome.

Halliday switched the image from his desk-com to the wallscreen. He magnified the section of the picture containing the guy he presumed was X – but all he came up with was a bunch of blurred pixels.

He sat back and thought about it. X had arranged to meet Canada outside the Arboretum, and then take her somewhere. So why then had they passed *into* the dome? Unless, of course, their destination was the dome itself, as unlikely as that appeared.

He put the wallscreen on fast forward, and slowed the image whenever figures appeared leaving the dome. He raced though the next seven hours, until twilight and then darkness settled over the dome, and still X and Canada had not emerged.

Which made no kind of sense at all . . .

He thought about trying to hack into the dome's security cameras, but decided not to waste his time. He'd ask to view the tapes when he went down there to take a look around.

He took Canada's address book from his jacket and trawled though the hundreds of names until he found what he was looking for. Jenny . . .

Jenny Murphy had an address in Yonkers.

He dialled the code into the keyboard of his desk-com and waited.

Seconds later the screen flared, showing a small, red-headed woman in her forties. 'Yes? Who is it?' He wondered, briefly, if this could be Canada's friend, Jenny.

'I'd like to speak to Jenny Murphy.'

The woman peered, suspicious. 'Who are you?'

Halliday hung his ID before the screen. 'Halliday, private detective. I'm investigating the disappearance of a friend of Jenny's.'

The woman looked worried and hurried away from the screen.

Seconds later she was replaced by an almost identical, albeit younger, version of herself. 'Yes?'

'Jenny Murphy?' Halliday asked. The girl was facially very much like the VR persona she'd used the other day, though the little that Halliday could see of her body lacked the womanly attributes.

He recalled watching her making love with David.

Jenny nodded. 'Mom says this is about Canada? What's happening?'

'That's what I'm trying to find out, Jenny. She was last seen leaving Thai Joe's VR Bar on Monday. You were with her in one of the sites—' He smiled as a startled look crossed her face. 'She met someone called X in Aphrodesia.'

Jenny reached out, and for a second Halliday thought she was about to sever the connection. Instead, she turned the volume down and looked guiltily over her shoulder.

'What do you know about X, Jenny?'

The red-headed girl shrugged. 'Not a lot. Nothing, in fact. Canada met him in one of the sites. They hit it off and met pretty often.'

'What tag does Canada use in VR? I assume she does use a tag?'

The girl nodded. 'Usually Ice, sometimes Snow. Canada, see?'

'Never Maple Syrup?'

The girl pulled a face. 'Clever.'

'So how come this X character knows Canada's real name?'

Jenny blinked. 'He does?'

'He used it in Aphrodesia.'

The girl coloured. 'How do you know that?'

'Ever heard of playback, Jenny?' Halliday smiled. 'So, how did he know her name? Is she in the habit of giving it out to strangers in VR?'

Jenny shook her head. 'She might have told X – they met pretty often.'

'She didn't say if she knew him in the real world?'

'No. I'm sure she would've mentioned it.'

'She didn't tell you where she was going with X?'

Jenny shrugged. 'Canada said that X was taking her to a real great VR Bar. It was a private place. You couldn't link in from any other Bar.'

Halliday nodded. 'And you haven't heard from her since Monday?'

Jenny nodded, pale-faced now. 'That's right.'

'One more thing. Do you have David's com-code?'

She smiled out at him. 'Which David would that be? I know a few.'

'The David,' he said, 'you were enjoying yourself with in Aphrodesia last week.'

Blushing, she typed the code onto the screen and stared at Halliday. 'Will that be all?'

'Thanks for your time, Jenny. Hey, and watch who you talk to in VR, okay?'

He cut the connection. He tapped in David's code and spoke to the boy. He knew no more than Jenny about Canada's disappearance. Like Jenny, he hadn't heard from Canada since she vanished, and he had no idea as to the true identity of the mysterious X.

Halliday thanked him and cut the link.

He sat in silence for five minutes, then got through to the police headquarters and asked for Jeff Simmons.

Seconds later, a plainclothes officer with a heavy, florid face and silver hair stared out at him. His expression changed as he peered. 'Christ, Halliday. That you?'

'Jeff, how's things?'

'Where've you been, man? What is it? Six months, more?'

'Been busy, Jeff.'

'So . . . This is a social call, right? You thought we'd grab a beer, catch up on old times?'

Halliday smiled. ''Fraid this is business. I'm working for a client whose sister went missing last week. This is between you and me. My client doesn't want the cops involved, for her own reasons.' He outlined the details of the case.

'You come up with any leads?'

'I think I'm onto something.'

Jeff Simmons gave a wry smile. 'I'll do what I can to help.'

'Would you look through the files, see if any other kids've gone missing in similar circumstances?'

'I'll do that, Hal. Drop by any time and I'll fill you in.'

Halliday arranged to meet Simmons around four, cut the connection and sat back. It was daylight outside and he was dog tired. By rights he should hit the sack with the fan running and catch up on some lost sleep. The image came to him of Canada Artois, giving herself to X on the hillside in Aphrodesia.

He'd take the Ford down to the ferry terminal and go over to Liberty Island, take a look around and see what he could find.

Then he'd call in on Jeff Simmons and stir a few old memories.

Six

Sergio Mantoni hurried down the spiral staircase to his basement VR chamber. The jellytank occupied the centre of the
room, its curving crystal cover set flush with the white-tiled
floor. He set the co-ordinates for the site he required, then
undressed and eased back the cover.

He applied the leads to his arms and legs and pulled the
faceplate over his head. This would be only his second
immersion in this site, and he was apprehensive. It was his
personalised zone, manufactured by Lew Kramer and his
team over the past six months to Mantoni's exacting specifications. No one else but he could enter the site: it was his
own private playground.

His first immersion, a week ago, had not gone well. Perhaps
he'd been expecting too much. He had looked forward to the
day for so long that he should have known the reality of the
site would fall short of his hopes. Perhaps it would be different, this time. His initial disappointment forgotten, perhaps
he would be able to better appreciate the miracle that Kramer
and his team had managed to perform.

He stepped down into the tank, his foot breaking the
surface tension of the jelly with a prolonged sucking sound.
He sat down and lay back, sinking slowly into the warm,
protective custody of the gel.

Over the course of the next thirty seconds, he lost awareness of his body. He was deaf and blind, a point of consciousness afloat in an infinity of darkness. He felt a quick heat pass
through his head, and then his senses were flooded with an
overload of sight and sound, smell and tactile sensation.

He was standing on the corner of a busy New York street.

Broadway and Houston, it looked like – though subtly altered compared to how he recalled the intersection from the last time he had ventured into the city.

He stared at the bustle around him, the verisimilitude of crowds and cars thronging the streets and sidewalks. He could smell the unaccustomed reek of gasoline in the air, the nostalgic aroma of frankfurters from the stall on the corner. For a long minute he just stood on the curb, buffeted by hurrying pedestrians, and looked about him in wonder.

The program had inserted him into the site at the point when he had exited on his last visit. He looked at the array of control decals on the back of his hand. The array allowed him to tailor the events of the site to his own desires. He had given Lew Kramer instructions to manufacture the site to follow a rigorous timeline, a series of events which he, Mantoni, could chose to alter at any moment. It was the ultimate God-like omnipotence, which he had hoped would give him more than a mere cathartic release from the tyranny of his memories.

But he knew, now, after his first experience of the site last week, that this was an impossible dream.

He crossed the street, along with a crowd of other pedestrians. He had forgotten quite how busy the streets of New York had been, how once upon a time it was impossible to just walk across the street whenever you felt like it. You had to wait for the lights to change at a crossing. He had forgotten, also, quite how noisy it had been, with the canyons between the buildings packed with thousands of cars, trucks and cabs. It was a revelation now to watch the reckless careering of so many speeding vehicles.

He walked along the street, gazing up at the buildings on either side. This was the time before holo-façades became all the rage. He recognised buildings long since demolished, beautiful edifices dating from the end of the century before last. The fashions worn by the constructed citizens in this site, likewise, seemed to belong to a distant era. Women wore conservative long dresses, and men black, high collared suits, like a herd of fashion clones.

He looked down at his own body. He too was wearing a smart three-piece suit with the obligatory high collar. He looked at his hands, the expanse of his chest. Like the world around him, he was twenty-five years younger. He paused and gazed at his reflection in a store-front window. He was almost thirty, handsome if painfully naïve-looking. He hurried on.

He came to the Grosvenor Building. The liveried doorman saluted, murmured his name and held open the vast glass door. Mantoni stepped inside, sinking into the lush carpeting of a lobby overgrown with palms. He took the elevator to the penthouse suite, his heart hammering an apprehensive tattoo.

He stepped from the elevator and approached the genuine timber door of his apartment. He found a key – an old-fashioned metal key, for chrissake – and inserted it into the old-fashioned lock.

This was the first time he had entered his old apartment. On his first insertion, he had met Bo at Maxim's restaurant and spent three hours marvelling at her resurrected beauty.

Now he paced around the lounge, taking in his old possessions, the books and holo-discs, the paintings he and Bo had collected and which, after what had happened all those years ago, he had sold off in a bid to banish the painful memories.

Even now, Bacon's triptych filled him with nausea.

He heard a sound from another room, the bedroom: the click of the walk-in wardrobe door. A second later a high clear voice called out, 'Serge, is that you?'

He told himself that this was nothing more than a lie, a magical fantasy conjured in his hallucinating sensorium. The world around him did not really exist, and the woman calling him from the bedroom was no more than a ghost in time.

But although he knew this to be a fact, the evidence of his

senses convinced some part of him that he had been miraculously transported back in time to the year 2015.

He heard footsteps as she padded from the bedroom, and he braced himself for the shock of her arrival.

His heart kicked as she appeared in the doorway. For a second he was breathless, the sight of her making him dizzy as his vision blurred and his legs weakened. He sat down on the arm of the settee and smiled across at her. 'Bo . . .'

She wrinkled her nose at him. Her dark hair was piled on her head and fixed into position with a couple of chopstick-like things. She wore a short kimono, belted at the waist but open to reveal a lot of tanned skin.

He was unable to bring himself to say a word.

He watched her as she crossed the room and slipped a disc into the sound-around unit, then moved to the window and gazed out.

He could smell her scent in the air. As the opening bars of some modern symphony swelled from the speakers, she hummed along, the long fingers of her right hand playing the keys of an imaginary piano.

Christ, but Lew Kramer had got it so right.

The Bo Ventura before him was nothing more than a construct. It . . . she . . . was an infinitely complex program built up from visual records of the holo-star who, for two brief years earlier this century, had been engaged to Mantoni. Kramer had had a lot of visual data to help him create a convincing simulacrum, the half dozen holo-movies she had made, the hundred-plus interviews she had given to the voracious news media. The sound of her voice, too, had caused Kramer and his team no problem to recreate. What had been more difficult, and where Mantoni's knowledge of his lover had come in, was the programming of the construct's personality, its likes and dislikes, its conversational strategies, its very personality.

For long weeks Mantoni had gone over his time with Bo, recounting to Kramer and his techs the memories of the holo-star. With these details they had built up a repertoire of her behavioural traits, her moods and intellectual responses. It had been a traumatic month, reliving such painful memories, and more than once he wondered at the wisdom of exhuming the ghost of the woman he had once loved.

Then, a week ago, he had met the resurrected Bo Ventura for the very first time.

And the pain of being with her again had been almost too much.

Now she turned and approached the settee. She was tall, over six feet, and more than half of her attenuated length seemed to consist of slim, tanned legs. He recalled thinking, all those years ago, that she possessed more beauty than seemed fair, in a world largely made up of ugly people. And yet she was unique among the many stars he had known in the industry. It seemed incredible, but she had not allowed her beauty – and how the world responded to her beauty – to affect her. In an industry riddled with vanity and conceit, Bo Ventura remained down-to-earth and level-headed, forever aware of her incredible good fortune. Her response to finding herself the most feted holo-star in America had often been naïve, but always genuine. He thought that that was why he had loved her so much.

She sat on the settee and pulled him from the arm, then straddled him and ran a hand through his hair.

The weight of her on his lap, the scent of her body . . .

His heart hammered and he wanted to cry out his pain.

'Dinner at the Korsteins tonight, Sergio. The usual crowd will be there. No doubt Charles will be trying to get me high on dust.'

Mantoni smiled. 'You know how he loves to watch you laugh when you're high.'

She wrinkled her nose. 'Like a performing puppy dog.'

'So we'll stay clear of the stuff.'

She kissed his nose.

He recalled that in a world where drugs of all varieties had been on constant offer, Bo had been almost religiously abstemious. She had tried dust and spin and other substances along with him, and while she said she had enjoyed their effect, she had never clamoured to repeat the experience. Perhaps once a month she might agree to share something with him in the privacy of their apartment. She'd had a good effect on him, putting a brake on his naturally addictive personality.

Later, without her, without brakes, he had gone downhill, fast.

He reached up, thumbed the kimono from her shoulders, and stared at her small breasts. They were as delicate as rose buds, and never failed to churn his stomach with a combination of lust and a more cerebral response to their aesthetic perfection.

She ducked forward and bit his lips, pulled away and smiled at him, then darted forward again, biting, licking, moaning softly to herself.

He felt something expand in his chest and resisted the urge to cry out in pain and rage.

He carried her to the bedroom.

Later, as she lay sleeping beside him, he propped himself on his elbow and stared down at the woman he had loved so long ago. She lay on her back, naked, arms above her head in an unconscious pose of submission.

Bo Ventura had been the first woman he had really and truly loved – the person beside whom all his other loves, the women he had thought he'd loved in his youth – paled into insignificance. When she had entered his life, he knew that he had found his perfect partner, knew he would never look any further.

Twenty-five years later, he recalled what it had been like back then, the heady careless days seemingly free from worry and concern over what the future might bring. His holo-production company was going from strength to strength, and he was engaged to the most beautiful woman in the world. If only his young self could have looked ahead . . .

With the back of his hand he caressed the flesh between her breasts, and then her stomach, drawn tight as a drum-head between the projecting bones of her pelvis.

Why was he torturing himself like this? What had he hoped to achieve in bringing her back to this ersatz, virtual life?

Over the past ten, fifteen years he had lost himself in an excess of flesh, using women one after the other and making it a rule never to see the same one for any longer than a week – and breaking that rule only on one, very painful, occasion.

He had been amazed, initially, at the ready supply of young women willing to be lured by nothing more than his power and prestige – and in time he came to despise his partners almost as much as he despised himself. They wanted only what he had to offer in terms of parts in holo-dramas and ads, while from them he wanted only the increasingly stale consolations of the flesh.

Then VR came along, and Mantoni began using the sex sites, and he indulged his appetites with a variety of partners who, out there in the real world, might have been anyone at all. He was able to take pleasure from the sites for two hours a night without the messy emotional consequences of relationships in the real world.

And then Lew Kramer's team had begun researching into the possibility of recreating historical figures in VR, and the idea had occurred to Mantoni to bring his old love back to life.

Perhaps he had hoped to invest his life with some meaningful human contact, after the impersonal sex of the past decade or more. He would renew his affair with the only woman who had ever meant anything to him.

He should have known that the past cannot be recreated, that the dead cannot be brought back to life.

He should have known that he would only succeed in torturing himself.

She stirred, squirming with pleasure at his touch. She opened her eyes and smiled up at him. He pulled her to him, finding her lips with his own.

He had recreated Bo Ventura so that, when the technology allowed, he would be able to leave the real world behind and exist forever in the safe domain of virtual reality. He had dreamed that one day he might live with the woman he loved in a past edited and abridged, and purged of tragedy.

She pushed him onto his back, taking him in her right hand as she squatted over him, easing him into her with that most sensuous of tactile communions. She moaned with pleasure, leaned forward and attacked him with her mouth.

Mantoni closed his eyes and felt tears sting his cheeks.

The only trouble was, the technology was lagging behind his dreams. He could spend only twelve hours tanked with Bo – which was eight hours longer than the safe upper limit imposed on the VR Bars. His techs were nowhere near extending the safe upper limit to a hundred hours, as Kramer had promised six months ago. Nor had they succeeded in making significant headway with the time-extended zones. At present, the ratio was in the region of six to four. He had tried it himself, spending six hours tanked while only four hours passed in reality. It was so insignificant a differential as to be effectively useless.

These failures he could tolerate, but the lack of success on the pharmaceutical front he found more difficult to accept.

If his chemists succeeded in creating a drug that could target specific memories and erase them from his consciousness, then he would be on the threshold of entering a virtual heaven.

He could have his mind wiped of his memories of the past, specifically of what had happened to Bo, all those years ago. He could have erased from his mind the knowledge that he was in VR, even, effectively travel back in time and live the rest of his life – however long that might be – in an altered, improved version of the past.

But the brutal fact was that there was no way his chemists could produce the miracle drug, no way he could have the pain of what had happened on that day, twenty-five years ago, wiped from his memory.

Bo climaxed. She screamed and dug her nails into his chest, and her face twisted in a grimace of tortured ecstasy.

Mantoni pulled her to him and gasped with the pain of the lie he was living.

Later, as she dozed again in his arms, he asked himself if the brief hours of passion spent with Bo were worth the agony. Being with her like this only brought back the terrible memories of that night, the hopeless abyss of loss he experienced thereafter. To make love to her like this was to be reminded that the Bo in his arms was no more than a lie, a fantastically complex, but nevertheless dead, version of a once real person – a ghost in the cyberverse.

He was about to hit the quit decal on the back of his hand when Bo reached out and touched his face. He smiled down at her.

'What do you think my chances are, Serge?' she asked, with the naïveté of a little girl.

His stomach churned. He lowered his face to hers and kissed her lips. 'I think you'll win,' he said. 'Your performance was stunning. There's no one else to come near you . . .'

She squealed in delight. 'You think so? You really think so? What shall I wear, Serge?'

He laughed, and promised to take her shopping.

Lew Kramer and his team had programmed a provisional timeline into this site. Events would proceed as they had twenty-five years ago, and on the night of the awards ceremony Mantoni would act to change history, to ensure that what had happened on that fateful night did not in this reality come to pass, to save Bo Ventura's life.

He had thought it might provide some psychological catharsis, some way out of the hell that was his life . . .

But how could he save the life of someone who had never really lived?

He hit the quit decal on the back of his hand, and the bedroom scene, and the vision of Bo's face, smiling up at him, vanished in an instant. He struggled upright through the thick weight of the gel, aware of his cries as he pulled off the faceplate and stepped from the tank.

He showered quickly, then dressed and left the VR room.

He sat on the lowest step of the spiral staircase, pulled his com from the inside pocket of his jacket, and got through to Lew Kramer.

Seconds later the tech's miniaturised face showed on the com screen.

'Sergio – how can I help?'

'Lew, I want the Bo construct deleted,' Mantoni said before he could change his mind.

Kramer stared at him. 'Deleted? You mean . . .?'

Lew knew full well what he meant. 'That's what I said, Lew. I want it erased as of now, understood?'

'But all the work we've put into the Bo construct—'

It was unlike the usually malleable Kramer, a born yes-man if ever there was one, to raise objections. It was a measure of all the hard work that had gone into developing the Bo construct that he could bring himself to voice dissent.

'It won't go to waste, Lew. The expertise you gained from . . .' He stopped, then. 'Look, I'm not debating this. I want the damned construct erased, okay?'

'Ah . . . couldn't we store it some place, somewhere you can't access it?'

He stared at the tiny, concerned face. It was a possibility, of course. But the temptation would be to ask Lew for the code some time in the future, to sneak back to the construct like some perverted masochist.

'No way, José. I want it deleted. And that's an order.'

Kramer nodded. 'Very well—' he began.

Mantoni cut the connection.

He pocketed the com and sat on the step, contemplating the order. Of late, he hadn't thought himself capable of feeling so much emotion. His excesses of the past decade, he thought, had inured him to such weaknesses. It was ironic that it was the ghost of a dead woman who had succeeded in resurrecting sentiments he had considered long buried.

He stood up but instead of climbing the staircase to the ground floor of the villa, he made his way along the corridor.

He came to a second timber door and passed into the white-tiled room.

He knelt beside the jellytank set flush into the floor, and stared down at the young girl floating within the suspension gel.

Lew had assured him that subjects were safe in VR for up to forty hours, before neural dysfunction occurred.

The girl was naked, and perfect, and as he stared down at her he realised that he was weeping.

Seven

Halliday stood on the gravel path before the Liberty Island Arboretum. The dome rose gracefully before him, its hexagonal panels reflecting the dull pewter of the overcast, for all the world like the upper eighth of a vast sphere embedded in the soil of the island.

Over the course of the past couple of months the island had become even more of a tourist attraction. It had always been popular with visitors, especially tourists from overseas lured by the symbol of all that was American and free, the Statue of Liberty. The irony was that, since the Georgian Avenging Force had planted a bomb beneath its robes two months ago – in retaliation for what it saw as Federal apathy in the aftermath of the Atlanta meltdown – the toppled statue had attracted even more tourists. It made sense, Halliday thought wryly. Now the statue was more accessible, and visitors who suffered vertigo need not endure the dizzying climb.

It was the first time he had seen the statue in the horizontal. Until the bombing it had been a familiar landmark, often glimpsed from various locations around the city, and he had missed its presence since the bombing.

Supine, the statue had about it an impressive solidity and bulk it had never possessed in the perpendicular. It lay like a toppled chesspiece adjacent to the dome, its green torso cracked where it had been ripped apart and then welded together. Its face, miraculously undamaged, stared into the sky with unmoved serenity. Crowds of Filipino and Indonesian tourists flocked around the grounded giant like scavengers around the corpse of a once fearsome and mighty animal.

On the lawn before the statue stood a line of street musicians, magicians, a few beggars . . . a rogue's gallery of penniless entrepreneurs, one of whom must surely have seen, and perhaps even remembered, the man who had met Canada on Monday afternoon.

Halliday worked his way along the row, tipping each one generously before starting a conversation. A few stared at him as if he were speaking a foreign language: they had the blank expressions of drug addicts and he knew he was wasting his time. Others were perfectly rational – these were the musicians, mime artists and magicians – but remembered nothing of what after all had been just another humid afternoon. People were meeting on the island all the time. There had been nothing noteworthy or remarkable to distinguish the rendezvous of X with the girl.

He came to a tall, emaciated man in his fifties, performing a series of clever sleight-of-hand and visual tricks. The magician juggled bean bags with mesmeric dexterity and made them disappear in mid-air, so that at first it seemed he had failed at even the simple act of juggling – when in fact he had performed a miracle. Halliday watched in admiration, entertained to the point of forgetting his interrogation.

The man tossed the last bean bag above his head, and when it failed to obey gravity and return he pulled a pantomime face of Pierrot-desolation.

Halliday stared into the air, but the bean bag had truly vanished.

The magician assumed a clown's smiling face for Halliday, who dropped twenty dollars in his upturned stove-pipe hat.

'The man who seeks will find, if persistence is his watchword,' the magician said, raising a long gloved finger.

Halliday smiled. 'You don't believe in failure?'

'Mephisto believes in nothing,' said the man, 'but persistence.'

'How do you know I'm seeking something?'

'Aren't we all seeking something, my friend?'

'Then perhaps you can help me?' Halliday said. 'I'm look-ing for—'

Mephisto closed his eyes. 'The man who met a young girl outside the Arboretum on Monday afternoon.'

'How the hell—?' Halliday began.

The man smiled. 'I heard you asking the beggar three along. He's deaf, and you had to raise your voice. There is no such thing as magic, my friend, only illusion.'

Halliday smiled. 'I'll remember that,' he said, turning.

'As a matter of fact, I did see them.'

Halliday stopped and stared at the magician.

'The girl stood and watched me for perhaps ten minutes. She tipped me fifty dollars.'

'Did you see the man who met her?'

'I could not tell if it was a man or a woman.'

'But surely—'

'You see, he or she was wearing a chu.'

Halliday regarded Mephisto dubiously. 'You could tell?'

'There are certain factors that give away the lie,' Mephisto said. 'A certain swagger of the user, a confidence they adopt that comes from thinking they are invincible in disguise – and this demeanour is rarely in keeping with the appearance of the persona they adopt.'

'So the person who met the girl, was he or she in the persona of a man or a woman?'

'A man, middle-aged, dark-haired, perfectly nondescript. The girl entered the dome with him, or her.'

'Did you see them come out?'

'I left at three,' Mephisto said. 'May I ask why you are asking?'

Halliday showed Mephisto his identity card.

'A private detective,' the magician said. 'A man who attempts in vain to order the chaos of existence.'

'I wouldn't put it quite like that,' Halliday said. 'I'm look-ing for a missing kid.'

'I wish you luck,' said Mephisto. 'And remember: persistence.'

'I thought you said that chaos couldn't be ordered?'

'I'm sure you will find the girl,' he said, 'but like all of us she will remain forever lost.'

Halliday smiled and shook his head. 'Thanks.'

Before he turned, Mephisto lifted a finger to the sky. 'Look!' he cried.

Six bean bags fell from the air and into Mephisto's hands. He shrugged and began juggling.

Halliday laughed and headed for the Arboretum.

He had never before visited the dome: it seemed a futile exercise to look at copies of objects that possessed less reality than his memories.

A party of schoolchildren hurried through the arched entrance before him, chattering excitedly. He passed inside and gazed around. Once, years ago, the dome had housed a hundred varieties of real, living trees; now it was filled with artificial mock-ups and holograms. They were, admittedly, state of the art, and no doubt the kids found them interesting and educational, but to Halliday the dome had the dead atmosphere of a museum of ancient history.

He strolled around the spiral pathway towards the centre of the dome and the main exhibit, the facsimile representation of a Coast Redwood, *Sequoia sempervirens*, which towered so high that Halliday was forced to crane his neck to make out the upper branches. He imagined a time when the tree had covered vast stretches of the West Coast, and wondered what it might have been like to stand amid a sprawling forest of redwoods.

He heard a tour guide telling a group of children, 'Some of these trees lived up to two thousand five hundred years. The last specimen of Coast Redwood died in the year 2031 . . .'

He moved away, following the spiral back out towards the edge of the dome and the padded seats where elderly tourists rested and admired the artificial view.

So why had X arranged to meet Canada at the dome? Could this have been their destination?

He wondered if there was some subterranean area beneath

the Arboretum, known only to X, some mysterious labyrinth . . . He smiled to himself. Desperation was leading him to ever more fanciful supposition.

He found a redundant guide, a young woman eating a burger, and flashed his identity. He produced the pix of Canada Artois. 'I understand she visited the dome on Monday afternoon?'

The woman took the pix and examined it closely. She passed it back. 'I was on duty Monday, but the number of visitors who pass through here . . .'

'She was with a dark-haired, middle-aged guy.'

The woman shook her head. 'Sorry. Maybe one of the other guides . . .'

Halliday indicated the entrance. 'Is that the only way in and out?'

'The rear exit's straight opposite, behind the stand of willow.'

Halliday looked around the dome. Positioned on stanchions at strategic intervals, he made out a dozen security cameras.

He pointed. 'I'd like to take a look at the tapes—'

The woman looked at him. 'Which day did you say? Monday?'

She shook her head. 'Your luck isn't in, friend. The tapes are reused every twenty-four hours.'

Halliday nodded. 'Thanks.' He moved off, heading for the weeping willow.

So X and Canada must have cut through the dome's rear exit on their way to wherever they had headed. Halliday experienced a sense of anticipation as he followed a gravel path, ducked and backhanded aside plastic fronds of willow.

He came to the exit, a door with a bar-opening mechanism. He lifted and pushed, and the door swung outwards. He stepped from the dome and found himself on a short flight of steps overlooking the edge of the island. A pier jutted out into the water, and at the shoreward end of the pier was a mock-timber building bearing a neon sign, empty of colour at this time of day, announcing the Liberty Island VR Bar.

He recalled from Canada's diary that she had tanked in the Bar on more than one occasion.

But it made no sense at all. Why would X go to the trouble of taking Canada to a Bar she already knew about and frequented? And anyway, hadn't Jenny said that X was taking Canada to a private VR Bar, which couldn't be accessed from any other?

Of course, the Bar might not have been their destination at all. There were a few other buildings scattered along the foreshore, concessions selling tourist gifts and curios, a restaurant and a boat-hire kiosk.

Halliday made his way down the steps and strolled along the shore. A gang of kids hung around outside the VR Bar, smoking and joking among themselves. Occasionally customers came and went. Compared to Thai Joe's and other Bars, it was a secluded and quiet place. He walked on, past the restaurant, the boat-hire kiosk . . . and that was the extent of the real estate at this end of the island.

So where had X taken Canada Artois?

He retraced his steps, turned past the VR Bar and strolled along the jetty, loose boards rattling underfoot. The sea was calm, its drab undulant surface mirroring the grey pall overhead.

He came to the end of the jetty and stared out across the water towards Manhattan, the ranked high-rises marching across the skyline like so many blocks on a graph.

He turned and regarded the swelling dome, the fallen statue and the VR Bar.

He walked back towards the shore. As he passed the Bar, something occurred to him. It was a long shot, but he was at that stage of his investigations where even long shots were worth following up.

He recalled an entry in Canada's diary – she had met X at the Liberty sex zone more than once. Perhaps there was a chance that at some time of the day or night, X might return to the Liberty sex zone. If so, then Halliday might be able to trace him.

That was a big if, and he could think of another: X might be traceable only *if* he adopted the same huge-membered persona each time.

Halliday didn't exactly relish the prospect of entering another sex zone – one where this time he could be seen – but Vanessa Artois was paying him good money to try and find her sister. He owed it to her. He could always hide behind an assumed persona.

He stepped through the sliding glass doors and entered a plush carpeted area like the lobby of an exclusive hotel. A receptionist behind an imitation-timber counter smiled with feigned charm and said, 'If you're already a member, sir, step right through—' She indicated a pair of swing doors to her left, '—but if you're a day visitor or wish to become a member, please sign here.'

He remembered that he had Canada's VR cards in his pocket and pushed through the swing doors. He found himself in a waiting room much like that in Thai Joe's, though smaller. No one was waiting in the chairs provided. A girl in a blue two-piece uniform approached him with the same company smile.

'I'll take your card and show you to your booth, sir.'

Halliday fumbled through the cards and handed over the appropriate one. She unlocked a booth and held open the door. 'Have a pleasant trip, sir.'

Halliday stepped through and consulted the screen set into the wall. He touched the menu bar and a listing of the hundreds of zones on offer scrolled down the screen in alphabetical order.

He touched: *Sex Zone: Eros Island*.

Another menu bar appeared, this one listing soma-types. He chose the body of a man in his early twenties, blond and well-muscled – everything, he realised, that he was not.

He stripped, applied the leads and slipped the faceplate

over his head, and stepped into the jellytank. He sat down and lay back. The gel sealed over him with the viscous flow of honey. He felt his senses leaving him one by one as he floated, weightless. He closed his eyes in anticipation.

He felt the sudden switch of transition jolt his senses, and when he opened his eyes he found himself on a paradisiacal tropical island. He was aware of the sun burning his skin, the fine white sand beneath his bare feet. He was garbed in a blue default robe and was standing on a perfect beach. Too perfect, he realised. Surely no tropical island had ever existed quite like this one: it was an idealised representation of paradise conjured for the inhabitants of a dour and sun-starved metropolis. Before him a lagoon like crushed sapphire scintillated under the sun, and a long, curving beach seemed to extend for miles. Inland, gentle foothills rose towards a distant range of mountains, their peaks capped with improbable snow, bright against the blue of the cloudless sky. A landscape of easy clichés, Halliday thought – but why criticise a venue merely for providing customers with a luxurious setting in which to enjoy themselves?

Along the foreshore was a series of low timber villas, with naked men and women lounging on the verandas. Behind them, in the open-plan rooms, Halliday made out activity groups of people moving together with the common purpose of dancers. From time to time men and women emerged from the rooms and sat on the verandas, resting a while before rejoining the fray.

Occasionally people materialised along the beach, appearing like localised heat hazes above the sand, gaining solidity before finally establishing and walking off towards one of the villas. Everyone appeared to have adopted a similar soma-type, inevitably young and physically well-developed, as if the collective unconscious dictated the desirability of a common athletic archetype.

Feeling self-conscious, and finding it hard to accept that he was in disguise, Halliday left the beach and strolled up the grassed incline. When he came to the crest he saw before him a shallow swimming pool. Situated in the pool were small climbing frames and other contraptions. He watched a group of men and women wade into the pool and climb onto the apparatus. Within seconds they were disporting themselves in bizarre and contorted bouts of sexual gymnastics. Halliday stared, drawn by the novelty of the acts as well as the simple fact of the raw sexuality on display.

A naked woman lay in the shallows of the pool, watching the activity. She saw him and waved, and he was startled by the woman's resemblance to his ex-girlfriend. She was Oriental and childishly slim, her bobbed hair parenthesising massive, wide-apart eyes. For a heart-stopping second he thought that it was indeed Kim, for some reason electing to appear here as herself.

She stood and stepped from the pool in one fluid and graceful motion. Though she shared Kim's basic soma-type, there were differences. Her breasts were bigger, hips fuller . . . He recalled the first time he had entered VR. He had been with Kim, and she had programmed herself a sexier, more voluptuous body, thinking it would please him. He tried to banish the memory.

On her way towards him, the woman plucked a default gown from the ground and wrapped it around her body, a show of modesty at odds with the exhibitionist nature of the surroundings.

'Hi, I'm Caroline. Your first time here, right?' Her smile was dazzling and, like everything else about her, dauntingly perfect. It struck him only then that he, too, represented a similar example of desirable sexuality. The thought was precisely opposite to how he felt about himself.

'Is it that obvious?' he said.

She shrugged. 'Most first timers are watchers, until they're initiated. So – ' that winning smile again, 'do you have a tag?'

He almost told her his real name, then remembered himself. 'David,' he said.

'So, Dave – mind if I call you Dave? – you never been to a sex zone before?'

'First time,' he admitted.

'Come on, then – I'll show you around, give you the Caroline guided tour of Eros Island. No tips required, but appreciated.'

She took his hand, the warmth of it in his own palm startlingly real. Her touch sent a charge through him, a realisation of the possibilities . . .

They strolled towards the first villa. 'You tank into other zones, Dave?'

'Not often.'

'So what made you chose Eros Island?'

'It was recommended. A friend. So I thought . . .'

'Why not give it a go? Hey,' she squinted up at him. 'How old are you in the real world? Young, I bet?'

He temporised. 'Old enough to gain access to this zone.'

'But still young . . . I bet you've never done it before. I mean at all, even in the real world. Hey, c'mon. That's okay. We all had a first time.'

He changed the subject. 'You come here a lot?'

She squeezed his hand. 'As often as I can,' she said. 'Like, every day. I'm a regular.' She laughed. 'An old hand, Dave.'

They passed the first villa. Caroline stood on tiptoe and peered in, frowning. 'Bor-ing. That's just a common or garden orgy room, a mass fucking session without much subtlety. Same goes for most of the villas along here.'

They strolled on, passing villas that echoed with the cries and moans of the participants within. Halliday caught glimpses of improbable combinations, Gordian tangles of limbs, something about the sight of such an indistinguishable mass of flesh less erotic than he would have imagined.

'Now the next couple of establishments,' Caroline went on, 'are real rough-houses. I mean, serious S&M joints. If I were you I'd leave well alone. I mean, I know this is VR, but some of the things that go on in there can leave marks on a young boy like you.'

'Thanks for the warning.'

'Say, don't mention it, Dave. All part of the service.'

109

They passed the S&M villas, the activities within veiled behind incongruous lace curtains that did nothing to conceal the screams and cries.

'We hurry on,' Caroline said, 'passing these gross scenes, and finally arrive at something altogether more pleasant, don't you think?' She smiled at him.

These were smaller villas, one-room affairs equipped with king-sized beds and little else. Caroline led him by the hand to one of these, up the steps and onto the veranda. She sat beside him on a long couch and drew her legs up beneath her, watching him. He detected a trace of amusement in her eyes.

'So you come here every day,' he said, 'but you don't like the group sessions?'

'Oh, I have nothing against watching them, but I never join in. There's no subtlety involved, David, no intimacy.' She smiled. 'I prefer one on one, where I can get to know my partner.'

'Do you really think that's possible, in VR?'

'Probably not. I mean, it's probably impossible to get to know the real person – the person beneath the persona, but we can kid ourselves that we're establishing something more than just a passing connection. We can dream.' She reached out a small, pink foot and touched the flesh of his thigh, smiling at him as she did so.

He looked away and suddenly wondered what kind of person she was, out there in the real world. He had been deceived by her assumed beauty, her expertise in this unfamiliar realm. Beneath her words he detected a lonely person, someone who needed the ersatz reality of VR in order to form relationships, however fleeting and doomed.

She was watching him, both her feet now rubbing his thigh beneath his gown. 'I always think that part of the pleasure is the anticipation, Dave. The lingering over the initiation. The knowledge of what we will eventually do . . .'

He swallowed, trying to find a reply.

She smiled at his awkwardness. 'But of course, you

110

wouldn't know that, would you. Christ—' she exclaimed to herself, 'am I a lucky girl today.' She moved towards him, kneeling, reached out and unfastened his gown. It opened, revealed swollen biceps. He stared down at his responding body. He should have known that the soma-type he had assumed would be well-equipped, but quite how well surprised him.

Caroline gasped and stared. She pulled off her gown and straddled his lap in one quick movement. He held her waist, aware of his ludicrously swollen penis standing erect between them. She pushed forward her belly, trapping him with an exquisite sensation of warmth. Something turned in his stomach, a surge of lust almost like sickness.

She climbed from him and grabbed his hand, pulled him from the couch and into the villa. She ran to the bed, the sight of her tapering back and full bottom reminding him of the other evening, in the real world, when Vanessa Artois had undressed on the wallscreen.

Caroline sprawled on the bed, laughing loud and opening her legs with unabashed invitation. Halliday knelt before her, reached out clumsily, and felt the contact of flesh like an electrifying force. When she embraced him and rolled him onto his back, squatting over him as she took his penis in her hand and guided him into her, Halliday reminded himself that none of this was real . . . Then he forgot the thought, which seemed ludicrous as soon as it occurred to him. As Caroline ground him to climax and dug long nails into his chest, he realised that there was nothing more real than the fact of experience . . . whether that experience was in the real world or in VR.

He lost track of time as Caroline coaxed him over and over, before they both lay exhausted on the bed, only their fingers touching as if unable to relinquish contact, however briefly. Later she rose from the bed and pulled him out onto the veranda. She sat on his lap on the couch, her head on his shoulder. He found himself stroking her short, jet black hair, reminded of similar times with Kim.

111

He gestured out at the island, touched her cheek.

'Caroline?' he said.

'Mmm,' she murmured, content.

'Does this . . .?' He tried to collect his thoughts, marshal his words. 'I mean . . . does it *mean* anything?'

She looked up at him. 'Does what mean anything?'

'This. The island, what we just did?'

'Of course it means something! It's two human beings, sharing. Giving and receiving affection.'

He shook his head. 'But ultimately it has no meaning beyond the confines of this zone. It can't develop, become a meaningful and lasting relationship. I can never really know you.'

'David, that isn't what VR's for. We come here to enjoy ourselves. To have fun.'

'It's a replacement for what we can't get out there, in other words,' he said at last. 'It's a refuge for inadequate people.'

She reached up and stroked his chest. 'David, why so analytical? Don't you realise that people need this place and places like them? Humankind has always had fantasies – the sex zones are a way of playing out those fantasies in safety.'

'But the ideal situation would be to play them out with those we loved,' he said.

It was a while before she replied. 'Perhaps that's impossible for some people,' she said. 'Perhaps they're old, or ugly, or disabled. Perhaps they have difficulty in attracting partners, of finding love . . .' She paused and looked up at him. 'I can't begrudge people like that their moments of pleasure.'

'Put like that, you're right. Of course not . . .'

Perhaps he was so condemnatory of the whole experience, he thought, because he no longer had Kim with whom to share the real thing.

'You said you come here a lot,' he began.

'Please, don't condemn me.'

'I wasn't going to.' He waited, staring out across the fore-shore to the dazzling blue of the lagoon. 'You must know all the regulars?'

She shrugged. 'There are a few people who assume the same personas, so of course you get to know them.'

'I'm looking for someone, a guy who sometimes goes under the name of X.'

She pulled away from him and stared. 'Hey, and here I was thinking you were young and innocent. So that's it – you're bi?'

He smiled. 'I need to locate him. We have to talk.'

She shrugged. 'X?' she said. 'It could be anyone. What's he look like?'

'About forty, small and very tanned. Bald-headed. He wears a gold nose-stud and—'

'And he has a chopper about yay long?' She parted her hands like an exaggerating fisherman. 'Well, perhaps not.' She revised her estimation.

Halliday felt a quick stab of triumph. 'That's him.'

'Sure I know him. He goes by the tag of Big Ed.'

'He's a regular?'

'Most midnights, swaggers into the zone and lies on the beach awhile, sunning his dick and eyeing the scene.' She regarded him. 'You seen this guy at other zones, Mr Dark Horse?'

'Something like that.'

'You wouldn't stand a chance with this body,' Caroline told him, tapping his chest. 'He goes for girls, skinny young kids new at the game. 'Course, you could always assume the persona of a teenage girl if you're that desperate for a big pecker.'

He smiled. 'I'm not. We just need to talk, is all.'

'Then like I said, most midnights.' She closed her eyes and rested her head on his chest.

Halliday sat in paradise, a beautiful woman on his lap, and considered what she had told him. The next thing was, how best to go about approaching X, or Big Ed, or whatever his damned name was? The prospect filled him with apprehension.

Five minutes later he heard the chime of a time-limit

alarm. Caroline sat up. 'Cripes, that's me! Four hours and it goes just like that!' She snapped her fingers.

She stood, bent over and kissed his lips.

'I wonder if we could . . .' He stopped himself. He had been about to ask, contrary to everything he had said earlier, if perhaps they might meet again.

Caroline smiled at him. 'David, why limit yourself when so many opportunities are waiting in here?' She shook her head. 'I never repeat, no matter how great it was. Ciao, David!'

She touched the exit decal on the back of her hand, and before Halliday could say goodbye, or even thanks, she vanished. He was suddenly and impossibly alone on the veranda.

He sat for a while, the unfamiliar sensation of the sun strange on his borrowed flesh. In minutes, even seconds, he would be back in the real world . . . He smiled to himself. If he were honest, he could fully understand the attraction of the zone, and why the people came back again and again.

He tapped his exit decal and instantly the tropical paradise disappeared. He sat up in the jellytank, the sudden transition disconcerting, and blinked through the faceplate. It seemed as if his time in the sex zone was already a thing of the distant past, a dream he had enjoyed that was now gone for ever.

He climbed from the tank and showered, scrubbing the gel from his body. He dried himself, dressed, and stepped from the booth.

As he was crossing the waiting room, the door of an opposite booth opened and a technician pushed out an old woman in a wheelchair. Halliday held open the swing door, and the woman, impossibly bent and emaciated, looked up at him with rheumy eyes. As she was wheeled across the lobby, the receptionist behind the desk waved and called out, 'See you tomorrow, Carrie.'

The old lady raised a frail arm and waved. 'You bet your bottom dollar!' she said. 'Ciao!'

Halliday stared. 'Caroline?' he said.

114

The woman looked up at him and laughed. 'Dave,' she said. 'Must say, you sure looked better on Eros Island!'

Halliday watched as Caroline was wheeled out of the VR Bar towards the ferry terminal.

Eight

The police headquarters was situated in the old public library building on the corner of Fifth Avenue and 42nd Street. The hallway was the only part of the building to have survived the renovation. Around it, the wood-panelled chambers had been hived off into a warren of corridors, cramped offices and interview rooms, the majority of them windowless. Halliday showed his identity card to the clerk at reception. The atmosphere of the building – the air of sanctity of the aged precincts cheapened by the grim business of law enforcement, as if a cathedral had been taken over by the Stock Exchange – brought back a slew of memories and mixed emotions.

He passed through the security check and made his way down a curling flight of steps into the basement, where the Missing Persons Department was inconveniently tucked away.

Half a dozen clerks worked at flickering com-screens in the outer office. Halliday made his way to the door at the far end of the chamber, which gave onto a small, dark room lit only by a wallscreen.

When Halliday knocked and entered, Jeff Simmons swung round on his swivel seat, upped the lighting and massaged his dazzled eyes.

'Good to see you, Hal. Coffee?'

'Could kill a cup.' He collapsed into the seat across the desk from the lieutenant.

Jeff found a chipped mug and poured a thick sludge from a pot on the desk. He passed it to Halliday. 'You look rough, Hal. You okay?'

'I'm fine.' Until he'd sat down, he hadn't realised how tired he was.

Jeff laughed. 'Thought you said you'd be here at four?'

'I did. What time is it?'

'Almost six. Where you been?'

'Six? I never realised. Been in VR.' He was surprised to think that he'd spent . . . what? . . . nearly three hours with Caroline on Eros Island. It had passed in a flash.

'How's business, Hal?'

'What business?' he laughed. 'I get by. Whenever I start thinking about quitting and getting a real job, something comes along. You?'

'You know how it is. You crack a case and begin to think it's all worthwhile, then a week later a missing kid turns up with her throat cut and you start thinking about getting out again.'

Halliday remembered when the lieutenant had a head of hair as black as midnight. Now he was grey. That was what the job did, aged suckers unwitting enough not to quit when the going was good . . . Not that he was patting himself on the back for getting out. He'd quit one pisser of a job and landed himself in another.

'Hey, I looked in the files like you asked me.'

'And?'

'Turns out that over the past year six kids've gone missing after being seen frequenting VR Bars.'

'That's interesting—'

'Don't get your hopes up, Hal. We've closed all the cases. The kids were the victims of a serial rapist. We nailed him in a shoot-out a month back.' Jeff swilled the dregs in his coffee cup. 'So, who's your kid?'

'Missing sister of the VR star, Vanessa Artois, who doesn't want publicity. Which is why she didn't go through you. Been gone two days when I'm hired.' He shrugged. 'I traced the kid to the sex zone of a VR Bar. She's been really getting into it for a couple of months. Couldn't get enough of the places. I watched her in playback yesterday.'

117

Jeff laughed. 'And they say our job's all hard work!'

Halliday smiled and shook his head. 'Call me a stiff, but I mean, she's still a kid.'

'Don't tell me. My eldest's sixteen, now. Christ knows what she gets up to at her local Bar.'

'Anyway, Canada met this guy they called X, arranged to see him on Liberty Island.'

'You saw the guy?'

'This was in VR, remember? No doubt he was using a persona. Small, well-muscled, bald. And when he was through talking . . .' Halliday shook his head. 'You should have seen him and Canada go for it.'

'You traced them to Liberty Island?'

'She took the ferry to Liberty and met Mr X outside the dome. After that I lost them. I know they went into the dome, but then they just vanished.'

'What about the VR Bar? Maybe he took the kid inside?'

'I thought of that – but why the hell would he take her to a place she could link to from any Bar in town?'

'Good point.'

'Anyway, I checked into the Liberty Bar. Tanked into Eros Island and guess what? Our Mr X, or Big Ed as he calls himself, is well-known on Eros. Tanks in around midnight most nights.'

'If VR evidence were admissible in court, we could just stake the place and take him in on suspicion.'

'But what evidence would we have that the Mr X who lured Canada was the same guy we picked up? He'd just claim he saw the guy in VR, liked what he saw and assumed the same persona . . . Also,' Halliday went on, 'we'd be wasting our time staking the Liberty. He uses Eros Island, but he might be linking in from any Bar in the city.'

The cop was silent for a time. 'So where do we go from here?'

Halliday stared at the disc of cold coffee in his cup. He looked up. 'If this Big Ed's the same guy who took Canada, I have an idea.'

118

'Go on.'

He went through the scenario in his head. 'Okay. I tank into Eros, assume the persona of a young, skinny, pretty girl – he likes them young and skinny, apparently. But I play coy, don't let him touch me.'

'That'd be going too far in the line of duty.'

'Instead of Big Ed doing the luring, it'll be me who's luring him. I'll make a few visits, get talking to him. I'll try to arrange to meet him in the real world.'

Jeff pushed out his lips, considering. At last he nodded, tentatively. 'Okay, it might work. And there's no risk to you. But when we stake the rendezvous point do we grab Mr X and hope he talks, or do we follow him in the hope he leads us to the kid? Always assuming, of course, that she's still alive.'

'I haven't followed it through that far.' Halliday paused. 'Let's sleep on that one, think about it later.'

'What about back-up? I could detail someone.'

'You don't fancy it yourself?'

Jeff hesitated, then nodded. 'Okay, why not? Look, you say he tanks around midnight? Call me tomorrow at eleven and we'll make arrangements, okay?'

'I'll do that.' Halliday finished his coffee and stood up. 'Hell, it feels like I'm back with the force. If anything crops up, I'll be in touch.'

'Likewise, Hal. Talk to you later.'

Halliday saluted. He left Jeff gazing at the wallscreen, walked up the steps and out through the cavernous hallway.

A twilight the colour of an old bruise was gathering over the eastern skyline. The sun was a rare visitor to the city, even in the height of summer. Halliday recalled the summers of his childhood, which seemed in retrospect to have extended forever in a haze of golden sunshine. He supposed that the grey apology that passed for daylight now meant that he was spared the sunlight's cruel illumination of a city falling to pieces.

As he stood on the steps and gazed out at the sparse traffic on Fifth Avenue, the nightly rain began. Within seconds a noisy deluge was pounding the tarmac. He remembered his arrangement to meet Vanessa, punched her code into his com and waited as the dial tone rang out.

'Hello? Hal, is that you?' Artois stared up at him from the tiny screen, frowning. He was surprised that she appeared even more beautiful than he recalled – after the surfeit of perfection on Eros Island he had doubted that anything in real life could pass muster.

'Hey,' he said, 'why aren't you wearing the chu?'

'Because I'm in my hotel room, dummy. I've been waiting for you to call.'

'I've been busy.'

'You come up with anything?'

He hesitated. 'I have a lead or two. I'll tell you about it. Can we meet?'

She glanced down at her watch. 'Okay, but just for an hour or so. I'm due to meet my agent for dinner at nine.'

'An hour's fine.' Even as he said it, he felt obscurely disappointed. 'Do you know Carmody's, the bar on 42nd?'

'Sure.'

'I'll meet you there in thirty minutes. And wear the chu, okay?'

'How will you recognise me?'

He smiled. 'I won't. Surprise me.' He cut the connection.

He hurried down the steps through the driving rain, ducked into the Ford and drove the three blocks to Carmody's.

The bar was going through a mid-evening lull in trade between the exit of the after-work drinkers and the arrival of the evening's serious revellers. Halliday was the only customer. He sat at the bar and ordered a Ukrainian wheat beer, Barney's old favourite. The coffee at police headquarters had brought him back to life: now he needed something to mellow him out.

The beer was good, a big improvement on the Chinese

120

crap that Thai Joe served. He finished the bottle and ordered another, staring at his reflection in the plate-glass mirror behind the bar and contrasting his appearance in the real world with the persona he'd assumed on Eros Island. After the afternoon session with Caroline, he could see the attraction of VR, but he found it hard to understand how people allowed themselves to become addicted to the depersonalised fantasy world of the zones. Having said that, he was obviously in a minority: new VR Bars were opening up all over the city, to satisfy the public's voracious appetite for the ersatz experience of a painless other world

He was wondering how much to tell Vanessa about her sister's involvement in the sex zones when the door opened at the far end of the bar, admitting a squall of monsoon rain and a big guy in a long raincoat. Halliday turned back to his beer. It wasn't Artois – unless she'd gone and bought herself a total-body chu.

Two minutes later a woman ducked into the bar, gasping after a run and shaking rain from an umbrella. She was shorter than Artois – which ruled her out – thin-faced and nondescript. Halliday drained his glass and signalled for a third bottle. He told himself that he would have to slow down if he wanted to stay awake until dawn, when he could sleep and so maintain his nocturnal life-cycle.

The woman stood next to him and signalled to the bartender, then turned and smiled. 'Come on, Hal. Sleeping on the job?'

'Vanessa?' He shook his head. 'I could've sworn you were taller than . . .'

Artois looked at the empty beer bottles on the bar before Halliday. 'You're drunk, Hal. I took your advice and ditched the heels.'

Halliday peered at the ugly, rather mean-mouthed woman next to him. 'Can I get you something?'

'Make mine a white wine, dry.'

He ordered, and they moved to a secluded booth at the far

end of the room. Artois pulled off her chu and shook out her long black hair. The revealed face was, after the ugly disguise, even more beautiful than he recalled.

He looked around nervously. 'Perhaps it'd be better if you remained disguised.'

She gestured to the guy in the raincoat at the bar.

'That's Baynes. Sticks to me like a limpet. There's another one outside. Expensive, but pretty effective. They said I was okay to be myself in the bar just so long as the place wasn't full.'

Halliday nodded and took a drink. 'Not that I'm complaining. I mean, I'd rather look at you than Ms Sour-Face.'

She smiled, the movement of her long, generous lips devastating. She reached across the table and lightly brushed the back of his hand with her finger-tips. 'Thanks for the chu, Hal. It's the best present a girl could ask for.'

He wondered if she was playing a game. 'Yeah?'

She reached into her coat for the controls. 'Look, these are the disguises I've assumed over the past few days.'

She held up the chu, and the contorted mask hanging from her fingers showed a succession of different faces. It was like a speeded-up film showing all the women who had sat in the same seat during the course of the past day, a dizzying optical illusion his brain found hard to accept.

He noticed a commonality between all the faces. None of them displayed the kind of glamour he might have expected a VR star to adopt.

'All of them are—'

'Plain Janes, right.'

'So? I don't understand.'

She looked at him. Sometimes her gaze seemed to exhibit depthless pity. 'What do you think it's like,' she asked, 'being beautiful?'

He smiled. 'It's not something I've ever really thought about.'

'I'll tell you, Hal. People don't see the real person, the person I am underneath this face. They're either intimidated

122

by my beauty, or challenged, or envious – or they're so captivated by it that they want it: they want to possess that beauty, to be seen possessing it, and not because they feel anything for me, the real person.' She pulled a long cigarillo from a pack and gestured.

Halliday shrugged. 'Life's tough,' he said.

She went on, 'It's difficult to establish meaningful relationships, Hal. There's a lot of reasons for that. One is that I work in a shallow and meretricious industry, and the men I meet are all vain and stupid. But another is that the men I date soon realise that I'm a real person with faults and flaws, not the perfect VR queen they thought they were getting . . . So it ends in tears when they can't accept my humanity and I'm ridiculously attracted to theirs . . .' She blew out a long plume of cannabis-fragrant smoke. 'Then again, there's the simple thing about being noticed all the time. People think that because they recognise me, they somehow own shares in Vanessa Artois. You become public property. This thing—' she tapped the case beneath her coat, '—has allowed me to be free for the past few days. You can't imagine how wonderful that is.'

'I'm pleased for you.'

She sipped her drink. 'Hey, enough of my problems. I didn't come here to bitch. What have you found out?'

He nodded, buying time. 'Okay. I have a couple of leads. Not a lot, but more than we had two days ago.' He paused, considering the best way to go about telling Artois that her kid sister was not the innocent little college girl she might have assumed.

'You said that you'd bought Canada a VR card the other month.'

Vanessa nodded. 'That's right. A one-month entry to the Cyber-Tech place in TriBeCa.'

'Well, she was already using the Bars.'

She shrugged. 'That's understandable. No doubt her friends are all users. How did you find out?'

'I found some cards in her room the other night.'

She looked at him, cigarillo stalled before vermilion lips. 'Cards, as in *cards*, plural?'

'About fifteen of them, for Bars all across the city.'

She exhaled a long plume of smoke. 'Christ. I mean . . . is she addicted? I never noticed anything, and I know what you're going to say: I was never about long enough to notice. But believe me, Hal, she seemed perfectly okay . . .'

Halliday shrugged. 'She's addicted, or let's say she's habituated. Canada and a group of friends. They were tanking every day for the past few weeks.'

'You traced where she went in VR?'

He regarded his beer, at last looking up to meet her gaze and nodding. 'Yes. Yes, I did. She spent a lot of time in the sex zones, Aphrodesia, Eros Island . . .'

Artois reached out with her cigarillo and tapped ash into the tray. 'The randy little slut,' she said, but there was a hint of grudging admiration in her tone which surprised him.

'Group sessions with her friends, casual acquaintances . . .' He wondered if he told her this to shake her from her complacent acceptance of her sister's actions.

'You actually watched them at it?' she asked, amusement in her eyes.

'I had to enter a playback session to trace her.'

'Did you enjoy the experience?'

'Frankly, I found it hard to take.'

'Hal, they're kids for chrissake. Canada's fifteen. She's growing up, becoming a woman. I'd rather she explored her sexuality in VR than in some of the orgy rooms around the city.'

'I thought you were taking it rather well.'

She took a long pull on her cigarillo. 'To be honest, Hal, it's not the sex that worries me. She can fuck the ass off whoever she wants – it's the fact that she was tanking every day that concerns me.'

'I can understand that.'

'But it was the sex thing that shocked you, wasn't it? The

124

fact that they were just kids. Is that what bothered you? That they were doing things you weren't?'

He looked into her eyes. 'If I'm honest with myself, yes. That probably was part of it. Perhaps I was envious of their lack of inhibition.'

'I'd rather Canada lost her inhibitions in the sex zones, learned how to handle herself sexually, rather than grow up repressed.'

Halliday looked into his beer. 'But what you can't learn in the sex zones is what sex – a sexual relationship – really entails. I mean, there's no real emotion in VR, no commitment.'

Artois was nodding, as if conceding the point. 'Okay. VR can be dangerous if you become addicted to it and don't make the graduation to real life, but I still say that the sex zones can be a valuable learning experience.' She paused. 'Hell, I don't know why I'm arguing about this. The thing is, is this why she's gone, Hal? Because she's addicted?'

He shifted uncomfortably. 'That's a possibility. I don't know.'

'So you traced her to a sex zone. What then? Do you know where she went after that?'

'She took a taxi from El Barrio. I watched it on surveillance cameras but lost track of it downtown.' He felt guilty for shielding her from the truth, but he didn't want to see her hurt.

'So, we're really no nearer finding out where she might be?'

'That's about right.' He looked up, met her eyes. 'But I'm working on it.'

She smiled. 'Sure you are, Hal. I have every confidence in you. '

She looked at her watch. 'It's time I wasn't here.' She reached out a hand and touched his fingers. 'Thanks for everything. I'll catch you later.'

He nodded. 'Later,' he said.

He watched as she arranged the chu over her head and slipped from the booth with a quick wave of her fingers. At the bar, her bodyguard quickly downed his drink and climbed the steps before her.

Halliday ordered another beer and sat in the silence of the empty bar. He'd go back to the office, get a take-out from the stall where Casey worked.

His thoughts were interrupted by the buzz of his com. He propped the device against the beer bottle on the table before him. 'Halliday here.'

A woman looked out at him. It took him a few seconds before he recognised the small, dark, pretty face framed in the screen.

'Anna . . .?'

His sister smiled. 'Hal, good to see you.'

'Hey, thanks for the book. It arrived yesterday. I'll make time to read it, okay?'

'Hal . . .' She was peering at him. 'Didn't the hospital get in touch?'

'What?' His stomach flipped. For a second he thought that it was his sister herself who was in hospital. Then he guessed. 'What is it?'

'I've just heard. It took them a while to find my code. Dad died yesterday, Hal. Heart attack. He was out walking. It was pretty much instantaneous.'

Halliday nodded, trying to assess his feelings. Perhaps it was an indication of his strained relationship with his father that he had to actively consider how he felt about the news of the old man's demise. There was no sudden, spontaneous sensation of loss, of grief.

Anna was saying, '. . . so sudden he can't have been aware . . .'

Halliday recalled their last meeting, when his father had talked for the first time about the fire, all those years ago, that had killed Anna's twin sister, Eloise. For the very first time, then, he had begun to see his father as a human being. That had been six months ago, and Halliday hadn't

126

bothered to contact him once since then. He felt a quick, involuntary stab of regret.

'The funeral's the day after tomorrow, Hal,' Anna said. 'I hope you can make it.'

'Sure. I'll be there.'

'I'm flying in from Seattle in the morning. I'll see you there.' She gave him the address of the crematorium and the time of the service.

He nodded. 'You okay?'

She gave a sad smile. 'I'm fine. It's strange. You know, we were never that close, and I knew this would happen one day . . . But the odd thing is that it's still a hell of a shock. I think of our relationship, and how I could have done things to make it so much better.'

He shrugged. 'Don't blame yourself, Anna. It takes two to make these things work.'

'I don't know. Maybe if I'd made the effort, he might have been moved to meet me halfway.'

Halliday smiled at her. 'Typical writer. Always analysing. Let's face it, he was a cold old man who didn't much want contact from us—'

'He said he did. Six months ago he chastised you for not calling more often.'

He gestured. 'That was just to make me feel guilty.'

She gave a quick laugh. 'Hey, listen to you. Now you're doing the analysing.' She sighed. 'Okay, I've got to go, Hal. I'll see you the day after tomorrow.'

He wanted to ask her about her life in Seattle, her writing, but such questions in the circumstances didn't seem appropriate. He nodded. 'See you then, Anna.'

She smiled and cut the connection.

Halliday sipped his beer and listened to the mood music.

Nine

Sanchez returned to consciousness by slow degrees.

He was aware of having awoken two or three times before: he recalled fevered images of Kat staring down at him, of someone else peering into his eyes with some device or other. He had flashes of Kat feeding him bagels dipped in tomato soup, of her mopping his sweat-soaked brow. On these occasions he had been in pain, a pounding agony that affected not only his head but the rest of his body in a measured syncopation matching the beat of his heart.

He had no idea how long had elapsed when he finally awoke without experiencing pain. He was lying on the mattress in the corner of Kat's room. The windows were blacked out – Kat had sprayed them with black paint when she'd moved in – and the only light came from a glowing com-monitor. Kat hunched before it, touch-typing feverishly.

He sat up, amazed at the absence of pain. He felt good, able to face the future.

'Kat.'

She turned quickly and stared at him. 'Sanchez. How you feeling?'

He smiled. 'I'm okay. Fine. How long . . .'

'You've been out two days.' She turned on a light beside the mattress and sat down cross-legged beside him. She picked up an old, torn T-shirt and mopped his brow.

'What happened?'

'They found you in there. They located O'Donnell's program and scoured it. I'm sorry. I couldn't pull you out in time.'

He shook his head. 'Hey, no worries. I'm alive, aren't I?'

'Only just. We got a doctor in, one of our own people. He said if you'd been in there seconds longer . . .' She smiled and shrugged.

He recalled only fleeting images of his time in the Mantoni zone: the rural idyll, the man and the woman, his disguise as a rat. He tried to recall what he had overheard, but his memory seemed to have been affected by whatever had happened to him in the tank.

He closed his eyes, briefly, willing himself to recall. He had the vague notion that he had overheard something of importance.

He felt a hand touch his and he opened his eyes.

Kat was smiling down at him, her expression sad. She squeezed his fingers, and her show of affection both surprised and delighted him.

'Thought I'd lost you, Sanchez,' she said, more to herself. 'Thought you'd died a tank-death, kid.'

He felt himself falling, slipping again into the sea of unconsciousness. He woke later, very briefly. Again the room was illuminated only by the partial glow of the monitor. He heard the sound of sobbing, looked around for Kat. She was sitting against the wall, staring at a pix in her hand, and crying.

He tried to open his mouth to speak, but he was so tired . . . He felt himself, against his will, falling asleep.

When he awoke again, it was light. Sunlight cascaded through the small window in the door, and sparkling shafts of illumination rapiered into the room where the window paint had been scratched.

Sanchez sat up, calling for Kat. She was not in the room. He felt a moment of irrational panic. He wanted to see her, to have the reassurance of her presence.

He looked around the room. There was so little, he thought, that denoted anything at all about the person who lived here. There were few personal possessions, no decorations, paintings or posters. Kat had no music system, not even a holo-unit. There were plenty of com-rigs of various types and designs, but these were the tools of her trade. The only things he noticed in the room that could definitely be said to belong to Kat, that indicated some aspect of her character, were the aerosol cans of spin that littered the floor.

Then he saw the pix. It lay face-down on the floor beside the mattress. He reached out and picked it up. The pix showed the head-and-shoulders shot of a young man, perhaps in his early twenties. He had a prominent nose and Adam's apple and a riotous mass of black hair.

Sanchez heard the sound of footsteps on the fire escape. The door opened. He dropped the pix and lay back.

Kat entered the room, arms enclosing two bags of provisions. She moved to the kitchen and called out, 'How you feeling, Sanchez?'

'Fine,' he said. 'Actually, hungry. Starving.'

'I'll fix you something.' She appeared at the door, smiling at him. 'Omelette do?'

'That'll be great.'

They ate on the mattress, Sanchez sitting back against banked pillows, Kat cross-legged beside him. He surprised himself with how hungry he was. He was at that stage of recuperation where the pain was a distant memory, where all he could think about was getting active again.

Not that he'd ever been that active, but sometimes he'd gone out into the night with a spray-can and daubed Virex graffiti on walls and hoardings . . . Some fucking protest, he thought. But it had proved a cathartic release in lieu of more positive action.

'Met our new controller, Sanchez. Guy calls himself Levine. He says we ought to lie pretty low for a while, what with Heller and Rodriguez both dead.'

He recalled Kat's response to the news of Heller's death the other day. 'It's the game that matters, not the players,' he quoted her own words now.

She looked at him. 'I was stressed, okay?' she snapped. 'I wasn't feeling well.'

He felt himself colour and said, 'Okay, sorry,' and hated himself for being so weak.

'Levine said there were new plans on the way, new tactics.'

'Let's hope they're an improvement on the old,' he muttered.

'He said that Mantoni and the others have realised the threat we pose. Until now they thought we were a bunch of disorganised eco-freaks.'

'Aren't we?' he said. 'Disorganised, I mean.'

She gave him a withering look. 'Doesn't it give you hope that all over the city, all over the country, dammit, there're whole bunches of like-minded individuals fighting alongside us?'

He sighed and lay back against the pillows. 'Sometimes it seems like we're so isolated, fighting a losing battle.'

'The very nature of our organisation, Sanchez, our battle against the big companies, dictates that we operate in cells. That way we can't be infiltrated, or rather if we are, we lose only two members at a time. Of course it seems like we're making no headway, but revolution is a slow process.'

He stared at the grease on his empty plate. 'Sometimes I look at the city and I think everybody wants the VR experience. It's a tide too strong to turn. What can we do to persuade Joe Public to stop tanking?'

Kat was silent for a while. 'We'll win, kid,' she said, with such conviction that Sanchez almost believed her. 'It might take time, but we'll beat the bastards.'

The silence stretched. Sanchez glanced across at the pix on the floor. He gestured towards it. 'Who's the guy?' he asked. He knew that, when she told him it was her lover, he'd experience an uncontrollable stab of jealousy.

She reached out and picked up the photograph, sat regarding it for a long minute. 'Was my brother,' she said in a small voice. 'Joe.'

'What happened?' He disliked himself for asking, but he felt pleased that the guy was not Kat's lover.

131

'Joe worked for Cyber-Tech,' she said in little more than a whisper. 'He was high up in the organisation, a real whizz kid. One of the best.'

'You two were close?'

She was a long time replying. 'He believed in VR,' she said at last. 'He believed in its power of democratisation. He said that in VR everyone could be equal. He was a naïve fool in many respects. We had major league arguments. But, yeah, we were close.'

'What happened to him?'

She shook her head. 'He died a tank-death. I never found out all the details, but he was working on a top-secret project and he died in the tank. They wouldn't even let me see his body.'

He wondered if her solicitude for him, after his near miss in the tank, had been nothing more than transferred grief for the death of her brother.

'That why you joined Virex?' he asked, and wished he hadn't.

She flashed him a look of pure malice. 'Sometimes, Sanchez, you can be so crass it's unbelievable. You think I joined Virex because my brother died a tank-death and I wanted to get back at the people responsible? Didn't you hear me? I said we argued about VR, its long-term effects and consequences. Joe's death had nothing to do with my opposition.'

'Hey, okay. I'm sorry. You're right, sometimes I'm a fucking fool, okay?'

He saw her looking around the room, searching the floor for a canister of spin. He hoped she wouldn't find one. Out of her head, she was never very communicative.

She moved to the kitchen and came back with half a bottle of Jack Daniels instead. She poured two measures into dirty mugs and passed one to Sanchez.

'So what about you? How'd you find yourself here?'

He took a mouthful of rye and felt it burn a trail down his oesophagus. He smiled. 'I worked for Tidemann's,' he said.

132

'R&D. I was no whizz kid, like your brother. A drone, never really had it up here. Straight out of college, I thought VR was the next great thing. Yeah, maybe like Joe I saw its equalising power. Trouble is with us romantics, we always underestimate the corrupting power of the vested interests in control of the medium.' He paused and took another swig. He looked up at Kat. 'I found out some worrying things at Tidemann's, Kat. Like how the high-ups in the company envisaged an indefinite immersion period. They forecast a time when those who could afford it would practically live in fucking VR. Imagine the possibilities for total corporate control and manipulation in that scenario.'

'That's what they're all pushing,' Kat said. 'Mantoni and Tidemann and the others. We know that the four-hour limit's merely a starting point. Soon the authorities'll relax the laws and it'll be twelve hours, and after that . . .'

Sanchez smiled to himself. 'I just didn't like the way all this power was tied up in these mega-companies,' he said. 'It gave me the screaming shits.'

'How'd you find Virex?'

'I didn't. They found me.' He smiled. 'I was headhunted, can you believe that? I moved from a sinecure at a cool half million a year, to living like a pauper and working for the underground.'

'But at least you know you're doing the right thing.'

He laughed, without humour. 'Yeah,' he said. 'Sure.'

She finished her drink and took the plates into the kitchen. Sanchez lay back and closed his eyes. For a time, there, he'd felt himself getting closer to Kat.

When he opened his eyes again, the room was in darkness and Kat was hunched before a glowing monitor, her fingers hovering over the touchpad.

'Kat?'

'Just going over the route you took the other day,' she said. 'Trying to work out how they traced us.'

'O'Donnell's program was clumsy, is how.'

133

She ignored him. From the set of her shoulders, the intensity of her attention to the screen, he could tell that she'd upped herself with spin again.

He closed his eyes, and for no reason he could work out he was once again in the Mantoni rural zone. He recalled, then, what the guy and the woman called Pablo had discussed.

He sat up. 'Kat.'

She ignored him.

'Kat, listen.'

'Can't you see that I'm busy, Sanchez? Just lie back and go to sleep, okay?'

'No, This is important. The other day, in VR, I overheard something. I saw this guy and this other persona. They were talking about assassinating someone . . . But this guy, I recognised him. Or rather, I didn't recognise him at the time. But it's just come back to me . . .'

'So who was he?'

Sanchez shrugged. 'Mantoni. The big-shot VR guy. Sergio Mantoni.'

As he spoke, he remembered something else. 'Hey, wasn't Vanessa Artois involved with Mantoni a while back?'

Kat had screwed around in her seat and was staring at him. 'Sanchez, just what the hell are you raving about?'

'In the zone, I overheard Mantoni talking to this guy, only in VR it wasn't a guy but this beautiful blonde. Anyway, he was talking about how this programmed assassin was going after Artois – ' He leaned forward. 'Christ, have you caught the news lately? Is she dead?'

Kat was shaking her head. 'Not that I've heard, Sanchez, but then I don't dig all that celebrity shit.'

'It'd make headline news, Kat. The death of Vanessa Artois.'

'I've heard nothing.'

Sanchez closed his eyes. 'The blonde Mantoni was with, she said Artois was in the office of some private operative in El Barrio.' He tried to recall the guy's name. 'Halliwell, something like that. No, Halliday. Specialises in missing persons.'

'You sure this isn't some dream? You really heard this? Mantoni wanted Artois dead?'

'That's the impression I got. Weren't they an item, a while back?'

Kat shrugged. 'According to the media, but who the fuck knows, or cares?'

'If we can pin this on Mantoni . . .' Sanchez began.

Kat laughed and turned back to the screen. 'You don't stand a chance, Sanchez. Mantoni's powerful. He has the cops in his pocket. What proof do you have?'

None, he thought. Not one fucking shred of proof. Still, wouldn't it be satisfying to let Mantoni know that he, no-hoper Sanchez, was onto him?

He wondered if he should go to Halliday with what he'd overheard. Maybe the detective could help?

He told Kat what he was planning.

She peered at him. 'You up to it?'

'I feel fine. I'm okay.'

She was sceptical. 'And what do you say when he asks how you overheard Mantoni in a supposedly secure zone?'

Sanchez shrugged. 'I just tell him I'm a lone vracker. Why should he suspect anything else?'

Kat was shaking her head. 'Nothing'll come of it, kid. It won't stick. Mantoni could fall in a sewer and come out smelling of roses.'

'I can't just let it slide. I need to find out what the hell's going on.'

Kat turned back to the screen. Sanchez looked around for his clothes, then stood unsteadily and dressed. He was a little dizzy, but he put that down to the Jack Daniels. His head felt fine.

He moved to the com-screen by the window, accessed GlobalNet and typed 'Halliday' and 'Missing Persons' into the search facility. Seconds later an address in El Barrio appeared on the screen. Sanchez memorised it.

'I'm outta here,' he said. 'Wish me luck in the jungle.'

135

'Luck,' Kat murmured, but her attention was wholly on the screen in front of her nose.

He left the apartment and walked to the Canal Street subway station. It was nine in the evening, and the air was heavy with the stale heat of the day. The subway was like a sauna, and the press of humanity riding uptown gave him the jitters. In every face he saw suspicion; every smart suit denoted some undercover FBI stiff working to eradicate every last Virex member. He felt immense relief when he quit the train and walked into the sultry night, the streets bright with the make-believe show of holo-façades.

He turned onto a street lined with fast-food stalls and bustling with customers, like some scene from an Oriental VR-drama. He found Halliday's office five minutes later, after asking at a chop-suey kiosk.

He climbed a staircase that stank of bleach and stale cigars and paused, unsure now that the time had come to meet the detective. He wasn't good with people, and how long had it been since he'd last spoken to a stranger?

He thought of what Mantoni had said in VR, and rapped on the pebbled glass of the door.

There was no reply, so he tried the handle and pushed open the door. A guy sat behind a desk, hurriedly pushing something into the top drawer. By the smell of it, Sanchez guessed he'd interrupted the detective's supper.

Halliday was small, mid-thirties, with a dishevelled mop of dark curls and the drawn expression of someone who worked too much and ate too little. It was the first time he'd met a private eye in the flesh, and somehow Halliday didn't conform to the image of the tough, hard-bitten stereotype so beloved of the dramas.

He gave Sanchez a quick once-over, then leaned across the desk and offered his hand. 'Halliday. How can I help you?' His handshake was firm, but not intimidating. He was surprisingly soft-spoken, too, and Sanchez lost some of his habitual uneasiness in the presence of a stranger.

Halliday indicated a chair and Sanchez sat down. 'Ah . . . I suppose I should explain why I'm here?' he began, stuttering despite the fact that he felt he could get along with the detective.

Halliday smiled. 'You want I should find someone who's missing, right?' He gestured. 'That's what I'm here for. Just take your time and tell me about it, okay?'

'Ah . . . well, it isn't quite like that.'

'So tell me how it is, Mr . . .?''

'Sanchez.'

'Take it easy and tell me why you're here, Mr Sanchez. Don't worry, I charge by the hour and there's no fee for preliminaries.'

'Well . . .' Christ, but he wished he wasn't so nervous. He was intelligent, eloquent in his head, but whenever it came to articulate what he wanted to say he invariably fouled up.

Halliday saw his discomfort. 'How about a coffee?'

He poured two mugs of black coffee and passed one across the desk. Sanchez took the mug in both hands and sipped. It tasted good; he needed a caffeine hit after the rye he'd shared with Kat.

'A couple of days ago,' he said, 'sometime after dark, someone came to see you. The VR star, Vanessa Artois.'

Halliday rearranged his position in the swivel chair. He was obviously trying not to let his interest show, but Sanchez saw his blue eyes widen at the sound of the star's tag.

'What if she did?'

Sanchez swallowed, wondering how best to phrase what he had to say. 'I . . . someone was trying to kill her.'

Halliday leaned forward, clasping his solid, square hands on the desk before him. 'How do you—?'

'Someone hired an assassin, a drone or something like that. I don't know, exactly. It was programmed to kill—'

'How the hell do you know about that, Sanchez?'

'Did they get her? I mean, I haven't heard any news. I thought, if she were dead, then I'd've heard something.'

'The laser missed by a fraction. Hit the chair you're sitting in. What do you know about the shooting?'

137

'I overheard something – the guy who was hiring, and the guy who programmed the assassin. They were talking about the hit as it was happening. They mentioned Artois by name, and the programmer said she was here.'

Halliday sat back in his swivel chair, massaging his unshaven jaw with a slow, deliberate gesture. 'Where were you? I mean, how'd you get so close to two guys discussing a hit? In my experience, people don't broadcast facts like that.'

This was always going to be the problem, Sanchez knew. How to convince Halliday of what had happened without divulging that he'd been in VR at the time.

'I just overheard them, okay? It doesn't matter where—'

'Com-link, right? You listened in on a communicator conversation?'

Sanchez nodded, relieved that Halliday had given him a way out. 'That's right.'

'So, is that it? You heard these two guys discussing the hit, and then what?' Sanchez could see the light of suspicion in the detective's eyes.

'I . . . I know who one of the guys was,' he said. 'I mean, I recognised the voice.'

Halliday was nodding. 'Right. You recognised the voice.'

'He was asking the woman about the assassin—'

Halliday massaged his eyes. 'So you overheard two guys discussing a hit on the com, and you say one of these guys was a woman?'

Sanchez felt like curling up and disappearing. He should have come out with the truth at the start.

'Okay, so I didn't overhear them on the com. I was in VR.'

Halliday shook his head, as if to clear it. 'You were in VR and you overheard two guys, one of whom was a woman, planning a hit. Tell me if I've got it right?'

Sanchez nodded. 'Right.'

'So, can you tell me this, Mr Sanchez, why are two criminals discussing a hit in some public VR site?'

Sanchez shifted, uncomfortable. 'It wasn't a public site. It was a restricted zone owned by one of the big VR companies, and I was vracking into it illegally.' Sanchez sat back, deflated.

Halliday let the silence stretch. He, too, sat back, sipped his coffee and regarded Sanchez evenly.

'You make a habit of vracking into secure zones owned by VR companies?' the detective said at last. 'You could get your fingers burned bad.'

'I'm a vracker, Mr Halliday. I started hacking on the Net, and when VR came along . . .'

'It was a natural progression, right?'

'Something like that.'

Halliday nodded, regarding Sanchez with a penetrating gaze. 'You said you recognised one of the guys?'

He nodded. 'The guy who was doing the hiring, who wanted Artois dead. He's the head of Mantoni Entertainments, Sergio Mantoni.'

Halliday regarded him for what seemed like an eternity. He set his mug down very precisely in the middle of his desk, next to a tiny bonsai tree, and looked up.

'Do you have any proof of this, a recording, visual or audio? Anything that'd corroborate what you're telling me?'

Sanchez spread his hands. 'I . . . There was no way I could record the insertion. Mantoni protects against that. And when I was discovered, I had to get out fast. His techs sent bugs after me, almost got me. I quit just in time.'

'So I've only your word for what you saw in there?'

'I wouldn't lie.'

'Why have you come here with this, Mr Sanchez? And don't tell me you're just doing your good citizen bit.'

Sanchez licked his lips. 'I . . . what would you have done, in the situation? I heard someone discussing the assassination of a VR star, I heard your name . . . I couldn't just sit back and do nothing, especially when I knew who was responsible.'

Halliday regarded him, as if attempting to come to some

conclusion. Finally he nodded. 'I'll look into it, Mr Sanchez. I'll be in touch at some point. If I could have your address . . .'

'Is that necessary?'

'Unless you've got anything to hide,' Halliday said. He smiled. 'Don't worry. I won't inform the cops of what you do in your spare time. That's between you and me. I'm more interested in nailing whoever wants Vanessa Artois dead.'

Sanchez gave Kat's address in Chinatown. As he was about to stand up and make for the door, the detective said, 'You say you're a vracker, right? You can hack your way into any site?'

'Well, not every one. But most.'

Halliday nodded. 'That's interesting, Mr Sanchez.' He passed a business card across the table. 'If you need anything in future, just call. And thanks for the information.'

Sanchez nodded and headed for the door. When he looked back before stepping from the room, Halliday was regarding the tiny tree on the desk before him, a frown creasing his face.

Sanchez made his way out into the warm night. He thought of Kat, and the sanctuary of her apartment. He would return and tell her that he was still feeling bad.

Perhaps she'd take pity and allow him to stay a while longer.

Ten

As soon as Sanchez left the office, Halliday got through to Vanessa Artois. Her face, her own face, appeared on the screen of his desk-com.

'Vanessa, you free at the moment? We need to talk.'

'I'm just finishing coffee with my agent. What is it?'

He hesitated. 'Something's cropped up, Vanessa. It's important.'

She looked shocked. 'Is it about Canada?'

He shook his head. 'The shooting the other night.'

She glanced at her watch. 'Look, give me half an hour, okay? We can meet in the bar of my hotel.' She gave him the name of a hotel on Broadway and signed off.

Halliday considered what Sanchez had told him. There was no way of knowing if the little guy had been telling the truth, of course. But as far as Halliday was concerned he couldn't ignore the possibility that for whatever reasons it was Sergio Mantoni who wanted the VR star dead.

He activated his desk-com and accessed GlobalNet. He scrolled through pages of information about the producer: Sergio Mantoni had made his name with holo-dramas, and then was one of the few successful media moguls to make the switch to VR Entertainments. He owned his own production company, as well as a chain of VR Bars across America and Canada. Much of what Halliday read was the usual media hype of the rich and famous, though one or two articles did mention that Mantoni was a demanding taskmaster who was hard to work for. He was fifty-five and a multi-millionaire. He had never married after the woman he'd been engaged to, the holo-star Bo Ventura, was shot dead by a fan-turned-assassin twenty-five years ago.

He was about to log off when he came across a news report that claimed, in typical media hyperbole, that millionaire tycoon Sergio Mantoni and superstar VR diva Vanessa Artois were conducting a clandestine affair. The report was date-lined March 2038, just over two years ago.

He sat and stared at the screen, considering.

He scrolled through page after page of information about the producer, compiling a list of names of the people who had worked closely with him over the years.

For the next fifteen minutes he attempted to contact a dozen people in the VR industry, fellow producers, directors and writers. If he could speak to people who knew Mantoni, he might be able to gain a mental picture of the man, perhaps even learn a little about his private life.

A couple of contacts had died, others were tied up with work and unavailable. He reached the private secretary of a director who had made half a dozen holo-films for Mantoni's studio over ten years ago. According to an article on GlobalNet, the men had been close friends for a while. Did that mean, Halliday wondered, that they were no longer that close?

'I'm afraid Mr Karel is very busy at the moment—' the secretary said.

Halliday hung his old police ID card close to the screen. 'I'm sure he'd find time to help with my investigations.'

The woman consulted something off-screen. 'He'll be available for an hour, and an hour only, tomorrow afternoon at four. He's working at his home studio.''

'And where is that?' He made a note of the address, thanked the secretary for her help, and cut the connection. The interview would fit in perfectly with his father's funeral.

He killed the desk-com, quit the office and drove downtown. It was almost midnight, and all along Broadway the holo-façades glowed in the darkness like an fleet of ocean-going liners. He left the Ford in a sidestreet and made his way to the hotel bar. A guy in a raincoat stood chatting to the bartender. One other person was in the bar, a red-headed woman seated in a plush booth.

Halliday bought himself a beer and looked across at the woman. She had not seen him. She sat with her long legs crossed, smoking her trademark cigarillo.

The plain-faced woman looked up when he slipped into the booth. 'Halliday. You said something's come up—'

'We need to talk.'

She made no move to take off her chu, and Halliday was thankful. He had to admit, though, that speaking to Artois in the guise of a stranger was an oddly disconcerting experience.

'I need to ask you about your career, if that's okay?'

She took a long draw on her cigarillo, watching him through the lazily curling tendrils of smoke. 'Ask away, Hal.'

'I feel like I'm interviewing you for a part,' he said. 'I suppose you've done a thousand auditions, over the years?'

'A thousand? Seems like millions.'

He took a swallow of beer. 'How'd you get the initial break? You started in holo-dramas?'

'Is this part of the audition, Hal? Or are you really interested?' She smiled and shook her head. 'I began as a serious stage actress. I trod the boards, applied the grease paint. I studied acting – I mean real acting, not the shit that passes today.'

'How'd you make the switch?'

'I had an agent. He got me a small part in some crummy holo-drama, then another. Work started to come in. Small roles at first, working for the independents. I was . . . what? Twenty? I thought that was as good as it was going to get.'

'Then Imperial signed you up, right?'

She nodded. 'A three-year deal, five big-budget dramas. I thought I'd made it. I'd be a star. Well . . .' She paused, regarding her wine glass. 'I suppose I was. I was cast in the best roles in the biggest dramas with the biggest and best

143

producers, and the people loved me. I was happy. I was acting in really great holos . . . and you know what happened then, of course?'

Over the period of a few months, earlier this year, the production of holo-dramas had been cut back drastically. The trade took a nosedive.

He nodded. 'VR happened.'

'VR happened,' she echoed, her eyes far away. 'VR technology became faster and better and cheaper, and suddenly everyone, or nearly everyone, could afford to tank. The production moguls saw a good thing when it came along and invested heavily in the industry, developed Interactive Drama Entertainment. You remember the first production, the *Ides of March*? How tacky . . . It got better, took off, and the holo industry died on its feet.'

She stopped there, stabbing out the butt of her cigarillo into the ashtray.

'You were taken up by a VR company.' Halliday paused, watching her. 'How did you come to work for Sergio Mantoni?'

'My agent, again. I signed a contract with Mantoni Entertainments.'

'I've heard that Mantoni's quite an interesting character.'

She matched his gaze. 'You could say that.'

'Didn't he start out in holos?'

'Originally, way back. Then he and his backers saw where VR was going and got in on the ground floor. They bought a few small VR companies, built them up, and effectively killed their own industry. Mantoni Entertainments became the leader of the field and Sergio one of the richest men in the country—' she stopped, staring at him, '—and I was no longer acting.'

'But I thought – I mean, you work in VR.'

'Work? You call that work? I'll tell you what happened, Hal. Mantoni had me contracted to his company. I didn't really think about it. I mean, I was being paid, wasn't I? Mantoni promised me fabulous roles in future productions, but all I did was what I thought were publicity shots. So I waited . . . and the work never came in, because there was no work. Real work. I mean, Vanessa Artois was starring in all the big VR Interactive Drama Entertainments, and she was as popular as ever – people loved taking part in a Vanessa Artois drama, but all the while, all I had to do was sit on my butt in New York, attend the occasional publicity session, media call, all that crap.'

'So who was taking the part of Vanessa Artois?' Halliday asked.

She lit another cigarillo. 'No one was, dummy. The Vanessa Artois in VR, the Vanessa Artois thrilling and moving all the punters with her inimitable acting skills, was a computer-programmed construct with my face and body and manner-isms. The hell of it was this program acted just as well as me, because for chrissake it *was* me!'

Halliday shook his head. 'I knew they used computer animations, but I thought that most of the acting—'

She interrupted. 'Well, think again, Hal.'

He hesitated. 'I read in Canada's diary that the studio was putting pressure on you.'

She nodded. It was a while before she spoke.

'The contract I signed with Mantoni Entertainments almost a year ago runs out next month. Technically, in a perfect world, I should be a free agent then. In the real world, the world Mantoni has by the balls, I'll be no such thing.'

'Why's that?'

'Because Mr Big Shot Mantoni's taking the case to court. He claims that he now owns the rights to the image of Vanessa Artois, since it was his company, his billions and expertise and management, that made me what I am.'

'It'll never stand up in a court of law.'

When Vanessa raised her eyes he saw that she was on the verge of tears. He wanted to reach across the table and touch her hand, make some futile and insignificant gesture to show her that he cared.

He just sat, paralysed at the thought of how she might interpret such an innocent gesture.

'Hal, Hal . . . that's not the point. He probably knows it won't stand up. That's why he's doing it. He has teams of attorneys like you wouldn't believe. They can tie the case up in the courts for the next ten, fifteen years. And all that time I'll be contractually obliged not to work for anyone else – not even some tiny two-dollar arthouse holo-company, not even a damned touring stage troupe.'

Halliday nodded. 'Tough situation.'

'Yeah, you can say that again.'

He looked up from his beer, staring at her. 'Look, is there any reason why Sergio Mantoni might want you dead?'

She stared at him. 'What?'

He shrugged. 'A couple of leads I'm following: one of them suggests that Mantoni might have – I said *might've* – hired the assassin. I don't know, but I gotta think of every possibility.'

She was shaking her head. 'He's a twisted bastard, Hal. But he wouldn't do a thing like that.'

He thought about what he had to say. 'Listen, you said yourself that it isn't you who acts in these VR entertainments.'

'Meaning?'

'Meaning, you aren't indispensable.'

She stubbed out her cigarillo in the ashtray, and Halliday saw that her hand was shaking. 'That's no reason why he'd have me killed.'

Halliday tipped his glass and regarded the foamy ellipse of beer. He looked up. 'But think of all the publicity. Famous VR star dramatically slain. You'd become an icon, a tragic symbol of the fucked-up world we live in. Who was that Brit royal totalled in Paris at the end of the twentieth century? Look what happened to her – canonised by the masses, or rather by the news media, in it for the bucks. Your VR dramas would still come out, and the citizens would love it. Mantoni'd make mega-bucks.'

'You've been watching too many bad holo-dramas, Hal. You're looking for motives where none exist.'

'Okay, so it is fanciful.' He paused, watching her, and then said, 'There was a rumour, some time ago, that you and he were attached.'

She shrugged, avoiding his gaze. 'For a short while, that's all. It was nothing. Affairs between producers and stars are a dime a dozen.' She smiled across at him and changed the subject rather too rapidly for his liking. 'So what now, Hal? Where do we go from here?'

'I need to meet Mantoni, talk to the guy. You know how I can contact him?'

Vanessa looked thoughtful. 'He's appearing at the Cassini Awards ceremony tomorrow.'

'Where've I heard that name before?'

'It's the VR equivalent of the holo-Oscars. Mantoni will be there.'

'I could gatecrash the party, have a quiet word.'

'I can get you in there. I'm up for the best lead actress award.'

'Even though it was a computer construct that—?'

'You see how much it stinks? They want a real, live, flesh-and-blood actress to collect the award, though.'

'I don't like the idea of you endangering yourself like that.'

'I'd be appearing as myself for what, twenty seconds when I step from the limo? As soon as I'm inside, I'll use the chu.'

'I'd rather you didn't go, Vanessa.'

She looked at him. 'And how will you get in to meet Mantoni without me?' she asked.

He thought about it. He'd contact Szabo, tell them what they'd planned. Szabo could have his best men on hand when the limo drew up, covering all angles.

He nodded. 'Okay, we'll do that.'

'Good.' She smiled at him. 'And don't take this the wrong way, Hal, but go and buy yourself a new suit and charge it to my bill, okay?'

'I already have a suit.'

'So treat yourself to another one. And don't argue.'

He smiled. 'How about another wine?' He signalled for a glass of white wine and a bottle of wheat beer.

'How's Casey?' Vanessa asked when the drinks arrived.

He shrugged. 'She's a mixed-up sixteen-year-old street kid who thinks she's ugly and has the hots for someone who hasn't even noticed her.'

'Just like every other sixteen-year-old on the planet.'

'How can I tell her that? She's hurting and all I can do is suggest she talks to this guy instead of admiring from afar. And guess what? She wants a chu to change her appearance.'

'You're kidding?'

'She told me she'll trade the coat you left the other night. Which reminds me, I should have brought it along.'

'Forget it. She can have it. A present.'

He smiled at her. 'I'll tell her. She'll appreciate it. But I won't let her trade it in for a chu.'

'Tell her from me that she doesn't need one.'

A silence developed, not at all awkward. She looked across at him, something hesitant in her expression. 'What?' he asked.

She gave a contemplative moue. 'I . . . I was just wondering. What are you doing tonight? I mean, it's no fun on your own in a big hotel room.'

He felt his mouth dry suddenly, as if he were a teenage kid on his first date. Christ, the kind of woman he'd only ever dreamed about in fantasies was asking him back to her room, and all he could do was think of excuses why he should refuse.

'I . . . thanks. You know how it is. I need to work. I have a lot to do before dawn.' He couldn't bring himself to look up, into her eyes.

'Sure. I understand. Don't worry about it.'

They were both embarrassed now and Halliday cursed himself.

She finished her wine, looked at her watch. 'It's late. I didn't realise.' She smiled. 'Got to catch up with my beauty sleep, Hal.' She stood to go. 'The limo's due to pick me up at the Plaza tomorrow night. I could meet you outside the building at seven thirty.'

'I'll be there.'

'Thanks for everything, Hal. If you need anything,' she said, 'just give me a call.'

She hurried from the bar, closely followed by her minder.

Halliday sat and stared into his glass, at that stage of pleasant drunkenness when he could laugh at his failings, the missed opportunities. Perhaps, later, he would begin to regret.

Before his thoughts turned maudlin, he drained the last of the beer, settled the bill and left the bar.

He drove slowly back to El Barrio, easing through the crowds spilling onto the streets. It seemed to him that there were a lot of couples out tonight. He thought of Kim, and then considered Vanessa's invitation, and cursed himself.

His office was illuminated by the glare of the wallscreen when he walked in. Casey had left an endearingly concerned and misspelt message in massive letters: Were are you HAL? Wated up for hours. Wake me up when you come in. C.

He made himself a coffee and sat down in his swivel chair. He lodged his feet on the desk, sipped the coffee and considered the evening.

He pulled the keyboard towards him, tapped into GlobalNet, and accessed the holo-drama archive. Seconds later the wallscreen flooded the room with garish pastel light, the images slightly blurred in the transfer from holo-vision to flatscreen reception. From time to time Halliday reached out and froze a scene, then sat back and stared at the still.

He must have dozed off. He was woken by someone shaking his shoulder. Casey was yawning massively, hair tousled. 'I told you to wake me up when you got back, Hal.'

'Only just got in,' Halliday said, sitting up.

'Liar,' Casey said. 'I heard you snoring.' She helped herself to a cup of cold coffee and pulled a face. She squatted on the chesterfield and nodded to the frozen image on the screen, smiling to herself as if she'd discovered Halliday's greatest secret.

'What's that doing, Hal?'

He squinted at her through one tired eye. 'Not a lot, Casey.'

'You seen her lately?' She was smiling.

Halliday looked at the giant full-face image of Vanessa Artois, from the love scene in what was regarded as her greatest holo-drama, the '35 remake of *Casablanca*.

'Last night.'

'You got it bad, Hal. Her holos on the 'screen? I worry about you, sometimes.'

'Don't bother. By the way – she says you can keep the coat.'

She let her mouth drop open above her folded knees. 'I can? Hey, that's great.'

'But,' Halliday went on, 'she says that if you trade it in to buy a chu, she'll be around to take what, by rights, is hers.'

'That's not fair!'

'And also, she told me to tell you that you don't need a chu.'

'Says her. Ms Perfection.'

'Be grateful you got the coat, Casey.'

She jumped up and crossed the room.

'Where you going?'

'Where do you think? Work.'

He looked at his watch. It was almost seven. He must have been dozing for hours.

Casey was splashing her face at the faucet in the corner of the room. 'How's your boyfriend, Casey?'

She looked up, water dripping. 'Not my boyfriend.'

'Then do something about it. Be brave. Ask him out.'

'Deal,' she said. 'If you ask Vanessa out.'

He smiled. 'Okay, Casey.'

She stopped by the door, surprised 'You mean it? You're really gonna ask her out?'

'You bet. And when I do, you've got to ask your guy out, too.'

She opened the door and gave him a big smile. 'Bye, Hal. Get some sleep.' She slammed the door shut and thumped down the steps.

Halliday took one last look at the face on the wallscreen, reached out and erased the image.

He made his way to the bedroom. Vanessa's coat lay on the bed. He stretched out beside it, brought the fabric to his nose, and inhaled the scent of her perfume.

Eleven

The crematorium was a low, red-brick building dating from the end of the twentieth century, situated about a mile along the Long Island coast from his father's weatherboard house.

Halliday braked the Ford in the near-deserted parking lot overlooking the bay. The funeral service would not be well attended, judging by the lack of cars, and despite himself he felt an involuntary stab of sadness. As he made his way to the entrance of the chapel, he realised that he had known nothing about how his father had lived the last years of his life. During his adolescence, he had seen his father as a cold, remote, unemotional figure of unbending authority. To the best of Halliday's knowledge he'd had no friends, and after the death of his wife very rarely ventured from the house. He had read a lot, and watched television, and later holo-vision.

How tragic other people's lives seemed in retrospect, he thought.

He passed into the chapel and was surprised to find that perhaps thirty people occupied the seats on either side of the central aisle. He looked around, but could see no sign of his sister. He made his way to the front of the chapel, uncomfortably conscious of being identified both as his father's son and as someone who should be mourning. As he took his seat on the hard bench, it came to him why he was so uneasy: he imagined his father's acquaintances pointing him out and thinking to themselves that he was the son who had never bothered to visit his ageing father . . . The guilt, like a curse that could not be escaped, had begun already.

He took a quick look over his shoulder at the silent congregation. He recognised two or three faces from the past, neighbours from along the coast, a shopkeeper. Seen like this after a interim period of twenty-five years, the visible evidence of the ageing process seemed shocking, yet another fact of existence that seemed so arbitrarily unfair. On the day when the fact of his mortality should have been emphasised by his father's death, he thought it ironic that it was the sight of faces from the past that filled him with such sadness.

Movement beside him put an end to his morbid thoughts.

Anna, trim in a jet-black trouser suit, slipped onto the bench beside him and took his hand in a tight, silent squeeze. He looked at her and smiled, wanting to say something in greeting but constrained by the ambient silence: to have said something now would be to commit an act of sacrilege.

At a sound from the rear of the chapel, the congregation rose. A military padre, in uniform and incongruous dog collar, preceded the coffin up the aisle. Six uniformed soldiers carried the coffin in severely precise slow-step, halted and lowered it onto trestles at the altar. The coffin was draped with the Stars and Stripes, a gesture that seemed to Halliday unnecessary, the imposition of nationalism on the private occasion of a funeral almost insulting.

His father's black beret and leather gloves were arranged on the flag, as if he might be along at any second to reclaim them.

His father had served in the United States Army for more than thirty years, working his way up in some obscure branch of intelligence which he had never spoken about to Halliday. Even so, he was surprised that the funeral would be military – it was as if his father had been killed in action in some foreign conflict, not of a heart attack fifteen years after retirement.

'We are here,' the padre began, 'to celebrate the life of Charles Edward Halliday. Those of you close to Charles, family and friends alike, will be grieved by the passing of so loving a father and friend, but I would like to take this opportunity to invoke a note of celebration. Charles was for the last fifteen years of his life, since his retirement, a regular parishioner at the Kennedy camp . . .'

The words droned on in the heat of the chapel, and Halliday learned other new things about the man who had been his father; as surprising as the fact that he had been a believer was the notion that he had contributed to various charities in the locality, that he had a wide circle of friends in various walks of life.

Halliday wondered what he found so disturbing about the new side of his father revealed today; he should have been thankful that his father's later years had not been as lonely and loveless as he'd assumed, and yet he found himself resenting the man for failing to show towards his family the humanity he manifestly exhibited to others.

Between sermons, and a short eulogy by a friend, they sang hymns. Halliday mumbled along self-consciously, willing the service to finish so that he could escape the building and breathe the relatively fresh air outside.

As he watched the coffin disappear into the curtained recess, he considered his father's life and the events that had conspired to make the man what he had become. His wife had died in her forties, and not long after that he lost his daughter in the house fire . . . was it any wonder that he had closed in on himself, become distant with his surviving family, unable to exhibit emotions like love and tenderness for fear, perhaps, that the objects of his affections might go the way of the others he had loved and cherished? It was easy to say that his losses should have made him more humanely disposed towards his remaining son and daughter, but the fact was that they had not, and who was Halliday to criticise the man for taking the measures, perhaps even subconscious, necessary for his continued survival?

The service came to a close, and the congregation filed out into the humid afternoon heat. Even the breeze blowing in off the ocean did little to stir the stifling air. Halliday shook hands with the padre, hearing the man's murmured condolences and feeling like a fraud, as he smiled and nodded with a manufactured solemnity.

He was standing with Anna, not yet having said a word to her, when a tall, grey-haired woman approached and introduced herself as a friend of their father's. She was holding a gathering at her house up the coast, if they would care to attend.

Halliday wanted nothing more than to escape the accumulating guilt that seemed to fill his head like an incipient migraine.

Before he could cite pressure of work as an excuse to get away, Anna smiled, radiantly, took his hand and said, 'We'd love to come, wouldn't we, Hal?'

The house was one of the seafront mansions he had noticed on his last visit to Blue Point, six months earlier. A lavish spread was laid out in a vast room hung with chandeliers, and perhaps fifty guests helped themselves, then stood around in urbane, chatting groups.

Halliday poured himself a strong black coffee, noticed that the french windows leading to a patio were open, and slipped outside. He leaned against a marble balustrade, drank his coffee and gazed out over the undulating ocean.

'Hal, here you are.'

Anna leaned against the balustrade with her back to the ocean, a glass of sherry in hand.

He said the first thing that came into his head. 'I know it's a cliché, but I wish I'd made some effort . . .'

She smiled at him. 'What did you say over the com the other day? I was the one expressing regret, and you told me not to blame myself, that it would have taken an effort from Dad to make things work.'

Halliday nodded. 'I thought he didn't want to make that effort, but perhaps I was wrong? Listening to all that back there . . . it made me realise how much I didn't know him.'

She shrugged. 'He didn't want us to know him.'

'Because of what happened to Eloise? I wondered that. Even so, I can't help feeling guilty.'

155

'It's natural. I feel the same. I keep thinking, *what if*? But you're right, you know; my brother the private investigator is dead right – we couldn't have done a thing to make things better between us without him making some effort too, and he never made that effort, Hal. That's life.'

'Yeah. So . . .' He took another mouthful of coffee. He wondered why so much of what he said, and what others said to him, was no more than platitudes. Perhaps the only way to stay sane was to couch experience in the easy explanations of the banal and clichéd? Perhaps the truth was sometimes too painful?

'How's Seattle, Anna? How's the writing going?'

'Seattle's great. It's so clean out there. You really should come over sometime.'

He nodded. 'I'd love to.'

'I'm working on the rewrite of my second book. *Beyond Persephone*'s doing okay. The publishers are happy with sales. I'm writing what I want to write – that's the main thing.'

'And Kia?'

She laughed. 'Kia is Kia. You know her. She's working for a software company out there – we have a timber house in the hills overlooking the ocean. Did you know they're planting genetically modified spruce and pine up and down the coast? They forecast that in ten, twenty years there'll be whole forests of the things stretching from Washington state all the way down to California.'

Halliday imagined the scene and shook his head. 'That'd be one hell of a sight.'

She took a sip of sherry, watching him. 'So, how's things with you?'

He shrugged. 'I'm working hard.'

'You and Kim? What happened there?'

'Nothing. We never got back together.'

'I'm sorry.'

'It's gone and past. History. I'm over it.'

She was still watching him. He received the impression that she wanted him to tell the truth, open himself up to her. But how could he do that, when he did not possess the vocabulary, emotional or linguistic, to express his true feelings with any fidelity? The banal and the clichéd, he thought.

The moment when she might have probed deeper passed, and he was grateful. She said, 'So, you seeing anyone at the moment?'

He had the ridiculous urge to tell her that he was dating Vanessa Artois, the VR star, but stopped himself. It was the type of lie that only a lonely loser would tell, and he might be many things, but he was not lonely, or a loser, quite yet.

'There's someone. No big deal. I'm too busy with work to take it seriously right now.'

She nodded. 'So what're you working on, Hal? Anything exciting?'

He laughed. 'Only attempted murder, kidnapping, nothing much. Not the type of thing you'd like to write about.'

'How do you know that? Did you read the book?'

'A few pages.'

'Enough to know that you won't read any more.' She was smiling at him, mocking.

'No, it's not like that. Hell, my sister wrote a book – sure I'll read it.'

'Tell me about the case, then.'

He finished his coffee, considering. He talked her through the events of the past couple of days, the attempted murder of Vanessa Artois and the search for her missing kid sister. Stated so baldly, it sounded like a melodramatic episode from a holo-serial.

As he spoke, he remembered his appointment with Karel, the director friend of Sergio Mantoni. He looked at his watch. 'It's time I wasn't here, Anna. I'm meeting someone about the case at four.'

'Can't you stay a little longer?'

He frowned. 'I really must see this guy. How long you in New York?'

'I fly back to Seattle at six. I'll stay here awhile then get a cab. Say,' she said, reaching out and placing a hand on his arm. 'I really meant it when I said you should fly out, spend some time with me and Kia. You look like you could use a holiday.'

He smiled. 'I'll hold you to that. I'll see you later, okay?'

She placed her empty glass on the rail and held out her arms to him. 'Come here, Hal,' she said, and he moved self-consciously into her embrace.

'We're all we've got now,' she whispered into his ear. 'It's just me and you, now.'

He nodded, kissed her cheek, then smiled in farewell as he stepped through the french windows into the mansion.

He thought briefly about finding his hostess and thanking her, then dismissed the idea. He hurried through the gathering and out the front door to the Ford. No doubt his father's friends would have him down not only as the son who'd never visited his father, but the miserable son-of-a-bitch who left the wake without so much as a thank-you.

He accelerated from the drive and headed towards Manhattan along the coast road. As he drove, he thought about Anna, and how she had made overtures back there to bring them closer together. It was up to him, now, to make the effort and take up her invitation, perhaps get to know his sister better. Christ, it was about time he gave something of himself to someone else. But, even as he acknowledged this, he knew that it would be so very hard to do, that the least line of resistance was apathy and neglect, and that time would work to ease the guilt he felt on that score, too.

One hour later he parked the Ford on a sidestreet off Fifth Avenue and made his way across the street to the towering glass needle of the Tidemann Building.

Emmanuel Karel had his studio apartment on the fiftieth floor. Halliday took the elevator and stepped out into a corridor hung with a moving montage of holo-film and VR images. The effect, as he made his way towards the reception desk, robbed him of his sense of balance. By the time he reached Karel's secretary he was feeling distinctly queasy.

'Halliday,' he said, producing his police ID. 'We spoke yesterday.'

'Mr Karel will be with you in five minutes. If you'd care to go through and wait in the lobby . . .'

He stepped through a pair of double doors and found himself in the foyer of what looked like the domain of a megalomaniac. The walls were hung with dozens of blown-up images of a small, grey-haired black man in the company of men and women Halliday recognised as holo-stars and VR actors. Other pix showed Karel accepting the statuettes Vanessa had told him were holo-Oscars.

So the director, in his own right, was a big name. He wondered if he should have heard of any of the guy's films?

He was still wondering this when a door opened and a young man in a white suit leaned through. 'Halliday? Mr Karel will see you now. This way.'

He led Halliday along a corridor to an open-plan lounge with a wall-window overlooking Central Park. The room was full of com-screens and devices that might have been movie cameras, though sleek and streamlined like something from a futuristic holo-epic.

Two beautiful women – models, if their attenuated limbs and *don't-even-look-at-me* hauteur were anything to go by – sat on high stools by the window. One of the futuristic cameras was positioned before them, and from time to time, at the command of a small, casually-dressed man in his seventies, they altered their poses.

'Mr Karel,' the young man said, 'Mr Halliday to see you.'

Karel turned to Halliday and winked. 'Halliday. Be with you in a second. Okay, James, that will be all. Girls, same time tomorrow, okay? See you then.'

They climbed from the stools and strode from the room without so much as a glance in Halliday's direction.

When the man in the white suit and the models had vacated the room, Karel said, 'Doing the preliminary character shots for the latest VR interactive, Halliday.'

He recalled what Vanessa had told him yesterday about her roles being little more than computer-enhanced images of her physical likeness. 'Should I have recognised . . .?' He gestured towards where the women had exited.

Karel laughed loudly. 'You mean you didn't realise the brunette was Dina Carstairs? Where the hell've you been hiding yourself, man?'

Halliday looked around the room at the com-screen and cameras. 'I've never experienced a VR interactive, if that's what you mean. Pressure of work, and all that.'

'You should get yourself down to your local Bar,' Karel advised. 'There's nothing like participating in an interactive to forget yourself. Talk about cathartic. Think about it, man. You can take part in any of a thousand ultra-realistic adventure scenarios – you're the hero, you experience the thrills and spills you'd never have a chance of experiencing in the real world. Wars, exploration, adventure, love affairs . . .'

'You've sold it to me,' Halliday said. 'Next time I get a few spare hours I'll tank in and forget myself.' He'd meant to sound sarcastic, but the director took him at face value.

'You do that, Halliday. Personally I recommend *Death Threat III* or *Mercury Rising*, but then I would, wouldn't I?'

'Don't tell me, you directed them?'

'How'd you guess, Halliday?' Karel laughed. 'Care for a drink?' The director moved to a cold-cabinet in the corner of the room.

'A beer,' Halliday said. He wondered if the director's easy familiarity with strangers was part of his movie-world conditioning. He'd noticed the same thing among some actors, a casual bonhomie that often came across as nothing more than an extension of their innate exhibitionism.

Karel passed him an ice-cold bottle of imported German lager and nodded to a long sofa positioned before the window.

Halliday took the proffered seat while Karel hitched himself onto one of the high stools recently vacated by the VR stars.

'So okay, Halliday,' Karel said, 'how can I help you?'

Halliday took a swallow of lager. 'I'm investigating a case that might involve an old acquaintance of yours. I thought you might be able to tell me something about this guy.'

Karel tipped his own bottle quickly, holding it at the neck and forming his lips into a receptive pout as he eyed Halliday. 'I might at that,' he said. 'But let me guess.' He pointed at Halliday with the bottle. 'Don't tell me, the guy in question is none other than Mantoni, yes? Sergio Mantoni?'

Halliday nodded, impressed. 'Right on the nose. How'd you guess?'

'Wasn't hard, Halliday. Reckoned it was only a matter of time before Mantoni got his fingers burned good.'

'So what's he been doing that you know about?'

'Let's just say that in this business I hear a lot of rumours, and I knew Sergio well enough to know that some of 'em just might be true.'

'Like what?'

'Like, for instance, the drugs he doles out at his parties. Okay, so the industry's famed for its pharmaceutical excess, but Mantoni doesn't stint.'

'He uses?'

'He did. He had a bad habit, what, ten years back? Word is he's clean now. But he still supplies.' Karel tipped his beer. 'So what's he done this time, Halliday?'

He shook his head. 'That's between me and my boss at this stage. I want to get some idea of what he's like—'

Karel laughed. 'Where to begin? Listen, I was a good friend of Sergio's fifteen, twenty years back. I did a few holos for him. He was talented, not one of these producers who're nothing more than big money and big ideas. He knew the score artistically. It was a pleasure working with him. But he was . . . haunted, Halliday. Ever since the Civic incident.'

'When his fiancée was shot dead?'

Karel nodded. 'It screwed him bad. He never really got over it. He blamed himself, see, even though every shrink in Manhattan told him he did everything he could to save her.'

'He went off the rails?'

'You could say that. He got into women in a big way. For my money, he was trying to find a replacement for Bo, which was a big mistake, believe you me. I tried to tell him that, but did he listen? It got so bad I decided our friendship was over.'

'So bad in what way?' Halliday watched the director. He guessed the guy was enjoying himself, chewing over old times, bitching about someone he could no longer bring himself to respect.

'With the women, is what way, Halliday. Hey, I'm no prude. You can't be, not in this line of work. But he was using these women like slaves. He had charisma, see. Women fell for him big time. He rarely saw the same woman for more than a week, and some chicks couldn't take this. I know of one kid who slit her wrists after an affair with Mantoni. He didn't seem to be bothered about the feelings of others.'

'Sounds like some kind of guy,' Halliday grunted.

'He'd been damaged, and I guess the way he looked at it he could damage no one as bad as he'd damaged himself.' Karel shrugged. 'Ten years ago I said fuck you, man, and I haven't talked to the bastard since.'

Halliday nodded, finished his beer. Karel gestured at the empty bottle, ever the attentive host. 'How about another?'

He'd slipped off his stool and was crossing to the cooler before Halliday could reply. He stared through the wall window and considered his next question.

Karel passed him the beer and resumed his seat.

'So what do you know about his affair with the VR star, Vanessa Artois?'

'Artois? Now there's one classy dame,' Karel said. 'I heard the rumour. Heard it was full on. For the first time since Bo Ventura, he'd found someone he was serious about. But you know something, Halliday? I didn't believe it. I mean, I knew Mantoni well enough to know no woman could pull him round, not even someone like Bo's double – and Vanessa Artois was the walking, talking embodiment of Ventura.'

'What happened?'

'What happened? This babe was stronger than the others, is what happened. It was Artois who ditched Mantoni this time, and he didn't like it. Took it bad, so I heard.' Karel chuckled. 'Between you and me, I was so damned happy that he'd finally got a dose of his own shit, know what I mean?'

Halliday nodded. 'Sounds like he finally got what was coming to him.'

'And how! He retreated to his island, licking his wounds. Rarely leaves the place.' Karel finished his beer and eyed Halliday. 'Say, just what is it you've got on Mantoni, anyway?'

Halliday smiled. 'And how long would it remain confidential, if I told you?'

'Touché,' Karel said, pointing fingers pistol-fashion at Halliday. 'You got me sussed, man.'

Halliday finished his beer. 'One more thing . . . You don't think Mantoni would be the kind of guy to resort to violence?'

The director looked at him. 'Violence? In what way?'

Halliday shrugged. 'Against someone who'd crossed him in the past.'

Karel pursed his lips, shaking his head. 'To be honest, I can't see him committing personal violence, I mean the one to one physical stuff. That isn't his style. You know something, during all the years I knew him, I never saw the bastard lose his temper. Always gave the impression of impeccable cool and sophistication.'

Halliday stood up and made to go.

Karel went on, 'But I wouldn't put it past Mantoni to get someone to do the dirty work for him. Know what I mean?'

Halliday nodded. 'Thanks for your time. I'll be in touch if anything turns up, okay?'

Karel winked. 'See you around, Halliday.'

As he quit the apartment and took the elevator down to the street, Halliday considered what Karel had told him. So Vanessa had left Mantoni after a tempestuous affair, and he had taken it badly . . .? But was that, he asked himself, enough to provoke the tycoon into trying to kill her?

Twelve

Sergio Mantoni tanked and entered the security-coded site where he'd installed the girl.

It was the archetypal desert island, pristine and timeless: a fringe of lazy palms fronted by a crescent of fine white sand, and a placid expanse of sapphire sea which merged at the horizon with the equally blue sky.

Mantoni wore the persona he always used in her company. He leaned against the trunk of a palm and watched the group of revellers disporting themselves around the beach-hut bar.

She seemed to be enjoying herself, heedless of how long she had spent in VR. She was talking to a bare-chested young man and drinking from a long glass. She was barefoot and topless, wearing only a cheesecloth sarong.

The other partygoers in this site were all constructs, personas taken from the files stored in the data-banks at Mantoni Entertainment HQ. Little did the girl know, but she was flirting with nothing more than the visual icon of an intricate but lifeless computer program.

She looked up and saw him. He was gratified to see that her face registered what looked like genuine pleasure. She touched the guy on the chest, murmuring something to him, and danced across the sand towards him.

She raised her hands above her head, swinging her hips in time to the music belting out from the speakers. Droplets of alcohol splashed over the salt-encrusted skin of her radiant face.

'Ed! Great to see you. Come dance. We're having a wild time!'

He reached out, snared her, pulled her to him. Her breasts pressed his chest.

She giggled, drunk, leaned forward and planted a misplaced kiss on his chin. 'Thanks for bringing me here, Ed! 'S really great!'

'Hey, the least I can do, kitten.'

She stared up at him, her eyes attempting to focus. 'How long have I been here, Ed? A day, more?'

He slipped an arm around her shoulders and walked her down to the water's edge. Docile wavelets lapped the shelving sand. He sat and pulled her down next to him. She hiccuped and stretched out in the sun.

'I explained earlier,' he said. 'It's a time-extended site. It's still in the experimental stages, which is why we need volunteers. It might seem like a day has elapsed in here, but out there in the real world only a few hours have passed.'

She shook her head in drunken teenage wonder. She believed every word he said – but, then, why shouldn't she? 'That's like incredible, Ed. I mean . . . wait till this is released on the world. We'll be able to practically *live* in VR!'

She frowned, realising something. 'But . . . I mean, okay, so it seems like a day's passed, Ed, but you say only hours've elapsed in the real world. But . . . but you can spend only four hours in a tank, yeah?'

'That's the so-called safe upper limit imposed by the VR Bars. We've been pushing that for the past six months. The safe upper limit we've arrived at is around forty hours.'

She tipped her head back, showing a delicate length of perfect neck, and laughed. 'So I can party for a long time yet!'

She reached out, made to grab the front of his shorts. 'Hey, why don't we . . . There's some beach huts back in the trees.'

He smiled and stroked her cheek with the back of her hand. 'Later, okay? Right now, I need your help.'

She squinted at him, leaning back on one elbow.

'We need some parameters checking. There's a site we're developing, an historical site. We need volunteers to take the parts of famous people in re-enacted scenes from the past.'

'Hey, sounds kinda cool.'

He smiled at her. 'How would you like to play a holo-star for a night?'

'A holo-star?' She sat up and placed a hand behind her head, pushing up her long black hair. 'Do you think I'm good-looking enough, Ed? Wait till Van finds out!'

Mantoni closed his eyes in recognition of the awful irony of her words. He smiled. 'You ready to go, kitten?'

'Right now? But the party's just coming to life!'

'It'll still be going when you get back, believe me.'

She drained her drink and screwed the glass into the sand. She looked down at the back of her hand, tipsily trying to focus. 'Hey, you know something? I just realised – I mean, I realised earlier, then forgot.' She gave a most unladylike belch and pressed two fingers to her lips. 'Excuse *me*,' she said, mock serious. She lifted her right hand and shook it before his face. 'No exit decal, Ed. What's the score?'

'Don't worry about it. We're monitoring everything. We'll pull you out well before we reach the upper limit.'

'Hey, don't know if I want to be pulled out. I could party all year! That Chaz guy's kinda cute . . .'

Mantoni stood and held out his hand.

She stood unsteadily, laughing as she swayed, and he caught her. 'How'd we get there, Ed?'

He pointed up the beach. Before the tree line, hanging in the air like a doorway to another world – which in effect it was – was a dark rectangle.

They approached through the fine sand. She peered. 'Hey, I can see people through there. It's . . . it's like some kinda party!'

'The holo-industry awards ceremony,' he told her, '2015.'

'Smart,' she said. 'But, hate to point this out, Ed. Those dudes in there are dressed kinda formal. I mean, we can't walk in all casual like this, can we?'

He smiled and took her hand. 'Don't worry yourself about it.'

He took a deep breath, bracing himself. This was going to

be hard, but it had to be done ... He stepped forward, towards the portal, tugging the girl after him. 'Hey!' she squealed. 'I can't go topless—'

They stepped over the threshold.

She stopped, and he turned and smiled at the suddenly transformed young girl, and his heart began a painful, laboured pounding.

They stood before the stage in the Civic Theatre, surrounded by the great and the famous of the erstwhile holo-industry. The girl gasped and stared about her. 'Where's—' she began, looking around for the doorway through which they had just passed.

'Hey!' She raised her hands and stared in amazement down the length of her body. She was dressed in an ankle-length jet gown, scattered with sequins. Her hair was piled up and held in place by chopsticks, emphasising the length of her neck, the line of her jaw. She was no longer the merely pretty young girl of a few seconds ago. Now she was Bo Ventura.

She laughed. 'Like your suit, Ed!'

He pulled her to him, feeling the familiar weight of the woman he loved, the stomach-turning subtlety of her scent.

'Just act natural. When people come up and compliment you, just smile and murmur thanks. They'll say you were fantastic in your last drama. You say it was a great role to be playing. The usual platitudes, okay?'

'Gotcha, Ed. Hey, who am I supposed to be?'

He opened his mouth to tell her, and the words caught in his throat. 'Bo Ventura,' he said at last.

She pulled a quizzical frown. 'Say, wasn't she an old star, years ago?'

He smiled to himself. 'Not so old, really,' he whispered.

Just twenty-three, he added to himself.

They schmoozed. The kid took to it like a natural. Mantoni stepped back, metaphorically, and watched as if from afar. Kramer had done a great job of recreating the Civic of twenty-five years ago. The sight of the place brought back so many memories. He watched Bo Ventura ease her way through the admiring throng, bestowing smiles and the occasional air kiss, and he was transported back in time. It *was* the night of the award ceremony, all those years ago.

But, this time, he would be in control of events.

The guests took their seats around tables equipped with outsized bottles of champagne. Mantoni escorted the girl in Bo's guise to their table before the stage. They were seated with a host of famous media personalities – or, rather, personalities who had been famous twenty-five years ago. As Mantoni exchanged handshakes and kisses, he recognised a holo-queen now dead by her own hand, a director killed just last year from a drug overdose. A couple of other stars had never made the transition from holo-movies to VR, and had slid into obscurity.

Lew Kramer and his team had recreated the setting right down to the personalities of those present. Mantoni listened in on the conversations around the table, though perhaps that was not the right word. These people did not converse so much as hold forth. They spoke about themselves at length, often at the same time, like mirrors reflecting each other into infinity.

How ephemeral and evanescent was the much-sought-after status of fame. He had realised long ago that the industry was full of people driven by vanity and ego, shallow individuals as tawdry as the profession itself, whose only desire was to be feted by the crowds, as if mass approbation might go some way to assuage their insecurity and loneliness.

He had talked about their chosen profession for long hours with Bo. They had agreed that they hated ninety-nine per cent of the people involved. They told each other that they were not in it for the money, or the cheap adulation of the viewers.

They had been young at the time, and idealistic, and they almost convinced themselves that their work had been the very best they could produce.

Next to him, the girl – he could not bring himself to think of her as Bo – smiled as she listened to some leading man massaging his ego. Mantoni took her hand and squeezed, then turned his attention to the stage.

An old actor – a veteran of the cinematic industry – was announcing the minor awards, for best foreign holo, best independent production. The guests of honour at the tables chatted amongst themselves, occasionally turning to bestow half-hearted applause.

He leaned towards the girl and whispered in her ear, 'You're Bo Ventura, up for the best actress award. You played Ella in *Chicago Dreams*.'

He had lured Canada to Laputa as part of his vendetta against Vanessa Artois, little realising at the time that he might use the girl in the historical VR re-enactment. Shortly after Lew Kramer deleted the Bo Ventura construct, it had come to him how he might employ Canada in the role of his ex-lover. Canada Artois as Bo Ventura. It appealed to his warped sense of irony.

Now she looked at him. 'Did Bo Ventura win?' she asked. She was frowning, as if something had stirred in her memory.

Mantoni nodded. 'She won. When they announce the name, just walk up there and accept the award. Say that you'd like to thank the committee and everyone present, etc. . . .'

She stared at him. 'Hey, wasn't there some trouble that night? I remember something . . .'

'Don't worry about it,' he said.

She nodded, unsure, and turned to regard the stage.

As the awards were presented, Mantoni watched the likeness of his lover and thought back to this night twenty-five years before. He wondered if he had been able to see through the sham and artifice then, or if he had been wholly taken up by the occasion, his love for Ventura and his delight that she had been nominated for the award. Perhaps it was only hindsight, the wisdom of his years, that allowed him to see the ceremony for what it was.

And to think that, for the price of a tin-plated statuette, Bo Ventura had lost her life . . .

Two famous comedians were on stage now, announcing the award for the best actor. 'And the award goes to . . . Jeff Carnaby for his role in *Topaz Nights*!'

A tall, immaculately tanned dust-abuser – rushed straight from rehab clinic to attend the ceremony, if Mantoni recalled correctly – bounded up the steps and crossed the stage.

His acceptance speech lasted ten minutes, and as the seconds elapsed Mantoni glanced around the tables and the tiered seats. He knew who he was looking for, and when exactly he should make his move.

He had never told Lew Kramer why he'd wanted this particular night re-enacted – but Lew was no fool; he had known very well what Mantoni was planning. To his credit, he'd played dumb.

Carnaby came to the end of his address. He strode off stage with seeming reluctance, and behind him the double act laughed. 'Hey, Jeff – don't think you'll be nominated for that performance next year!'

The audience settled down. The comedians passed a big golden envelope back and forth in a corny *me – no, you* routine designed to heighten the tension.

At last one of the dummies snatched the envelope and slit it open. 'It's edge-of-our-seats time for six of the finest actresses the world has ever known. The nominations are . . .'

As the six names were read off, Mantoni turned in his seat and scanned the guests. He saw someone rise from the second row of seats and make his way, unobtrusively, down the aisle towards a half-empty table before the stage.

The guy was ridiculously young – eighteen, it transpired – with a fixation on Bo Ventura that had turned demented when she had failed to reply to his last sick letter.

'And the winner is . . . Bo Ventura!'

Twenty-five years ago, Sergio Mantoni had stood with Bo and they had embraced for what seemed like an eternity, and now he did the same with the Bo lookalike.

Then he had released her, let her go, watched her climb the steps, cross the stage, accept the award . . . and he had been unable to do a thing to forestall what had happened next, even though he had been peripherally aware of the young man at the far table as he stood and raised the pistol . . .

Now, as the girl moved from the table towards the steps, striding through the tumultuous applause as if born for the role, Mantoni stood and moved around the tables.

The girl crossed the stage, hands outstretched in anticipation of the embrace from the double act.

Mantoni approached the table where the young man sat. The guy was leaning forward, one hand reaching beneath his suit jacket.

On the stage, the Bo lookalike bent her knees to reach the microphone. 'I don't know what to say . . . This is just too much. I'd like to thank . . .'

For a fraction of a second, Mantoni glanced up at her, and something turned in his chest like the blade of a knife. He beheld Bo's sublime beauty and wanted to cry out in rage at the treachery of fate.

The young man was standing and pulling the pistol from his jacket. He took aim, sweating, his eyes wide in manic desperation.

Mantoni dived, hit the guy – but not before he managed to squeeze off half a dozen shots. As he tumbled to the floor on top of the killer, Mantoni looked up and saw the girl, centre stage. She was holding her hands to her face and screaming with shrill intensity.

He felt people around him, pulling him from the assassin. He stood and rushed up the steps and across the stage.

The girl who was Bo turned to him, one hand pressed to her chest. 'They hit me!' she screamed. 'I'm sure they hit me!'

He took her in his arms, wondering if it was fated for this night to go wrong, even in reprise, and whispered reassurances into her hair. 'It's okay, Bo,' he said, forgetting himself. 'It's only VR. You can't be hurt—'

He felt her stiffen, pull away. She was staring at him in a fair approximation of shock. 'You . . .' she began. 'You knew

171

. . . you knew this was going to happen!' She stopped, realisation showing in her eyes. 'The ceremony – Ventura. She . . . she was killed that night! You knew!'

She turned and ran.

Mantoni gave chase, across the stage, through the wings. Behind him, he was aware that the awards ceremony was going on as if nothing had happened, an act of eerie collective amnesia that he thought entirely appropriate to the event.

He caught up with the girl in the shadows and led her, struggling, around the back of the stage. Ahead he made out a portal. He touched his metacarpal decal, coding for the beach site, and seconds later the portal was flooded with bright sunlight.

He led the sobbing girl onto the beach, and on the instant of transition she was divested of the Bo Ventura guise. He felt the quick, tactile anomaly of her transformation in his arms as she became, once again, the pretty fifteen-year-old drama student dressed in nothing but a sarong.

He eased her down onto the sand where she sat and sobbed, head in hands. He sat beside her, stroking her back.

She looked up at him, tears tracking down her cheeks. 'That was sick! Why? Why did you do that?'

'We—please listen, we had to go through with it. We had to re-enact the crime. The police . . .'

Even to himself, the lie sounded corrupt, unconvincing.

She buried her face in her hands and sobbed.

He hurried over to the bar and fetched a drink, returned and knelt beside her.

He held out the glass. She looked up, lashed out and knocked the drink from his hand. She stood and screamed at him. 'Get away from me!' she cried. She turned and ran up the beach and vanished into the trees.

Mantoni remained kneeling for a time, sickened. Then he hit the quit decal, and the tropical sunlight was no longer beating down on his skin.

As he sat up in the jellytank, however, the knot of pain and self-loathing was still tight in his belly.

It should have been so different, he told himself as he climbed from the tank and showered. This time, he should have apprehended the killer before he had the chance to fire. He should have gained the cathartic satisfaction of wrestling the young man to the ground, while on stage the likeness of Bo Ventura had completed her acceptance speech. It would have done nothing to bring his lover back to life, of course, but it might have served in some way to heal the pain of remorse that had eaten away at him over the years. It might have proved a definitive act of closure.

He hurried from the villa, walked across the greensward and stood on the edge of the cliff, staring out across the sea to the distant coastline of New York.

He thought ahead to the forthcoming award ceremony, the Cassini Awards, presented to the best of the VR industry.

Vanessa Artois was nominated in the best actress category, though he was sure that she would not risk showing herself at the event.

Mantoni considered his options, then reached for his com. It was time to contact Pablo again.

Thirteen

Halliday stared at his reflection in the bedroom mirror. He was accustomed to the familiar image he had lived with for years, and the sight of this new man, with the two-thousand-dollar charcoal grey suit and smart haircut, made him ill at ease. He felt as if he were proclaiming a statement to the world that he had no intention of maintaining .

He heard Casey's footsteps thumping up the stairs. She kicked the office door open, arms overflowing with cartons of food.

'Stuff yourself time, Hal! We had lots left over, so Sue let me bring it home.' She deposited the food on the desk and came to the bedroom door. She stared at him, then turned back into the office.

'Hal!' she yelled. 'Where are you? There's a well-dressed stranger in the bedroom!'

Halliday moved from the mirror and stood in the doorway to the office. 'Very funny, Casey.'

'Oh, it's you.' She ripped open a tub and bit into a spare rib, fat dribbling over her chin. 'What the hell's happened to you, Hal? I mean, who's died?'

'What do you think, Casey? I mean, seriously.'

She hoisted herself onto the desk and sat, swinging her legs. She continued eating for a while, considering her reply and eyeing him up and down. 'Well, it's different. You look *different*, Hal. Like someone else.'

'You're not expressing yourself very well.'

She wiped her chin with the back of her hand. 'To be honest, I think I preferred the old Hal.' She stopped chewing and looked at him. 'You're not thinking of pimping me, are you?'

174

He had to laugh. 'That bad? You think I look like a pimp?'

She made a contemplative pout with her lips. 'Or a gangster. Can't decide which.'

'You fill me with self-confidence.'

'I fill you with Chinese take-out,' she said, indicating the cartons. 'Come and eat and tell me what's going on.'

He fetched a towel from the bedroom and tied it around his neck like an oversized bib. He pulled up the swivel chair and opened three cartons: chop suey, chicken satay, and rice.

'Some meal, huh?' Casey said

'Feast fit for a king.'

'So, you going to tell me what's happening around here?'

He chewed on a mouthful of chicken. 'You know this morning, just before you left for work – you said you'd ask your Chinese heartthrob for a date if I asked Vanessa?'

A spare rib made an emergency stop before her mouth. 'No . . .' she exclaimed.

'Go ask him if he's free any time, Casey.'

'You're kidding!'

'I'm not.'

'You're lying!'

'I'm telling the truth.'

'You didn't . . . You mean, you really asked Vanessa Artois, the VR star – you asked her for a date . . . and she *accepted*?'

'You sound like that's hard to believe.'

She shook her head, still in wonderment. 'Just a little, Hal. No, it's like, *impossible* to believe, to tell the truth. You're joking me.'

So he was lying – technically, Vanessa had asked *him* out – but it was an acceptable lie. And if the lie prompted Casey to go and ask her boy for a date . . .

'I'm serious, Casey. We're going to the Cassini Awards, then moving on to some cosy little bar, and after that, who knows?'

'Look, don't take this wrong, Hal. You're a nice guy and all . . . But she has the pick of all the gorgeous men in New York.

She works with superstuds every day. Admit it, you aren't exactly in that league, are you?'

He recalled what Vanessa had said yesterday about the men she had worked with. 'It just goes to show that looks and wealth aren't everything, Casey. So I might not be the most handsome guy in the city, and I'm sure not wealthy, but Vanessa obviously sees something in me.'

'Yeah . . .' Casey nodded her head slowly. She picked up another spare rib and stared at it. Then she looked sideways at him.

'This isn't some big put-on, make-a-fool-of-Casey time, is it?'

'If you still don't believe me, tune into Channel Fifteen tonight. The ceremony's on live. You'll see me step from the back of a stretch limo with Vanessa, walk down that red carpet in front of all the paparazzi and holo-station people.'

'I'll do that, Hal. I'll be watching.' He could see from her expression that she was still dubious.

He finished his chicken and looked at his watch. 'Time I wasn't here, Casey.' He pulled off the towel and mopped his mouth.

'You have yourself a good time,' she said.

He paused at the door. 'And once the show's over, you know what you have to do?'

'Sure,' she said, shy. She looked up. 'If I see you on that red carpet with Vanessa, I'll go and ask Ben what he's doing tomorrow night, okay?'

He smiled. 'Catch you later.'

He hurried down the stairs, walked to the main street and hailed a taxi, self-conscious in case he bumped into anyone he knew. He imagined Thai Joe's uproarious laughter at the sight of him.

In the back of the cab, motoring at speed through the glare of holo-façades along Park Avenue, the mood of levity left over from his joshing with Casey gave way to the stark reality of the evening ahead. He considered the words of the street magician, Mephisto, the other day: a private detective, a man who attempts in vain to order the chaos of existence.

He wondered if that was all his life had come to. He was in the line of work he was in because of a subconscious desire to set straight the disordered world around him, maybe even to order the contents of his chaotic psyche.

The cab drew up outside the Plaza building on Madison and Halliday told the driver to wait. A big limousine was parked by the curb ahead, the chauffeur walking up and down the sidewalk. Two minutes later another taxi pulled up and a woman climbed out. He recognised Vanessa's body, her long legs. She was stunning in a short black dress. Halliday paid the driver, ducked from the taxi and joined the VR star in the limo.

As the vehicle pulled into the street with all the grace of a liner drawing away from its dock, they sat in the spacious rear and regarded each other. Vanessa removed her chu, and as ever Halliday was amazed by her beauty.

'Are you really the Hal I was drinking with last night?' she said.

'Don't you start. I've had enough already from Casey.'

'You look good.'

'I could say the same about you. But I wish you'd put the chu back on.'

She pointed to the tinted windows. 'I'm safe in here, Hal,' she said. 'Don't worry.'

He glanced at her, recalled what Karel had told him earlier today. He wanted to ask her about her affair with Mantoni, but decided that now was not the right time.

Instead he said, 'What's the set-up?'

'Once you're in the auditorium you can sit down if you want, or mix in the area before the stage. There'll be waiters circulating with drinks and drugs. Mantoni will be there, pressing the flesh.'

'Describe him to me. '

'He's above average height. Slim for his age, mid-fifties.

He's had facial surgery, but he also wears a body chu to improve his figure. You'll take it from that that he's vain. But he's also very charming and sophisticated. A real snake, Hal.'

Halliday looked out at the passing holo-façades, then turned back to her. 'What's the score once we reach the Civic?'

'As soon as we're inside I'll slip to the loo and change. This is a reversible dress and jacket. Once I put the chu back on, I'll be unrecognisable.'

'What if you're called on to accept an award?'

She shrugged. 'There'll no doubt be an embarrassing wait while people rush around trying to find me. My agent will give the press some story about my being ill.'

Halliday stared through the window. He wondered what a woman with Artois' experience might possibly see in someone like him. And yet they seemed to get on well enough together – unless, of course, their rapport was nothing more than an act on her part. She had tasted the delights of New York manhood; now she was slumming it.

He told himself that he was being ridiculous. If she was attracted to him, it more likely had something to do with the fact that she was genuinely beguiled by the idea of an older, stronger, protector figure.

The limousine joined a long line of others queued along the street outside the Civic Theatre. Two minutes later they drew up outside the entrance. A crowd of photographers and holo-cameramen appeared outside the limo, scrambling for the best shot. Hovering police drones, domes flashing, issued warnings. The paparazzi reluctantly gave ground and moved back. A cordon of police restrained a crowd of eager fans and autograph hunters. Halliday looked around for Szabo's men whom he had requested to be on hand. He felt his stomach churn with apprehension. There was no sign of the bodyguards, which he supposed could be interpreted as a good thing.

'When we climb out, Hal, take my hand and smile at the

cameras, okay? We'll hurry straight inside and ignore all the calls to pose.'

He nodded, watching the limousine ahead disgorge its freight of tanned and immaculate VR puppets. The air outside the theatre exploded with the incendiary flares of a hundred cameras. Halliday heard pleas of, 'Over here! Bob, Maria – one more time!'

Seconds later their car eased to a halt and a liveried flunkey opened the back door. Vanessa squeezed his hand and slipped her legs from the vehicle, standing on the red carpet like some perfect version of womanhood, turning with a dazzling smile and reaching for his hand.

Halliday emerged into a lightning barrage of camera flashes and blinding halogens. He remembered Vanessa's instructions and gripped her hand, looking straight ahead and adopting a fixed grin. He realised that a good part of his apprehension was due to Vanessa: out here, as herself, she was easy prey for a hired assassin.

He heard screams from women in the crowd, the cries of newsmen imploring Vanessa Artois to halt and pose, and though he had known intellectually that Vanessa was in that exclusive coterie of human beings equally feted and hounded because they were media superstars, he had never really understood the reality of the fact.

He had time only to wonder if Casey was watching, and then they passed through the honour guard of press and fans and were in the lobby thronged with impeccably-suited men and daringly-costumed VR bimbettes.

Vanessa squeezed his hand. 'You were great, Hal!' She kissed him quickly on the cheek. 'I'll go change,' she whispered. 'See you after the show.' And then she was gone.

Halliday made his way into the tiered auditorium.

Its size, after the unpretentious lobby, surprised him. Banked seats stretched away on either side like the interior of a baseball stadium, the lighting dimmed the better to see the illuminated performance area far below. Most of the seats were taken and a murmur of hushed anticipation filled the air. Halliday paused before descending. The semi-circular stage was decked out like some improbable VR heaven, with rolling green fields stretching away in a passable imitation of infinity, a blue sky above with occasional puffballs of pure white cumulus. Centre stage was a podium, done out in the style of a rustic bridge crossing a stream, upon which those judged best in their category would be rewarded.

Before the stage a throng of guests stood in chatting groups, perhaps fifty men and women holding drinks and the occasional vial of legal recreational drug. Halliday made his way down the aisle, attempting to pick out Sergio Mantoni from Vanessa's description. The majority of older men in the gathering seemed to fall into the archetype of the senior media executive: they were all well-fleshed, silver-haired or balding, and tanned like a race of god-like Caucasians transported here for the evening from some equatorial paradise retreat.

Halliday entered the urbane and sophisticated fray. A waiter grazed his orbit, offering drugs on one tray and beer on the other. He accepted a beer and sipped sparingly as he gazed around at the assembled guests.

He had planned to find Mantoni and engage him in conversation, unconcerned if the VR mogul wanted his company or not. He would steer the conversation onto the subject of Vanessa Artois, try to assess from the man's reaction whether or not he might be implicated in the plot to kill her.

Before he had time to circulate, attention turned to the stage. A tidal wave of applause swept from the banked audience. Halliday turned and watched a woman appear from the wings. Judging from the enthusiasm of her reception, she was a star beloved of the VR-using public. She was a platinum blonde in her forties, severely tall and thin, as if the natural slimness of youth had been artificially maintained in middle age with a regimen of drugs and surgery. He thought he recognised her from advertisements for recent VR spectaculars.

She climbed the bridge and accepted the applause with a smile as artificial as her figure. 'Ladies and gentlemen, members of the awards committee, allow me to welcome you all here tonight on the occasion of the second annual Cassini Awards. You don't need to be told, but I'll tell you – it's you good people who keep our industry great!'

A burst of applause. Halliday looked around. Even the hard-bitten media moguls were lapping it up. He wondered if they were smiling with the cynical knowledge that it was all bullshit, or if they really believed such self-aggrandisement.

The first of the awards were presented. A variety of technicians stepped up to receive vulgar, gold-plated VR symbols in the areas of visual realisation, reality-matrixing and a dozen other fields new to Halliday. Oddly enough, the techs, perhaps the only people here tonight to deserve the plaudits, were the only ones to exhibit uneasiness during the presentations.

The actors who followed them onto the podium, to receive awards for their parts in so-called epics – their faces and body-types used as templates on which to fashion computer-generated VR actors – showed no such inhibition. They gave speeches and wept, hugged each other and made declarations of universal affection, taking this rare opportunity to exhibit their underemployed acting talents.

He thought of Vanessa, and her anger at her situation, and felt a sudden welling of affection towards her.

Preceding each award was a clip from the relevant drama, remastered from VR and presented as holo-graphics on the stage. Halliday watched them with a mounting sense that he was being excluded from something that everyone else seemed to be enjoying. The acting was wooden and unconvincing, the dialogue stilted, the dramatised situations clichéd and trite. He wondered if this was because the dramas were best experienced in their intended medium of VR, where the public could interact with the storyline. The more he watched, the more he realised that he was making unnecessary excuses for an essentially puerile and aesthetically bankrupt form of mass entertainment.

He smiled as he considered with nostalgia the holo-dramas of his youth.

He moved back through the audience, towards the front row of seats. If he failed to locate Mantoni in the next half hour, he'd ask someone to point out the tycoon.

He was about to take a seat when he heard a voice behind him. 'Halliday?' a gruff baritone enquired. 'Hell, it *is* you!'

He turned. One of the suits, indistinguishable at first glance from any of the others, detached itself from the throng and approached him, belly hammocked in a puce cummerbund, fleshy face almost the same complexion.

Chief Police Commissioner Reynolds was a bad advertisement for high office and good living. Halliday remembered the man as lean and fit, a hard-working Divisional Commander, before his promotion to City Commissioner five years ago. Now Reynolds appeared twenty years older and twice as heavy as his former self.

'I wouldn't have thought this was your kind of scene, Halliday.'

He shook the Commissioner's hand warily, aware of Reynolds' reputation since his promotion. 'I came as the guest of a friend in the industry,' he said. 'You're right – I feel like a fish out of water.'

Reynolds turned and gestured to the stage, where a beautiful blonde teenager was sobbing copiously into the microphone.

'VR,' he said to Halliday. 'I call it Veritable Rubbish, the whole lot of it. Never go myself. The thought of getting tanked just to participate in some third-rate story acted out by computer copies of human beings ... Call me old-fashioned, but I always preferred the holos.'

'I was just thinking the same thing.'

'Hey, I heard about what happened to Barney. I was shocked. But I bet you've heard similar futile sentiments over the months.'

Halliday shrugged. 'People say what they think you want to hear.'

A couple of years ago, Reynolds had been implicated in some bribery scandal involving the city public works, though no wrongdoing had ever been proven. Last year, he'd been photographed socialising with a known Mafia boss, though again no criminal charges had been brought. It was an open secret among those in the know that Reynolds could be bought, and often was – and the strange thing was that, for all Halliday knew of his former boss's misdemeanours, he found it hard to associate the man he had known with the corrupt official he so obviously was.

Beyond Reynolds, beside the stage, Halliday saw a familiar face. It was a second or two before he could place it. He smiled to himself – one of the plain thin-faced women Vanessa had programmed into her chu.

She was gesturing to him, pointing at someone nearby. Mantoni? Halliday shrugged, unable to decode her gesture.

The assembled guests turned to watch a love scene on stage. The knowledge that no actors were involved, that the drama was little more than a complex and incredibly realistic computer animation, robbed the scene of any real interest.

Reynolds grunted his disgust. 'And to think that some of my friends work at the highest level of this industry . . .'

Halliday sipped his beer. 'You don't happen to know Mantoni, Sergio Mantoni?'

'Know him? We cross swords frequently, Halliday. Actually, I jest. We're good friends.' He raised his voice and called, 'Isn't that right, Sergio?'

A tall man turned and smiled. 'Reynolds, I'd be desperate if I counted you among my friends.'

Halliday regarded the mogul. It was impossible to tell if he were wearing a chu. He stood over six feet tall and sported a close-cropped head of silver-grey hair. His face was tanned and unlined, his skin impossibly smooth for a man in his middle fifties.

Reynolds gestured to the stage. 'As appalling as ever, Sergio.'

Mantoni joined them. 'I should have known a Police Commissioner would have difficulty appreciating the finer renditions of human intercourse.'

Reynolds laughed. The put-down was obviously part of some ritualistic contest between the two men. 'I was telling Halliday here what a farrago of nonsense the whole VR thing is.'

Mantoni assumed an expression of pained forbearance. 'Reynolds, your criticism cuts to the bone. You should have more consideration for the feelings of your friends in the industry.' Mantoni turned to Halliday and smiled. 'Please excuse Reynolds' behaviour. He can sometimes be brutally forthright.'

'No good appealing to Halliday,' Reynolds said. 'He's another cop with no aesthetic appreciation.'

'An ex-cop,' Halliday corrected, 'with no aesthetic appreciation. Perhaps I haven't participated enough, but I can't see the attraction.'

Mantoni was nodding. 'Fair enough. None of us is obliged to appreciate what is after all just another form of entertainment. Fortunately, sufficient numbers do, globally, to make the American VR industry the most lucrative and influential in the world. Two and a half billion users can't be wrong, after all.'

Reynolds said, 'Big mistake, Mantoni. You can't presume that popularity equates to any criterion of artistic merit. In fact I'd say the reverse was true.'

Mantoni was looking around him as the Commissioner spoke, doing nothing to disguise the fact that he found Reynolds' argument of little interest.

He laid a hand on Reynolds' arm. 'Perhaps we can continue this discussion at some point over the weekend?' He pulled a gold card from his pocket and passed it to the Commissioner. 'Excuse me. There's someone I must talk to . . .'

Mantoni nodded to Reynolds and Halliday and slipped away. Reynolds snorted, holding up the card. 'I've had enough of Mantoni's damned parties for one lifetime, Halliday!'

'May I?' Halliday reached for the card, examining the silver text on the gold background. It was a simple invitation, without RSVP, to a place called Laputa Island.

He glanced at the Commissioner. 'You don't mind if I . . .?' He held up the invite.

'You're welcome to it, Halliday. I hope you enjoy yourself. Excuse me while I find another drink.' He moved off through the crowd, leaving Halliday alone.

He slipped the card into his pocket and looked around.

Mantoni stood nearby, drink in hand, staring up at the stage. Halliday manoeuvred himself towards the producer. 'Reynolds didn't introduce us,' he said, offering his hand.

Mantoni inclined his head and shook Halliday's hand. 'Another of the man's failings is his terrible social manners. Mantoni, Sergio Mantoni.'

'Halliday, Hal Halliday.'

Mantoni nodded. He had the sophisticate's ability of seeming interested in whoever he was talking to. 'You mentioned that you were an ex-officer. How did you find yourself in VR?'

'I'm not. I run an agency specialising in missing persons.'

'Halliday . . . That's why the name was so familiar. We share a mutual acquaintance.'

Halliday assumed an innocent expression. 'We do?'

'Vanessa Artois. She's one of my best actresses.'

Halliday sipped his beer. 'How do you know I'm working for Artois?' he asked, attempting to sound casual.

Mantoni smiled. 'I make it my business to keep up with the circumstances of my finest stars. Terrible business about her sister. I trust you're progressing with the case?'

Halliday tried to detect any trace of irony in the man's tone. He seemed, on the face of it, perfectly genuine. He had not known what to expect from the VR mogul; perhaps an arrogance and brashness altogether missing from Mantoni's solicitous demeanour.

He told Mantoni that he was following certain promising leads. 'I'm confident of closing the case pretty soon,' he found himself saying.

Mantoni nodded. 'You don't know how pleased I am to hear that,' he said. He glanced towards the stage. 'Ah, the highlight of the evening.'

The platinum-blonde woman was once again centre stage. 'The nominees for the category of best leading actress are Domini Paluka for her role in *The Dead Tide*, Persephone Greaves in *Towards Eternity*, and Vanessa Artois for her role in *The Promise of Tomorrow*!'

Applause greeted her words. Halliday glanced at Mantoni. He was staring up at the platinum blonde who was typing a code into a hand-held soft-screen. The woman feigned surprise as she read the name of the winning actress.

'And the winner is . . .' said the platinum blonde, 'Vanessa Artois!'

A surging tide of applause and cheers rose from the auditorium, testifying to the popularity of the winning actress. There was a delay of a second. Halliday looked around the gathered guests. There was no sign of the thin-faced woman in the short dress.

He looked up at the stage, and for a second thought that his eyes were deceiving him. He was suddenly aware of his heart, beating madly. From stage left came Vanessa Artois, taking long-legged strides and waving at the audience.

Halliday wanted to shout at her, ask her what the hell she was doing. He wondered if she'd had second thoughts about receiving the award, if someone on the organising committee had persuaded her . . . No, that was impossible. No one but she and Halliday was aware of her disguise.

She climbed the bridge and embraced the platinum-blonde

186

with all the false affection of her calling. Halliday recalled what she had said about the awards the night before, and found it hard to believe that he was really witnessing this.

She accepted the best actress award, held it above her head, and then lowered her wide, smiling lips to the microphone. 'You don't know how much this means to me,' she said in a husky whisper, and got no further.

Halliday heard the rattle of bullets, deafening in the confined space, and saw the actress stagger and fall to her knees. Seconds later, the stage was aswarm with security guards. It was a long moment before the audience could fully comprehend what had happened, and then the screaming began. Dizzy with shock and disbelief, Halliday turned and scanned the auditorium. There was only one place the killer could have fired from – high at the back where he would have been concealed in darkness.

He knew that he should not let basic emotions prevent him from doing his duty. He ought right now to be chasing the killer. He knew this, knew what he should be doing, but a cold paralysis had gripped him. He could only stand and stare at the knot of men and women on the stage as they milled around the body of the VR star.

He looked for Mantoni. The tycoon was standing before the stage, staring at the mêlée with appalled fascination.

Before Halliday could confront him, he felt a hand on his arm. He turned, alarmed. 'Hal! It's me. I'm okay!'

He stared at a face familiar from somewhere: the thin-faced persona Vanessa had used earlier.

In disbelief he took in the black dress, the legs that went on for ever.

'Hal! Pull yourself together! I'm okay!'

'Vanessa?' he said, dazed.

'It's me. I'm fine.'

He gasped and held her. 'Christ . . . Oh, Jesus Christ I thought—'

'Let's get out of here, Hal.'

'The bodyguards?'

'I don't know. I lost them somewhere. Do I need them right now?'

Halliday tried to gather his thoughts. 'Probably not. The killer must think he's got you.'

She stared at him, shaking her head. 'I don't think so,' she said.

'What do you mean?'

She looked around her. 'Not here. Come on.'

She took his hand and they hurried from the auditorium, past knots of pale-faced officials and weeping actresses. In the pouring rain they hailed a cab and made for Carmody's on 42nd Street. As the car raced through the lighted night, Halliday realised that he was still gripping Vanessa's hand.

'Vanessa?'

'It was a holo,' she said.

He stared at her. 'I don't follow—'

'The representation of me, on stage. I was standing about three metres away when I heard the shots. They went right through her, Hal. She was a hologram.'

He closed his eyes and saw the woman disguised as Vanessa fall again. 'I don't understand. Why would anyone—?'

'I think it was Mantoni. He must have set it up.'

'What makes you so sure?'

She hesitated, gathering her thoughts. 'Have you heard of Bo Ventura?'

'Sure, the holo-star engaged to Mantoni.'

Vanessa nodded. 'Twenty-five years ago to the week, Bo Ventura was gunned down in the Civic while accepting a holo-Oscar.'

'Jesus Christ. So he set this up as a kind of . . .' He recalled Mantoni in the auditorium, staring up at the stage.

'A re-enactment of some kind, Hal. Perhaps he also wanted to scare me into the bargain.'

'The guy's seriously sick.'

'You don't think I didn't already know that?' She laughed and squeezed his hand.

The cab pulled up outside Carmody's and Halliday paid

188

the driver. They hurried through the downpour and into the darkened sanctuary of the bar. Vanessa gripped his arm while he ordered the drinks, a wheat beer and a dry white wine. He carried them to a booth at the back of the room.

She sat down opposite and stared at him. 'So, what now?'

'Do me a favour,' he said.

'What?'

'Take the chu off. I want to see your real face.'

He stared at her as she removed the chu. Her midnight hair appeared as if by magic, the long and elegantly angled face, the familiar too-wide lips.

'Just wanted to make sure it was really you.'

She reached across the table and took his hand. 'It's really me, Hal. I'm okay. It'd take more than a few bullets to scare me.' She smiled, bravely, but he could see behind the bravado to the fear in her eyes.

'So, did you manage to talk to him?'

He took a long drink of beer. 'I was introduced to him by a mutual acquaintance, would you believe? He knew I was working for you.' He hesitated. 'We'll have to be careful from now on. If he puts a man on me . . .' He stopped. 'I don't want to lead them straight to you.'

She looked down at her glass. Something in her attitude, a tremulous hesitation as if she wanted to tell him something but could not bring herself to do so, made him ask, 'What is it?'

She did not raise her eyes to meet his. 'Yesterday,' she said in barely a murmur, 'when you asked why Mantoni might want me dead . . .'

'Go on.'

'I wasn't exactly truthful, Hal. I didn't tell you everything.'

He nodded. 'So . . .' He kept his tone neutral. 'Are you going to tell me everything now?'

She regarded her wine glass for a long time, and then said, without looking up, 'You asked if we'd had an affair. Well, we did, but it wasn't as brief or insignificant as I made out. I was with him for a number of years. Christ, I think I even

189

loved him. It's hard to tell, in retrospect, especially since I've come to hate him. I wonder how I could have been such a fool.'

'But you said you left him, right? You weren't so foolish that you couldn't walk out on him.'

Quickly she lifted her glass and took a long drink. Her hand was shaking so violently that the wine spilled. It was either a fine performance, or she really was in the grip of painful emotions.

'I left him because of something I found out,' she said. 'Something he told me.'

He nodded, feeling his pulse quicken.

She stared at him through eyes suddenly awash with tears. 'I . . . I always thought it was a strange relationship. He was almost thirty years older than me. He treated me like a child. I'd heard that he was a monster, that he enjoyed playing psychological games with his lovers. I wondered why he was so different with me.'

Halliday felt something expand in his head, dizzying him, a sudden premonition. 'Go on.'

'We had a row. I wanted to take a role in a stage play on Broadway, but he said it'd be demeaning. I was a world-famous VR star, after all. I couldn't be seen to be slumming . . . He said that he knew what was best for me. And then . . .'

'Vanessa?'

'Then I accused him of treating me like a child.' She stopped, then, and bowed her head.

'What did he say?'

'He said that I always would be a child, to him. Then . . . then he told me that I was his daughter.' She stared across the table, as if defying him to comment. 'Sergio Mantoni is my father.'

He nodded, exhibiting a calm he did not feel. His job was full of surprises, truths discovered and lies found out. He told himself that he should have been inured to shock, by now.

'So . . . Bo Ventura. She was your mother?'

She nodded.

'And the old couple in the pix, back at your apartment? The folks you said were killed in a plane crash?'

'They were my foster-parents. As soon as I was born I was put up for adoption. Neither Mantoni nor Ventura wanted kids. My adoptive parents never told me the truth.'

'And Canada?'

'She was their child. I know – we're not really sisters at all. But I grew up believing we were.'

Halliday massaged his jaw. 'So . . . You got into acting, and then Mantoni turned up?'

'Some coincidence, huh?' She laughed, without humour. 'No coincidence at all, Hal. I thought that maybe if I hadn't become an actress, I might never have met him. But the fact was, he would have wormed his way into my life.' She nodded and took a long pull on her cigarillo. 'So, when he signed me up five years ago to act in his holo-dramas . . . he came onto me. I suppose I was flattered, I was young, starstruck. He was older, but powerful and influential. It seemed natural, at the time.'

'You loved him?'

'He . . . he was good to me. As I said, I didn't know what he was really like, back then. I didn't listen to the rumours. Then we had the row, and he told me, and do you know something, Hal? I think he wanted me to know. I think the death of Ventura sent him over the edge.'

'He's one sick bastard, Vanessa—'

'Imagine putting me up for adoption, then tracking me down and seducing me like he did? He thought he had me where he wanted me, feeding from his hand. He didn't expect me to walk out on him.'

'How did he react?'

She pulled a face. 'He didn't like it. That's an understatement. The last time I saw him he said that no one walked out on Sergio Mantoni. He threatened that he'd kill me if I left him.'

She smiled, bleakly, across at Halliday. 'There,' she said. 'That's it, the truth, the whole truth, and nothing but.'

Halliday began nodding and kept on, lost for words.

'Well, Hal? Are you going to say something?'

He shrugged. 'There's not a lot I can say, Vanessa.'

'I hope this doesn't change anything . . . I mean, between us.'

'Don't worry. I'll still work on the case.'

Her glance flared. 'I didn't mean that.'

He took a drink of beer, avoiding her eyes.

'So,' she said, 'what now?'

'The first thing is that you leave the hotel where you were staying. Did you book in under your own name?'

She shook her head. 'Used a pseudonym.'

'Good. Don't even go back for your stuff. Leave it there and buy what you need. Then contact Szabo and terminate the contract.'

'I thought you said they were good?'

'They are. The best. But even the best are sometimes not good enough. I don't want to take any risks. Mantoni's rich and influential and he has contacts. If one of Szabo's men decides he needs a bonus and slips Mantoni the word . . .' He shook his head. 'I'm probably being paranoid, but I'm taking no risks.'

'I won't need bodyguards? '

'You're going to drop out completely. I mean, right out of the scene. You're going to disappear. Contact your agent and tell him you're leaving the country on holiday. Where do you usually go?'

'The past couple of years I've spent summer in the Caribbean.'

'Tell him you're going there for a while, and you don't know when you're getting back. Don't contact him again and make sure he can't contact you.'

He paused, wondering if he'd covered everything. 'Change your chu identity every day, along with a new outfit. And change hotels and your identity at the same time, okay?'

She was nodding. 'We're talking radical lifestyle change here, Hal.'

He smiled. 'The alternative is a lifestyle change even more radical – it's called death.'

'You say the nicest things to make a girl feel good.' She looked at him over the rim of her wine glass, but her eyes were smiling.

'Another thing. You probably don't need telling, but you might find yourself doing it without thinking. Don't frequent old haunts, don't go to any place you used before. Start afresh, as if you're a completely different person.'

She nodded. 'I'll do that.'

'And try to avoid public places, okay? The chus are pretty reliable, but they've been known to go haywire. Imagine if you're in a crowd and the chu decides to go kaput.'

She lifted her glass, her hand steadier this time. 'Just talking to you makes things seem better.'

'If we think of everything and make no mistakes,' he told her, 'we'll be okay.'

She regarded him. 'So we've planned my itinerary for the next few weeks. What are you going to do?'

'There's nothing I'd like to do more than stop Mantoni breathing.'

'Don't go getting yourself killed on my account,' she said. 'I mean, who'd protect me then?'

He nearly told her that she'd hire someone else, but stopped himself just in time.

He remembered the invitation card in his pocket, pulled it out and laid it on the table between them.

Vanessa's eyes widened. 'He invited you to Laputa?'

He told her about his meeting with Commissioner Reynolds. 'So what's Laputa Island?' he asked her.

'It's out beyond Staten,' she said. 'He had it built a while ago. He has parties there from time to time.' She stared at him, concern in her eyes. 'You're not going to go, Hal?'

'It'd be the perfect opportunity to find out more about him—'

'But he knows you're working for me! I mean, if he is responsible . . . It'd be dangerous, Hal.'

'Don't worry, I can look after myself.'

'Why not let the police handle it?' she said. 'Give them everything we know and forget about revenge.'

He laughed. 'Everything we know? How much is that? We have nothing in terms of hard evidence. No pix, no real witnesses, nothing to incriminate Mantoni in the slightest.' He thought about it and gave a bitter laugh. 'And listen to this, Mantoni and the Chief Commissioner of Police are big buddies. You think the authorities would really investigate big-shot Mantoni?'

She shook her head, staring into her wine.

They drank in silence for a while. At last Vanessa said, 'You know, last night when I asked you back . . .? I really wanted you to come. You probably thought I was frightened and wanted protection, and if I ask you tonight you're going to think the same.' She paused, shrugged. 'What can I say? If you want to stay the night, you're more than welcome.'

He thought of Casey, and her fear at asking the Chinese boy. He understood how she felt. The fear of rejection, the fear of allowing yourself to feel too much for someone . . .

'Hal?'

He looked up and shook his head. 'I don't understand, Vanessa. What can you possibly see in me?' He almost made a cheap jibe about her having a predilection for father figures.

'Jesus Christ, Hal,' she said with a fierce, whispered insistence. 'Don't demean me by thinking I can't make my own choices, or that I should be dating some handsome VR superstud. For chrissake, we get on well and I like you, and what matters is the person you are, not the person you're not.'

Perhaps that was the problem, he thought. He knew himself better than she ever could: she could only see his apparent strength, the bullshit tough-man image that went with the job.

She reached across the table and took his hand. 'Please,' she said. 'For me.'

He recalled getting back to the office last night and downloading one of Vanessa Artois' old holo-dramas, halting the action and watching her beautiful face and hating himself for being unable to take the opportunity when she offered it. He recalled the sensation of frustration and regret, and he had promised that if ever the opportunity arose again he would put aside his fears and grasp it. Because the alternative, if he failed to do so, was a placid acceptance of his situation, an easy inertia that could only lead one way.

He smiled and squeezed her hand. 'I'd like that,' he said.

She resumed the persona of the thin-faced stranger and they left the bar. They caught a taxi and Halliday told the driver to stop at an all-night store while Vanessa bought toiletries and clothing, dresses she would not normally wear but which would suit the demeanour of her alter ego. She left the store hauling a massive holdall and a smaller bag stuffed with soft-screen books and plastic magazines.

They continued to a small hotel off Broadway and booked in under the name of Mr and Mrs Williams, on vacation from San Francisco, if anyone should ask. They decided that Vanessa would move out in the morning, find another hotel, and make it her base for a day.

The room was spacious, with a wraparound window overlooking the lighted length of the street. Halliday moved around the room, looking for security cameras: there were none. Vanessa pulled off her chu, began unfastening her dress, and disappeared into the bathroom. Halliday listened to the jet of the shower and sat before the wraparound, staring out at the holo-façades diminishing in perspective like an architect's scale model of some fabulous dream city.

Tomorrow he would make his way over to Laputa Island and gatecrash the party, see where that avenue of investigation might lead. If he found nothing, could discern no way to persuade the tycoon to call off the assassin, then in order to save Vanessa Artois he would be forced to consider a more drastic course of action.

He opened the holdall Vanessa had bought at the store and

pulled out a soft-screen book. He turned it on and scrolled part way into the story. There were long chunks of narrative describing the thought processes of the central characters, interspersed with visual scenes where the characters talked. Halliday accessed a scene in a bar, a man and a woman sitting at a table, holding hands. They were declaring their love for each other.

Vanessa stepped from the bathroom wearing a short black kimono embroidered with red dragons rampant. He held up the soft-screen book. 'Strange,' he said.

'Why so?' She crossed to the couch and curled beside him, her long legs drawn up beneath her. She lay her head on his shoulder and looked at the book.

The scent of her freshly-washed body filled the air.

Halliday gestured to the text. 'Why all this?' he asked.

'Don't you read?'

'Sure, but not for pleasure.' He looked at her. 'You?'

She nodded and laughed. 'Don't look at me like I'm a freak. I find it relaxing, entertaining.' She moved her head on his shoulder and looked at him. 'What do you do for entertainment, Hal? Holos? VR?'

'I've never really got into VR. I watched plenty of holos as a kid. Now . . . I'm too busy now to bother with anything much.'

She slapped his arm playfully. 'That's terrible for the soul, Hal. We all need to relax, be entertained.'

He thought. 'Trees,' he said at last. 'A few days ago I downloaded a file about trees. I watch that from time to time. I find it relaxing.' He looked at her. 'And the bonsai you brought me, the oak. That's incredible. I spend a lot of time watching that.'

Her expression was amused. 'Watching? How can you watch a tree, Hal?'

He smiled, shrugged. 'It's beautiful and perfect and I just sit and stare at it, and it relaxes me.'

'Each to their own,' she said. 'I'm glad it brings you so much pleasure.'

He was amazed, when he thought about it, how relaxed he was now, talking to her. There was no pressure. They were enjoying each other's company. He liked the simple sensation of the weight of her body against his, the scent of her perfume and shampooed hair.

In retrospect he realised that it was fated not to happen, but at the time the chime of his com was as unexpected as it was unwelcome.

He pulled the set from the inside pocket of his suit jacket and Vanessa sat up, frowning.

Jeff Simmons stared out from the tiny screen. 'Halliday, you alone there?'

'What is it? '

'It's eleven thirty, Hal. I was expecting a call. I thought you said you were tanking tonight?'

'Christ, yeah. Okay. Where are you, Jeff?'

'Police HQ, Hal. Ready and waiting, if not exactly eager.'

'Okay . . .' He sighed, looked across at Vanessa and shrugged. 'I'll grab a taxi and pick you up in ten minutes.'

'See you then.' The cop cut the connection.

'What is it, Hal?'

He hesitated. 'I arranged to meet a colleague. We're following a lead. Look, I'm sorry . . .' He reached out and touched her shoulder.

She shrugged with sad resignation 'Will you be back tonight?'

'I'll do my best. If I can't make it, I'll be in touch.'

She nodded. 'Okay. I'll miss you.'

He wondered how much she meant that. He nodded and made to move away, but she pulled him back and kissed him as if in an effort to show just how much she really would miss him.

When she withdrew, he saw that her eyes were glazed with tears. He hurried out from the room and left the hotel.

He caught a cab and headed uptown. It was almost midnight and the traffic was sparse. The rain had abated, leaving the tarmac slick and smearing the neon illumination in abstract sprays across the road.

He sat back and stared through the window at the flickering procession of holo-façades, apprehensive now that the time had come to enter the sex site in disguise. He wondered what he was fearing most: the thought of meeting X on Eros Island in the persona of a young girl and having to entice him, or the possibility that the meeting might never come off.

Fourteen

Mantoni was staring out across the sea, considering the events at the previous night's Cassini Awards, when he heard footsteps behind him.

Stephanie stood to attention, soft-screen in hand, something about her severely upright posture denoting unflappable efficiency.

She had been his PA for almost five years now, and yet he could not claim that he knew the woman. She was good at her job, and that was all he asked of her. For all the emotion she showed in her dealings with him, she might have been an android. He received the impression, no doubt a product of his guilty conscience, that she had disapproved of him when she began work on Laputa five years ago. He had been at the height, then, of his dissolute phase; that was when the wild parties had begun, when his addiction to sex had consumed his waking hours, before he graduated to the delights of the VR sex sites.

'I'm about to send out the invitations for this weekend's party,' she said. 'Any last-minute additions?'

He almost told her to cancel the party – he was in no mood to socialise at the moment. Instead he shook his head. 'No, that'll be all for now.'

She nodded and returned to the villa.

He had started the parties over ten years ago, when they had suited his hedonistic lifestyle, his addiction to drugs and women. Over the past couple of years he had grown tired of the twice-monthly gatherings, and he often absented himself from proceedings. He was, he thought, becoming anti-social in his old age. The people he met seemed less interesting these days, which he knew was less an indictment of the people he met than of himself, and his own lack of interest in others.

He wondered if the facile pleasures of VR were to blame for his social apathy.

He stared out across the sea to Manhattan Island, and he went over the events at the Civic Theatre. After his failure to prevent the gunman in the VR re-enactment, he had tried another tactic. Perhaps he would gain some kind of perverse satisfaction in having a gunman succeed this time, in watching the holo of someone he despised being assassinated. He had considered, briefly, somehow staging a physical threat to the real Vanessa Artois, and being on hand to observe her reaction. Quite apart from the logistical difficulty of achieving this – Halliday was succeeding in keeping her well hidden – he doubted that he would gain the psychological satisfaction he was seeking.

The re-enactment at the Civic had been the real thing – but the fact was that it had done little to satisfy whatever was driving his desire for . . . what? Absolution? Catharsis?

On waking this morning, he had had the first inkling of an idea for the greatest catharsis of all, but for that to happen he would have to lure Vanessa Artois to the island.

Which, bearing in mind that he had Canada in the protective custody of VR, might not be that difficult after all.

He activated his com and called Pablo.

Seconds later an impassive, slab face appeared on the miniature screen. 'Sergio. How can I help?'

'We need to meet.'

'The usual place?'

'I'll be there in ten minutes.'

Pablo nodded, minimally, and cut the connection.

Mantoni made his way up the greensward to the villa. Once in the VR room, he undressed and readied himself for the jellytank. He entered the co-ordinates for the secure site and immersed himself.

He made the transition and found himself standing on a riverbank beneath a lowering oak, wearing the persona of a younger trimmed-down version of himself. There was no sign yet of Pablo.

He sat on a fallen log overlooking a bend in the river and waited.

He had been introduced to Pablo ten years ago by a mutual acquaintance. The Latino came recommended, simply, as someone who could sort out problems. Over the years, Mantoni had used Pablo's services on perhaps a dozen occasions, giving orders and awaiting results and not enquiring too closely as to how those results were achieved.

Pablo was a big Puerto Rican, and highly educated, and Mantoni had often wondered how he had found himself in his line of business. They had met in a quiet bar in SoHo in the early days, and later, with the onset of VR, rendezvoused in secure sites.

On these occasions, Pablo chose to appear in the persona of a mature blonde beauty, adding another layer of mystery to his already complex character. In the past they had sometimes made love beside the rolling river. In fact, the first time with Pablo had been Mantoni's first sexual experience in VR, the encounter which had moved him towards experimenting with the numerous virtual reality sex sites.

Along the riverbank, a patch of air shimmered like a convection current above a baking highway. As Mantoni watched, a figure materialised.

Pablo, in the guise of a stunning blonde, curvaceous figure emphasised by a tight floral dress, approached and sat down before him.

She – Mantoni could not bring himself to think of her as Pablo – fingered a strand of hair from her eyes and smiled up at him.

'Things are progressing on the Virex front,' she said in a cultivated New England accent.

'I'm delighted to hear that.'

'I've located a cell working in Manhattan.' She paused, watching Mantoni with liquid blue eyes. 'Do you want them warned?'

In the early days, Mantoni in his naïveté had assumed that Pablo's use of the verb *warned* meant merely that – until certain targets had turned up dead. After that, Mantoni had been reluctant to allow Pablo to warn anyone. He usually delegated the task, having Pablo contact his second-in-command for permission to go ahead with the warning.

But with Virex it was different. With Virex it was war, and in any war there were casualties.

He nodded. 'That might be the best solution,' he said.

The woman reached out and ran a hand along Mantoni's thigh. 'What did you want to see me about?'

He took the woman's hand in his own, halting its progress. There were times when he welcomed her overtures, but this was not one of them.

'I want you to put a trace on a private detective, Halford Halliday. He has an office in El Barrio.' He gave her the address. 'He's working for Vanessa Artois, the VR star. She's in hiding, and he's protecting her. I want to know where she is.'

'And then?'

'I don't know ... First of all, I want to know Artois' whereabouts. Once you've found that out, contact me and I'll tell you how to proceed. I might want her brought to the island.'

The woman made a moue of her perfect lips. 'That will cost, Sergio. She is famous, after all. She'll be missed. It won't be as easy as the kid.'

'We'll talk about it when you know where she is,' Mantoni said. 'And since when has cost ever entered into the equation?'

The woman smiled. 'I'll be in touch.'

Mantoni glanced at his metacarpal decal. It was almost midnight. The sight of the woman lounging in the grass at his feet reminded him of the pleasures awaiting him elsewhere.

'Surely you don't have to be getting away so soon?' she said.

Mantoni frowned. 'I have a business meeting,' he lied. 'I can't miss it.'

'Then maybe some other time?'

'Maybe,' he said.

'I'll be in touch.' The woman stood, smiled in farewell, and touched her quit decal. The air shivered, and her substantial form was gone.

He had become so accustomed to the protocols of VR that there were times, in the real world, when acquaintances said farewell and he expected them to vanish in an instant. He smiled to himself as he tapped a code into his decal.

He experienced a second of blackness, a quick heat in his head, and then he was elsewhere, and equipped with a new persona.

He stood on the golden beach of Eros Island, the familiar thrill of imminent conquest pushing everything else from his mind. He looked along the beach, and then inland, taking in the action.

Over the months in the sex sites his sexual preferences had undergone a marked change. He no longer found the ideals of physical perfection a turn-on; instead, he found himself going for younger girls, skinny teenagers with pre-pubertal bodies . . .

He had tried to analyse this preference. Perhaps it was simply that, with so much perfect, voluptuous flesh on offer, he was sated with what others considered to be the desirable optimum. Then again, perhaps it went deeper than that. In VR, nothing was as it seemed. A sexy sixteen-year-old nymphet might in reality be a shrivelled old man of eighty. Perhaps it was this hidden, subtle element of ambiguity that lent a frisson of excitement to encounters in the sex sites. Quite apart from the physical pleasures of indulging in the viscous delights of uninhibited sex, there was the added enjoyment of attempting to see through the various guises to the real world identities hidden beneath.

Mantoni had become skilled at discovering which personas were not what they seemed, and then trying to work out what they were in the real world, and why they had adopted whichever guise . . . It was, as sex had always been with him, ever since the death of Bo Ventura, a game of power and control.

He strode along the beach, assessing the talent on display.

Fifteen

Jeff Simmons ducked into the cab, took one look at Halliday's suit and raised his eyebrows. 'Hey, nice outfit, Hal. What's the occasion?'

'Long story,' Halliday said as the taxi motored uptown on Madison Avenue. 'What do you know about a guy called Mantoni, Jeff? Sergio Mantoni?'

'The VR big-shot? He's a buddy of Commissioner Reynolds. Mantoni keeps Reynolds supplied with horny starlets and Reynolds pulls the strings when the district attorney tries to drag him in on illegal drugs charges.'

'He supplies, right?'

'Not in a big way. He's no dealer or trafficker, but he does hand out the stronger stuff to friends. If that were you or me, we'd be doing a year for illegal possession.' Jeff looked across at him. 'Why do you ask?'

'You heard about the incident at the Civic tonight?'

The cop shook his head. 'Been in the office since two this afternoon.'

Halliday recounted the events at the awards ceremony. 'I'm pretty sure it had something to do with Sergio Mantoni. I think he was behind the shooting at my office the other night.'

'Mantoni?' Jeff whistled. 'You're kidding, right?'

'Wish I were. I had a tip-off the other day. Someone says they overheard Mantoni hiring an assassin. At the moment, that's all I have to go on.'

'You think it might be linked to Canada's disappearance?'

Halliday sighed. 'I don't know, but I suppose it's possible.'

To what end, though, he had no idea.

Five minutes later the taxi turned onto 116th Street. The flashing neon lights of Thai Joe's and the other Bars and clubs along the main drag were a familiar, tawdry sight after the sophisticated glitz of the Civic.

Joe waved from his sidewalk bar stool as the car pulled up outside. Halliday wondered if this was the only time when Joe rested, in the early hours when trade was slack. At every other hour of the day he seemed to be patrolling the sidewalk, extolling the virtues of his Bar to passers-by.

'Brought a friend today?' Joe grinned as they entered the Bar. 'Half-price if you introduce a friend, Hal!'

He slapped Joe's meaty hand in greeting and pushed through the swing doors. The plush waiting-room was deserted but for a couple of red-uniformed girls taking the opportunity to sit on one of the central couches and chat. They met Halliday and Jeff with smiles activated and escorted them to adjacent booths.

Before he entered, Halliday said, 'Eros Island is the sex zone on Liberty, Jeff. I'll see you on the beach.'

'I'll be myself,' Jeff said. He slapped his beer gut. 'But I might take the opportunity to shed a few pounds.'

'I'll be a skinny kid, around fifteen, sixteen. I'll signal once I'm there.'

'How will I recognise the guy?'

'He'll be small, tanned and balding. Well-muscled. If he isn't wearing a gown, you'll notice him.'

Jeff nodded. 'If he's there, I'll get out pretty quick and get the technical boys working to trace where he's linking from.' He regarded Halliday. 'You'll be okay in there?'

'I'll be fine. There's no risk, Jeff. If things get too hot, I'll just get out.'

'Okay, let's do it.'

Halliday stepped into his booth and activated the screen. The first menu listed over a hundred different sites and he selected Eros Island. Then a persona menu appeared. For the next five minutes he selected and refined his assumed soma-type. He began with the stock persona of a sixteen-year-old blonde girl, then worked to customise the appearance. He recalled what Caroline had said about Big Ed's sexual preferences: skinny, under-developed young girls with pale complexions and thin faces. He honed down the stock soma-type to these characteristics, then touched the command for Selection Complete.

He stripped and stepped into the jellytank, sat down and lay back. The gel sealed over him and he floated free. He closed his eyes in anticipation of the transition, and when it came he was surprised by the totality of the experience. Where before he had retained a male body with feelings and sensations no different from those he experienced in the real world, now he was plunged into a totally different soma-type, and it was as if he were inhabiting the body of an alien being.

He opened his eyes and stared in amazement at his thin golden-haired arms and delicately articulated fingers. He was aware of the rub of the default gown against his small breasts, a sensation at once raw and arousing. He felt lithe and trimmed-down, in control of a persona healthier and fitter than the person he had been.

He stood on the golden sand of a broad beach. He regarded the perfection of his bare feet as his toes scrunched the fine sand. He had always considered the process that allowed him to experience VR as something of a miracle: he had never claimed to understand the science that conducted the reality of the virtual world to his sensorium – the process that deceived the brain into being unable to distinguish between the real world and this hyper-real fantasy – and his ignorance made the experience all the more magical.

He sat down and looked along the length of the beach. Jeff, garbed in a blue default gown, had arrived before him and was sitting twenty metres to his right, watching a couple make slow and languorous love in the shallows of the lagoon.

Halliday caught his attention and waved. Jeff opened his eyes wide in a mock stare. He strolled over and knelt before Halliday. 'Christ, Hal. I'd never have guessed . . .'

'Apparently this is the type he goes for.' He stopped, surprised with his new high-pitched girl's voice. 'Hey, you look years younger yourself.'

Jeff parted his gown to reveal a tight, muscled stomach. 'Feel like a new man, Hal.'

'Don't say that around here,' Halliday said. 'You might get one.'

Jeff glanced along the beach, and then inland to the recreational pool. There were few people around. 'I've been keeping a lookout for Big Ed, but unless he's in one of the villas he hasn't shown yet.' He stood and stretched. 'I'll go and check. See you later.'

Halliday turned and watched Jeff as he sauntered past the pool, his attention taken by the intricate antics of a sun-tanned threesome.

He looked left and right along the beach. Apart from himself, the couple in the shallows, and a blonde woman sunning herself in the distance, the foreshore was empty.

Self-consciously, Halliday removed his gown, spread it on the sand and sat down. He made sure no one was watching, and then touched his belly and slipped his fingers lower. He marvelled at the realistic – well, he supposed it was realistic – sensation of pubescent sexual arousal. The experience was disconcerting – he felt almost guilty at the thought of enjoying the act of transsexual self-pleasure.

He turned onto his belly and stretched out. Jeff was standing outside one of the villas. When he saw Halliday looking, he shook his head and gave a thumbs-down signal. He moved along the line of villas, peering into each like a leisurely voyeur.

Minutes later Halliday noticed a patch of air ten metres away begin to distort and shimmer like a heat haze. As he watched, a man's familiar shape formed, gaining solidity in an instant. Halliday felt his heartbeat increase and looked away quickly.

When he looked again, Ed had slipped out of his gown and tossed it to the ground. He stood with his hands on his hips, gazing around at the possibilities on offer. His member hung loose almost to his knees, its size so improbable as to invite ridicule in a medium where soma-types were so adaptable. The guy had no sense of modesty.

Ed saw Halliday looking, and his gaze lingered. Then he strolled up the beach towards the pool, and Halliday experienced a quick stab of relief that he was being spared the man's attentions.

Which was contrary to why he was here, he told himself. He knew he would have to face Ed, sooner or later. He wondered whether he should make the move, approach him and begin some naïve conversation.

He decided to wait. Ed had obviously registered the presence of the slim girl. There was something studied about his bypassing of Halliday for the more adult pleasures of the pool: it was the action of a man well aware that he was toying with the lust of a young girl.

As Halliday watched, Ed slipped himself into expert synchronisation with the rhythm of the threesome. He looked away, aware of a squirm of involuntary arousal within his belly.

He wondered, then, if Big Ed might indeed be none other than Sergio Mantoni – or perhaps someone in the tycoon's employ?

Before he could speculate further, Jeff hurried past the pool and knelt beside him. 'That's our guy, right? I'll get out and see if the techs can work out where he's linking from.' He paused, watching the four frantically bucking figures in the pool. 'Christ, look at him go,' he said, something almost like admiration, or perhaps even envy, in his tone.

He nodded at Halliday. 'Hang in there, Hal.' He touched his exit decal and vanished.

Ridiculously, without Jeff's reassuring presence, Halliday felt a quick stab of unease. He told himself that he had nothing to worry about. He looked at the red circle on the back of his hand. Escape was but a touch away.

He stretched out and offered his slim girl's body to the heat of the sun.

He was on the edge of sleep, five minutes later, when he sensed that he was not alone. He opened his eyes, shielding his gaze from the sun, and made out the dark silhouette of Ed standing over him. Even from Halliday's perspective, Ed's member, foreshortened, was a monstrous thing.

Ed knelt and Halliday sat up quickly, backing away.

The guy gave an easy smile, holding out a hand as if to calm a frightened animal. 'Hey, not so skittish, kitten. I come in peace.' He reached for Halliday's hand, as if to shake.

Hesitantly, his apprehension obviously coming over as coyness, he took Ed's hand.

Ed gripped lightly, not letting go. 'I'm Ed,' he said in a slow Texan drawl. 'Pleased to meet you, ma'am . . .'

Ed retained his grip on Halliday's fingers, smiling all the while. 'And you are?'

Halliday swallowed and said the first name that came to him. 'Eloise . . . I'm Eloise.' As soon as he said it, he wondered why he'd given the name of his dead sister.

'Pretty name for a pretty girl, Eloise.' He released Halliday's hand and sat down beside him, propping himself on one elbow and smiling with accustomed ease.

'What do you think of this place, Eloise?'

'Well . . . It's certainly different. It's beautiful.'

'Hey,' Ed said. 'Don't tell me it's your first time here?'

Halliday nodded. 'Is it that obvious?'

He took a quick glance at Ed's penis, aware that Ed was watching. Semi-erect, it bridged the gap between them.

'You really are a shy little thing, aren't you?' Ed reached out and stroked Halliday's leg, his fingers brushing gently back and forth.

Halliday felt himself colour, and at the same time his young girl's body responded.

'Hey, chill out, kitten. It's always a bit scary, the first time. What brought you to Eros Island?'

He was fishing, Halliday realised, trying to determine if Eloise in the real world was really as young – and female – as her persona in VR.

Halliday played along. 'Some people I know went to the sex zones the other day,' he said in his piping voice. 'They said they had a great time.' He smiled and shrugged. 'I thought I'd take a look.'

'Why didn't you go with them, kitten?'

Halliday gave him a shy glance. 'They're a year older than me.' She shrugged. 'They don't associate with youngsters.'

He watched the guy's expression. Ed swallowed, nodded, his smile growing positively vulpine.

'Well, the great thing about Eros,' he said, 'is that there are no rules here. If you want to watch, but not take part, that's great. There's no pressure to join in. Then, when you feel confident, you do it. Simple as that, kitten. Absolutely no pressure.'

Halliday nodded. 'I think I'll like it here.'

'Say,' Ed said, and his hand squeezed Halliday's thigh playfully. 'I bet you're real pretty in the real world, too. What do you look like, kitten?'

'Oh,' Halliday shrugged his narrow shoulders in what he hoped would be taken as girlish modesty. 'Much the same, maybe not as pretty.'

Ed laughed. 'Hey, kitten, if you're not as pretty in the real world, you'd still be beautiful.'

Halliday laughed and lowered his eyes. Ed resumed stroking her leg. Halliday was torn between telling him to stop and wanting him to continue.

If the response of his body was anything to go by, he understood how Canada had found Ed's lure irresistible.

He looked up and smiled at Ed. 'What about you?' he asked. 'What do you look like in the real world?'

It was Big Ed's turn to shrug modestly. 'Much the same as what you see,' he said. 'Apart from one thing.' He grinned. 'Can you guess what that is, kitten?'

Halliday glanced at Ed's swollen cock. 'I couldn't begin to imagine.'

Ed laughed. 'In the real world,' he said, 'I haven't got a tan as good as this.'

Halliday covered his mouth with his small hand and laughed. He was becoming an accomplished VR actor. Wait till he told Vanessa.

Swiftly, seizing his moment, Ed slid his hand up Halliday's thigh, rubbing and pulling. To his astonishment, Halliday realised that he had opened his legs, allowing Ed's fingers greater freedom.

'There, that's how it is, kitten. This is it. How's that feel, Eloise?'

Quickly Halliday rolled away and drew his legs to his chest. He realised that he was panting, his breath coming in quick gasps. 'Not now, Ed. Some other time.'

Ed grinned. His cock was extravagantly prominent now. 'You want that there should be another time, kitten?'

'No. Yes – maybe. I don't know.'

'I come here every day around midnight,' Ed said. 'If you like, we could meet again. Same time, same place. No pressure. We'll go at your pace. You dictate. You tell me just what you want, and Big Ed'll be only too pleased to oblige.'

Halliday nodded. 'Okay, tomorrow. Promise you'll be here?'

'You bet your sweet little ass I'll be here, kitten.'

He reached out, took Halliday's fingers, and planted a gallant kiss. 'See you tomorrow, Eloise,' and then he was gone, up the beach, his erection preceding him like a flagpole.

Feeling at once aroused, sickened, and triumphant, Halliday hit the exit decal and in an instant Eros Island was no more.

He rose from the cloying grip of the gel, the images and sensation of his experience in the sex zone rapidly diminishing, becoming as distant as if they belonged to another lifetime on another world.

He stepped from the jellytank and showered, then dressed and left the booth.

Jeff Simmons was sitting on a couch, speaking into his com. When he saw Halliday, he cut the connection. 'How'd it go, Hal?'

Halliday sat down beside Jeff, leaned back and blew out a long breath. 'Christ! Well . . . it went, Jeff. I'm meeting him tomorrow at midnight.'

'Hell, you little vixen.'

'He's one smooth operator, Jeff. No wonder Canada followed him to wherever.'

'You sound like you enjoyed the experience.'

'I don't know. I mean I – Halliday – was repelled. But the body I'd assumed . . . I don't know how they do it, Jeff, but it felt authentic to me. I was in a girl's body, and the body wanted nothing more than to get it on with Big Ed.'

Jeff grunted. 'Rather you than me.'

Halliday thought back to reading Canada's soft-screen diary, and her entries describing her first experiences in the sex zones, the young girl's emotion fluctuating between trepidation at her daring, and unabashed delight at her desire.

Jeff raised his com. 'That was the tech team, Hal. While you were enjoying yourself with big boy in there, they were trying to find where he was coming from.'

'And?'

He shook his head. 'They couldn't work it out. Apparently, he wasn't tanking in any one of the city's hundred-plus VR Bars.'

Halliday stared at him. 'You telling me he was a computer-generated image?'

'The techs checked that one out and discounted it. The guy's for real.'

'So where's he linking from?'

'The only hunch they could come up with was that he was linking from a private tank somewhere. Illegal, but it's a possibility. They tried to put a trace on the link – they scanned the guy on Eros Island and tried to work back, but the guy had it all worked out. He's put scramblers on the link and the traces got lost in the static.'

Halliday thought about it. 'Do they think they'll be able to crack the link?'

'They're working on it, but to be honest they didn't sound too hopeful.'

'So let's just hope that it all works out tomorrow.'

'How you going to play it?'

Halliday laughed. 'Put it this way, I'm going to try to walk out of the encounter with my VR virginity intact. I don't know ... I'll meet him there and see how it goes. If he doesn't suggest we meet in the real world ... then I might have to come on to him. Ask if we can meet.'

'You don't want to make him suspicious.'

Halliday nodded. 'You're right. I'll let him make the first move. I'm pretty sure I've got him, though. What're you doing now, Jeff?'

The cop glanced at his watch. 'Officially I've been off duty for the past couple of hours.'

'How about a coffee? The office is just around the corner.'

They left the Bar, emerging into another sultry Manhattan night, walked along the main drag and turned right. They passed the row of busy food-stalls and a minute later turned under the sign for the Chinese laundry and climbed the steps.

The wallscreen was pulsing the pastel shades of a news broadcast across the darkened room when they walked in. Casey had obviously gone to bed and forgotten to turn it off, as she was in the habit of doing. Halliday left the screen burning, muted the sound and switched on the fan.

Only then did he hear the sobbing.

Halliday moved around the desk and found Casey lying face down on the chesterfield, her face buried in the cushion.

'Casey, what the hell—?'

She looked up at him. Her face was pulled into a tragic mask of such epic Greek proportions that it appeared comic.

'Casey, what's wrong?'

She could only stare at him. 'What's wrong?' she sobbed. 'You were there, weren't you?'

Before he could work it out, she went on, shooting a glance

214

past Halliday at Jeff. 'Who's that?' she wailed. She launched herself from the chesterfield and sprinted into the bedroom.

Halliday shrugged an apology to Jeff, indicated the percolator and followed Casey.

She flung herself full-length on the bed, face down and sobbing. He shut the door behind him and sat beside her. He found himself relishing what he had to tell her. How often in one lifetime do you get to impart incredible good news?

He reached out and took hold of her thin shoulders. Heartfelt sobs wracked her body.

'Casey, Casey . . . listen to me. It's okay. Everything's okay. Vanessa's still alive.'

She whirled around and shouted at him. 'I saw it, Hal! I was watching the fucking show! I saw you get out of that amazing car. I was so proud, Hal. Vanessa . . . Vanessa was so beautiful.'

'Listen to me . . .'

'And I watched the show and she won the award and then—then the bullets hit her, Hal. They killed her! I saw it! Oh, it was awful, it was so awful!'

He smiled and took her by the shoulders and shook her, gently. 'Listen to me. Stop crying. It wasn't Vanessa. A hologram accepted the award.'

'But I saw all the newscasts. I've been watching them all night! They all say that Vanessa Artois is dead!'

'Then they've got it wrong. Have you tuned into NYNC? They'll have an update, watch.'

He stood and moved to the door.

She stared at him with big eyes, hardly daring to hope. 'You really mean it, Hal? Vanessa's still alive?'

'Come and see what the screen says, Casey.'

'I don't want him to see me crying,' she said.

'Okay, watch it from in here.'

Halliday moved into the office. Jeff was sitting on the chesterfield, clutching a coffee and leaning forward to stare at the miniature oak.

215

'Some bonsai, Hal.'

Halliday typed a code into his keyboard. 'Present from Vanessa Artois.'

Jeff whistled. 'Great present! She must be stuck on you.'

'You know how it is,' Halliday said. 'Protector fixation.'

The wallscreen flared. He found a news channel broadcasting from outside the Civic. A front-man was ranting into a microphone.

'And the latest twist in tonight's events – earlier reports that VR star Vanessa Artois was killed in a hail of bullets are apparently way off the mark. Get this: we now understand that the incident was some bizarre reprise of the death of Bo Ventura, twenty-five years ago. We're trying to get hold of Sergio Mantoni for his comments. Don't go away!'

Halliday killed the sound and returned to the bedroom.

Casey was kneeling on the bed and peering through the door at the wallscreen, like a survivor on a life-raft sighting land.

'See?' Halliday said.

She turned to Halliday, her mouth open. 'Vanessa really is alive?' she whispered. 'She didn't die?'

He pointed to his eyes. 'Do you see any tears?'

Casey leapt from the bed and into his arms. She wrapped her legs around his waist and hugged his head. 'I thought she'd died. I mean, I *saw* it happen! All the news channels were full of how tragic it all was – but they didn't mean it. Just a big story for them. I was thinking of you, Hal. Your first date in how long, and she gets all cut up!' She pulled away from him, her face a mess of tears and dribbles.

He held her head between his hands and kissed her forehead. 'It's okay, Casey. Everything turned out okay.'

She smiled through her tears. 'You get to your cosy bar after the shooting?'

He smiled. 'Sure. We had a drink, and then she asked me back to her room, but . . . you know how it is, I had work to do.'

Casey was shaking her head in wonder.

'So today,' he went on, 'when you see your Chinese boy, you got to ask him out, okay?'

She nodded. 'I'll do that.'

'Good.' He deposited her on the bed. 'Now settle down and get some sleep, you hear?' He moved to the door.

She lay on her back, arms behind her head, and peered at him along the length of her body. 'Who's the guy, Hal?'

'A cop friend. We're working on the Canada case.'

'You think you'll find her?'

'Sure we will, Casey. We've got some good leads.'

She smiled. 'That'd be a happy ending, wouldn't it?'

He nodded. 'Sure would. Now sleep.' He closed the door behind him and rejoined Jeff. The cop poured him a cup of coffee. Halliday sat down in his swivel chair and lodged his feet on the desk.

Jeff sat back on the chesterfield. 'Who's the kid, Hal?'

'Don't look at me like that. It's not what you think.'

'She lives here, sleeps in your bed, and it's not what I think?'

'She's a stray. Found her on the fire escape last winter. I let her sleep here one night, and now she won't go away.' He shrugged. 'What do I do, Jeff? World stinks out there. Would you kick her out?'

Jeff made a maybe/maybe-not face.

'She's a good kid. Works at a Chinese stall and keeps me in food.'

Jeff nodded at the desk, still littered with the detritus of last night's take-out. 'See what you mean. Hey, good coffee,' he said, helping himself to another cup. 'You given any thought how we're gonna go about catching Big Ed?'

'I've been trying not to look too far ahead. I mean, one step at a time, right?' He shrugged. 'But sure, of course I have. Can't think of much else but the damned case.'

'So go on.'

'Way I see it is, we almost got him. Midnight tonight I go

217

in and wave my fanny around. With luck, he'll arrange for me to meet him out here in the real world. We stake the place out—'

'And that's where it gets real tricky, Hal. Until now it's been child's play. No danger, no risk. You show your butt and reel him in. When he arranges a meeting, that's when we got to make sure we don't mess up. What kind of stake out?'

Halliday shrugged. 'We have men waiting, drones and cameras. He turns up and we trace him.'

'You mean, like follow him to whichever hole he's crawled from?'

Halliday nodded. 'We get a surveillance unit out and we track him back to base.'

Jeff was silent for a time. 'What do you think Canada's chances are, Hal? I mean, let's be realistic . . .'

Halliday glanced at the bonsai. 'Look, if the cases are linked, if it is Mantoni who's kidnapped Canada, then maybe he's still holding her, right?'

'And if it isn't? If some sicko's got her?'

Halliday sighed. 'I've been upbeat about it with Vanessa,' he said, 'but if you're right, and some psychopath has got her . . .' He shook his head.

Jeff sipped his coffee, then said, 'Okay, so we set up surveillance. But what if Big Ed's clever? What if he turns up, finds no kid, suspects something and runs? How about this, he doesn't even turn up 'cos he's got the place rigged with cameras of his own, so he knows there's no kid. What then, Hal? We've lost our man.'

'That's assuming he's on the ball.'

Jeff leaned forward. 'Christ, Hal, we *gotta* assume the bastard's on the ball! We underestimate this punk and he's got us beat.'

'So what do you suggest?'

Jeff swilled his coffee round the cup a few times, finally looked up at Halliday. 'What does he want, Hal?'

'He wants Eloise, the kid.'

218

'He wants the kid, too right. And we – or rather you – have worked hard to get to the point where we've almost got him in our grasp. The last scene needs to be played perfectly, played just how he thinks it should be played.'

Halliday stared at Jeff, an uncomfortable premonition entering his head. 'What do you mean?'

'I mean, you arrange to meet him someplace in the real world, and instead of staking the place out with just cops and drones, we have cops and drones, but we *also* have what he wants, waiting there for him just like she said she would be. Live bait. We have a kid waiting, Hal.'

He was shaking his head. 'I don't like it. Too risky.'

'Not if we minimise those risks. Have cameras on all possible routes to the rendezvous point, rig the kid up with a monitor.'

It was a few seconds before Halliday could bring himself to ask, 'Who are you suggesting, Jeff? Who's the kid?'

'You're not gonna like this. But as soon as I saw her . . .'

'You mean Casey?' Halliday almost laughed. 'No way! There's no way I'll allow that.'

'There's gonna be no risk. We'll rig her up so the tech boys can follow her wherever she goes. We'll be right behind her. Just as soon as he leads us to base, we swoop. And Casey's had a stroll in the park.'

Halliday felt his pulse quicken. 'A hundred and one things could go wrong. It's a risk I'm not prepared to take. Put it this way, would you risk your daughter out there?'

Jeff rocked his head from side to side, deliberating. 'With today's technology, and maybe with the life of an innocent kid at stake . . . I think I probably would.'

'How do we know he won't do something to her there and then?'

'We'll be keeping visual contact all the time, Hal. We gotta go through with this. Think of the lives of the kids we'll be saving in future—'

'You're blackmailing me, Jeff. You're trying to make me feel bad.'

'I'm trying to make you see the reality of the situation. How many more kids does he have to abduct before you agree that we got to do something radical to get this guy?'

Jeff stopped there, and his focus slipped from Halliday to the bedroom door.

Halliday turned in his swivel chair and stared.

Casey lay her cheek against the woodwork, a sad, bedraggled figure in a soiled T-shirt and ripped panties.

'Let me do it, Hal,' she said in a small voice. 'I want to help Vanessa get her sister back.'

'Casey, honey,' Halliday said. 'Look . . . chances are that Canada's dead, okay? It's awful, but that's what it looks like from here.'

'You don't know that!' she cried. 'You don't know she's dead! She might be alive! And if she is, if she is alive, and I can help to get her back, then I want to do it. If someone risked themselves to get my sister back, if they did that for me, can you imagine how grateful I'd be?'

'That has nothing to do with it,' he began.

She went on, 'It'd be like all my dreams come true . . . Maybe if I help you get Vanessa's sister back, maybe one day I'll find my sister?'

Halliday closed his eyes, wondering where to begin to refute the flawed logic of her plea.

Jeff said, 'We'd make sure you were safe, kid. We wouldn't put you at risk.'

'How can you say that, Jeff?' Halliday said. 'The very act of setting her up as bait—'

Casey said, 'Will you tell Hal that we got to go through with it, sir?'

Jeff smiled. 'You got yourself one hell of a spirited kid here.'

'Well?' Casey said, staring at him defiantly.

Halliday shook his head. 'I don't like the idea one bit.'

'We gotta do it,' Jeff said. 'Put it this way, if we don't go ahead with this, and in a day or two Canada turns up dead . . . How you gonna explain that to your squeeze, then?'

'That's blackmail!'

'It's fucking reality, pal. 'Scuse the language, Casey.'

Halliday hung his head, going over the possibilities.

At last he pointed at the lieutenant. 'This goes wrong and I'll have your ass, Jeff. You get onto your tech boys and make sure the rendezvous is planned down to the very last detail. Drones, monitors, the works.'

Casey smiled to herself.

'And you,' Halliday said, glaring at her. 'Don't you look so goddamned happy. You're gonna be picked up by a maniac who'd just as soon strangle you and fuck you dead as give you the time of day. Just remember that!'

Casey winced and looked away, more at the tone of his voice than the content of his warning.

Jeff said, 'You made the right decision, Hal.'

Casey disappeared back into the bedroom.

Halliday massaged his face, suddenly dog tired, then stared at the cop. 'I damned well hope you're right, buddy.'

Jeff drained his coffee and placed the cup on the desk.

'It's been a long night. I gotta be going.' He raised his bulk from the chesterfield, clapping Halliday on the shoulder as he passed.

'Hey, Jeff,' Halliday said, looking up. 'The kid means a lot to me.'

'Sure she does. We'll do it by the book, okay? We gotta nail this bastard, right?'

'Yeah, right.'

Jeff nodded at him, and gave Casey a wave through the bedroom door as he let himself out.

Halliday pushed himself from his chair and moved to the bedroom. He stared in at Casey, not trusting himself to speak.

She had her back to him, fastening the old pair of jeans she wore for work. She sensed his presence at last and half turned. 'What?'

'You know very well *what*.'

She turned, ignoring him, feigning difficulty with the zip of her pants.

'You had no right to listen in on a private conversation, Casey.'

She twisted her thin body and stared at him. 'Listen in? I couldn't help hearing what you two were talking about. You weren't exactly whispering, you know.'

He felt an irrational anger welling inside him.

She continued staring. 'What's your problem, Hal? I mean, don't you want to catch this sicko?'

'What the hell do you think! But there's ways of going about it. I don't like the idea of putting you in danger—'

'I can handle myself!'

He tried not to laugh. 'Handle yourself? You sound like some naïve schoolkid. Listen up, Casey. You wouldn't stand a chance if that maniac tries to slit your throat down some back alley.'

'I've got to do something to help Vanessa get her sister back!'

'Grow up!' Halliday yelled. 'Live in the real world! Chances are Canada's been dead days already. I don't want you ending up buried in the same landfill—'

She looked at him, something very close to contempt in her eyes. 'Who do you think you are, Hal? You don't own me! You aren't my fucking father!'

He felt an inexplicable, impotent rage take control of him. He had to restrain himself from launching himself at her. At once he wanted to hit the girl, and hold her to him, and tell her that he cared.

Instead he just shook his head. They stared at each other. Casey was crying now, silent tears leaking from swollen eyes and rolling down her cheeks.

'Christ!' Halliday said, punched the door and stormed back into the office.

Seconds later, as he sat at his desk and tried to calm himself by staring at the bonsai, Casey hurried from the bedroom and out the door. He heard her footsteps on the stairs as she hurried to work.

He pulled the photograph of Anna and Eloise onto his lap and tried not to dwell on the coming events.

Minutes later he saw an indistinct shape through the pebbled glass of the door. The shape knocked, timidly.

Halliday moved to the door and pulled it open.

Casey leaned against the jamb, looking up at him. She merely smiled in tearful desperation and gave her thin shoulders a hopeless shrug.

Halliday reached out and pulled her towards him. She was so short, her head hardly reached his chest. He could not bring himself to speak, did not have the vocabulary to express what he was feeling. Instead, he just held her.

Sixteen

At nine that evening Halliday drove to the marina at Battery Park and boarded Sergio Mantoni's private launch.

A dozen other guests were making the crossing, rich-looking men and women immaculately outfitted in the latest designer fashions. Halliday thought he recognised a few faces from the awards ceremony. Already, a party atmosphere enveloped the guests as they laughed and chatted among themselves.

He found himself standing beside a portly, prosperous-looking man in his fifties, wearing a dark suit and carrying an overnight bag. As the engine caught and the launch chugged away from the quay, a young woman in a red uniform turned in her seat beside the pilot and spoke into a microphone 'Welcome aboard the *Prospero*, ladies and gentlemen. We'll soon be passing through the Narrows and at that point I'll tell you something about Laputa. Thank you for your attention.' She clicked off the microphone and addressed the pilot, the mute movement of her lips disconcerting after the volume of her previous words.

A babble of excited chatter arose from the guests. The man beside Halliday laughed. 'Laputa!' he said to Halliday. 'I'll give it to Sergio, he knows how to do things in a big way. I once called him a megalomaniac to his face, and he was offended. He sees absolutely nothing strange about the scale of his desire to control.'

Halliday raised an eyebrow. 'Control?'

'Everything. People, events, the island. Even,' he went on, leaning close to Halliday, 'reality.'

'Reality?' Halliday said.

'I take it this is your first trip to Laputa?' When Halliday nodded, he went on, 'You're in for a treat, then. Nothing is ever as it seems on the island, not even reality.'

'Reality?' Halliday repeated, looking sceptical.

'I can see you're puzzled.' He leaned forward again in a familiar manner that suggested he was bequeathing pearls of wisdom.

'Holographics,' he explained. 'Sergio is a magician with holographics. He pioneered the holo-industry back in the twenties, before getting into VR. But holographics has remained a pet hobby of his, as you'll no doubt find out.'

'I've heard a lot about his parties.'

'We're privileged to be invited, buddy. His events are famous worldwide. Hey, some royals are even queuing up to get invites.' He laughed and held out a meaty hand. 'Al Simioni, I'm in the construction trade.'

Halliday took the proffered hand. Simioni had the appearance and bearing of a Mafia boss. 'Halliday,' he said. He thought it wise not to admit to being an ex-cop and private investigator. 'I'm in VR.'

'One of Sergio's business buddies?' Simioni laughed and shook his head. 'Hey, you boys sure know how to put on one hell of a show! Some of your sites really kill me! And I mean that virtually!' He laughed at his joke and leaned forwards again with a confiding intimacy Halliday was coming to dislike. 'That's where I met Sergio,' he said, 'in one of the dungeon sites.'

Halliday nodded. 'I see his initials match his predilections.'

'Hey,' Simioni said, jabbing Halliday's shoulder, 'you know something, that never occurred to me!' He paused and gave Halliday a speculative once-over. 'What're you into, Halliday?'

'Me?'

'Don't be shy. Admit it. You'll find whatever you want on Laputa. Did you know Sergio's trying to gain independence for the island? There are some federal laws he's not too happy about. If he declares Laputa an independent territory, then he can legislate his own laws.' Simioni chuckled. 'Now that *is* what I call megalomania on a grand scale!'

They had left Manhattan in their wake and were heading through the Narrows between Brooklyn and Staten Island. On the horizon, in the twilight caused by the overcast, Halliday made out the tiny shape of an island.

The red-uniformed woman spoke into the microphone. 'Ahead and slightly to starboard you can now see Laputa. Conceived and designed by Mantoni and his team of architects in 2025, building work began two years later and was completed by 2035. Laputa is the base for Mantoni Holdings and Sergio Mantoni's personal retreat. On selected weekends throughout the year Mr Mantoni hosts festivities and celebrations . . .' She went on, describing some of the events Mantoni had hosted recently.

For the next twenty minutes Halliday stared out across the water as the island grew ever larger. As the launch approached, he could see that his first disbelieving impression was not mistaken: the gently contoured knoll of the island, set upon a base of blue-grey granite bedrock, was actually floating above the surface of the sea. Halliday felt dizzy at the optical illusion of an object of immense weight defying the laws of gravity. While his mind told him that what he was seeing was impossible, his eyes could only relay the incredible vision of the flying island of Laputa.

Beside him, Simioni was chuckling. 'Gets newcomers every time, Halliday! According to Sergio, Laputa was a floating island in some old book.'

Halliday was still shaking his head. 'But how does he do it?'

'Told you he was a holographics wizard. It's all an illusion. Laputa isn't floating at all. An image of the sea is projected onto the cliffs of the island, giving the illusion that it's flying. Simple really, but very effective. The first of many wonders in store tonight.'

Laputa was perhaps two kilometres across. Vast lawns sloped down to sheer blue slabs of rock. Dotted about the lawns Halliday made out groups of people, flower gardens, gazebos, ornamental features like waterfalls and fountains. Presiding over the island was a white, one-storey villa.

The launch throttled back, passing through the projection of shimmering waves. Ahead was a cliff-face, with a jetty and carved steps leading up to the lawn. Laputa had resumed the aspect of just another island – though one, Halliday reminded himself, designed by a millionaire megalomaniac.

The pilot eased the launch alongside the jetty and a red-coated crew member made the boat fast. The guests filed from the *Prospero*, crossed the jetty and made their way up the precipitous stairway. Halliday was the last off, and followed Simioni up the steps. The launch started up and turned out to sea, returning for other guests.

On the way up, halting behind Simioni while the fat gangster paused to regain his breath, Halliday reached out and touched the rock. It seemed genuine enough, but of course he could be certain of nothing on this island of illusion. Two minutes later they emerged from the defile in the rock and stepped onto the margin of the emerald lawn.

And, suddenly, they were no longer in the summer twilight of New York. Here, above the immaculate lawns and gardens of Laputa, the air was blue, and a warm sun shone down from directly overhead.

Halliday gazed into the sky with wonder.

Simioni was laughing. 'Some trick, huh?'

The guests made their way across the greensward towards the villa. Simioni joined them. Halliday was about to follow when a slim woman with close-cropped blonde hair, outfitted in the regulation red jacket and a short dress, appeared before him.

She was consulting a soft-screen, staring from it to Halliday and back again. 'Excuse me, sir. May I see your invitation?'

He drew the gold card from his pocket and passed it to the woman. Each card was numbered, and she was checking the number of his card against the guest-list on the soft-screen.

He wondered what she would do when she discovered that he was using Commissioner Reynolds' card.

She looked up, squinting at him. 'I'm afraid that this isn't your card, sir. I must ask you to leave.'

He produced his ID card and held it before her. 'Halliday. I'm working for Vanessa Artois. Contact your boss and tell him I need to see him, okay?'

The woman hesitated, then hurried away from him and spoke into a com. Once or twice she glanced back at Halliday as she relayed her massage to Mantoni.

She slipped the com into the pocket of her blazer and returned. 'Mr Mantoni said he will see you, Mr Halliday. He asked me to escort you to his chamber. If you'd care to follow me . . .'

They took a gravelled path across the lawn and past the villa. Guests sat on rustic benches in the sunshine, chatting and drinking from long, fluted glasses. A host of red-jacketed waiters and waitresses passed among them, offering drinks and small trays of drugs.

They climbed the canted east end of Laputa. 'I would have thought there'd be more guests,' Halliday said.

'There are,' the woman said.

He stared around the island. 'I don't see them.'

'The people out here are mainly holograms, even most of the waiters.'

He looked at the villa. It appeared too small to be the venue for a lavish weekend party. 'Everyone's in there?' he asked.

She shook her head. 'Not in the villa. That's Mr Mantoni's private residence.'

'Then where are they?'

She indicated the ground. 'Under our feet. All the guests are in the island. You see, Laputa is hollow.'

She pointed to the greensward rising before them. At the crest of the incline, at the very far end of the island, was a depression in the grass.

228

'If you follow the gravel path you'll find yourself walking gradually further beneath the surface of the lawn. Then you'll pass through the "ground" altogether and you'll be in Wonderland.'

He looked at her. 'Wonderland?'

'That's what Mr Mantoni calls it,' she said. 'You'll see why when you enter.'

She had stopped walking and looked at him. She looked as though she wanted to tell him something.

'Perhaps I should warn you, Mr Halliday. Mr Mantoni and Vanessa Artois go back a long way, and there's bad blood between them.'

'There is?' He watched the woman.

'Artois left Mr Mantoni a while ago. She got away. She was stronger than him, and he didn't like it. He's been trying to get back at her ever since.' She paused there. 'I really don't think you should get involved, Mr Halliday.'

'I am involved. I'm working for her—'

'You should tell her to leave the country, change her identity and leave the country. And then you should get away, too.'

He smiled. 'I couldn't leave her like that,' he said.

She gave him a pitying look. 'Are you and Vanessa . . .?'

'You get close to someone you're trying to protect.'

'A word of advice. Don't let Mr Mantoni hear that.' She pushed up the sleeve of her jacket. 'It's almost ten. If I were you I'd leave the island now. There's a boat leaving every hour.'

'I came here to see Mantoni.'

She shook her head, as if dismissing him. 'In that case, don't say that I didn't warn you.'

'You said there was an entrance some place around here.' He moved towards the depression in the grass, and after a second's hesitation the woman followed him.

He was unable to say quite when he realised that he was no longer walking on the ground – his viewpoint suddenly

229

lowered, and when he looked down he saw that his legs seemed to be mired to just below his knees in the gravel path.

They walked on, his eye-level sinking step by step, until he was up to his chest in the gravel. When he looked down, the ground seemed as solid as ever. He stepped forward, his line of sight breaking through the layer of gravel as he sank, like a diver passing beneath the surface of the sea.

It took a disorienting second or two for his vision to adjust to the aqueous half-light, and then he saw that he was walking down a night-time city street. He was back in New York, and though his brain knew that what he was seeing was a lie, nothing more than an array of brilliantly realistic holographic projections, his every sense was convinced. Every sense, he told himself, but touch. He reached out, and his hand passed through the solid-seeming wall of a derelict brownstone.

'Mr Mantoni likes to remind his guests of what they left behind,' the woman explained.

The street came to a dead end. A red-brick wall blocked the way. A door was situated in the middle of the wall.

She gestured. 'Open it, Mr Halliday.'

He stepped forward, turned the handle and pushed open the door.

A gentle wind blew in his face, freighted with the scent of a forest, wild flowers and new-mown hay. After the gloom of the city, the assault of the golden sunlight was a visual overload.

It was an idealised scene from a land far away and a time long gone, a scene of archetypal rusticity that seemed to call to something in Halliday's blood – a realisation deep within him that the world had once looked like this, but no longer, and the pain of understanding what was lost was like the apprehension of all loss, a tragic understanding of the irrevocability of change.

The vale stretched away to a distant horizon, a sweep of variegated tree cover, oak and elder and sycamore cladding

230

its left flank. To the right was a stretch of golden fields, hay freshly harvested and stacked in wigwam stooks to dry. Ahead was meadowland, cut through with the silver blade of a flashing stream. Birdsong played in the air, and over everything shone a forever-midday sun.

The woman pointed. 'Mr Mantoni said that he'd meet you in the back garden of the cottage beside the stream.'

They walked through the meadow towards a small, ivy-covered building. Here, on the stretch of land leading from the door in the wall to the riverside lodge, Mantoni had gone to special effort to create authenticity. Real grass and wild flowers grew, and the feel of them against his fingertips allowed Halliday to half-believe the lie of this subterranean rural wonderland.

He peered into the distance and made out other guests strolling among the wild flowers and through the forest. 'Are they all here?' he asked.

She shook her head. 'There are a dozen different worlds down here,' she said, 'and more than a hundred smaller chambers.'

They came to the cottage. Halliday reached out and touched the reassuring solidity of the honey-hued wall. The woman led the way down a path overhung with abundant flowers.

Mantoni, tall and immaculately suntanned, was standing on the lawn of the back garden, staring into the crystal river at his feet. He wore a dark suit and a white roll-neck shirt. Halliday tried to discern any resemblance to his daughter, but found none.

The woman cleared her throat. 'Mr Mantoni, Mr Halliday to see you.'

Mantoni turned and nodded. 'Halliday, do you make a habit of gatecrashing all the fashionable parties? Take a seat.' He indicated a timber bench on the lawn. 'That will be all, Stephanie.'

The woman nodded and departed. Halliday sat on the arm of the bench and lodged one foot on the seat. To have sat

231

down conventionally would have been to surrender to Mantoni's wishes – to ignore the invitation would have been overly confrontational.

Mantoni turned from the river and smiled. 'Seeing as you're here, Halliday, how can I help you?' His eyes, their intensity emphasised by the tan of his face, were a piercing, steely blue.

'I came to question you about Vanessa Artois,' Halliday said.

'Tell me, how is our mutual friend?' The tone of the question surprised Halliday. Mantoni did nothing to conceal his loathing.

'As well as can be expected, under the circumstances.'

Mantoni nodded, considering. 'Is she still in New York?'

'As if,' Halliday said deliberately, 'I'd tell you that.'

'And why is that, may I ask?' There was something about Mantoni's attitude, his entire demeanour, that Halliday found objectionable. He exuded all the overweening self-confidence and calculated asceticism of an intellectual on a late-night holo-show.

Halliday considered what he was about to say. He was conscious of the weight of his automatic, slung beneath his jacket.

'A few days ago,' he said, 'you were in what you thought was a safe VR site. You met with the programmer of a boosted-chimp assassin.'

Mantoni adopted a casual air, his hands in pockets, one foot lodged on a stone at the water's edge. 'You're certainly thorough in your investigations, Halliday.'

'You don't deny that you were behind the shooting?' he said, taken aback at the man's aplomb.

Mantoni regarded him. It was a while before he replied. 'What is there to deny? You obviously know that I instigated the incident.'

Halliday was tempted to pull his automatic and shoot him then, take the life of Mantoni to save the life of Vanessa Artois.

232

Something stopped him: certainly not any qualms about ending such a worthless life. Rather, he was amazed by the man's cavalier admission. It was almost as if Mantoni deemed it his right to place himself above the law, some supreme arbiter of who should live and die.

'Why are you trying to kill her, Mantoni?'

The tycoon gave his clever little smile. 'But I'm not, Halliday.'

'I thought you said—'

'I said that I instigated the *incident*.'

'Incident? It was more than just—'

'Do you think for a second that a man of my means and contacts would fail in the attempt to have someone killed?'

'You mean . . .?'

'I mean that I didn't want Artois dead. I merely intended to frighten her.'

'The laser missed her because she moved just at the right time.'

'Had it hit her,' Mantoni replied, 'it would merely have caused minor injuries. It wasn't a fatal charge.'

Halliday tried to retain his air of calm accusation. 'And I suppose the incident in the Civic – that was meant to frighten her, too?'

Mantoni gestured. 'What do you think?'

'You go to bizarre and sadistic lengths to scare your enemies.' Halliday shook his head. 'What has she done to you, Mantoni?'

'My reasons are entirely personal.'

Halliday stared at the man. 'Was it because,' he found himself saying, 'your daughter left you?'

Mantoni's attitude changed, suddenly. Something seemed to die in the man's eyes, as if his earlier confidence, his arrogance, had suddenly drained from his being. 'Get out of here, Halliday.'

Halliday smiled to himself. He wondered, then, whether he should mention the name of Canada Artois, to see how Mantoni reacted. He decided to keep the information to himself: it would be of no benefit to him if the tycoon knew he was under suspicion of kidnap.

Instead he said, 'You're so accustomed to ordering people about, you think you can get rid of me just like that.' He stared at the tycoon for long seconds. 'You really do think that you're above the law, don't you?'

'I don't think about the question much at all. I know that no prosecution brought against me, for any alleged offence, would be successfully completed. I have so much power and prestige that the judicial system of New York State is impotent against me.'

'There is one system of justice you can't fight, Mantoni.'

He smiled. 'And which system is that?'

Halliday moved from the arm of the bench and sat on the seat, casually. He slipped his hands beneath the flap of his jacket and sat back.

He drew the automatic from its holster and lay it across his lap, regarding the dull metal of its short barrel for a count of five seconds before looking up.

'The justice of the streets, Mantoni. Okay, so you're above the law. You've got everybody in your pocket from the Commissioner down. But then one day some two-dollar hack like me thinks enough is enough. And this guy does something about it.'

'Is this what you expect me to do, Halliday?' Mantoni raised his hands in the air. 'Do you want me to plead for my life?'

As he raised the automatic he thought of Vanessa, and wondered if he could go through with the killing.

Mantoni held out a hand. 'Don't shoot—' he began.

Halliday aimed.

'Because if you do, you'd be wasting your time. You don't think for one second, do you, that I'd risk meeting you in the flesh?'

At that second Mantoni disappeared.

Halliday experienced a sensation then of sickness, defeat and disbelief.

Where the tycoon had stood, Halliday made out a tiny silver airborne projector, perhaps the size of a bee. As he watched, it took off over the river and out of sight.

The scene was empty of threat, of menace, and yet Halliday felt that the entire fantastical representation of this rural idyll was corrupted with something evil beyond words.

He wanted to get out as quickly as possible, and yet at the same time he hardly had the strength to move.

He looked at his watch. If he hurried he might make the hourly boat.

He left the garden, climbed through the sloping grassland.

He had assumed there would be a wall where he had entered from the holographic city street, but there was no such thing. He thought at first that Mantoni was playing a game – he would imprison him in here, indefinitely, for his amusement. Then he saw the giant oak at the crest of the rise. Set into the girth of its great trunk was a small door. Halliday hurried towards it.

He paused before the oak and took one last look across the forested vale, then pulled open the door and stepped out into the grim city street. As he walked the street narrowed, became a mere footpath between dank brick walls. He came to the aquarium gloom where the sunlight invaded the projection. He covered his eyes as the light grew brighter, looking down as his head, shoulders, and then torso and legs emerged through the gravel path.

He hurried down the greensward and past the villa, towards the defile in the rock that led down to the jetty and the boat that would take him away from Laputa.

Seventeen

Mantoni stood in the middle of the holo-chamber and stared about him. One hour ago this space had been filled with images of a rural idyll, forests and wheatfields and a slow-flowing river. Now the projectors showed the interior of a vast auditorium, banked seats and a wide stage area. It was a representation of the Civic Theatre, though the Civic not as it was today but as it had been twenty-five years ago.

He walked towards the stage. He had stilled the projectors, and the effect was so unnatural as to be almost surreal. Minutes ago the guests in the auditorium had been circulating like the colourful tesserae of a kaleidoscopic mosaic, smiling at every photo-opportunity, exchanging exaggeratedly animated conversation. Now it was as if a spell had been cast, magically halting the suited men and gowned women in mid-sentence, mid-gesture. Mantoni moved from one group of frozen figures to the next, stopping from time to time for a closer inspection of the miraculously immobile guests. Wine glasses were halted before parted lips, arms were raised in what in continual motion would have been part of a perfectly ordinary gesture, but which, isolated in an instant, seemed melodramatically grotesque. He stopped before one group of actors where a wine glass had fallen at the very second the images had been stilled. The glass hung in the air as if by magic, tipping a jewelled spray of spumante droplets. An eerie silence filled the chamber, and Mantoni had the odd sensation that he was trespassing on something he had no right to behold.

At a table near the stage was the holo-image of Bo Ventura,

and seated beside her the image of himself, much younger. He was holding her hand and staring into her eyes.

He turned away, as if the image was too painful to contemplate. Across the floor was the table where the assassin had been just seconds before firing. The seat he was about to take was empty, awaiting his arrival.

Mantoni turned, taking in the entirety of the complex projection. The stage was set, he realised. All that was required now was the presence of the players.

He stopped before the stage. Here, on this very spot, his holo-projection had faced the private detective, Hal Halliday. Mantoni had been not too far away, controlling his image and relaying the conversation.

When the detective had pulled the gun and taken aim, he had experienced a sensation almost of orgasmic release. The image, of his holo-projection under threat, had struck something deep within him, a profound psychological chord, which at first worried him because he had been unable to rationalise the feeling. Then, when he thought through his reaction, he came to understand why he considered the image so right, so fitting. It was because the tableau stood as a potent symbol of retribution, of what perhaps should have happened had Halliday fired. He had almost wished, on realising this, that he had been standing in the projection's place – and it had given him an idea, had crystallised in him a notion he had been moving towards, without quite realising it, for the past few days.

His com buzzed. 'Mantoni here.'

The solid, expressionless face of Pablo gazed out at him. 'Sergio, there's been developments.'

He was aware of his pulse. 'You've traced Artois?'

Pablo gave his head the merest shake. 'No, but you might be interested in what I have found out. We need to meet.'

Mantoni nodded. 'Ten minutes,' he said, and cut the connection.

He took one last look around the holo-chamber, then rode the elevator to the basement of the villa. In the VR room he stripped and immersed himself in the jellytank, conscious of his anticipation as the gel sucked him down.

As ever, when he materialised on the riverbank, Pablo had not yet arrived. He took his customary position on the fallen log and counted off the minutes.

The image of the woman materialised what seemed like an age later, establishing from a blur like a heat haze. She sat on the grass a couple of metres before Mantoni, the hem of her dress riding up her bare thighs.

'You haven't traced Artois?'

The woman shook her head. 'Not yet, but I'm working on it. Halliday's clever. He's got her changing hotels every day, and she never tells him where she is when they're talking on the com. I know because I've bugged his office.' She hesitated. 'I have an idea how to trace Artois, but I'll need a chu loaded with her likeness.'

Mantoni nodded. 'It's yours. Anything else?'

'That should be enough.'

'Okay, so . . .' Mantoni tried to keep his eyes from the woman's cleavage as she leaned forward, smiling. 'You said there's been developments?'

The woman winked. 'And how. Like I said, I've bugged Halliday's office. I've been listening in on some of his conversations.'

'And?'

'And I've come up with something you might find interesting.'

Mantoni sighed. 'And something which, let me guess, you'll want paying for, above and beyond the usual fee. Am I correct?'

The woman smiled, at once lascivious and cunning. 'There are payments, and payments, Sergio.'

'What do you want?'

'Can't you guess?'

'You, my friend, are seriously warped. If you're right, and what you have is interesting, then okay.'

'You're a darling man, Sergio.' She sat up, pushing a strand of hair from her face. 'I understand you've recently met a chick called Eloise, right?'

Mantoni tried not to let his surprise show. 'How do you know that?'

The woman laughed. 'I have my methods, Sergio.'

'You said you've bugged Halliday's office? He's been monitoring me in VR, right?' The thought was worrying.

'You could say that,' the woman said. 'About this Eloise – she isn't what she seems.'

Mantoni nodded. His instinct had told him as much when he'd talked to the kid the other night. There had been something about her mannerisms, her coyness. Young girls in VR were never usually as nervous and shy as Eloise had been. He'd guessed he was chatting up some old pervert.

'Don't tell me,' Mantoni said. 'You've managed to find out who Eloise really is, right?'

The woman smiled. 'It wasn't that difficult, Sergio. Like I said, I've been listening in on Halliday.'

'So he's been doing the detective work?'

She laughed. 'You could say that,' she said. 'You see, Halliday is Eloise.'

Mantoni nodded, trying not to let his concern show. 'Very clever,' he said.

'He discovered that Canada met Ed in VR and arranged to meet him on Liberty. He decided to appear on Eros in the guise of a kid, hoping to attract your attention.'

'What does he want?'

'He's set it up with a cop. The next time you meet Eloise, she'll try to set up a meeting in the real world. Halliday hopes you'll take her back to wherever you're holding Canada—'

'But if Eloise is Halliday,' Mantoni began.

'They've got someone to play her part, some kid who's living with Halliday. They'll rig her up with some kind of tracking device and follow her, or at least that's the plan.'

Mantoni massaged his jaw, considering. What if he played

along with Halliday's little plan, allowed the detective to find out where he was holding Canada? He need never leave the island; he could use holograms to do the work.

The police would be no problem. He had Reynolds in his pocket, after all.

The woman was smiling. 'So, what do you think?'

Mantoni checked his decal. He had a couple of hours before he was due to meet sweet Eloise on Eros Island. He reached out and cupped the woman's jaw in his right hand.

'I was hoping,' she said, 'that Big Ed would be around.'

Mantoni tapped the code into his decal and underwent an instantaneous transformation. His eye-level dropped, and he found himself in control of a more compact, muscular body.

The woman stood quickly and removed her dress.

Mantoni reached out and pulled her towards him.

Eighteen

Halliday hurried from the marina and made for the parking lot. He waited until the launch had pulled away from the quay, taking more guests over to Laputa. Confident that Mantoni had assigned no one to follow him, he found his Ford and drove from Battery Park.

As he passed through the gaudy holo-façades lining Bowery, the wash of pastel light sliding across the hood and up the windscreen, he tapped Vanessa's code into his com.

Her real face appeared on the tiny screen. 'Hal!' She leaned forward. 'You went to the island? What happened?'

'You still at the same hotel?'

'I'm moving out in the morning. Did you see Mantoni?'

He ignored the question. 'We need to talk.'

'We can meet in the hotel bar.'

'See you in five minutes.' He cut the connection.

He turned right along Houston Street and made for the Dorchester. There was only one solution to the problem, as far as he could see. They might run, they might try to hide up somewhere, but he was in no doubt that, sooner or later, Mantoni would find them and continue his psychological warfare. The only answer was to accomplish what he had failed to do tonight, and eliminate Mantoni. That would be more difficult than he had at first imagined. Mantoni was no fool. He'd be wary of Halliday in future, careful not to leave himself vulnerable now that Halliday had shown his hand. He would employ stand-ins, use holographics to conceal his actual presence.

Somewhere, the real, live flesh and blood Sergio Mantoni lived his real, flesh and blood life – and that location was where Mantoni was vulnerable. It was as simple as that. More difficult, Halliday knew, would be to establish that location.

He parked three blocks from the Dorchester and took a circuitous route to the hotel bar, to ensure that he was not being followed. He bought a wheat beer and carried it over to a booth at the rear of the plush saloon. There were three couples in the room, and two unattached women. As Halliday sat down with his drink, one of the women moved from the bar with a glass of white wine: apparently middle-aged, silver-haired, a nondescript professional taking a nightcap. She slid into the booth opposite Halliday and smiled. 'Great to see you, Hal.'

He reached across the table as she made to remove her chu. 'I'd rather you left it on, okay?'

The silver-haired woman nodded. 'Did you see Mantoni?'

'Not in the flesh. I spoke to his holograph, and unfortunately you can't shoot a holograph.'

'What happened?'

He considered how much he should tell her. He took a long drink of beer, the ice-cold liquid cutting through his thirst. 'I confronted him, told him I knew he was behind the shooting.'

She looked appalled. 'What did he say?'

Halliday released a long sigh. 'That's the hell of it, Vanessa. He openly admitted he was responsible. That was the frightening thing. He sees it as his right to persecute you for having the guts to leave him.'

'You've got to understand Mantoni, Hal. He craves power – he needs to control those around him.' She shook her head and smiled at him in an attempt at bravery. 'So how long does this go on, Hal? Me running from hotel to hotel . . .?'

'Hey, we'll beat him, Vanessa. Believe me, I'll get the bastard sooner or later.'

'Was I fortunate when I walked into your office.'

He smiled. 'I was thinking the same thing.'

She looked him straight in the eye. 'Stay the night, Hal. No excuses this time. Stay with me.'

He sensed that her request was genuine, motivated not so much by fear but by a real need to be with him.

'Vanessa . . . you don't know how much I'd like that.'

'Then what's stopping you?'

'We have a lead regarding Canada. She met someone in one of the sex zones. We think this is the guy who took her.' He talked her through his meeting with Big Ed on Eros Island, the plan to set him up with Casey in the real world. He looked at his watch. It was eleven thirty. 'I'm meeting someone working on the case at midnight.'

'You think Canada's okay?' she asked.

'Listen, Vanessa. We think it might be Mantoni who kidnapped her.'

The stranger's eyes widened in alarm. 'Mantoni?'

'It's only a theory. We might be wrong. We'll know more in a few hours.' He finished his drink. 'Like I said, we're following a lead.'

'I want to know what happens, Hal. Contact me tomorrow, okay?' She looked into his eyes.

'I'll call. We'll meet somewhere. Have you decided on the next hotel?'

'I thought I'd treat myself to a little luxury, why not? The Carlyle, off Madison.'

'I'll try to meet you there tomorrow sometime.' He stood. 'Time I was moving.'

She stood with him and reached out. 'Hey, you think I'm going to let you get away without a hug?'

She came into his arms, and the pressure of her body against his made him regret that he was leaving. Hell, why couldn't he drop the case, leave the country with her, start a new life . . .? He realised he was fantasising.

When she kissed him, he wished that it would go on for ever.

'Good luck, Hal,' she whispered.

He pulled away, nodding in confusion, and hurried from the bar. He stepped onto the sidewalk, the humid night air doing nothing to clear his head. Houston Street was busy, crowds milling outside the restaurants and VR Bars. It was almost midnight, and he realised that for the first time in weeks the rains had failed to arrive that night. He wondered if it might be an omen.

He drove uptown, away from all the glitz and rich citizens out to enjoy themselves. Ten minutes later he reached El Barrio, passing the legion of homeless sleeping on the sidewalks.

Jeff Simmons was waiting for him at Thai Joe's, perched on a bar stool with a small bottle of Chinese beer clutched in his fist. He pushed the half-full bottle away and nodded to Halliday.

'It's all on the next hour or so,' the cop said. 'You okay? You look strung out.'

'I'm fine. Things'll go fine, Jeff.' He'd hardly had time to consider how he'd play it with Big Ed on Eros Island. Let him do the talking, play coy, keep his default gown covering his cute young body. Drive the bastard crazy thinking about what awaited him in the real world . . .

'Let's go for it.'

'See you in there.'

Once in his booth Halliday touched the screen and tapped in the serial number of the soma-type he'd used the other day. A rotating full-length representation of the girl's naked body appeared on the screen. He shortened her hair, thinned her face a little, so that she more resembled the image of the girl Big Ed might, if all went to plan, be meeting in the real world. The thought filled him with apprehension.

A minute later he stepped into the jellytank and lay back. He closed his eyes, feeling the warm embrace of the gel seal around him. He felt the quick, disorienting nausea pass through his head, and was suddenly aware that he was no longer inhabiting the body of a thirty-five-year-old male.

He opened his eyes, and he was on the golden beach of Eros Island.

The long crescent of sand was deserted, and this time no cavorting couples played in the shallows of the lagoon.

Inland, though, the recreation pool was crowded with perhaps two dozen men and women, squirming together like a bucket of suntanned maggots. There was activity in the villas further beyond. Halliday made out glimpses of moving figures through the doors and windows.

He sat down and drew his knees to his chest, scrunching his toes into the granular sand. Along the beach, the air shivered as someone materialised. Halliday sat up, heart thumping, then relaxed as a thinned-down, younger version of Jeff Simmons established on the beach and walked inland, not even so much as glancing at Halliday/Eloise.

Five minutes passed, then ten. Halliday considered the possibility that Big Ed might not show. Perhaps out there in the real world something had happened to prevent him turning up. Perhaps he'd had second thoughts about the skinny street kid . . . How many other willing young girls did he meet every day in the various sex zones . . .? What if he failed to appear, Halliday asked himself. Then, he decided, he would turn up at midnight every night in the hope of coming across the kidnapper.

He wondered if something he'd said to Ed last night had given him away. Had he let slip some comment or observation that, to him, was innocent enough, but to Big Ed, well practised in the dissimulation and deceit of VR, had set the alarm bells ringing?

The more he considered that, the less he thought it possible. Ed had been well and truly suckered by little Eloise. The expression on his face, as he said farewell to Halliday, had testified to that: he'd been practically smacking his lips like some cartoon wolf.

An hour passed. Perhaps every ten minutes new revellers materialised along the beach, and each time Halliday sat up and stared with a mixture of apprehension and anticipation. Once or twice he was approached by men and women, but Halliday just closed his eyes and feigned sleep.

He considered the possibility that this was a ploy by Big Ed. He would keep Eloise waiting, making her all the more eager for him when he did eventually show. He was dealing with an experienced kidnapper, he reminded himself; someone adept at letting the girl do the running until she found herself caught.

He was beginning to think that Big Ed was never going to appear when, five metres up the beach, the air shimmered and a figure took on substance. Halliday watched, prepared for another disappointment. He was surprised when Big Ed materialised and gave him a casual wink. He smiled in return and waved shyly. Big Ed shrugged off his gown and strolled down the beach, cock nodding as if in lazy acknowledgement of whoever might be watching.

'Hey, kitten,' Big Ed said.

'Hey yourself.'

He knelt beside Halliday, reached out and chucked his chin. He sat down and then stretched out, leaning on one elbow and staring out to sea.

He looked at Halliday, one eye screwed shut, and nodded at his default gown. 'Aren't showing off your pretty little body, Eloise?'

Halliday smiled. 'Didn't want anyone else getting too interested,' he said.

'Saving it for Big Ed, hey?'

'Maybe,' Halliday said with assumed teenage hauteur, 'maybe not . . .'

Big Ed lay back and stared into the sky, hands linked behind his head. 'Hey, Eloise, where you live in the real world?'

Halliday thought about that one. 'Here and there,' he said.

'Where you from originally? You a New Yorker?'

He shook his head. 'Chicago.'

'So you're all alone in the big, rotten apple, kitten?'

Halliday nodded. He could see Big Ed's slow, calculating expression. 'So . . . what you do with yourself out there in the real world?'

Halliday shrugged. 'Oh . . . not much. I don't know many people here.'

'No friends?'

'A few . . .'

Big Ed was nodding his understanding, biding his time, and when he spoke next it was all Halliday could do not to smile in triumph. 'Hey . . . how about this? How about we meet, out there in the Big Apple? I could show you the city, take in a meal, a show. Hey—' he held up a hand. 'No big deal, right? I mean, this place here's for getting it on. Out there in the real world we'll just be friends.'

'Well . . .'

'C'mon, kitten. We'll talk, have a good time. So okay, I might be a bit older than you . . . but what does age matter between friends?'

Halliday played at thinking about it, pulling at his pink, perfectly formed toes and frowning. At last he asked, 'Where can we meet?' in a whisper.

'That's the girl!' Big Ed reached out and stroked his cheek. 'What you doing later this morning, say ten?'

'Nothing . . .'

'Ten it is, then. You know Fort Hamilton?'

He squinted at Big Ed. 'Isn't that Brooklyn?'

'You got it. I'll meet you on the steps of the Wilson library building, okay?'

Halliday was aware of his little girl's heart, ticking like a time bomb behind his skinny ribs. 'I'll find it.'

Big Ed caught something of Halliday's enthusiasm, grinned broadly himself. 'Okay! On the steps, then. Ten on the dot, kitten. I'll show you the sights.'

Halliday smiled at him. 'Sounds great.'

Big Ed winked. 'Give you the time of your life, Eloise. Hey, better go get myself some shuteye before the big date.' He punched Halliday's shoulder, 'Catch you later, kitten.'

Halliday waved fingers. 'Later, Ed.'

He watched Big Ed sit up and touch his exit decal. Seconds later, Halliday was alone on the beach. He turned quickly, looked inland.

Jeff was sitting on the grass of the foreshore, ten metres away. He hurried over. 'Well?'

Halliday gave the thumbs up. 'We got him! On the steps of the Wilson library, Fort Hamilton. Ten o'clock this morning.'

Jeff nodded. 'I'll get the tech boys sorted, Hal. I'll bring some of the team round to your place, say seven? Get Casey rigged up with the monitors.'

'See you then.'

'I'm outta here, Hal. Catch you later.' He touched his decal and shimmered out of existence.

Halliday lay back on the sand, enjoying the sensation of the warm sun on his face. He felt a rare elation coursing through his body – or rather Eloise's body. He'd get out, dress and find a bar and have a few beers in celebration. The thought cheered him. Alone, in a darkened bar, with an ice-cold beer . . .

He quit Eros Island and rose slowly from the tank, the cloying grasp of the gel retarding his motion. He showered and dressed and left the booth. It was one thirty, the dead of night. He considered having a beer at the bar here, but the possibility of encountering Thai Joe and his perpetual enthusiasm, even at this unlikely hour, decided him against it. He needed peace and quiet, the solitude of his own company.

He went to Olga's at the end of his street, the cellar bar quiet at this time in the morning. Mood blues played soft, the beer was good, and Halliday sat in a padded booth in the half-light and drank six bottles of Ukrainian wheat beer, slow.

He knew the elation would wear off, in time, and he needed the soporific of drink to ease the apprehension that would follow.

It was after four by the time he left Olga's and made his way along the street. He climbed the steps to the office, tripping only once, and with exaggerated care opened the door so as not to disturb Casey. The bedroom door was ajar, and Halliday leaned against the jamb. In the overspill from the flickering wallscreen he stared at the sleeping girl. She was lying on her belly, naked because of the heat, one arm around the comfort blanket of Vanessa Artois' silver Gucci coat.

Halliday eased the door shut and brewed himself a coffee.

He sat on the chesterfield with his feet on the swivel chair, sipped the coffee and allowed his drunken thoughts to wander. He thought back six months, to the ugly little drowned rat he'd let shelter from the rain for one night, just one night. Now she had taken over, imposed her routine, and Halliday went along with it . . . He actually *enjoyed* her company, for chrissake, her warped wit and irreverence and sheer vitality . . . At first she'd been just another nobody, a face in the crowd, and then somehow, miraculously, she became someone with a character, a distinct and infectious personality, and the hell of it was, the bottom line was, he was really scared, shit scared, of what might happen, but at the same time he told himself that they had to go through with it, they had to . . .

Nineteen

Sanchez fell through a psychedelic fractal landscape like a diver through a coral sea. He was without bodily sensation, without substance, merely a viewpoint through which his mind observed the strange, multicoloured world of the Tidemann Corporation's VR core.

Kat had been reluctant for him to venture into the jelly-tank again so soon after the last scare, but Sanchez felt that he had to lay the ghost. If he didn't prove to himself that he was greater than his fear, then he would be no use at all to Virex. Grudgingly, Kat had agreed to let him tank, but she'd promised to pull him out at the slightest sign of danger.

Her solicitude had been another indication that her attitude towards him was slowly changing. For the first few days of their working relationship, Kat had treated him like some subnormal kid, quick with the sarcastic jibes and put-downs. Then, ever since the burn in the Mantoni core, she had been less caustic, more concerned. They'd talked for hours about their pasts, their opposition to the virtual reality craze that was sweeping the world.

Once or twice Sanchez had wanted to reach out and hug Kat to him; she was a sad and vulnerable woman who concealed her pain behind a front of world-weary cynicism. But Sanchez was beginning to see past the disguise to the real woman within, and he liked what he saw. He had restrained himself from touching her, for fear of rejection, but he wondered how long that might last.

He heard Kat's voice, 'You're approaching Tidemann's code core, Sanchez. I'm following you in with the virus. I don't know what you're looking at in there – but from my point of view it's all encrypted data. God knows where we'll be planting the virus, or what damage it'll do . . .'

They had elected to go ahead with the insertion after Levine, their new controller, had contacted them. He'd said that his fellow Virex controllers had elected to continue with the O'Donnell virus, the same one that had failed in the Mantoni zone. Kat and Sanchez had been selected to target Tidemann's, if they wanted to take the risk.

Sanchez had been all for it, while Kat was not so sure. They'd talked long into the night before Sanchez had finally won her over. They had to take risks; they were facing opposition that was not only rich and powerful, but also ruthless. They had to use everything within their means to defeat the enemy.

Kat guided him through a spacescape of expanding, polychromatic novae; each flare, he knew, was a zone, an area within Tidemann's core controlling a multiplicity of VR sites that citizens all around the world could access. Destroy these, and Tidemann VR would grind to a halt, until their techs could repair the damage and restore the core to working order.

'This looks like a big one, kid. I'm slipping you straight in, releasing the virus, and then getting you out immediately. No messing around this time.'

He tried to prepare himself for whatever visual overload was about to hit him. To suddenly enter a zone was like opening your eyes to an explosion of primary colours after a lifetime of blindness. There was no way he could not be shocked and awed at the sudden influx of pulsating visual information.

He dived towards a rapidly expanding ball of fiery orange light, and it was as if a supernova had exploded in his head. He was flying over a crazy landscape of brilliant primary colours. He stared down at the passing terrain and tried to make sense of what he was seeing, but the images were disconcerting: purple trees, meadows daubed blue, and a sky the colour of marmalade: then he understood. He was in a

251

site he'd heard Tidemann's was experimenting with, one of the realms loaded with the visual information laid down in certain schools of art. He was in the middle of a neo-Fauvist panorama, where all shapes were recognisable, but the colours were *wrong*.

The sight was too much, and he tried to close his eyes – but the information was being relayed directly to his visual cortex and there was nothing he could do to shut it out.

He saw something on the horizon. At first it was no more than a speck. He thought it was a bird, a bird flying towards him at speed . . . and expanding incredibly as it did so.

Only then, with the thing perhaps a hundred metres from him, did he realise that it was no bird. It *looked* like a bird, a hawk or something similar, but it was heading straight for him as fast as a missile.

Then Kat's voice sounded in his head. 'Christ!' she cried. 'Hold on, kid! I'm pulling you out.'

The hawk was almost upon him, seemed to hit him. He was aware of an explosion, as if something had detonated right before his eyes, tearing the world apart. He experienced a second of searing pain familiar from the Mantoni core when the techs had released the anti-insurgency bug. Tidemann's had evidently located his presence and launched an attack.

Then he was no longer in the zone. He was in darkness, and sensation returned to his body. He was sitting up in the tank, forcing his way through the restraining medium of the gel.

Kat was with him, helping him stand and step from the jellytank. He pulled off his faceplate and the sensors. It was a few seconds before he could make out her words. 'Are you okay, Sanchez? They detected the fucking virus, sent something after you! It's a miracle you got out in time.'

He stood, naked and dripping with slime, and to his amazement Kat hugged him to her.

'I'm fine, Kat. I'm okay.' He held his dripping arms away

252

from her, as if fearful to embrace her slight, boyish body. 'I'll go shower. I could kill a coffee.'

She released him, only then realising that her black T-shirt and leggings were plastered with gel. She laughed. 'I'll go and . . . I'll change, and then fix you that coffee.'

Embarrassed, he hurried to the bathroom and showered.

When he returned ten minutes later, Kat was hunched over the com-monitor, a pot of coffee steaming beside her. She poured him a mug and one for herself.

'They were onto us, kid. They eradicated O'Donnell's virus before it did any harm. We're just wasting our time, risking our fucking lives.'

He reached out, took her hand, and held her delicate fingers for what seemed like an age. He took his coffee and moved to the mattress, hoping that Kat might join him.

After staring at the screen for a minute, she killed it with an angry gesture, picked up her mug and sank onto the mattress beside him.

Her head found his shoulder.

Sometimes, he wondered if what he was doing, pitting himself against the combined might of the VR industry, meant anything compared to the simple pleasure that other people seemed to take for granted – the pleasure of being close to another human being. Sometimes, Sanchez just wanted to retreat with someone he could love, someone who loved him, and let the whole stinking world go to Hell.

He smiled to himself. If everyone had that insular, self-interested attitude . . .

'Sanchez . . .' Kat set her coffee aside, reached across his chest and held him, her face close to his. 'What if we fail, kid? What if we can't do anything? Have you thought about that?'

'I have nightmares, Kat. We're living in VR, a perfect world, and we can't get out, and the environment is wholly controlled by the companies.'

Kat was laughing.

'What?'

She said, 'Sounds a bit like *this* reality, kid.'

He grunted an acknowledgement. 'Yeah, only ten times worse.'

'It's getting that way.' She stopped and stared at him. 'Why don't we admit it, there's nothing we can do. They're too powerful. And you know what they say about power . . .?'

He almost suggested, then, that they leave the city, move upstate, find a farm and live the simple life. He was saved the embarrassment of Kat's rejection by the buzz of her communicator.

Kat sighed and struggled from the mattress. She found her com beneath a drift of old clothes.

It was Levine. 'We need to meet.'

She nodded. 'Go on.'

He told her where and when.

'We'll be there.' She cut the connection, looked at Sanchez and shrugged.

They took the subway from Canal Street to 68th. The carriage was crowded and hot, and Sanchez wanted nothing more than to get back to the apartment. He caught the glances of the other commuters, looking at them, and experienced a wave of pleasure at being considered Kat's partner.

They quit the subway at 68th Street, crossed Fifth Avenue and entered Central Park beside the zoo. Sanchez took Kat's hand, holding tight as they entered the vast, inimical, open space of the park.

Levine was waiting for them, seated on a park bench beside the lake and staring out across the water. He was a prosperous-looking grey-haired man in his fifties, dressed in khaki chinos and an expensive white shirt: in the real world he might have been a top-ranking executive in some multinational corporation.

In the Virex set-up he was a controller, a link-man who passed on information from the contact above him to his allotted cell, no more important in the system than Sanchez or Kat.

He nodded first to Kat and then to Sanchez.

Kat squatted on the tarmac, hugging her shins. Sanchez sat on the bench beside Levine.

'The O'Donnell virus failed on all fronts,' he began in a cultured mid-Atlantic accent.

Kat nodded. 'Tell me about it. The other day, Sanchez nearly burned good. Today, I got him out just in time.'

'They're onto us. They seem to be one step ahead of our techs. Word is they're taking us seriously and pumping millions into anti-sabotage software.'

'That's what you got us here to tell us?' Kat began, eyes flashing.

Levine shook his head, unperturbed. He looked from Kat to Sanchez. 'I'll be brief. The consensus of opinion among the cells across the country is that the tech approach is failing. We have two options. Persevere with the technical assault, or abandon it and adopt a strategy of direct action.'

'Which means, exactly?' Kat asked.

'Sabotage. Terrorism. We target the companies, the HQs, communication networks. We destroy them physically.'

'Radical,' Sanchez said. 'It's almost a sign of desperation.'

Levine nodded. 'We've been driven to desperate measures by our failure on the technical front, and in light of information coming from our contacts in Tidemann's.'

Sanchez felt something turn in his stomach. 'What information?'

'Tidemann's technical staff have succeeded in developing some pretty advanced software. They're confident that soon they'll be able to abolish the restrictions on immersion limits.'

'You mean to say,' Sanchez said, 'that soon we'll be able to tank indefinitely?'

Levine nodded. 'It's what we've always feared – why many of us joined Virex. It'll be the perfect opt-out for those who can afford it, those who've had enough of this reality. They'll be able to live in VR, indefinitely.'

Kat said, 'I thought . . . word was that it'd be another, five, ten years before they made the breakthrough.'

'Tidemann's think they'll have the new system on-line in six months, maybe a year,' Levine said. 'Our informants tell us that their techs have developed a method of permanently maintaining the body in VR.'

'Jesus Christ,' Kat said. 'It'll be the next big thing. Why live in this world when you can opt for a tailor-made paradise?'

'So you see why we're thinking of scaling up our operations? I want to know how you feel about this. Are you willing to remain with us if we move into direct action?'

Kat was nodding her head slowly, looking up at Sanchez.

'We need to think about it,' Sanchez said. 'Talk it over. We'll get back to you.'

Levine nodded. 'And another thing. As well as the companies outwitting us on the technical front, they've taken to exterminating certain of our members. Rodriguez and Williams were killed last week, and of course your former controller. We've lost ten operatives over the past month. I'm advising you to hire security. Don't worry about the cost – Virex will foot the bill. Not only are we no longer safe in VR, we're finding it increasingly difficult to maintain ourselves in the real world.'

Sanchez nodded. 'We'll look after ourselves,' he said, with a confidence that surprised him. 'I'll arrange a bodyguard, Kat.'

'I'll contact you in a day or two for your decision about our next course of action. I hope you can see your way to joining us.'

He nodded to Kat and Sanchez, then stood and made his way around the lake towards the exit.

Kat moved to the bench beside Sanchez, and sat quietly with her head on his shoulder. He smiled and closed his eyes. He could get used to her doing this.

'What do you think, kid?' she said.

'I know someone who can advise us on security,' he said. 'Halliday, the detective I saw the other day.'

'I meant about direct action.'

'Oh . . .' Sanchez opened his eyes and stared at the water. 'I don't know. Perhaps it's the only way forward. We aren't winning on the technical front.'

Kat sighed. 'It's almost an admission of failure, if we resort to violence.'

'It's not violence against people,' he pointed out. 'We'll be targeting property, company offices.'

'Even so . . .'

'Look at it this way, you could say that what we're trying to do with the viral insertions is nothing more than violence. Software violence, but violence just the same.'

'Yeah. Okay.'

He looked at her. She was staring at a duck on the water. 'You're frightened of what might happen to us?'

She smiled, without humour. 'Suppose I am.'

He put an arm round her shoulders and squeezed. 'What did Levine say? Ten Virex operatives have died in the past month? We're already in danger, Kat.'

'I just wish we could get our message over before it's too late,' Kat said.

'Perhaps people'll take notice when we start blowing up some real estate,' Sanchez said.

Kat stood up and tugged Sanchez to his feet. 'C'mon. Let's go.'

They took the subway downtown and got off at Canal Street. As they were about to turn down the alley towards the apartment, Kat stopped.

'What?'

'You go ahead. I need to get something, okay? A surprise.'

He watched her run across the street and enter a Chinese supermarket. He smiled. Chinese food was his favourite.

He turned, heading for the apartment, then stopped. On the corner of the alley, leaning against the wall as if waiting for someone, was a big Latino guy with a thick Zapata moustache. He glanced at Sanchez as he passed, and Sanchez felt his scalp prickle. He recalled what Heller had told him

257

the other day, before the assassin struck: he thought he was being followed by a big Mexican-looking guy.

He continued down the alleyway and told himself he was being paranoid, jumpy after what Levine had said about the other operatives.

As he approached the fire escape, he looked back. The guy was still there, studiously examining the state of his fingernails.

Sanchez hurried up to the apartment and let himself in. He sat on the mattress and tapped Kat's code into his com. Seconds later she answered. 'Sanchez, what is it?'

He found his voice. 'Don't come back to the apartment, Kat. I think we've been followed.'

'What? How do you know?'

'I don't. It's just that ... Look, let's play it safe, okay? Contact Levine and tell him we need to get out, arrange for someone to move the equipment.'

'Okay, fine.'

'Is there somewhere safe you can stay?'

'Sure. I know somewhere.'

'Go there. Don't come back here, okay? I'm getting out straight away. Be in touch.'

'Sure. Sanchez – take care, okay?'

'I'll be fine.' He cut the connection. From the pocket of his camouflage trousers he pulled the card that Halliday had given him the other day. He'd call the detective later, when he was safely away from here.

He pocketed the card and looked around the room.

He'd get out and stay in a cheap hotel somewhere – wouldn't even go back to his place in Brooklyn. He had few possessions, anyway. Nothing he was too attached to.

He tried to think if Kat might need anything. She was a woman of very few possessions. He saw the bottle of Jack Daniels next to a canister of spin on the table beside the com monitor.

He picked up the rye, left the spin, and stepped out of the apartment.

He hurried down the fire escape, wondering if he was being ridiculously jumpy. He reached the alley and stopped. The big Latino pushed himself away from the wall with studied nonchalance, turned and walked down the alley towards him.

Sanchez told himself that there was a simple explanation. The guy lived along here, of course. But something about his casual, unhurried approach . . .

He turned, his heart thumping in fear, and almost ran down the alley away from his pursuer.

Twenty

Halliday was dozing on the chesterfield when Jeff Simmons knocked on the door and entered the office, calling his name.

He started and looked up, disoriented by the arrival of the big, slab-faced lieutenant, accompanied by two strangers, until he realised what was going on.

'You guys help yourself to coffee.' He indicated the percolator. 'I'll get Casey.'

He pushed himself from the chesterfield and banged on the bedroom door. 'Hey, Casey! Get up!'

Jeff introduced Halliday to the two techs, but a combination of alcohol and nerves caused Halliday to forget their names almost immediately.

Casey, bleary-eyed and still out of it, appeared half-naked at the door. She stared at the roomful of men, squeaked and quickly slammed the door shut. Three sets of eyes moved in unison to Halliday.

He shrugged. 'Don't think she was expecting company.'

When she appeared again she was dressed in shorts and a T-shirt. She smiled shyly at Halliday, then waved fingers at the strangers. 'So today's the day, huh?'

She poured herself a cup of coffee and curled up on the chesterfield, yawning. 'Sunday's my day off, too. Only day I get to lie in, and here I am playing mouse.'

Halliday slumped in his swivel chair. 'You could always pull out, Casey.' He looked challengingly at Jeff. 'We could follow the guy back without her.'

'*If* he shows himself when she isn't there,' Jeff said.

'Hey,' Casey piped up, 'I want to do this, Hal. I thought you agreed.'

Halliday held up a tired hand. 'Okay, okay. Let's do it.'

'When you've finished your coffee, Casey,' Jeff said, 'the techs here'll rig you up with a couple of monitors so we can follow you, okay?'

'Hey,' she said, draining her mug and standing up. 'I'm all yours.'

The first tech opened a case and pulled out a silver filigree apparatus like a chu. Casey stood in the middle of the room, arms in the air, T-shirt hiked up to show off her skinny belly, while the techs strapped the silver band just below her ribcage.

She sensed Halliday's concern and gave him a big, warm smile. He tried to return it.

'You want she should be armed?' one of the techs asked Jeff.

'Hey, yeah!' Casey cried. She made a gun of her fingers and shot the techs. 'Pee-ow, pee-ow!'

Jeff looked at Halliday.

'You gotta be kidding, Jeff. You give those things to cops who've been on the range, not sixteen-year-old kids.'

'No shooter,' Jeff said.

'Aw,' Casey moaned. 'What if this pervert tries to do something to me?'

'Don't worry,' Halliday said. 'We won't be far away. That right, Jeff?'

'Sure thing, honey. We'll be tracking you every centimetre.'

'This is a powerful radio transceiver,' one of the techs explained to Casey and Halliday, indicating the device strapped around Casey's midriff like a corset. 'Has a range of over fifty kay. This—' he held up a small disc, 'is a back-up. Do you have shoes and socks?'

'Have,' Casey admitted. 'Hardly ever wear 'em, though.'

'I think you should today. This'll slip into your sock, just to be on the safe side.'

Halliday fetched a pair of red bobby-sox and a worn pair of runners from the bedroom. Casey slipped the disc into her right sock and pulled it on. She forced her feet into the runners and walked up and down the room. 'Feels kinda strange wearing runners, Hal.'

He smiled. She looked kind of strange in the runners, too, like a wild animal forced to wear shoes.

'So what's the story?' she said.

Jeff said, 'Hal'll fill you in on the background, what you need to know, when we're driving over to Brooklyn. That way you won't forget anything.' He looked at Halliday. 'We'll drive in an unmarked car to about a kay from the library building. At ten minutes to ten, Casey transfers to a taxi, one of our cars. We set off and take up positions across from the library. It's an old office complex I scouted earlier. We've got the whole area rigged, officers posted in every direction and a team of drones at the ready. At ten, Casey shows up and stands on the steps until Big Ed shows. When Casey and our mark set off, my men follow inconspicuously, in whatever manner is applicable. Hal, you and me'll follow either by car or on foot, in microphone contact with the immediate tailers. We find out where our man has his base, and then we confer and consider the best possible course of action.'

'I don't want Casey too long anyplace with that sicko,' Halliday said. Casey rolled her eyes at him.

'We'll do what's best for the kid, Hal, don't worry.'

'I'll be fine, Hal, really I will. Shoulda seen some of the streetlife I had to fight off before I ended up here.'

'This guy's in a different league, Casey,' he said quietly. 'I don't want you doing anything foolish, you hear? No heroics.'

Casey nodded. 'No heroics.'

'Okay.' Jeff looked at his watch. 'All set?'

They filed down the stairs, Casey in front of Halliday. He held the nape of her neck, squeezing with reassurance. In the back of the unmarked police car she snuggled against him, and something about her lack of chirpiness now suggested that her earlier vivacity had been nothing but an act.

She found his hand and held on tight.

They headed downtown through the quiet Sunday morning streets, making for Brooklyn Bridge.

'You don't need to do much talking when you're with this guy,' he said. 'You act shy – he'll be expecting that. Story is that you met in a sex zone, Eros Island.'

She looked up at him. 'Me, in a sex zone? Mr Halliday, what kind of girl do you think I am?'

'He came onto you, and you agreed to meet him in the real world. Your name is Eloise, and you live on the streets.'

'Which streets?'

'Doesn't matter. I didn't mention that in VR. Make something up, if he asks. You're from Chicago and you're alone in New York. Now, his name is Big Ed – that's the tag he uses in VR. His persona in VR is a short, well-tanned guy in his forties, balding, with a moustache. We think he wears a chu in the real world, so we don't really know how he'll appear.' He looked at Casey. She was nodding seriously. 'You got all that?'

She repeated it all practically verbatim, Halliday correcting her on a couple of minor points. 'Good. That's great. So we're all set.'

She increased her grip on his hand, and they rode in silence for the next twenty minutes. They crossed the bridge into Brooklyn and motored down street after street of drab tenement buildings. The driver slowed.

In the passenger seat, Jeff pointed. 'That's our cab up ahead. Pull in behind it.'

The tech eased the car to a halt behind the taxi. Jeff looked at his watch. 'A quarter to,' he said, screwing round in his seat and looking at Halliday. 'We'll give it five minutes and then it's action stations.' He gave a big wink to Casey. 'Hey, don't worry, kid, okay? You've got the might and expertise of the NYPD behind you.'

Casey pulled a face. 'Think I *should* be kinda worried,' she said, 'some of the stories Hal's told me 'bout the force.'

They lapsed into silence. The seconds seemed to crawl by.

Casey examined her bitten fingernails, last week's pink nail polish chipped and flaking.

Halliday wondered, suddenly, if she had kept her promise to ask out the Chinese boy, Ben.

Jeff sighed, looked at his watch again. 'It's ten to, Hal, Casey. Let's get going. Hang in there, kid.'

She nodded, biting her lip. Halliday gave her a quick hug, kissed her forehead. 'See you soon, okay?'

She said nothing, merely nodded again, a sure sign she was frightened now that the time had come to act. She climbed out of the car and walked quickly to the cab in front, looking ridiculously thin in her T-shirt and tight-fitting shorts. Halliday found himself wondering, with a lump in his throat, why she wore such tight shorts when she had nothing of a butt to show off.

She jumped into the back of the cab and it pulled away from the curb. Jeff nodded to the tech. They set off and took the first left, then the first right, along narrow streets between high-rise office buildings.

Jeff began tunelessly humming some piece of classical music. Halliday smiled to himself. Back in the old days, out on a case, whenever things got tense Jeff would begin humming.

'Hey, what is it again?'

'Beethoven. "Ode to Joy". Remember it?'

'How could I forget it, Jeff? Still sounds like you're ill.'

Jeff grinned without humour. 'To tell the truth, I don't feel that good.'

Halliday nodded. He knew what Jeff meant. Himself, he wanted to lean out the window and vomit.

The car pulled into the side of the narrow street. Jeff and the techs climbed out. Halliday followed. Jeff had the keycard to the sliding door of a delivery bay. They passed into the gloom of an empty warehouse. Jeff led the way, Halliday following and the techs behind him. They climbed a flight of stairs to the second floor and approached a wall of dusty windows. The techs pulled objects like communicators from their cases and tapped the touchpads. Jeff passed Halliday an earphone, screwing his own into his left ear. Halliday inserted the 'phone, hearing nothing but faint static.

He looked through the window, across the street to the library building. The cab drew up, deposited Casey, and pulled away. She looked up and down the street, then walked up the steps and peered into the double doors of the library. She walked back and forth along the top step, kicking her heels. Seen at this remove she looked about eight years old, tiny and vulnerable. Halliday wanted to rush down and take her in his arms, hurry away from this place and the imminent threat from Big Ed.

The street was quiet, for which he was grateful. A few old couples were out taking a quiet Sunday morning constitutional, along with a guy walking a dog.

Halliday looked at his watch. It was one minute to ten.

Jeff was speaking. He pointed through the window. 'The microwave mast repairman on the corner, he's one of ours. That bag lady on the opposite corner, one of ours. We have half a dozen other cops round and about, all ready to follow on foot. Six drones are ready and waiting, concealed around the area. We have a dozen cars waiting for action, everyone rigged up with monitors and microphones.'

Halliday nodded. For some reason, none of this reassured him in the slightest.

Suddenly, the static in his earphone cleared. He made out a voice, and his heart began a laboured pounding. 'O'Brien here. A cab's just pulled up on the corner of 80th and 4th – a guy's climbing out. Walking towards the library building.'

Jeff spoke into his com 'Check, O'Brien. We've got him.'

Halliday leaned forward. He looked along the street. Someone was approaching along the Sunday-quiet sidewalk. It was Big Ed – or rather a real-world version of Big Ed, taller than his VR persona, not as bulkily-muscled or tanned, but the same smiling, confident face, moustache, bald head, the same arrogant swagger. Halliday wondered if he was wearing a chu, reckoned that it'd be more than likely.

'O'Brien here. He's approaching the girl.'

Jeff said, 'We see him.'

Big Ed walked up the steps. Halliday watched as Casey turned, arms folded defensively high across her skinny chest. She nodded at something Big Ed said. He could imagine his opening line. *Hey kitten, lookin' wonderful* . . .

They talked briefly. Big Ed reached out once or twice, stroking her cheek, chucking her chin. Casey cowered away, avoiding his eyes.

Ed gestured along the street. Casey nodded.

As they walked down the steps, Ed slipped a possessive arm around her narrow shoulders and quite suddenly, irrationally, Halliday wanted to shoot the bastard dead.

Casey looked across the street, up at the window from which they watched.

'Don't do that, girl,' Jeff whispered. 'Don't do anything to make him suspicious . . .

Halliday realised that he was sweating, his face slick, his palms oily. He wanted to do something, to act. The worst of it was the knowledge that he was powerless; all he could do, like everyone else, was watch and wait.

He watched. Casey and Big Ed strolled along the street, for all the world like . . . like a father and daughter, perhaps. Except that something in the young girl's body-language belied the comparison. She still had her arms tightly folded, and her posture was hunched, afraid.

They turned the corner, disappeared from sight, and Halliday's stomach lurched.

In his ear: 'Havel here. I have them. Walking down Union Street.'

Halliday watched as the microwave repairman closed his toolbox and moved around the corner.

One of the techs was peering at his tracking device.

'Everything working smooth this end. I have them on Union Street.'

'What now?' Halliday said. The question came out as barely a croak. His mouth was dry. He realised that he was shaking

266

uncontrollably. Christ, even on Laputa, confronting what he had assumed at the time was a real-life Mantoni, he'd not felt as nervous as this.

'Now we sit tight and see what gives,' Jeff said.

The tech said, 'I have a good fix. Two hundred metres away and moving.'

In Halliday's ear, another surveillance cop reported, 'Rodriguez here. Our man and the kid're passing now. Corner of Union and Pascoe. They've turned left. We have no one down there. I'm following.'

Jeff spoke into his com. 'Take it easy, Rodriguez. Don't go spooking our man. We're tracking them on the monitor, remember.'

'Got it, sir,' Halliday heard Rodriguez say in his earphone. 'I'll take it easy.'

Jeff looked at the tech, who nodded and formed a circle with thumb and forefinger.

'Where's he taking her?' Halliday said.

What if, this time, Big Ed decided he wanted a little immediate fun? He had this skinny defenceless kid, didn't he? Why not take her up some quiet back alley, beat her up . . .?

'Rodriguez here. They've turned down an alley between the International Commercial bank and the Anderson Building. The girl's spooked. She's not going with him . . .'

Halliday sank to his haunches, his back against the wall, and held his head in his hands.

'They've stopped. Our man's talking to her. Persuading her, it looks like. Okay . . . it's okay. They're moving on, down the alley.'

Halliday closed his eyes. A part of him wished that Casey had refused to go, then, had turned and fled.

Jeff was speaking into his com. 'Don't follow them immediately, Rodriguez. Wait till they're out of sight, then proceed with caution. Got that?'

'Loud and clear.'

The tech said, 'They've turned left at the end of the alley.

They're . . .' He peered at the screen of his tracking device. 'They're descending, sir – looks like they're going down a spiral staircase, by their movements.'

Jeff said, 'Rodriguez, get down that alley and turn left. Stop when you come to a spiral staircase. Our man's descending.'

'On my way,' Rodriguez said.

'They're no longer descending,' the tech reported. 'They're walking now, along a straight stretch parallel with Pascoe Street but on a level about five metres lower. I don't know what it is.'

Jeff looked at Halliday. 'Any ideas?'

'Some kind of subway? An underpass?'

Jeff said, 'Rodriguez?'

'Rodriguez here. I'm at the top of the staircase. Going down real slow. It's a waterway down there, sir . . . I'm at the bottom now. I can just make out our man and the girl, about two hundred metres ahead. They've just passed into the shadow of a bridge. I've lost them.'

'Follow carefully, Rodriguez.'

'You got it.'

Jeff touched Halliday's shoulder. He opened his eyes. He was imagining Casey's fear at being led through a maze of backstreets and alleys . . . He should never have let Jeff talk him into the scheme.

'Let's go,' Jeff said.

They left the building, Jeff leading them through a front door this time and across the street. One tech accompanied them while the second went for the car. They passed the library and turned down Union Street towards the junction with Pascoe. They were in a commercial district. Many of the tall buildings around here were clad with holo-façades bearing colossal company logos and advertisements.

As they walked, Jeff looked at Halliday. 'Hey, chill out, Hal. It's going okay. We're gonna nail this bastard any minute now.'

They turned down Pascoe and approached the International Commercial Bank. Halliday experienced a strange kind of relief merely at being on the move, at the simple fact of getting physically closer to Casey.

Jeff spoke into the com. 'Report, Rodriguez.'

'I'm following along the path of the waterway. Some of it's open, with buildings on either side, other stretches are covered by bridges, roads and whatever. I can't see our man and the girl. I'm taking it easy.'

Halliday was aware that his pace had increased. They came to the mouth of the alley and turned. They passed down an enclosed passage, their footsteps ringing.

A second later the tech came to a halt and stared at the screen of his monitor. 'They've stopped – they aren't moving, sir.'

Jeff spoke into his communicator, 'Rodriguez! Our man has halted, do you read?'

'Check, sir. Can you give me a reading?'

Jeff looked at the tech.

'They're four hundred and fifty metres from the spiral staircase,' the tech reported.

Jeff relayed this to Rodriguez.

'Check,' Rodriguez said. 'I'm about three-fifty metres from the staircase now, and proceeding with care. There's a bridge ahead. I guess they've stopped on the other side . . .'

Halliday looked at Jeff, heart hammering. It came to him, with a sudden, sickening realisation, that it was Casey who had stopped. She had refused to go on, was arguing . . . He wondered how Big Ed might react to that.

'Why the hell have they stopped, Jeff? It doesn't make sense.'

'I don't know. Maybe he knows he's been followed. Rodriguez!' Jeff shouted into his communicator. 'Take it easy, okay? Our man might know you're onto him.'

'Pretty sure he doesn't, sir. No sweat, I'm taking it real slow.'

Halliday looked at the tech. 'Still no movement?'

'Not a twitch.'

Jeff led the way down the darkened alley. They came to a

269

concrete staircase and wound their way down to the stinking, scum-laced surface of the waterway. They hurried along the narrow path in single file, their way illuminated by the weak light filtering down between the high buildings on either side.

Rodriguez's voice sounded in his ear, and Halliday stopped.

It was this moment he had been dreading all along. Now that it had happened, had gone horribly wrong, it seemed to conform to some terrible inevitability they should have foreseen and prevented.

'Jesus Christ . . .' Rodriguez said, the voice soft, urgent, in Halliday's ear.

'What!' Halliday said. 'What the hell's happening?'

'Rodriguez!' Jeff shouted.

'I've found the tracking device, sir. It's on the path, along with her clothes. Christ . . .'

Halliday set off. He sprinted along the path, losing his footing more than once, almost slipping into the waterway. Ahead, he made out the shape of the plainclothes cop, kneeling on the path.

He came to a halt, panting. He was aware of the arrival of Jeff and the tech, behind him. He stared at the torn T-shirt on the path, the discarded shorts, the ripped remains of the filigree tracking device. Further along the pathway was her left runner, sole up. The other floated like a miniature boat on the surface of the water.

Pain filled his chest, a choking ache. He wanted to scream, to accuse.

Then he saw the sock, so tiny and bright against the dark stone of the path, and the thought of Casey, naked but for one sock, for some strange reason struck him with remorse and brought acid tears to his eyes

Rodriguez reached out for something.

'What is it?' Jeff said.

Rodriguez picked up a soiled pad of gauze, gingerly took a sniff. 'Christ . . . Chloroform.'

Halliday turned on Jeff. 'We should never have done it, Jeff! For chrissake!'

Another voice sounded in his ear. The second tech, back in the car. 'I have a signal! They've moving along the waterway at speed, heading towards the bay.'

'Jesus,' Halliday said. 'The other sock! The monitor's in the other sock!'

'They're on some kind of boat,' Jeff was saying. 'Let's get back to the car.'

Halliday found himself, with an involuntary action that later surprised him, picking up Casey's discarded T-shirt, shorts and the single red sock. He followed Jeff, Rodriguez and the tech as they ran back along the waterway and clattered up the spiral staircase.

The car was waiting for them at the end of the alley.

Halliday climbed in the back, Jeff in front beside the second tech. 'Follow 80th as far as 5th, then turn south. The waterway comes out somewhere by Fort Hamilton park.'

The tech gunned the engine, accelerated along Pascoe. Halliday watched the passing buildings, the occasional pedestrian, in a confused daze. He realised that he was clutching Casey's old T-shirt, tight.

He recalled something, some detail that had come to him when Rodriguez had first mentioned the waterway. He had lost it, then, with the discovery of Casey's clothes . . . But it came back to him now.

'The waterway, Jeff. A boat!'

Jeff screwed round in his seat and stared at him.

'Listen Jeff. Big Ed, or X, or whoever the hell he is – he took Canada through the Liberty Arboretum and disappeared.'

'I don't see—'

'There was a jetty beyond the dome. He had a boat waiting. He took her somewhere aboard a boat.'

And he thought he knew just where . . .

Jeff took the monitor from the second tech and peered at

271

the screen. 'They're moving fast. Almost reached the Park. Let's move it!'

They accelerated along 5th. Ahead, the flat expanse of the scrubby park came into sight. They screeched to a halt and piled out. Halliday sprinted across a stretch of threadbare greensward to a line of railings and leaned over, staring down to where the mouth of the waterway merged with the greasy swell of the channel between Brooklyn and Staten Island.

Seconds later a small motorboat emerged in a flash of silver and raced away, bouncing, beneath the toll bridge and out across Gravesend Bay. In that second Halliday tried to make out figures through the tiny portholes of the covered cabin, eager for just one glimpse of Casey.

The motorboat diminished rapidly across the dark waters of the bay, heading out to sea.

Jeff was speaking into his com. He turned to Halliday. 'The techs have still got the trace, Hal. The bastard won't get far.'

Halliday saw something fly from the mouth of the waterway at speed. He gripped the rail, staring. The drone was one of the latest designs, a sleek manta ray, faster than the regular patrol models. It chased the motorboat across the choppy water, a second drone following close behind.

As he watched, Halliday saw someone emerge from the cabin of the boat. He heard the muffled sound of gunfire, and a second later the first drone exploded in a spectacular burst of flame and metal cladding.

The figure fired again, winging the second drone. It careered crazily through the air, finally lost the fight to remain airborne and plunged towards the sea. It skipped three times across the water before sinking beneath the waves.

The boat sped away, vanishing towards the horizon.

Jeff's com buzzed.

He spoke into the mouthpiece, listened intently. 'That's good. Well done. We could use some good news.'

He clapped Halliday on the shoulder. 'The techs have

plotted the course of the boat, Hal. It can only be heading one place . . .'

Halliday waited, already knowing what Jeff was about to tell him.

'It's making for Laputa Island,' he said.

'Mantoni's island,' Halliday said in little more than a whisper.

Jeff walked away, speaking hurriedly into his com.

Halliday watched the motorboat until it disappeared from sight. A part of him wanted to follow the boat to the island immediately; another, more rational part of him knew the absolute futility of that course of action.

Mantoni was a master of holographic illusion. It would be almost impossible to locate Casey on Laputa, just as it would be impossible to discover the precise whereabouts of Sergio Mantoni.

He felt despair welling within him, and the bitter taste of . . . not defeat, he told himself. He was not defeated, yet. He would go over to the island at some point soon, and he would do his best to bring Casey back, find out what had happened to Canada. The bitter taste he experienced was the knowledge that the odds were stacked against him, that the chances of succeeding were diminishingly slight.

He thought of Sanchez, the vracker who visited him the other day. Perhaps if he contacted Sanchez, persuaded him to hack into the Mantoni core . . . Was it possible that they might happen upon details of the island, plans of Laputa's vast interior? Perhaps, Halliday thought, Sanchez might be able to access and close down Mantoni's holographic projections . . .

It was a long shot. He'd see what Sanchez thought.

Jeff returned. 'I got through to Deputy Commissioner Rankin,' he said. 'I briefed him on everything that's happened. I told him that we suspect Casey, maybe even Canada, is being held on the island.'

'What did he say?'

Jeff hesitated, unable to bring himself to look Halliday in the eye. 'He said he'd pass the information on to Commissioner Reynolds.'

'I thought he might.'

Jeff laid a hand on his shoulder. 'C'mon, Hal. I'll drive you back to the office.'

'Not the office. Can you drop me in Chinatown?'

'Sure thing. Chinatown it is.'

Halliday followed Jeff to the car and they crossed Brooklyn Bridge to Manhattan. He was silent, thinking ahead. They reached Chinatown and Jeff came to a halt on Canal Street, busy with pedestrians. 'Hal, we'll get Casey back, okay?'

'Sure we will, Jeff. I'll be in touch.'

He stuffed Casey's discarded clothing into the pockets of his jacket, climbed from the car and headed towards the address Sanchez had given him the other day. The apartment was situated above a busy Chinese restaurant, and the only entrance was by way of a back alley lined with overflowing trash cans and containers of discarded, rotting vegetables.

He came to a fire escape which gave access to the apartment he was looking for, and looked up as someone emerged from a door on the second floor. The guy hurried down the escape, a big Latino in a black leather jacket and green chinos. At the bottom he passed Halliday with a quick glance and hurried along the alley towards the main street. Something about the guy's attitude, his haste as he left the apartment, alerted Halliday.

He hurried up the fire escape. The door to the vracker's apartment was open, and an oddly familiar smell leaked out. It was a second before he recognised it: the astringent, chemical reek of VR jelly.

He pushed the door open further, and a sluggish tongue of gel oozed over the threshold. He stared into the cramped room, through a haze of smoke. A jellytank had stood in one corner, shattered now, its gel spilled and covering the floor. Banks of computer consoles and terminals lay smashed and gutted in the goo; the fusion of shorted electrics and burning gel created a sharp, adenoid-pinching stench.

'Sanchez?' he called, knowing he was wasting his time.

He stepped through the gel, into the room, and looked around the tiny, darkened apartment. There was no sign of Sanchez.

Coughing at the stench, he emerged into the fresh air and made his way down the escape. As he turned on the steps, he saw something ten metres further along the narrow alley.

He hurried down the rest of the steps and ran towards a stand of overflowing trash cans. He slowed as he saw that he had not been mistaken. The legs protruding from behind the piled rubbish belonged to the vracker, Sanchez.

Halliday knelt, reached out and removed a greasy take-out tray that covered the guy's face.

His expression was serene, seemingly untroubled. Halliday wondered if he had been aware of his impending death. Judging by the laser wound that had severed his jugular and sliced down and through his upper chest, he must have died instantaneously .

Halliday looked away, remained kneeling for a few seconds, then stood and made his way towards Canal Street and the subway station.

Twenty-One

Halliday woke late that night.

He lay on his back, still fully clothed, and blinked up at the cracked ceiling. For a fraction of a second he was blissfully empty-headed. Then, with sickening speed, the memory of Casey's abduction rushed in to fill the void.

He had known that he should never have given in to Jeff's demand that they use Casey as the lure. Risking her had been nothing but a damn fool gamble. His regret had nothing to do with wisdom after the event . . . Christ, he could have used a bit of wisdom before the event, this time.

The image of Sanchez, lying dead in the alley, rose in his mind's eye like something from a particularly gratuitous holo-drama. He recalled the nervous, geeky kid in his office mere days ago and wondered if his death was related to what he'd overheard in VR.

The bedside angle-poise threw the room into blessed shadow. He could smell Casey's body odour on the sheets, the cocktail of sweat and old, cheap perfume. Beside the bed was a pile of her discarded underwear and T-shirts, and next to it the few possessions she had garnered while living here: a stack of comics, a plastic watch she never wore, a holo-cube of some famous VR star.

If anything happened to her, he thought, the only physical evidence that she had ever existed would reside in this pathetic pile of old clothes and cheap trash. Sixteen years, a hell of a short life. There was something fatalistic about the fact that all her travails and troubles so far should lead her to a brutal and meaningless end.

She would live in his memory, of course – whatever good that would do her – before fading as memories tended to do. Christ, it was only six months since Barney had died, and sometimes Halliday had trouble recalling his face. In a year or so from now, he wondered, would Casey exist only as a fleeting recollection?

He considered her life and energy, her cutting humour. He told himself that he'd remember her.

He sat up suddenly, massaging his eyes and telling himself that he was being needlessly pessimistic. There was time yet, hope . . .

On top of her piled possessions was a pix of Casey and her sister. They were sitting on the stoop of an ancient, tumble-down weatherboard house. He picked up the picture and stared at it for what seemed like a long time.

The screen in the office chimed. He pushed himself from the bed and trailed through to the next room, still holding the pix. He slumped in the swivel chair and touched the screen. Jeff Simmons' face flared, then distorted, before settling. He looked out, unsmiling.

Halliday massaged his eyes. 'Jeff, any news?'

'I've been talking to Commissioner Reynolds.'

'And?' Halliday sat back, interpreting Jeff's brief silence. He knew what was coming.

Jeff shook his head. 'I talked him through the case, the evidence we've compiled. I requested a warrant for a squad of men to go over and search the island.'

'Let me guess. He turned it down, right?'

'He questioned whether we could definitely implicate Mantoni. I told him we monitored the boat right to the island. He said that wasn't evidence enough.'

'What more evidence does the bastard want?'

'I told him we needed to search the island, even if only to eliminate Mantoni from our enquiries.'

'What did he say?'

'He said he'd contact Mantoni. He got back to me about ten minutes ago. Mantoni told him the claims are preposterous.

He invited Reynolds over to the island to take a look for himself.'

'But Reynolds and Mantoni are best buddies!'

'Yeah, yeah. Tell me about it. You know what Reynolds said when Mantoni invited him?'

'I can guess.'

'I get the impression Reynolds didn't want to embarrass a friend. He said he'd send a cop over to question Mantoni's staff about any possible sighting of a silver motorboat.'

'That's great, Jeff. That's really great. We've got Casey somewhere over there on the island, and Reynolds doesn't want to embarrass a friend! You know what's gonna happen: lone cop goes over, pokes about, then goes back to Reynolds and reports a clean island. End of story.'

Jeff was quiet for a time. 'So what do we do?'

'I know what I'm doing, but I don't think you'll like it.'

'Go on.'

Halliday hesitated. What the hell had he to lose? 'I'm going over to the island to get Casey back. If that means shooting Mantoni in the process, that's fine by me.'

'You can't go alone—'

'You volunteering?'

Jeff licked his lips, looked around his office. He leaned towards the screen. 'Not in my official capacity as a cop.'

Halliday shrugged. 'Either way, you'll be implicated if Mantoni survives.'

'If he doesn't, I was never on the island, okay?'

Halliday nodded. 'Deal.' He paused. 'This is gonna be no chicken shoot, Jeff. The bastard won't just let us walk onto his island like tourists. He's got a complex array of holographs at his disposal. He'll be damned hard to find.'

'How are we gonna handle it?'

'There's two ways we can do this. We go in nice and polite and make enquiries, and get nowhere—'

'Or we go in on the quiet, see what we can see.'

Halliday nodded. 'We could always go in separately – you the Mr Nice Guy, "sorry to bother you, just following up a

278

line of enquiry . . ." while I go in on the blindside, if there is a blindside.'

'That sounds favourite. When are we going?'

'Give me an hour, two, okay? I need to make plans, contact someone with a boat. I'll be in touch.'

Simmons nodded and cut the connection.

Halliday sat and stared at the blank screen. The reaction from Reynolds was expected; Jeff's loyalty not so, but damned welcome. If they got to the island in darkness, scouted about before sunrise . . . Then he remembered something Mantoni's PA had told him: it was always daylight on Laputa. So, they'd arrive in the dead of night and the sun would be shining, and they'd just have to make a daylight search.

He wondered if Mantoni would resort to shooting dead a cop and a private eye. Halliday smiled to himself. If it was to protect whatever it was he was doing on the island, then Mantoni would shoot anyone.

He unlocked the bottom drawer of his desk and pulled out a pair of heavy, mean-looking automatics.

The thought of actively doing something to get Casey and Canada back served to give him hope, banish the mood of despair he'd woken with.

He was moving to the bedroom, meaning to freshen himself with a cold water wash, when his com chimed. He returned to the office and picked it up from the desk.

Vanessa stared out from the tiny screen. He just hoped she wouldn't ask if he'd managed to locate Canada.

'Hal, how's it going?'

'Fine. Okay.' The sight of her face filled Halliday with the sudden desire to be with the VR star. He wondered where she was and peered, trying to make out the background. Some bar, by the look of it.

She saw his expression. 'I needed to get out, Hal. I wanted a drink. The past few days . . . it's getting to me.'

'I wish you'd wear the chu, Vanessa."

' 'Sokay.' She gestured. 'I . . . I've been careful.'

279

She was slurring her words. Halliday peered. 'Are you drunk?'

'That's what I was calling about. I changed hotels today, Hal – this morning. Thing is . . .' All of a sudden she looked pathetic, a lost child. 'Thing is, I can't remember which one, Hal.'

He thought. Yesterday she had told him the name of the hotel she had planned to move to. 'The Carlyle, off Madison. Vanessa, get your chu working and get back to the Carlyle, okay? I'll see you later.'

'The Carlyle.' She nodded, smiling. 'Thanks, Hal.'

She cut the connection.

Halliday sighed and regarded the automatics on the desk. This time tomorrow, the case could be wrapped up. Mantoni dead, no longer a threat to Vanessa, and Casey safely back here where she belonged; and as for Canada . . . He tried not to dwell on what might have happened to her.

He moved to the bedroom and ran the cold water, dousing his face and feeling suddenly refreshed. As he towelled himself dry he went through what he had to do before making his way to the island. He had a contact who knew people with a boat. He'd arrange to meet them at Battery Park, along with Jeff Simmons. He had protective armour somewhere, his own jacket and one that had belonged to Barney. He'd take it along for Jeff, just in case.

He really should call Vanessa back and explain what he had planned, just in case it didn't work out. The thought was appalling, but he had to think of every possibility. If he didn't return from the island, then Vanessa should leave New York, preferably the country . . . He'd give her ten, fifteen minutes to get back to the hotel and then call her.

He stepped into the office and sat behind his desk. He picked up one of the automatics and dismantled it, polishing its barrel and stock with an oil-streaked chamois. He reassembled it and laid it aside, then repeated the process with the second automatic. The slow, repetitive routine was therapeutic, helping to concentrate his mind on the task ahead. He finished cleaning and snapping together the second weapon, then arranged a row of spare cartridges on the desk-top. The guns were heavy – he'd need his old pilot's jacket, specially adapted to carry them. He fetched it from the bedroom and slipped it on, and then inserted the guns into the slings. The charges followed, sliding into a bandoleer stitched up the inside flap of the jacket.

He sat back, picked up his com and tapped in Vanessa's code.

She was a long time answering.

She appeared at last, her hair wet, the noise of a shower in the background.

'Sorry, Hal. Just taking a shower. Good to see you.'

He smiled. 'You made it back quick. Sobered up?'

She blinked at him, fingering a strand of wet hair from her forehead. 'Excuse me?'

'I said, have you sobered up?'

She laughed and shook her head. 'What are you talking about, Hal? I haven't had a drink for over a day.'

His heart felt as though it had suddenly stopped. 'You didn't call me about fifteen minutes ago?'

She stared at him. 'No. Of course not. I've been in the shower—' Her half-amused expression changed to alarm. 'Hal, what is it?'

'Christ. Oh, Christ.' He tried to gather his thoughts. 'Where are you?'

'The Carlyle. I told you yesterday. The penthouse suite.'

'Listen to me. Get dressed and use the chu. Leave the hotel and meet me on the corner of Madison and 34th, okay?'

She nodded 'What's happening?'

'Nothing. It's okay. Just get out now, okay? I'll be over straight away.'

'Hal, I wish you'd tell me—'

'Hurry up!' Something in his tone alarmed her. She nodded and cut the connection

He ran to the door and hurried down the stairs, the automatics heavy beneath his jacket. He told himself that there was no way he could have known, no way he could have foreseen that Mantoni would use someone in a chu . . . It had been perfectly plausible. Why shouldn't Vanessa go out for a drink, to relieve the stress, and forget the name of her hotel?

Perhaps if he'd been fully awake, or less strung out with the events of the day . . .

He jumped into the Ford and revved it away from the kerb, u-turning in spectacular fashion and accelerating along the street. Ten minutes to reach the Carlyle, he estimated. If Vanessa had shifted herself, she would be waiting for him. If, that was, she'd managed to get out in time . . . Mantoni would have had his man already in the city when he made the bogus call. Right now some hired killer might be in the Carlyle, stalking Vanessa.

He was presuming, of course, that Mantoni had hired a hit-man, a killer. But what if he had no intention of killing her? What if this was merely another episode of his vendetta against his daughter? Rather than killing Vanessa Artois, perhaps he was planning to kidnap her?

The thought was almost as frightening.

He calmed himself with the thought that Mantoni's hench-man would be looking for Artois, and Vanessa would have booked in under an assumed identity – and she'd be wearing the chu.

It all depended, he realised, on the tactics employed by Mantoni's man. He could hardly ask for the room numbers of all the single women in the hotel, or barge into every room in search of someone who just might be the VR star. So he'd either go straight to the security room, disable the guards, or . . . Halliday felt his stomach lurch. If the bastard was clever, he might make an educated guess that someone of Vanessa Artois' background would rent the penthouse. It'd be the first place he'd check.

If, that was, the guy reached the hotel before Halliday.

Of course, if Vanessa moved it and got herself out of the damned place fast, then they were home free.

One hand gripping the wheel, he reached inside his jacket, pulled out an automatic and clicked off the safety catch. He tried not to look too far ahead, to fill his mind with plans that might prove unnecessary. He'd take the situation as he found it, make second by second assessments and trust his luck and instinct.

He approached the corner of Madison and 34th and slowed, looking for Vanessa on the sidewalk. An icy sweat gripped him. There was no sign of her on the corner, or on any of the other corners. He looked along the street – no sign of her there, either. Halliday braked the Ford outside the Carlyle and leapt out. He was about to run into the hotel when he saw the silver Cadillac parked further along the street. It was not the car that he noticed so much as its driver. She sat with her head laid back against the rest, her eyes closed. She wore the red uniform of Mantoni's staff.

Mantoni's PA, Stephanie . . .

Dread clutched at his stomach. So Mantoni – or whoever – was already here

He sprinted up the steps and into the hotel. The lobby was deserted this late at night. There was no one at reception. He looked behind the desk. A woman stared up at him from the floor, arms and legs bound tight, her mouth gagged.

Halliday knelt and ripped away the gag. 'Where the hell did he go?'

The woman was too shocked to speak coherently. 'In— in . . .'

'In security? Through there?'

She nodded, wide-eyed in fright.

Halliday took off. He pushed through a swing door and found himself in a long corridor. The third door on the right was obligingly marked Security. He kicked it open, automatic drawn and levelled. A security guard lay on the floor, dead, blood from a head wound pooling on the carpet.

He ran back down the corridor and into the lobby, he crossed to the elevators and scanned the lighted panel above the first set of sliding doors. The lift was not in use. He pressed the open command and looked around the lobby. As the doors sighed open, he grabbed a chair and laid it on the threshold, effectively stopping the doors from shutting and disabling the elevator. He moved to the second elevator and punched the controls.

Long seconds later the doors sighed open and Halliday stepped inside.

He drew the second automatic and, one in each hand, watched the doors slide shut and the lighted indicator rise slowly from floor to floor.

He arrived at the top floor and the doors opened. He was in a short corridor, a pair of gold-painted double doors to his right. He sprinted to the doors and turned the handle. Locked . . . He tried to think. Would Vanessa have bothered to lock the doors while making a rapid exit?

He stood back, aimed, and destroyed the lock with a short blast, then kicked open the door. He ran into the room, found the bedroom with Vanessa's case open on the bed. He checked every room, sure now that he'd find her, dead. He didn't know whether to feel relieved when he found nothing. He went through the rooms again, in case Mantoni or his henchman had concealed the body.

He returned to the bedroom, and only then saw the key-card on top of the suitcase. Jesus Christ . . . The doors had been locked from the inside.

The movement of the curtain spun him around, automatics ready. The lace curtain billowed in the breeze. He ran to the window and dashed the curtain aside. The window was open, giving access to the fire escape.

So Mantoni, or whoever, had taken Vanessa. At least, he reasoned, it gave him a chance.

He climbed through the window and ran down the fire escape, jumping the steps and swinging himself around the turns. He came to a narrow alley, dark and midnight-silent.

He remembered the car. The silver Cadillac. He ran down the alley, calculating his chances of reaching the car in front of the hotel before it departed.

He had almost gained the corner when he heard the scream. It came from behind him, way along the alley past the fire escape. He heard it again, a women's strident, terrified cry. He turned and ran. Ahead, in the darkness, he made out two figures writhing on the ground – the struggle illuminated by the pastel flicker of a malfunctioning chu as it phased through a manic sequence of facial options.

In the faint light he made out the form of a man, restraining Vanessa. Halliday aimed and fired, clipping the assailant's shoulder and spinning him away along the alley. Vanessa crawled towards the wall on her hands and knees, gagging. As the man climbed to his feet, Halliday fired again and missed. A return laser shot caught him by surprise, as if he'd expected no resistance. The cobalt lance missed him by centimetres, the heat passing like a fireball over his head.

He fired again. He thought he heard a cry, indicating that he'd scored a hit. The man slumped into a sitting position against the wall, staring at Halliday as he attempted to lift his weapon.

Halliday fired, instinctively, and six bullets tore into the guy's chest. He stepped forward, staring at the dying man: it was the Latino he'd seen leaving the vracker's apartment yesterday, the bastard who'd killed Sanchez.

He ran back to Vanessa and pulled her to her feet. She clung to him, sobbing. Her face strobed with a myriad identities.

'You okay?'

'Fine. I'm fine. I . . . I thought he was going to kill me.' She took a long, juddering breath. 'I managed to trip him. Thank God you turned up.'

'We've got to get out of here. Follow me.'

She tore off the malfunctioning chu and became Vanessa Artois once more.

Halliday was already running, gripping Vanessa's hand and pulling her along after him. They reached the end of the alley and ran around the corner, Halliday ignoring the glances of passers-by.

They reached the Cadillac and Halliday pulled open the passenger door. The woman behind the wheel turned suddenly, alarmed.

He jumped in, covering the woman with his automatic. Vanessa climbed into the back and slammed the door.

'Drive!' Halliday ordered. 'To the marina. There's a launch waiting, right?'

The woman nodded, too frightened to speak.

'Okay, let's get there.'

Shaken, the woman obeyed. She pulled the car from the kerb and accelerated. They headed downtown, towards Battery Park.

Vanessa leaned forwards between the front seats. 'Would you mind telling me what's going on, Hal?'

'Mantoni's got Casey,' he told her. 'He took her yesterday,'

'Mantoni?' Vanessa said. 'How—?'

'We think he's also holding Canada.' He saw the look of startled hope on her features, then turned to the woman. 'Have you seen a young kid on the island with Mantoni, slim, dark, about fifteen?'

The woman thought about it. 'Four or five days ago . . . there was someone. I thought she was older than that. She was there of her own free will, Mr Mantoni's guest. What's happening?'

Halliday ignored the question. 'Who else is on the island, besides Mantoni? What about staff, bodyguards?'

'When there's no party scheduled, the island's deserted. Mr Mantoni lives there alone.'

Vanessa reached through the gap in the seats and took Halliday's hand.

He pulled out his com and got through to Jeff Simmons. 'Jeff, there's been developments. Can you meet me at the Battery Park marina as soon as possible?'

'I'll be there, Hal. What's going on?'

'We're on our way to the island. Apparently, Mantoni's alone there.'

Jeff nodded. 'That's what I like to hear. See you in five minutes.' He cut the connection.

Minutes later they arrived at Battery Park. The woman braked beside the quay. Mantoni's launch rose and fell on the light swell, its neon lights bright in the darkness. Halliday climbed out, closely followed by Stephanie and Vanessa.

A car engine sounded in the darkness. Halliday turned, almost expecting one of Mantoni's hired hit-men to appear, laser blazing. A taxi drew up and Jeff Simmons joined them.

'Good to see you, Jeff,' Halliday said. 'Let's get going.'

They hurried down the quay and boarded the launch. Halliday moved to the cabin. The pilot, a young guy in the red uniform of Mantoni Entertainment, looked up from a soft-screen, startled, as Halliday appeared in the doorway brandishing his automatic.

'Where's the radio?'

The pilot pointed to a two-way set mounted beside the wheel. Halliday ripped it from its moorings and tossed it over the gunwale. He turned to the pilot. 'You armed?'

The guy shook his head, staring at the automatic as if mesmerised.

Halliday frisked him, found nothing. 'Okay, let's get moving. Laputa, and step on it.'

He returned to the deck as the launch powered up and eased from the quay. He took Vanessa's hand in his, leaning against the gunwale and staring ahead to where the island of Laputa would eventually appear. Jeff Simmons joined them. Mantoni's PA, Stephanie, stood beside the stern, staring back at Manhattan as the lights receded.

Jeff looked at him. 'You still planning to nail the bastard?'

Halliday nodded. 'He's not going to get out of this alive, Jeff. He's more powerful than you imagine. He'd get himself off whatever charges we brought against him, despite the evidence.'

'All we have to do now,' Jeff said, staring out across the water, 'is find him.'

Vanessa gripped Halliday's arm. 'Hal, why do you think Mantoni took Canada?'

He shook his head. 'To frighten you? It makes sense.' He tried a reassuring smile. 'Don't worry. We'll get her back.'

Vanessa nodded, matching his smile with a brave version of her own.

Twenty minutes later Laputa appeared in the darkness, and Jeff Simmons whistled in amazement. The sunlit island rose from the darkened sea like an optical illusion. 'Some place,' Jeff said.

'You haven't seen the half of it. The island's hollow. Inside it's a series of holographic chambers. Mantoni's personal kingdom.'

The launch throttled back and edged towards the jetty. Halliday passed one of the automatics to Jeff and levelled the other, scanning the jetty and the island above for any sign of life.

Twenty-Two

Sergio Mantoni stood on the edge of his island and stared across the sea to the distant, glowing filament of Manhattan. Pablo had set out one hour ago, and he should have called by now with confirmation of his successful bid to apprehend Vanessa Artois. With both Artois and the kid, Casey, held on Laputa, Mantoni would be assured of luring Halliday.

He considered what he might do if Pablo failed with Artois. If this happened, then he would contact the detective, tell him that Casey was fit and well and awaiting him on the island. He would have to go through with the show without Artois present to witness the final act.

He told himself he was being needlessly pessimistic. Pablo would produce the goods, as he always had in the past. The show would go on.

He felt frustrated that he could not call Pablo and find out what the hell was going on. In anticipation of his arrival, Mantoni turned and strode up the greensward towards the villa.

For the past few hours, ever since finalising his destiny in his mind, he had felt detached from reality, as if he were existing at one remove from the world around him. The fact of the physical no longer governed his thoughts or actions; it was as if he had been set free from the shackles of experience, of all apprehension of what the future might hold. He knew what would come to pass in the immediate future – the only series of events that now concerned him – and this knowledge gave him for the first time in so many years a deep and abiding sense of peace.

He moved through the villa to the bedroom and unlocked the door.

Canada Artois lay on the bed, dressed in the same blue jeans and white blouse in which she had arrived on the island five days ago. She was sleeping peacefully, the youthful glow of her cheeks suggesting that her extended VR experience might never have happened.

He drew up a chair and sat beside her. 'Canada . . .' He reached out and took her hand, and recalled holding her small, warm hand in the Civic Theatre VR site, when she had been in the persona of his lover, Bo.

'Canada, wake up.'

She stirred. She woke slowly, blinking up at the ceiling, and finally turning her head to look at him.

A slight smile played around her lips. 'Hi,' she murmured. 'Who're you?'

'Who do you think, kitten? How're you feeling?'

She gave a small laugh. 'Is it really you, Ed?'

'It's really me, kitten.'

'You look different in the real world.'

'How're you feeling?'

She pushed herself into a sitting position, then leaned back against the banked pillows. 'Okay, I suppose. A little tired, but okay. How long was I in there for?'

'Two days, real-world time.'

'Seemed like about a week to me!' Her expression clouded. 'Hey, what you did in there . . . at that theatre place. What was all that about?'

'As I told you, it was a re-enactment. We had to stage the incident for the benefit of police investigations—'

'But I thought they caught the guy who killed the actress . . .'

He nodded. 'They did. But they wanted it restaged for reasons of security.'

She shook her head, as if puzzled by the whole idea, but didn't argue. She looked at him. 'You could have told me what was going on, Ed,' she said. 'I mean, the shock when that maniac fired—'

He squeezed her hand. 'We needed it to be spontaneous, kitten,' he said. 'I'm sorry if it frightened you.'

She smiled. 'Guess I'm okay. I survived, didn't I?'

He raised her hand and kissed her fingers. 'I want to show you something, Canada. You up to walking?'

'Sure. I'm fine.' She sat up and swung her legs off the bed. He had to assist her as she stood, weak after so long in the tank. He walked her from the bedroom and down the hall.

'Where we going?'

'Shh, you'll see.'

They stepped into the elevator and Mantoni slipped an arm around the girl's shoulders as they dropped into the heart of the island. The doors parted to reveal a plush corridor. He eased her from the elevator and along the corridor, into a spacious auditorium. They paused on the threshold.

She gasped, as if in wonder. 'Where are we? Why are all the people—?'

'Holograms,' he explained. 'We're in the holo-chamber in the island. Come, I'll show you.'

He walked her into the reconstructed Civic, through the stilled mêlée of a hundred frozen guests. Canada paused from time to time, staring at the statue-like forms of the men and women.

'They look so real!' she said.

They moved towards the stage, passing the table where, twenty-five years ago, he and Bo Ventura had awaited the outcome of the awards announcement.

The holographic image of the VR star, Bo Ventura, sat on the edge of her chair, her smile frozen, pearly teeth and glowing skin caught in vital perpetuity.

He looked away and assisted Canada up the steps of the stage. They crossed towards a dais, and an armchair situated beyond it. He gestured Canada to sit down, and she obeyed.

A small table stood beside the armchair, and on it were a bottle of wine and two glasses. As Canada curled up in the chair and gazed around her at the auditorium, he poured the wine and passed her a glass.

'So what now, Ed?' she asked. He could see the first glimmer of uncertainty, maybe even apprehension, in her eyes.

She took a long drink of wine and Mantoni smiled.

He knelt before the chair and took her hand. 'Twenty-five years ago,' he said, 'I was engaged to Bo Ventura. We planned to marry—'

'Bo Ventura? But wasn't she the actress—?'

He smiled. 'I could have prevented the shooting, if only I'd acted a little quicker. I saw the gunman, but it was too late. I could do nothing to stop him.'

She was staring at him, her eyes searching his face.

'You're . . . you're Mantoni. Sergio Mantoni. You and Vanessa . . .'

'I loved Vanessa almost as much as I loved her mother.'

Canada's eyes widened in alarm and surprise. 'Her mother?'

'Bo,' he said.

She shook her head, her lips twisted into a sour expression. 'Bo Ventura was Van's mother?' she said, incredulous.

'And I was her father.'

The girl struggled to move from the armchair, but the effects of the drugged wine hauled her back. She sagged, gasping. She was having difficulty, now, in keeping her eyes open.

He reached out and stroked her hand. 'I wanted my affair with Vanessa to be everything it was with Bo, but that was impossible, of course. They were different people, souls forged by different conditions.'

Her head jerked upright as she tried to keep awake.

He went on, 'When Vanessa walked out . . . it destroyed me, Canada. It was the end of a dream. I truly loved her, but perhaps I was deluding myself, and she was aware of that delusion.'

292

'What do you want with me?' she said, slurring her words.

He brushed her cheeks with the back of his hand. 'Don't worry. I won't harm you. You're safe with me, please believe that.'

She began to cry, her lips forming an exaggerated grimace.

Mantoni's com chimed. He pulled it from his pocket and strode to the far end of the stage. 'Pablo, is that you?'

The tiny screen was in darkness. Peering, he made out the indistinct outline of a head.

'Sergio . . .' It was barely a whisper.

'Pablo, what's happening?'

'I didn't get her, Sergio. The detective, Halliday. He . . . This is the end, Sergio.'

Mantoni saw a smile playing on the shadowy face, as if in acknowledgement of his melodramatic parting shot. Then the screen lost focus as Pablo dropped the com, and Mantoni heard a long groan and a last desperate cry of anguish.

He felt his heart thudding. He cut the connection and considered. Across the stage, in the armchair, Canada Artois was unconscious. He returned to her, knelt and stroked her soft cheek with the back of his hand.

He left the auditorium and rode the elevator to the ground floor of the villa, then stepped outside into the artificial sunlight and walked across the greensward to the edge of the cliff.

The outside world showed as an area of enclosing darkness, with Manhattan on the horizon a symbol of all that he had fled.

Without Pablo he had no hope of accosting Vanessa Artois, so he would be forced to proceed without her. He had wanted her to be present, to watch the final act of the play in which she had taken such a vital part – but that was not to be. Reality had the perverse habit of never delivering the expected conclusion.

He would contact Halliday, tell him that he had Canada Artois and the kid on the island, and then wait for the detective to make his move.

He was pulling the com from his pocket when he saw the launch appear through the darkness, perhaps a hundred metres from the jetty.

As the vessel approached, he made out a number of figures on the deck. He recognised the tall shape of Vanessa Artois and beside her the stockier form of Halliday. They were accompanied by another man, and Stephanie.

Mantoni felt elation course through him like expensive champagne. Perhaps, after all, he would have the finale he so desired.

He hurried from the cliff-top and entered the villa.

He took the elevator to the basement. Next to his VR room, where Canada had spent the past two days in the tank, was a smaller room. He unlocked the door, bracing himself for an attack.

It never came. The girl cowered in the corner, curled in a protective foetal ball. She was dressed in the oversized trousers and shirt he had found for her yesterday, when Pablo brought her to the island.

She stared at him with tear-filled eyes. 'What do you want?'

He paused in the doorway, aware of her pain, her fright. He shook his head. 'It's okay. You're safe. Halliday's on his way.'

She stared at him, as if unwilling to believe what he was saying.

He reached out a hand. 'Come, follow me. I'll show you.'

He moved from the door, leaving it open, and seconds later she appeared timorously on the threshold.

He coaxed her into the elevator, for all the world like a frightened animal. As they rode to the ground floor, she pressed herself into the panel, as far from him as she could get, and stared at him with fearful, accusing eyes.

He stepped from the lift and walked through the hall and out of the villa. He paused on the steps, and seconds later the kid appeared, blinking in the sunlight.

'Where is he?'

Mantoni pointed across the greensward to the steps that led down the cliff-face. 'He'll be here in a matter of minutes.'

She moved away from him, fearful. 'I can go?'

He smiled. 'Tell Halliday that I'll meet him in the chamber,' he said. 'He knows where I mean. And tell him to bring Vanessa along too, okay?'

She nodded, then slowly backed away, as if fearful to turn lest he should shoot her in the back.

At last she turned and fled across the greensward, and her headlong flight to freedom filled Mantoni with a foretaste of his own imminent liberation.

He watched her go, then made his way to the elevator, and the finale in the reconstruction of the Civic Theatre.

Twenty-Three

As the launch edged sidewise towards the jetty wall, Halliday gripped his automatic and scanned Laputa Island. The jetty and the cliff-face were bathed in the harsh magnesium glare of floodlights. Above, the island shone with artificial sunlight like some improbable surrealist improvisation.

Jeff climbed over the gunwale and made the launch fast, and Halliday gestured Stephanie into the wheelhouse with the pilot. 'Stay in there and don't move until we come back.'

He saw a flash of something in her eyes, nascent disobedience. Then her gaze dropped to the automatic in his hand and she nodded. He pulled the cabin door shut behind Stephanie and the pilot, then moved to Vanessa.

She was holding the gunwale against the rise and fall of the swell, the wind blowing a strand of hair across her eyes. 'I want to come with you, Hal. Canada's somewhere on the island.'

'You're staying here. It's too dangerous up there. Christ knows what Mantoni would do if he saw you.'

'But Canada—' There was a note of desperation in her tone.

'There's nothing you can do to get her back that me and Jeff can't,' he said. 'I'm not prepared to have you risking your life. Think about it. Stay here until we come back.'

She glanced at the wheelhouse. 'What about those two—?'

She was interrupted by a cry from Jeff, on the jetty. 'Hal . . . Up there!'

He turned and looked up at where Jeff was pointing with his automatic. A figure had appeared in the cutting where the steps approached the greensward.

He stared, hardly able to bring himself to believe what he was seeing. Even as Casey scrambled down the steps, outfitted like a street urchin in oversized trousers and shirt, he told himself that this was another of Mantoni's tricks. The Casey figure was no more than a hologram, a lie of light designed to undermine his resolve.

Then the girl jumped the last few steps, landed on the jetty and sprinted across to him. The force with which she hit him and hung on, pressing her face to his chest and whimpering in tearful relief, told him that she was no hologram.

He took her head in his hands and examined her, aware of some powerful emotion welling within his chest and making coherent speech impossible.

'He—' she began, stuttering with the after-effects of shock. 'He ler-let me go. Ser-someone on the island. He said he'd meet you in the chamber – you'd know what he mer-meant.'

'Casey, slow down. Was it Mantoni?'

'I don't know. He was tall. Short grey hair.'

'Mantoni,' Jeff said.

'He said he'd meet you in the chamber.' She stopped, then went on, 'He said he wanted Vanessa to come with you, too.'

Vanessa climbed from the launch and hurried over, taking Casey in her arms.

Jeff Simmons scanned the cliff-top, automatic ready. 'What the hell do you think he wants?'

Halliday shook his head. 'Christ knows.' He looked at Jeff. 'Do you really think he'll be in the chamber, or is that a bluff?'

Jeff shrugged. 'Impossible to tell.'

Halliday touched Casey's cheek. 'Did he say anything about Canada? You didn't see her up there?'

She shook her head.

Jeff said, 'We've got to make a move.'

'Mantoni didn't say what he wanted with me and Vanessa?' Halliday asked Casey.

'He just said he wanted to meet you both in the chamber.'

Halliday nodded. 'How do we do this, Jeff?'

The cop considered. 'Okay, we've got to presume he's watching us. Surveillance cameras. He'll know our every move. Even so, if he's alone up there ... we'll have a numerical advantage.'

He recalled what Mantoni's PA, Stephanie, had told him earlier. 'According to the woman, he's alone.'

'So one of us goes in first, followed a minute later by the other. We make for the chamber, play it from there.'

Halliday wished he'd brought the body armour along: he'd been in such a hurry to get out and save Vanessa that he'd clean forgotten it.

'Okay. Let's do that.' He turned to Casey and Vanessa. 'Stay on the jetty and make sure those two don't leave the launch, okay? We'll be back.'

'What if they try anything ... ?'

Halliday glanced at Jeff, who reached into his jacket and produced a small handgun. He passed it to Vanessa. 'If they try to leave the boat, wave this about.'

She took the gun as if it were a poisonous snake. She made to reach for Halliday, stayed the gesture and smiled instead. 'Take care, Hal.'

Tearful, Casey just watched him as he moved to the steps. He climbed quickly, aware of his pulse, the butt of the automatic slick in his grip.

He emerged from darkness into the sunlit greensward as if he had stepped from one world to the next. Behind him, Jeff called out in surprise, shielding his eyes. 'Some place,' he said. 'How do we get to the chamber?'

Halliday gestured. 'Beyond the villa. There's a hollow in the grass. Follow me.'

As he led the way up the sloping greensward, past the whitewashed villa towards the stand of artificial elm at the east end of the island, Halliday could not banish from his mind the idea that they were walking into a trap.

But what, he asked himself, was the alternative?

They paused on the edge of the depression. An air of stillness and calm pervaded the island; nothing moved. After the constant activity of New York, the lifeless hush and serenity of Laputa was disconcerting.

'I'll go first,' Halliday said. 'You simply follow the gravel path. You'll find yourself in the reconstruction of a city street. Then you'll come to a door in the wall, if it's the same as last time.'

The thing was, there was no guarantee that anything within the island would be the same as it was before. Mantoni was the master of illusion: on Laputa, he controlled reality.

'And when we find Mantoni?'

'First, we try to find out if Canada's okay—'

'And then we shoot first and ask questions later?'

Halliday could not help but smile. 'There's nothing I'd like more. But we'll assess the situation. Play it by ear.'

He was about to step onto the gravel path when he made out a movement behind the trunk of one of the nearby elms.

As he watched, disbelieving, Sergio Mantoni stepped out from behind the tree and approached them.

Jeff raised his automatic.

Mantoni halted three metres from Halliday. He was dressed flamboyantly in a white tuxedo, and exuded all the calm confidence and sophistication Halliday recalled from their previous encounters.

'Where is Artois?' Mantoni asked.

'You must take me for a complete fool, Mantoni,' Halliday said. 'If you thought for a second—'

'Oh, let me assure you that I mean her no harm,' Mantoni said. 'No harm at all. I merely want her to witness the final act—'

Jeff interrupted. 'Where's the kid, Mantoni?'

'Canada? She's safe and well. You'll find her, in time.'

'What do you want with us?' Halliday asked. 'What's happening in the chamber?'

Mantoni ignored the question. 'Call Artois on your com,' he ordered. 'Tell her to join us, now.'

'She's staying where she is, Mantoni. If you think I'd risk—'

'If you don't call her,' Mantoni said with impeccable calm, 'then I'll kill Canada.'

Halliday glanced at Jeff, who nodded minimally.

He reached for his com and got through to Vanessa. Her face appeared in the tiny screen, a study in fear. 'Hal? What's happening?'

'We need you up here,' he said.

'Is Canada . . .?' she began. 'Is she okay?'

'We don't know. Mantoni wants you to join us. We've no choice in the matter.'

'I'm on my way.' As she cut the connection, her face fading from the screen, Halliday had the feeling he'd made a terrible mistake.

Before them, Mantoni smiled. 'It wouldn't be the same,' he said, 'if Artois was not on hand to watch the finale.'

'Where's Canada?' Jeff asked. 'What the hell's—?'

Mantoni raised a hand, as if to deflect the question, and Jeff misinterpreted the gesture.

He fired, hosing half a dozen shots into the tycoon's chest.

Halliday told himself that he should have known.

Mantoni remained standing, his white suit umblemished by the hail of bullets, his smile unaffected.

'What—?' Jeff began.

The Mantoni hologram performed a mocking bow. 'When Artois gets here,' he went on, 'make your way down to the chamber. I'll be waiting.'

He disappeared, and suddenly they were alone on the greensward.

Halliday turned and watched as Vanessa, accompanied by Casey, emerged from the steps and hurried towards them.

'We heard the shots,' she said. 'What happened?'

'False alarm,' Jeff said. 'I tried to shoot a hologram.'

Vanessa shook her head. Beside her, Casey gripped her hand, white-faced. 'What does Mantoni want with me?' Vanessa said.

'He talked about some kind of finale,' Halliday said. 'He said he wanted you to watch it. Don't ask me what the hell he was going on about.' He turned towards the gravel path. 'I'm going in. Give me a minute and then follow, okay? Jeff, bring Vanessa and Casey with you.'

What was the alternative, he asked himself, when Mantoni had threatened to kill Canada?

He stepped onto the gravel path and advanced, moving through the surface with every step. His eye-level fell, and seconds later he was looking along the plane of the ground.

The next step took him beneath the gravel path. He walked on, and his eyes adjusted. He looked ahead, along the length of the mean city street, to the wall and the door at its centre.

Slowly he approached and paused before the door. He looked behind him. Ten seconds later he saw the shadowy trio of Jeff, Vanessa and Casey appear, first their legs and then the rest of their bodies. He waved; Jeff raised his automatic in acknowledgement.

Halliday pushed open the door in the wall and peered through.

He blinked in surprise. He had expected to see the rustic scene from the other day, the sunlit fields and forest.

Instead, he was greeted by the interior of some grand building. He saw the stilled holograms of a hundred people, a stage, banked seating . . . and he knew then what this was, or rather what this reconstruction was.

The Civic Theatre – but not the Civic as he recalled it from the other night. There was something dated about this representation, or perhaps it was the fashions of the guests who filled the auditorium, that told him he was witnessing a historical recreation.

Cautiously, automatic ready, he advanced into the area before the stage. He passed the frozen figures of a dozen beautiful men and women, images of the famous and infamous of what might have been twenty-five years ago. They were like ghosts in time, their immaculate physicality preserved in a tableau at once sad and tragic.

A dead, impending silence filled the chamber.

He paused in the centre of the auditorium and gazed ahead. He should have guessed that Mantoni would occupy centre-stage.

The tycoon stood beside a dais in a white tuxedo identical to the one his hologram had worn, his hands slipped casually into his pockets. He smiled down at Halliday, as if with genuine delight that he had made the party at last.

Halliday wondered if this image of the tycoon was, like the first, no more than a hologram.

Only then did he see Canada. She sat slumped in an armchair to Mantoni's left, and it was impossible to tell whether she was unconscious or dead.

'Where's Artois?' Mantoni said.

'Is the girl alive?' Halliday found himself saying. 'You don't think I'd risk Vanessa if you'd already killed the girl?'

A strange expression, part exasperation, part disgust, crossed Mantoni's features. 'She's alive, Halliday. Look.'

Mantoni stepped towards the armchair, reached out and took Canada's chin in his hand. The girl groaned.

Halliday knew, then, that the Mantoni before him was the bona fide, flesh-and-blood tycoon, not the image of some hologram. Even then, even as he was taken by the desire to shoot Mantoni dead, he feared a final twist. Could it be that this was not Mantoni at all, that the real Mantoni was waiting in the wings until he made just such a rash mistake?

He heard a sound behind him and turned.

Jeff Simmons, with Vanessa and Casey cowering behind him, emerged from the mêlée of sophisticated holograms.

Halliday looked back at Mantoni. 'What do you want?' he asked.

Mantoni smiled. 'I'm so pleased you could all make it to my little gathering,' he said.

Vanessa came to Halliday's side and gripped his hand. She gasped when she made out her sister, unconscious in the chair.

302

Jeff moved off to the left, automatic ready. Halliday felt a hand on the small of his back – Casey.

'Vanessa,' Mantoni said, 'it's so good to see you again. I hope you'll forgive the coercion necessary to bring you here. There are some things that require desperate measures. I trust you'll find the following little drama instructive.'

'What do you want?' Jeff called out.

'What do I want?' Mantoni's tone was reflective. 'I suppose I want to show you the degree of my pain, and the lengths I am prepared to go to to assuage that pain.' He looked around the auditorium, his expression lost in some recollection of the past.

'Twenty-five years ago,' he went on, 'Bo Ventura was shot dead in the Civic Theatre, and I was unable to do anything to prevent the murder. Tonight I will atone for my inability.'

He reached out and touched something on the dais, and instantly the auditorium came to life. A hubbub of polite chat filled the room, discreet music played; the guests were galvanised into movement. The effect, Halliday thought, as he gazed around him, was as if an act of magic had been performed, as if so many shop-window mannequins had suddenly been invested with life. It was impossible to tell the hologram men and women from the real thing, from Vanessa and Jeff and Casey . . .

His attention was drawn once again to the stage as Mantoni picked up an envelope from the dais and quickly opened it. 'And the nominations for the best actress award are . . .' As Mantoni read out the names, Halliday glanced across at Jeff and shook his head. The cop nodded, lowered his automatic. Beside Halliday, Vanessa was weeping.

'. . . and Bo Ventura in *Chicago Dreams*.'

A breathless hush seemed to descend over the gathering, and Mantoni announced, 'The winner is . . . Bo Ventura!'

From a table near the stage, a tall, physically perfect vision of womanhood rose and strode forward to collect her award. In the woman's poise, something about her grace and attenuated limbs, Halliday was reminded of her daughter . . . and, beside him, Vanessa gripped his hand and fought back choking sobs.

Bo Ventura ran up the steps and crossed the stage towards Sergio Mantoni. Halliday stared, appalled, aware that he was witnessing a moment in history – in more than one sense – as Bo Ventura moved to embrace Mantoni.

Except, of course, Ventura was a hologram. Instead of embracing, their forms merged, Halliday could only watch in dizzy disbelief as the image of Bo Ventura, overlaid upon the reality of her one-time lover, turned towards the audience. Their faces comprised a ghastly super-imposition, an optical illusion which the eye could not take in simultaneously; instead, Halliday made out first one face, and then the other.

And then Mantoni turned, his white tuxedo moving like a ghost within the form of Ventura, and drew something from his pocket. As Halliday watched, frozen, the tycoon raised a pistol, and aimed across the stage towards the unconscious form of Canada Artois.

For an eternal, painful second, the image held.

Then Vanessa screamed and lunged forward. She held the gun in both hands, arms outstretched, and began firing.

Perhaps six shots hit Mantoni in the torso, and as many more missed the target altogether. His tuxedo bloomed with a florid Rorschach blot of blood. He staggered backwards, his form in death parting company with the lifeless holographic image of Bo Ventura.

Vanessa Artois stopped firing and dropped the gun, as if in horror at the act she had committed. Halliday rushed to her side, caught her as she sagged, and held her upright.

On stage, Sergio Mantoni sank to his knees, his hands pressed to the bloody mess of his chest, and Halliday thought he saw a smile of satisfaction cross his face as the image of Bo Ventura moved towards the microphone and spoke in a husky whisper, 'I'd like to thank everyone here tonight for awarding me this honour, but most of all I would like to thank Sergio . . .'

The tycoon fell forward, and Halliday released Vanessa. He felt a hand in his, and slipped an arm around Casey's shoulders as they watched Vanessa cross the stage and kneel before her sister.

'Told you it'd be a happy ending,' Casey said in a tiny voice. 'Didn't I tell you, Hal?'

Halliday smiled to himself, then moved with Jeff and Casey towards the reunion playing itself out upon the stage.

Twenty-Four

Halliday sat at his desk, listening to the monsoon rain drumming on the fire escape. Three days had passed since the finale on Laputa Island, and for three days he'd spent hours just staring at the miniature oak on the desk before him.

His desk-com buzzed. He sat up. 'Yeah, Halliday here.' He peered at the screen.

'Hal.' Vanessa Artois stared out at him. 'Are you in the office?'

'Yeah. Yeah, I'm here. Where're you?'

She laughed. 'You sound out of it. Is it okay if I come up?'

'Sure. I'll fix you a coffee.'

'See you in a second.' She cut the connection.

He watched her walk into the room a minute later, and he wondered if it was just a week ago that she had first stalked into the office, tall and beautiful and predatory.

He remained behind the desk.

She sat down, crossing her long legs. He thought he saw something in her eyes, a shadow of sadness that would never be erased. 'Hal, it's good to see you.'

'You too.' He pushed a mug of Colombian roast across the desk.

She saw the miniature oak and smiled. 'You still watching the tree?'

'All the time, Vanessa.'

She reached into her shoulder bag and produced a silver envelope, and Halliday experienced a flashback. One week ago she had passed him a similar silver envelope, containing a pix of her sister – her foster-sister, he reminded himself.

306

'How's Canada?' he asked.

'She's fine, Hal. No lasting effects from her time in VR.'

'That's good to hear.'

'She's waiting outside, in the limo. We're heading for the airport.'

'Holiday?'

'I landed a contract in Hollywood. There's a real live theatre company out there, putting on the classics. Would you believe it? I'll be acting again before you can say grease paint.'

'Good for you.'

She smiled and passed him the envelope. 'There's a cheque in there, Hal. I know money can't buy what you did for me, but it's a token. I hope you think it's enough.'

'I billed you, Vanessa. That was my fee.'

She laughed. 'Okay,' she said, 'consider the surplus a little gift. If you hadn't turned up in the alley . . .'

He shrugged, leaving the envelope on the desk before him, unopened.

'And you traced Canada back to the island . . .'

A silence developed between them. How could he begin to tell her that it'd been less his good judgement that had brought a successful end to the case than pure good fortune?

Vanessa looked up from her coffee. 'I had to do what I did down there, Hal. I had to kill—'

He reached out and took her hand. 'I know, Vanessa. Believe me, you did the right thing.'

'I keep thinking about it, wondering if there might have been some other way.'

Halliday squeezed her hand. 'I know it's hard,' he said, 'but try to put it behind you. Get on with your life.'

She nodded and smiled, sadly. Perhaps she had hoped for more from him than mere platitudes. 'I'll do that.'

He recalled what she had asked him, last week: how could he live with the knowledge of having taken a life? Well, now she would have to live with that terrible knowledge, and some understanding of this fact showed in her eyes.

307

She finished her coffee and looked at her watch. 'My flight's at ten, Hal. I'd better be going.'

'I'll see you out.'

He followed her through the door and down the narrow staircase. The monsoon deluge pounded on the sidewalk. A small crowd of hardy souls had gathered around the black limo parked outside the Chinese laundry.

Vanessa turned to him in the covered entrance. 'Thanks again for everything, Hal. I won't forget what you did.'

Without waiting for a cue from Halliday, she stepped forward and embraced him. Her lips found his briefly, and he wondered whether, somehow, things might have turned out differently. Perhaps if he'd accepted her invitation to stay the night in the hotel, a few days back?

He watched her move to the limo, slip inside in one svelte, practised movement. He raised a hand in farewell as the car started up and cruised away from the kerb.

Across the road, Casey and her boyfriend were holding hands beside the food-stall where she worked. She waved at Halliday, quickly, then resumed her conversation with Ben.

Halliday waved in return, and made his way back to the office. He sat in the swivel chair, looked at the bonsai, and then noticed the silver envelope on the desk.

Curious, he opened it. He'd billed Artois for thirty thousand dollars, which included all the hours he'd worked on the case, and his expenses.

He withdrew the cheque, read the figure inscribed in her perfect copperplate hand. He read it again and shook his head.

The cheque was accompanied by a very short note.

Thank you Hal. Love, Vanessa.

He lay the cheque on the desk and leaned back in his swivel chair.

Half a million dollars . . .

He could retire on that, if he invested wisely. Buy a small place upstate and spend the rest of his life drinking good wheat beer and tending his garden.

He thought of all the things he could buy Casey.

The desk-com buzzed, surprising him.

'Yeah, Halliday here. Missing Persons.'

A dark-haired woman with a thin, pale face stared out at him. 'Halliday? Look, you don't know me. I found your name and number on the com of a dead friend of mine. Guy called Sanchez. You knew him?'

Halliday leaned forward. 'Sure, I remember Sanchez,' he began.

'Good. Great. I'm Kat. I've been trying to trace his killer. Thought you might be able to help.'

He thought about it. 'Sure thing, Kat. I think perhaps I can, too.'

'Also,' she went on, 'I might be able to put some work your way. You interested?'

He hesitated, glanced at the cheque on the desk.

At last he nodded. 'Always interested in work,' he said.

'Good. When can I see you, Halliday?'

He arranged a day, a time, and cut the connection.

He looked around the rundown office, wondering why the hell he'd agreed to see the woman.

He smiled to himself, knowing that Barney would have understood. He lifted the bonsai tree onto his lap, sat back and stared at its unique and exquisite perfection: he had gained something from staring at the oak over the past few days, an inner peace that came from knowing that the tree, though isolated, was independent; though alone, was strong.

Outside, the rain continued to fall.